Susan Carlisle's love affair with books began in the sixth grade, when she made a bad grade in mathematics. Not allowed to watch TV until she'd brought the grade up, Susan filled her time with books. She turned her love of reading into a passion for writing, and now has over ten Medical Romances published through Mills & Boon. She writes about hot, sexy docs and the strong women who captivate them. Visit SusanCarlisle.com.

Karin Baine lives in Northern Ireland with her husband, two sons and her out-of-control notebook collection. Her mother and her grandmother's vast collection of books inspired her love of reading and her dream of becoming a Mills & Boon author. Now she can tell people she has a *proper* job! You can follow Karin on Twitter, @karinbaine1, or visit her website for the latest news—karinbaine.com.

D1143899

A DADDY
SENT BY SANTA

SUSAN CARLISLE

MIDWIFE UNDER
THE MISTLETOE

KARIN BAINE

MILLS & BOON

First Published in Great Britain 2018
by Mills & Boon, an imprint of HarperCollins*Publishers*
1 London Bridge Street, London, SE1 9GF

A Daddy Sent by Santa © 2018 by Susan Carlisle

Midwife Under the Mistletoe © 2018 by Karin Baine

ISBN: 978-0-263-93383-3

A DADDY
SENT BY SANTA

SUSAN CARLISLE

MILLS & BOON

To Katie

CHAPTER ONE

PAXTON SAMUELS' DECISION to leave Boston had been calculated. Volunteering for the temporary medical position in western Oklahoma hadn't given him pause. It was his ticket out of the emotional nightmare his life had become. He needed this change in scenery, some privacy. Desperately.

With his experience and training in emergency care and family practice, the temp job was a perfect fit for him. That it was halfway across the country from Boston only added to its appeal. Still, he'd not anticipated driving through a blizzard at the end of November in the middle of nowhere. He'd been prepared for culture shock but not this blowing snow and endless road. The unexpected brutal weather notwithstanding, the move was well worth the effort. It got him away from his parents' demands as well as the media's fascination with the spectacular failure of his wedding, which had been hailed as the "social event of the year."

He searched the empty white plain for any sign of civilization but only spotted an occasional tree. According to his GPS, Last Stop, Oklahoma, should only be a few miles ahead. Visibility was becoming so bad he had thoughts of pulling over until it improved. Still, he couldn't shake the worry that if he did so the rapid snow accumulation would strand him. He had to push on.

Moments later the terrain rose enough to obscure the road ahead. Paxton topped the small rise and instinctively stomped on the brakes. The back end of his sports car fishtailed. He yanked his foot off the brake, steering the car into the spin, and the vehicle straightened. In control again, he slowed to a stop and surveyed the wreckage before him. Blocking the road was a huge combine tractor lying on its side, a truck smashed against it.

His job as local doctor was starting sooner than he'd thought.

Paxton parked on what he guessed was road, making sure two of his tires remained on the pavement. Locating his cell phone, he called 911. The dispatcher answered and he reported the wreck, its location and that he was a doctor.

"Help is on the way," the dispatcher said, and ended the call.

Opening the door, Paxton shuddered at the bone-cutting blast of wind and snow that assaulted him. He snatched his heavy wool overcoat from the front passenger seat and jerked it on. Reaching in again, he pulled out his medical bag. Pushing the door closed with his hip, he shoved his empty hand into a coat pocket and lowered his head against a biting gust. His toes curled in his shoes in an effort to generate heat as he trudged toward the accident.

Reaching the pickup truck, he skidded across a patch of black ice, doing a little twist and turn, before he smacked his hand against the truck to catch himself. When his feet were firmly beneath him, he worked his way to the cab and peered through the driver's side window.

The man inside was slumped forward, his head against the wheel. Paxton knocked on the glass. The man moved slightly but didn't straighten. Grabbing the door handle, Paxton pulled it open and touched the man's shoulder. In a firm but caring tone he asked, "Hey, are you okay?"

The man moaned and attempted to sit up.

"Easy." Paxton gripped his shoulder to hold him in place. "Don't move. I'm a doctor. Can you tell me where you're hurt?"

"My head."

"I want you to remain still."

Swiftly Paxton assessed his head injury. Delving into his open bag and pulling out a packaged four-by-four bandage, he tore it free of the wrapper and pressed it over the man's bleeding gash.

"Someone will soon be here to help you. I need to check on the other person."

The man muttered, "Okay."

Making his way to the overturned tractor, Paxton stabilized himself by pressing a hand on the side of the truck. The cold metal felt like sharp pins beneath his fingers but fear of falling overrode the pain. What light he had was disappearing fast.

At the tractor cab, he rubbed his hand in a circle across the window. From what he could make out there was one young man lying on his side, not moving. Paxton would have to climb up onto the side of the cab of the hulking piece of machinery, then lower himself inside to properly assess the unconscious man's injuries. He studied the tractor. It wouldn't be easy.

Strapping his medical bag over his shoulders, thankful for the growing wail of an approaching siren, he carefully made his way around to the exposed undercarriage. To get inside he'd have to open the cab door. He examined the bottom workings of the engine for a footing. No help there. Even if he could find something to stand on he still couldn't swing high enough to grasp the cab handle. The metal step to the cab was just above his head but not large enough to do him any good. On his best day he couldn't pull himself up within reach of the door.

He looked at the front tire of the tractor suspended in the air. That was his way in. Using the inside rim of the tire for foot support, he hefted himself up on the exposed axle then onto the side of the engine hood. Crawling on hands and knees, he located the latch. At least the engine was still warm enough to give his hands some relief.

Reaching the door, Paxton kneaded his fingers to get them flexible then tried the handle. At first it wouldn't budge. Using his palm, he hit it. His teeth clamped together as pain shot through his arm. After one more knock the handle shifted and he swung the door back. Warmth greeted him but soon vanished into the frigid twilight.

He looked down at a teen, who still hadn't moved. "Hey! Are you okay?"

No answer.

The siren grew louder. Relief washed through him. There would be help soon. In Boston he didn't get tractor accidents so this was a new one for him.

Getting on his belly, Paxton leaned in from his waist until he could touch the closest part of the boy's body, which was his thigh. There was still heat there. He was alive. Carefully Paxton pulled himself back. He didn't need to fall in and cause more damage to the boy or to himself. Sitting on his butt so he could go in feet first, he braced one foot on the side of the seat's backrest and the other on the dash. Leaning as far forward as possible, Paxton just managed to put two fingers on the teen's pulse point just below his jaw. It was faint. If the boy was going to live he needed help soon.

The siren stopped. The strobe of the lights reflected off the cab. Help was finally here.

Pulling his bag strap up over his head, he placed his medical duffel on top of the backrest and against the cab window behind his patient so it wouldn't slide out of his reach. He opened it and one-handedly found his stethoscope. Getting it into his ears, he placed the bell on the teen's chest. A thrill went through him. A heartbeat was there.

As Paxton was reaching for the boy's head a voice snapped, "Don't touch him!"

Looking back over his shoulder, all he could see was a face surrounded by a white cap trimmed in white fur. Echoing that command were rosy lips pulled tight, a small flared nose and wide glaring dark eyes.

"Don't move him!" Lauren Wilson hung over the edge of the cab, using the tone of voice she'd perfected to stop her two-year-old son from doing something that could harm him.

She couldn't have some good Samaritan making matters worse. The situation was bad enough as it was. Her attention zeroed in on the stethoscope the man held. Amazement rocked her. It couldn't be. Luck was with her.

"You wouldn't happen to be Dr. Samuels, would you?"

"I am, and I'm glad to see you. Do you have help coming?"

"I'm your help. Name's Lauren." He didn't look too impressed. "I also have Rick with me. He's a police officer," she added.

"We've got to get this boy and the other man—" he nodded toward the truck "—taken care of. Where's the ambulance? This fellow needs to be gotten out of here and on his way to the hospital."

This wasn't the type of doctor she'd been expecting. Someone older, less attractive. With graying hair and narrower shoulders. There wasn't enough light to tell if his eyes were light blue or green.

Last Stop's longtime physician, Dr. Barden, had retired after forty-five years of service. He'd given up on finding a permanent replacement and had settled for coaxing doctors to at least fill in for a few months at a time, yet often there were no volunteers. The town and neighboring area needed a full-time doctor in residence. Lauren was the only nurse and medical professional for sixty miles. She helped where she could during emergencies until assistance arrived, but the town deserved more. Emergency medical aid was too far away in the absence of EMTs or a resident physician.

Lauren looked over the top of Dr. Samuels as his attention returned to the patient. She had no doubt he was just one younger doctor meeting his medical school loan requirements. He would soon be gone. But for now she was glad to have him and tonight in particular.

Lewis Williams, the teen who was folded against the cab windshield, she'd known all her life. From the looks of him Dr. Samuels was right. They needed to get him to the hospital right away. "Rick," she called down, "it's Lewis Williams. We need to get him out of here. We're going to need lights, blankets, possibly a rope and your help up here. Throw me my bag." She grabbed it as it sailed through the air. Lauren looked down at Dr. Samuels, who was wearing an expensive-looking coat and no head covering. "We need to get his neck stabilized before we move him."

"I realize that, but I don't have a neck brace with me."

"I have one." She pulled her bag closer. Unzipping it, she reached for the neck ring and handed it to him. He was already working his way around the steering wheel and farther into the cab when she said, "Hold on a minute. I'll climb in and help you."

The confining space would be difficult for two to maneuver in but it would take both of them to get the neck brace into place. Fear clutched at her chest as she eased her way inside.

Young Lewis had just earned a university scholarship. His future was bright. Now this. He reminded her too much of her husband. Young, smart and willing to work hard for what he wanted. Then to have it all destroyed by an explosion. She was brought out of her morbid thoughts by the doctor.

"I want you to support him while I check his head wound. We don't need to make any sudden movements that could make matters worse."

He seemed to be talking to himself as well as her.

"The light is going. And this weather..." He glanced up.

She watched snowflakes settle on his cheeks and forehead. Even in the dimming light, she registered he wasn't the average man in looks or attitude. The few single young women in the area would be fighting over him. He was still speaking and she forced her wandering attention back to the crisis at hand.

"If we don't get him out of here we're gonna have to worry about hypothermia on top of all his other injuries. What's the ETA on the ambulance?"

"Under an hour from the time it was called."

He muttered an expletive as his head jerked around. "That long!"

"The closest hospital is over sixty miles away. In this weather…" She hadn't meant it to sound so harsh, yet it was the truth.

His mouth dropped in disbelief, although whether it was because of the distance or her snapping, she wasn't sure. It might have been comical in any other situation.

His expression went from resigned to determined as he turned back to their patient. "We've got to try and shorten that time or this boy may not make it."

Terror shot through her. Not another wasted life. She couldn't stand another one of those.

He commanded, "Hand me that brace."

She did so then placed a foot on the side of the seat to support herself as she climbed down farther into the cab. By the time she'd gotten situated, he was working the brace around Lewis's neck with one hand while supporting himself with the other against the cab roof. Using her free hand, she helped him get it into place then secured it.

"Good. Now I want to have a look at his head. At least get a four-by-four over the wound. Can you get your arm around his shoulders and pull him toward you while I lift his head?"

The action would put her in an awkward position,

but she would try. Lauren nodded. "Hold on a sec." She reached into her bag and pulled out a square paper package, put it between her teeth and tore it open then handed the gauze to him.

Moving her foot on the seat to the floor, which put her in contact with the doctor from hip to foot with the steering wheel column between them, she was stable enough to reach both arms around Lewis and pull him against her chest.

At the same time the doctor used his hands to support Lewis's head. "Good." A second later he said, "It looks like he's taken a good shot to the temple. I'm concerned about his brain swelling. He's still not regained consciousness. You got a blanket in your bag of tricks?"

Just as he said that Rick called, "Lauren, catch." A blanket fell into the cab. She passed it to the doctor as another hit her on the head.

"Rick, we're going to need the rope and you up here," she called.

"What're you thinking?" Dr. Samuels asked as he tucked the blankets around Lewis.

"Tie the rope under his arms and have Rick pull him out as we push and steady him."

"Sounds like a plan. He needs to be in a warmer place than this. I need to check for any broken bones."

"Lauren, here you go," Rick yelled from above them as he lowered an end of rope to them. "Just got a message the ambulance is still twenty minutes out."

Dr. Samuels uttered another word under his breath that she wouldn't want her two-year-old to hear, or repeat.

She announced, "Rick, it's going to take us a few

minutes to get Lewis secured, then on my word I want you to pull. We'll help from down here."

Seconds later Rick was holding his flashlight over them.

"As I lift can you get the rope in position?" Lauren asked Dr. Samuels as she wrapped her arms around Lewis once more.

"Yeah." The doctor wound the rope around Lewis and tied it off.

"I'm going up to the door to make sure he doesn't topple over the side as we pull him out." She started her climb, but her foot slipped. She fell against Dr. Samuels. His body was hard and his strong hands grabbed her at the waist. "Sorry," she muttered.

"You get a handhold and I'll help you out," he ground out.

Once she was on the engine hood, Lauren remained on her stomach, twisted around and grabbed the rope. Rick laid the flashlight down and stationed himself behind her. "Okay, on three. One, two, three."

Lauren wrapped her hands around the rope. She pulled with all her might until her muscles burned with the effort. Between her and Rick pulling and Dr. Samuels pushing, Lewis's head came over the door edge then his shoulders.

"Wait. Hold him steady. Let me get hold of him." Using her legs, she dragged Lewis while Rick pulled and the doctor lifted. Lauren kept working until Lewis almost lay across her, his back to her front.

Rick hurried to help her. With Lewis on the engine hood, they rolled him on his side, placed a blanket beside him, and gently positioned him on it before bundling him up and tucking it around him. Cracking all the heating picks she had, she placed them along his side then put another blanket around him. Now they had the chore of lowering him to the ground.

Dr. Samuels, with his bag across his shoulders, hoisted himself out of the cab. He must be freezing in his less-than-suitable clothes, but she hadn't heard a complaint or seen a wince.

With Lewis wrapped burrito-style, she grabbed the rope and tied it around his thighs and shoulders. They couldn't have Lewis slipping out of control.

"This isn't the first time you've done this," Dr. Samuels observed from behind her.

"No." She didn't slow to look at him. "Rick, you ready?"

"Ready."

The doctor grabbed the rope. "What do I need to do?"

In the dim light provided by Rick's flashlight and the running police cruiser headlights she could see Dr. Samuels' fingers were turning dark. He would need attention as well. But that would have to wait until Lewis was taken care of. "We need to keep the rope taut between us as we lower him so that he remains as level as possible."

He nodded.

"On three. One, two, *three*."

Slowly they lowered Lewis a couple of feet to Rick's waiting hands. Minutes later Lewis was on the ground and she was climbing off the tractor. She had just reached the pavement when she was bumped. The doctor had slipped. Seconds later they were sprawling entangled in the snow.

He was the first to recover. His arms were around her and his face close. "I'm sorry. Are you hurt?"

She blinked. "No."

"Good." He scrambled to his feet.

Lauren followed his lead.

"We need to get Lewis out of the elements and see where that ambulance is." He hurried toward Rick, who was untying Lewis.

"I have the cruiser running so it's warm. The back seat is clear," Rick informed them.

As he and Rick carried Lewis around the back of the tractor to the waiting car, Lauren rushed to the far side of the vehicle. Opening the door, she climbed in as Rick laid Lewis's shoulders on the seat. She placed her arms under Lewis's armpits and pulled him toward her. As she did so Dr. Samuels helped by pushing from his end. She kept going until the boy lay across the seat. Before she could straighten up, the doctor joined her on her side.

"Let's get a set of vitals on him," he said with authority. "Rick, could you see to the guy in the truck? The best I could tell, he just has a head wound. I'm not sure how serious. Also, check the ETA on the ambulance."

The doctor was good with issuing orders, but he had stood back when she'd been the one giving them earlier. Hadn't arrogantly assumed command of the situation as other male doctors might have done. She appreciated his unspoken acceptance of her as his professional equal.

Lauren went to the other door, leaving him room to work. Putting down her bag, she removed her stethoscope and blood-pressure cuff. Lewis was so thin there was a chance she could get a reading from his calf. She didn't want to remove the blankets or his jacket unless absolutely necessary. Instead she pushed at Lewis's pants leg in an effort to get it beyond his boot top. Succeeding, she placed the cuff around his leg. With relief, she found it just fit.

"His heart rate is erratic. It wasn't when I first checked," Dr. Samuels said. "BP?"

"One forty-three over one hundred and two."

He shook his head. "We've got to get him to a hospital. We don't have time to waste. Can you get a temp while I check on Rick?"

"Yes."

He disappeared into the night through the blinding snow.

Finding the thermometer, she closed the door to keep the heat in and carefully moved around to Lewis's head and ran the electronic instrument over his forehead. Ninety-six. The acid taste of panic filled her. Lewis was well on his way to hypothermia. With a grateful heart and elation knowing no bounds, she saw the lights of the ambulance arriving.

Dr. Samuels came up behind her. "Go help Rick get the other man here while I report to the EMTs. I may need to ride in with Lewis."

Lauren didn't miss the concern in his voice or him blowing on his cupped hands. He was in pain as well was her guess. Would he shorten his stay in Last Stop after this adventure?

Paxton couldn't remember the last time, or if there had ever been one, he'd done this much physical activity during patient care. He worked out regularly, but he was going to feel tonight's exertions in the morning when he tried to get out of bed.

The lights of the ambulance had been a happy sight. Rick was helping the other man out of the truck when he left to meet the EMTs. He feared Lewis was going to end up having just as many issues from the prolonged exposure to the elements as he did from the actual accident.

When the first EMT approached, he introduced himself and gave a quick report of his examination of the man in the truck, then went into detail about Lewis's care. The second EMT hurried to them with the gurney. Paxton went around to Lewis's feet and crawled across the seat as the other two men worked Lewis's shoulders onto the gurney. Minutes later they had him strapped down. Rick joined them, helping the EMTs get Lewis into the ambulance. As soon as the EMTs had Lewis secured inside, they immediately started working on him. Paxton was told he couldn't ride in the ambulance. He responded, "Then I'll see you at the hospital."

He watched the ambulance leave and returned to the cruiser to check on his other patient. Lauren and Rick had sat him in the back seat. "I'm going to follow the ambulance in my car," he told her.

"No, you're not," Lauren said in a firm voice that reminded him of his mother refusing him a cookie before dinner when he'd been a child. "I'm going to see about your hands after I get through with Mr. Thompson here. We've got to take him to the hospital as well, so Rick is driving."

"I'll call someone to come get your car. Are the keys in it?" Rick asked.

"Yes." Paxton just experienced another element of culture shock. He'd never have left his keys in his car in Boston, even if he'd been the first medical person on the scene of a bad accident.

"Now get in the back seat," Lauren ordered. "I need to have a look at your hands. You probably have the beginnings of frostbite. Are they numb?"

He had no choice but to admit, "Yeah, they are."

"Let me see." She grabbed a flashlight and shone it on his hands. "Ooh, the tips are already turning white. You should've been wearing gloves."

"I have some in my suitcase but didn't take the time to find them."

"Next time you need to." She pulled off her gloves and stuffed them in a pocket of her coat before reaching for his hands. "Bend them for me."

He started to argue but with the way he felt and her tone of voice he thought better of it. Doing as she instructed, he was disappointed to find his fingers wouldn't move. She was right, he had all the signs of frostbite.

To be ordered around by someone other than his parents was a new experience. Now that the adrenaline rush was over he was starting to register intense pain. He'd overextended his body in addition to his exposure to the increasingly frigid temperature.

He watched as she turned his hands one way then the other. Her fingers were strong and sure, yet tender. She'd pushed back her coat hood. Snowflakes hung like stars in the night sky in her thick dark hair. Even in the shadowy light he could tell she was pretty in a natural, wholesome way.

"You might as well do as she says because you won't win," the injured man leaned out to say.

"He's right. Get in. We need to get going. I'll work on your hands in the car," Lauren said.

Paxton climbed in next to the man, welcoming the warmth inside despite the still-open door. He attempted to kick off his shoes, but pain shot up his leg. His toes hurt but with the car heat on they would recover soon.

"Let's go, Rick," Lauren called to the policeman, who

was doing something near the tractor. She closed the door and headed to the other side of the car.

Somehow the sound of her soft, slow drawl and unusual tone that could only be native to the region took his mind off his pain. Who was this young woman who lived out in the middle of nowhere? And why did she? After Gabriella's mistreatment of him, he was surprised that he'd even wonder about a woman, but curiosity about Lauren did keep his mind off his discomfort.

Lauren got into the front passenger seat and closed the door. She swiveled in her seat and said, "Give me your hands."

"Again?"

"Yeah. I need to start warming them. You are familiar with frostbite care?" she asked, a little irritated note in her voice.

"Of course I am."

"Then you know I need to bring the feeling back slowly. I don't have any more heat packs so I'll need to hold them between mine. Body heat is the best."

He glanced at the man next to him to see his reaction, but he had his head back and his eyes closed. In a few minutes Paxton would rouse him to make sure he wasn't unconscious from a concussion, but first...

Paxton extended his hands.

Lauren took them between her smaller ones and held them but instead of rubbing movements she blew on them. Her gaze met his, held. Her eyes were as black as the sky he'd so often lain under in Africa. Unspoiled, huge and comforting. There was look of caring he'd not seen in a woman's eyes in a long time. Was he destined to judge every woman by Gabriella? He hoped not. Lauren blinked and the moment was gone.

"You were good out there," he said with true admiration.

"Thanks." She looked pleased with the compliment. Did she not get many of them?

"You know, I'm used to being the one who gives the orders." He watched a slow smile light up her face.

"I know. I heard a few of them tonight."

"I think you're pretty good at them as well." He knew his grin was more grimace than smile.

Rick climbed into the driver's seat. "Everyone ready?"

"Where're we headed?" Paxton asked when they were riding down the road.

"Lippscomb, Oklahoma. Closest hospital. By the way, I'm Lauren Wilson." She nodded to the driver. "This is Rick Moore. That's Art Thompson beside you."

"And I'm Dr. Paxton Samuels. Feel free to call me Paxton."

"You're our new temporary doctor. Tough way to start your month," she said, giving him a reassuring smile.

"I won't argue with that." But everything about the last few weeks had been tough as well.

She continued to blow and after a few minutes she looked at him. "I forgot to mention that I'm your nurse. So this probably won't be our last adventure together."

He wasn't sure if that sounded ominous or inviting, but it was definitely intriguing.

CHAPTER TWO

LAUREN BLINKED AT the bright light coming from the hospital emergency department entrance. The ride hadn't been the worst one of her life but it had been uncomfortable. She'd spent most of it with her body twisted toward the back and her arms between the seats, holding Paxton's hands while she blew on them.

They were strong, capable hands. She had already learned that. His fingers were long and tapered down to well-manicured nails. They weren't as soft as she'd expected. Something about them made her think of security. That he could take care of himself and anyone else he cared about.

As they'd driven she'd seen him studying her, his face faintly lit by the dashboard lights. Tingles of self-awareness had flickered through her, as though she were a specimen under a microscope. She feared he was analyzing her both in appearance and intelligence, and passing judgment. Did she fall short or measure up?

They were to the outskirts of Lippscomb before he said, "You can stop. I have feeling now."

"That's good but you're not out of the woods yet. You'll still require medical attention to make sure there hasn't been further damage." She struggled to conceal her relief. Her back hurt and she had become ever more aware of him as a man the longer she'd held his hands.

More disturbing were her sharp memories of his body pressed against hers in the cab and when they had been entangled on the ground. Despite the bitter weather and her thick clothing, she'd been conscious of his warmth and his body against hers. Was it because she'd not let a man so close in such a long time? What was this odd reaction she was having to a stranger? Whatever it was she had to put a stop to it. Nothing about it was healthy.

Rick had done a good job of driving but the going had been slow. The snow had slackened but the bitter wind had picked up. When Rick stopped at the emergency department door Lauren hurried inside to let the staff know they had arrived. Earlier Rick had radioed ahead, telling the hospital they were on their way.

She headed straight for the unit desk, which was draped with garlands and red and gold Christmas balls. The clerk, wearing reindeer antlers, looked up.

"Hey, I'm Lauren Wilson from Last Stop. I've got two patients in the car. One needs a wheelchair."

Lauren didn't wait for her response before returning to her patients.

Paxton, as she suspected, had climbed out of the car in order to assist their patient.

She rushed to him. "I'll take care of Mr. Thompson. You should be concerned about your hands."

"He's my responsibility," Paxton growled through pain she was sure he was trying to hide.

"And you're mine," she snapped.

Glancing behind her, Lauren was pleased to see the unit staff hurrying toward them with a wheelchair.

She pointed to Mr. Thompson. "He needs the chair."

Mr. Thompson settled into his chair and Paxton walked into the hospital beside him. She and Rick followed close behind them. When Paxton reached the unit desk he said, "I'm Dr. Paxton Samuels. I need to speak to the attending."

Lauren hurried forward. "I'll take care of giving report. You're a patient as of now and you need to worry about having those hands properly tended."

"They're fine."

"Doctors never make good patients," she muttered.

"I heard that," Paxton said with a glare. "I'm sure my fingers have recovered."

"I think we need to get a second opinion. Last Stop needs a doctor with good hands."

He gave her a stricken look then nodded. "Okay, but I want to be informed about my patients."

"Not a problem."

"Hey, Lauren," Henry, a doctor and friend who was wearing a Santa hat on his head, said as he came up the hall toward them.

"Hi, Henry." She gave him a smile.

"What do you have for us tonight?" Henry looked at Paxton with curiosity.

"You've already gotten one of our accident victims, Lewis Williams. Head trauma and hypothermia. We have another head trauma, Art Thompson—" she pointed toward a cubicle where he'd been taken "—in there who needs to be seen."

"I'm Doc—" Paxton tried to butt in.

Lauren didn't slow down. She gestured to Paxton. "This is Dr. Samuels. He's a possible frostbite case."

Henry told a nurse who had just joined them, "Take him to trauma three and get him started on the frostbite protocol. I'll see the head trauma you brought in first. Lauren, come with me and tell me what's going on."

Throughout the brief exchange Paxton looked from her to Henry and back again. He appeared puzzled by their discussion. A couple more times he made noises as if he was going to interrupt but before he could utter anything the unit tech pushed him away.

Lauren stowed her outer clothing behind the nurses' station and joined Henry in Mr. Thompson's room. He was sitting up and talking to the nurse. Lauren shared what she knew about his case. A few minutes later they were on their way to Paxton's room.

"So, who is this Dr. Samuels?" Henry asked.

"Our new temp doctor until we can find someone to permanently replace Dr. Barden. Dr. Samuels was on his way to Last Stop and came up on the accident. He wasn't well dressed for the occasion. I can't complain about his care and quick action, though."

She and Henry stepped into Paxton's cubicle. He was sitting in a chair with his hands in water.

"How's Lewis doing?" he asked before either of them could say anything.

"He's in a room," Henry stated. "He still hasn't regained consciousness. We scanned for swelling but saw nothing. It's just a waiting game now."

"And Mr. Thompson?"

"He seems to be recovering. He has a handful of stitches and we're going to keep him overnight for observation." Henry stepped closer to Paxton. "Now it's your turn. I'm Dr. Henry Fields and I understand you're a doctor as well."

"Dr. Paxton Samuels."

"I hear you're going to fill in at Last Stop."

"Yeah, if I ever get there," he said in a grouchy tone.

Henry gave a dry chuckle. "I've heard of the difficulty. So, tell me, how're your fingers? Our winters are pretty brutal here."

"Better."

"Good to hear."

Paxton lifted his hands out of the water and flexed his fingers. He looked directly at her. Lauren's middle fluttered. He had deep green eyes. Green like the plain in the spring. Their new doctor was handsome.

"I had good care on the way here."

Henry glanced at her. "I have no doubt you did. I should admit you, but Mr. Thompson took the last bed. The best I can offer you is a spot in the waiting room. You really should have someone checking on you every couple of hours."

Rick stuck his head into the cubicle. "Lauren, I've been called out. I've got to go. I'll pick you up in the morning or get someone to come get you." He raised a hand and was gone.

He didn't even give her a chance to respond. She and Dr. Samuels were stuck in Lippscomb.

Paxton's unnerving eyes met hers. "Isn't that our ride back to Last Stop?"

She nodded. "Yep. I guess we're staying the night in the waiting room."

"What about that hotel across the street? I saw it as we pulled in. Surely they have rooms." Paxton was in no mood to sit up all night in a brightly lit public area.

Lauren shrugged. "I guess that'll work. The weather is too bad to ask anyone to come get us."

"He's—" Henry indicated Paxton "—going to need you to check on him a couple of times during the night.

I'm concerned he might spike a fever." Henry looked at her then at Paxton. "And you, I want you to promise you'll keep your hands covered for the rest of the winter season. You'll have trouble again if you're not careful."

"Thanks. I'm well acquainted with frostbite, as I'm from Boston. We have the cold and snow as well."

"Then you know it's nothing to mess around with." Henry wasn't letting his patient intimidate him.

Lauren shook her head in disbelief. Could this evening get any more interesting? "Then we're going out in the weather again." She winced. "More fun in the snow."

"It looks like it."

Lauren imagined Paxton's arrival in Oklahoma was far above and beyond his Bostonian expectations.

"How soon can I get out of here?" Paxton asked Henry.

"As soon as you're ready." Henry made a note on the chart he held. "After you have your hands wrapped. They need to be that way for at least twenty-four hours. I don't want you using them until tomorrow. I'm going to prescribe you a little something for pain. Call me with any problems."

Paxton didn't look pleased with that directive but he didn't argue. "Understood."

Henry nodded to her and Paxton, then left. A few minutes later a nurse wrapped Paxton's fingers individually in gauze.

As soon as she left Paxton said, "I'm ready to go." He stood and started pulling on his coat.

Lauren assisted him with getting his arms into it, then adjusted the weight around his shoulders and buttoned it. The rigid posture of Paxton's body let her know he wasn't used to people doing things for him and he didn't like feeling incapable. She pulled his collar up around his neck.

A funny feeling came over her and she looked up to see him intently watching her. Her gaze met his. A pang of awareness ran through her.

His hair was still damp and mussed, a large lock of it having fallen over his forehead, giving him an endearing disheveled appeal. He was a good-looking man, not in a glossy magazine manner but in the subtle way of someone who had confidence in who they were and what they wanted.

"Can we go now?" he asked with arched eyebrows.

Had she been staring at him? She backed away. "I need to get my coat and bag on the way out. I left them at the nurses' station." They walked to the unit desk. There she went around to a cubby and gathered her things. "Jane," she said to the unit clerk, "do you know where we can get some scrubs?"

The heavy woman in her mid-twenties said, "Yeah, but I'm really not supposed to hand those out."

"I'll bring them back, I promise. If I don't, you can charge me for them."

Jane pursed her lips and gave her a sideways look. "In this case…" She went into the storage room. She soon returned with green scrubs sealed in clear plastic. "Sorry, I only have one set left, in extra-large."

"Okay. We'll make them work." Lauren took the package, then turned to Paxton. "You ready for this?"

"I've been ready," he grumbled.

Apparently he'd had all he wanted for a day. She looked at him. His eyes were bloodshot, underlined by the bruise-like evidence of exhaustion, and his mouth was a tight line. She glanced at his hands all wrapped in white. He deserved to be testy.

Pulling on her coat, she zipped it closed and put her bag over her shoulder. The large automatic glass doors opened as they approached. A blast of cold rolled in. Lauren shivered and murmured, "All we have to do now is manage to not slip on the ice."

Paxton grunted and hunched against the wind, putting his hands into his coat pockets.

She picked her way down the curved drive to the street while keeping an eye on him. All he needed was to fall. Thankfully the street lights gave off enough light to make visibility good and the snow had slowed to drifting flakes. The motel was straight across the four-lane street from the hospital. They waited for a car to pass then as quickly as possible walked toward the window with the glowing orange neon sign that read "Office."

"How often do you get snowbound with a patient?" Paxton asked.

"I'd have to say this is a first."

"I'm not surprised. That's my life lately. A lot of firsts."

Lauren wasn't sure what that statement meant but it didn't sound good by the tone of his voice. Keeping a steady pace, they kept moving. The situation was movie-worthy. They would laugh about this one day.

Lippscomb Motel was a nineteen-fifties-style place, where the one-story building formed a horseshoe and the parking was in front of each room. All the slots appeared taken. What were they going to do if there were no rooms? Return to the hospital. She should have thought to call. They had no choice now but to ask.

Making it to the entrance first, she opened the glass

door, letting him go in ahead of her. The warmth of the lobby greeted them.

A bald-headed man wearing a T-shirt despite the weather stood behind a counter with a tiny, sad-looking Christmas tree on it. A TV blared in the background.

"Can I help you?"

"We need a couple of rooms for the night," Paxton stated.

"Don't have but one," the man said off-handedly.

Lauren had been afraid of that.

The man continued, "The storm has us all full up tonight."

"We'll take it," Paxton said before she had a chance to say differently.

She pulled her wallet from her bag.

"I've got this." Paxton put a card on the counter.

Regardless of the circumstances, it didn't quite sit right with her to have a man she hardly knew pay for their hotel room for the night. Somehow it seemed sleazy. She was a professional taking care of a patient who happened to be a male, she sternly reminded herself. There was nothing immoral about that. It was necessary.

A minute later the man returned Paxton's card and gave her a plastic keyring with the number three on it. "The heat won't be on, but it shouldn't take long for it to warm up."

She shuddered at the thought of going back out in the frigid night and to a cold room but she had no choice.

Walking under the awning, they made their way to Room Three. Her feet were wet and cold and all she wanted to do was have a hot bath, call Shawn and crawl into bed. She was pretty sure Paxton had a similar desire.

Unlocking the door, Lauren pushed it wide and let

him enter, then quickly closed the door behind them. It wasn't much warmer inside than out. She left Paxton in the middle of the room lit only by the porch light coming through the thin curtains. Going to the lamp sitting on the table between two beds, she clicked it on. The room was much as she had expected.

The beds were standard size with headboards fixed to the wall and a small, well-worn sofa set against a wall with a cheaply framed picture above it. There was a built-in desk with a chair and beside it a clothes rack attached to the wall, level with her head, to serve as the closet.

She was confident it was a major step down from what Paxton must be used to. To his credit, his face didn't look as disgusted as she expected. It leaned toward pitiful. He'd had a hard first day on the job. Yet he'd been more than efficiently competent under the circumstances. Too bad his tenure at Last Stop would be brief.

He sank onto the side of the bed closest to the door.

"Let's get some heat going in here." She hurried to the wall heater located under the only window. It made a clang when she turned on the fan and cranked the thermostat up as high as it would go. "Hopefully it won't take too long for it to heat the place."

"That would be nice. I'm starting to fear that I might never be warm again."

"I'll see if there's a heater in the bathroom." Somehow she had assumed personal responsibility for him. He was new to town. She wanted him to appreciate where she lived, to make a good impression. Even though he was only going to stay a short while she didn't want his time there to leave negative memories. Granted, it had been his choice to come to Oklahoma but still she wished it could have been more welcoming than the last few hours had been.

It was a relief to see there was a heater in the bathroom as well. She turned it on high. When she returned to the main part of the room Paxton still sat in the same spot. That could only be an indication of how bad he felt.

He looked at her. "Sorry about the room situation but at least you don't have to get out in the cold to check on me. We're both adults, I believe we can handle one night together in a hotel room. You needn't worry. I'm no threat, especially tonight."

She wasn't as worried about him as she was about making a fool of herself around him. A shiver went up her spine. He was watching her.

"I can handle it if you can. Uh…you hungry? I could call for some takeout. There's a pizza place next door."

"Yeah. I could do with something to eat."

"Pizza do?"

"Sure. Anything at this point would be great."

She clasped her hands in front of her. "I'm sorry. This wasn't an ideal way to start a new job. Not very hospitable of the weather."

"Can't control that. I've been through difficult times. Let's just say that today was mild compared to some things I've dealt with."

She'd had her share of difficult times as well. Like losing a husband. Being a single mother. Maybe Paxton wasn't as soft as the fine cut of his coat or the brand name of his shoes implied. After the last few hours she suspected that, like his hands, his life had had some rough spots. "I need to make a phone call then I'll go get that pizza. I'll just step in the bathroom to talk."

* * *

Paxton wasn't sure exactly when he'd entered this sur-
real vortex in time and space where his life had gotten
completely out of his control, but he had to find a way
to take back some degree of it soon. If two weeks ago
someone had predicted that he would be in Oklahoma
stranded in a motel room with a pretty young woman
who turned out to be his office nurse as well as his personal caretaker during a blizzard, he would have called
them a quack. He should be on his honeymoon in the
Mediterranean. With a cheat.

He listened to the soft burr of Lauren's voice. "Hi,
sweetheart. I'm not going to make it home tonight. I'll
see you tomorrow." There was a pause. "I love you too."

So she had a boyfriend. He noted she hadn't told the
guy she was spending the night with him in a hotel room.
Paxton harrumphed. As if he could do anything about
it even if he had a chance. All he could think about was
getting a hot bath and climbing into bed. The medicine
he'd been given made him want to do nothing but sleep.

When Gabriella had pulled her final dramatic stunt,
he'd never believed it would lead to him having potential
frostbite and spending the night in a seedy motel with a
woman. He and Gabriella had been an off-and-on couple most of their youth. Their families were close, ran in
the same social circle of longtime Bostonians with the
correct pedigrees. As adults, it seemed that both sets of
parents had expected them to marry. Paxton had cared
about Gabriella and had believed she'd felt the same
about him. His parents had been encouraging him to
marry her for years. For once he had been doing something they blessed.

He'd always been a bit of a rebel in their eyes. He'd

gone to a West Coast college instead of the Eastern one all the family members had attended. Between college and medical school, he'd secretly applied to the Peace Corps and spent a year helping in a North African medical clinic. His parents had been vocally displeased. They had anticipated he would finish his medical training and join the clinic that held their family name. Many a time he'd seen disapproval on their faces. It wasn't until he and Gabriella had become engaged that he'd finally felt they were proud of him. Apparently, and most disconcertingly, Gabriella had found him wanting as a potential mate.

Lauren emerged from the bathroom, slipping her cell phone into her pants pocket. She definitely caught his interest with her glorious mass of long dark hair, smooth skin with cheeks still rosy from the cold and those dark eyes that were intelligent while at the same time tender and caring. Even with her heavy coat on, he suspected there were nice curves beneath. Lauren's wholesomeness was appealing after Gabriella's contrived sophistication.

"I'm going to go see about some food now. I'll be back as soon as I can."

Feeling a vulnerability he hated, he had no choice but to ask, "Uh…before you go, could you help me out of these damp clothes?"

Her eyes widened and her full-lipped mouth went slack.

Where had her thoughts gone? He held up his bandaged hands. "I don't think I can unbutton my coat. Or my shirt for that matter."

It rubbed him the wrong way to need her help. How did it look? Here he was the new physician in town who was supposed to take care of others and he couldn't even take care of himself. He wasn't making a good impression, he was sure. If he wasn't careful Lauren would be the one people turned to instead of him.

Her look had changed from one of surprise to sympathy as she looked at his hands. "I'm sorry. I should've thought. Doesn't make me look like much of a nurse."

"I'd disagree with that. I saw you in action today." He stood.

Lauren appeared small and fragile in front of him but there was strength there, he knew. Her warmth seeped into him as she continued into his personal space. A handful of her hair fell over her face, stirring his awareness further. What did it feel like? Was it as silky as it looked? He inhaled. She smelled of the outdoors. Fresh, clean. Alive.

"Well, let's get your coat off, then I'll help you with your shirt." Her fingers worked the buttons of his jacket, opening all of them before pushing it off his shoulders and throwing it on the bed.

She hesitated before her hands moved to his shirt.

Paxton didn't miss the tremor in her hands. "This isn't your first time to undress a ma…uh, patient?"

"No. I trained in a big hospital." A firmness had entered her voice. "Cut a number of patients' clothes off as well."

Was she reminding him this was strictly business for her? Which it should be. But her hair looked so silky. That wasn't something he should be thinking. Even if being strangers was keeping them apart he still couldn't take a chance on being rejected. His self-esteem was battered enough. Besides, they were going to be working together. "I don't think that will be necessary this time."

Her gaze held a twinkle as it met his for a second before she continued to work the buttons of his shirt.

He couldn't deny his body's reaction to her standing so close. Whether he knew her or not. He suddenly felt warm all over. From his vantage point her movements were the efficient and functionary ones of a nurse except for the tremor of her hands. At least he wasn't the only one affected. "I'm sorry you have to do this. It's embarrassing to be so helpless."

Lauren worked quickly. "Hey, it happens to all of us sometime. It's just your turn this time."

"That doesn't mean I have to like it."

She smiled. It was a nice one. "I'd just put it down to this entire evening being unusual." Her tone turned matter-of-fact.

As she finished he said, "Now I'm reaching for a new level of mortification." Would his male ego survive this? "I hate to say this but I'm going to need help with my pants button as well."

Lauren smiled. "I've heard that it's good for a doctor to be a patient every once in a while. It gives them more empathy for their patients."

"Then I'll have that in abundance." His disgust rang loud and true.

She freed his pants button. "I think you can handle things from here. And I'm hungry. I'm going after that pizza."

He was hungry too, and on the verge of being turned on.

Seconds later a draft of wind brushed over him before the door closed and he was alone. Paxton eyed the bed. He was going to lie down while she was gone. His fingers tingled as if little pins were being pushed into his skin. Maybe if he raised them above his heart they wouldn't hurt so much.

A bath could wait. He finished removing his clothes, leaving them in a pile on the floor. Removing the pants of the scrub set from the package, he pulled them on. Lauren could have the top.

He slipped between the cold sheets that made the skin of his bare back ripple. Piling one pillow on top of the other, he placed them above his head before he pulled the covers into place. He raised his hands and rested them on the pillows. He shivered until sleep took him. The only time he'd been warm in the last two weeks had been when Lauren had stood near him.

Lauren made her way across the parking lot, grateful for the chilling wind after the hot moments she'd spent with who was in essence her new boss, a stranger. Her credibility as a nurse had never been more in question than when she had been undoing Paxton's pants. Thoughts that were better left dormant had been projected in 3D, full-color, jumbo size.

She'd glanced at Paxton to find a wicked gleam in his jade-colored eyes. Heat rushed to her cheeks at the memory. That had been no patient and nurse moment. It had been about two people attracted to each other on the most basic of human levels. She'd hurried through the process with shaking hands. Even as she'd unbuttoned his shirt her blood had hummed with ultra-sensitive awareness. She had left it hanging open, but not before she'd noticed his chest had a light dusting of hair over well-formed muscles. She forced herself to swallow.

It had been too long since she'd been with a man if her overreaction was any indicator. It wasn't like her not to remain professional in that type of situation. It was a relief to get some fresh air, even if it was still snowing.

There hadn't been a time in her life she could remember when she'd been so affected by a man. Even undressing her husband hadn't made her hands tremble. She and Paxton hadn't come anywhere near having sex yet her nerves were still humming as if they had. This instant attraction wasn't a feeling she was familiar with.

Lifting her face to the night sky, Lauren let the few flakes of falling snow settle on her hot skin. Paxton wouldn't be the last doctor to fill in. He wasn't going to stay long, and she certainly wasn't going to let history repeat itself. She'd left town with a man before and she didn't plan to do that again. With her next relationship, she would know the man long enough to know she could trust him. She deserved fidelity. Shawn needed a stable life. That she would give him.

Mark had been a brash young man who had come to town with an oil company. He'd led the team planning to take a number of the wells deeper. She'd been swept off her feet.

Before she'd known it, she was married and on her way out of town with him to his next assignment. She'd dreamed of leaving Last Stop all her life and when she'd got the chance she'd been thrilled. She'd happily packed her bags and left with fairy-tale dreams. At first, everything had been great. They'd moved every three to four months and she'd found every new place exciting but increasingly lonely.

More than once she'd feared Mark wasn't being faithful. He'd always assured her that he was but while at a party she had been approached by a woman who'd told her she'd been seeing her husband. Their marriage had gone from bad to worse.

Only because they'd moved again and she'd discovered she was pregnant had she stayed. She'd told Mark the morning of the accident she was pregnant and had wanted him to find a job that would let them settle down, so they could work on their marriage and be a family. They'd fought, him stating he wanted no part in her plans. That afternoon he was gone. An explosion on the oil rig had killed him and five others.

Lauren had returned to the only place she'd ever really known as home—Last Stop. She'd used Mark's life insurance money to finish nursing school and had made a home for Shawn and herself. He was her life now. No guy passing through town was ever going to turn her head again. Especially some fancy doctor from Boston.

Enough of those thoughts. She had food to get. The pizza place only had a lone young man working. She ordered a large pepperoni pizza and sat down to wait. It had been so long since she'd felt anything for a man. Henry had been asking her out for a couple of months and she had been putting him off. Then in had come a man she knew nothing about and bam! She'd babbled and tingled all over. It just wasn't right. Yet there was an excitement between them she couldn't deny.

Half an hour later she returned to the hotel room with a pizza box in hand and two cans of drink in a bag. She knocked lightly on the door, giving Paxton a heads-up that she was entering. Digging the key out of her pocket, she opened the door. She pushed inside, expecting to find him watching TV. Instead the chair was empty and Paxton was softly snoring in the bed. Compassion filled her. He must have been exhausted after driving all day, then the adrenaline rush of the accident followed by the dangerous brush with frostbite.

Lauren placed the food on the desk before taking the

spare blanket off the top of the clothes rack. She spread it over him. He mumbled, shifted and settled again. Picking up the TV remote, she returned to the desk chair with plans to watch a show while she ate. Paxton could have cold pizza. He needed his rest.

She finished her food, then picked up the scrub top he'd left lying on the bed. Placing the back of her hand on Paxton's forehead, she decided he was a little warm but not overly so. After turning the heat down in the room to a more reasonable temperature, she headed to the bathroom.

After the wonderful experience of a hot shower, she pulled on the scrub top, thankful it was extra-large and hung far enough down her legs to decently cover her. The idea of sleeping in her damp clothes or, worse, nude made her shudder. After hanging and draping their clothes around the room to dry, she sat on her bed. She'd decided that leaving the light on in the bathroom would make it easy to check on Paxton.

Lauren turned off the TV then looked at him sleeping in the next bed. He was resting comfortably. He'd turned on his side but his hands were still above his head. She could only think that they must have hurt. She couldn't help but feel sympathy for his plight. He looked miserable with his bandaged hands. Taking a pillow from her bed, she raised his head and tucked it beneath before easing him down onto it. Satisfied she hadn't disturbed his slumber, she adjusted the covers over his shoulders. Switching off the bedside lamp, she got into bed and was soon asleep.

A loud moan startled her awake. She jerked around to look at Paxton. He whimpered again, then kicked the covers back, leaving most of his body exposed. The scrub pants rode low on his hips. Climbing out of bed, Lauren reached out to touch his head. Heat surrounded him. Her heart thumped. He had a fever.

Grabbing her digital thermometer from her bag, she ran it across his forehead. It read one hundred and three point seven. She'd been afraid this might happen. Hopefully it would be a temporary situation and not require hospitalization. Returning to her bag, she found fever-reducing medicine then went to the bathroom, filled a water glass and returned to Paxton's bedside.

Lauren shook his shoulder. His skin was hot and dry. She bit her bottom lip as anxiety flooded her. This didn't need to turn into more than a fever. "Paxton."

He groaned but didn't open his eyes.

She shook him a little harder. "Paxton."

"Uh…?" His eyes opened. A glassy unseeing look filled with confusion.

"You have a fever." Her voice was firm. "You need some medicine. Will you sit up?"

He attempted to rise but fell back again, too weak to move. Lauren reached behind his back and supported him until he was upright enough to drink safely. Slipping the pills between his rosy, dry and cracked lips, she pushed them past his teeth onto his tongue, then pressed the glass against his slack mouth to encourage him to drink. He took a sip.

"You need to drink all of it. You're dehydrated." She coaxed him to comply by offering him the glass again.

He took two more swallows before he collapsed back against the pillow.

Carefully freeing her hand, Lauren set the glass down in order to pull the covers up over his torso and straighten them around him. Paxton had fallen back into a fitful sleep. She dampened a washcloth and applied it to his forehead.

His eyelids fluttered open then closed. He moaned and pawed at the washcloth until it slipped off, but Lauren returned it. She pulled the desk chair up next to the bed then went to re-dampen the cloth. The medicine should kick in soon. Sitting, she lifted the covers from his chest enough that she could sponge him off in an effort to lower his temperature.

She looked at him closely. He really was a fine-looking man. A shadow of his beard was beginning to show, giving him a devil-may-care look. There were small laugh lines around his eyes. She liked people who laughed. There wasn't enough of that in her life. She watched her hand move the cloth over his chest, appreciating the ripples of the muscles beneath his skin. He must do some type of workout to keep them that toned. Even his biceps were well defined.

Sometime later, Paxton started to shake with chills. Pulling the blanket off her bed, she placed it over him and tucked it around him. At least his fever had broken. She dampened the washcloth again and continued to sponge him off.

He murmured something Lauren couldn't understand and thrashed around. Then said, "Gabriella, how could you?"

Lauren rested her hand on his shoulder, hoping to get him to relax. "Shh, you're okay. Everything is all right."

He eased back against the pillow.

When he was calm, Lauren checked his temperature. The reading was normal and she returned to bed.

Who was Gabriella? His wife? Girlfriend? What had she done? Why was he out here without her?

CHAPTER THREE

PAXTON OPENED HIS eyes to the dim light of morning coming through faded curtains. Where was he? Oh, yeah, a hotel room. He looked at his hands, still bandaged. At least he wasn't feeling any pain.

Turning his head, he saw Lauren sprawled out on the bed next to his with one leg out from under the sheet. The scrub shirt had ridden up, leaving an expanse of shapely thigh visible. Beautiful. Was Lauren's skin as smooth as it looked?

He looked away. Ogling a woman while she slept wasn't his style. Especially women he didn't know. She'd been kind to him and deserved better. After what Gabriella had done he should be leery of women. Yet there was something about Lauren.

Seconds later she rolled over and met his gaze. "You're awake. How're you feeling?"

"Like a bus hit me."

She grinned. "I'm not surprised. Your fever was pretty high last night."

"It was?"

"Yeah, but the medicine brought it down."

He raised his hand to his forehead, taking the washcloth off. "What's this?"

"I was trying to make you more comfortable."

He looked at the chair then at her. "Did you sit up with me?"

"For a little while."

Great. Once again she had been taking care of him. Could he seem more pitiful? She had to have been just as tired as him last night, yet she'd been up caring for him. "Thanks. I'm sorry you had to do that."

Lauren shrugged. "Not a problem. You could probably use another dose of medicine now." She made a move to get up, then jerked the sheet over her hips, her look meeting his. Seconds later she wrapped the sheet around her, picked up her clothes off the desk and headed for the bathroom.

He couldn't help but grin. Despite Lauren's appearance of complete control, she could be set off kilter.

Within minutes Lauren emerged from the bathroom, but she didn't look at him. Instead she headed straight for her bag with a glass of water in hand. Bringing it and some pills, she handed them to him. He swung his legs over the side of the bed and sat up unsteadily.

One of her hands instantly came to his shoulder. "Whoa, no quick moves until we know how you feel."

There was that helplessness again. The hits to his self-esteem just kept on coming.

She stood over him while he swallowed the medicine.

"You do know I can do this by myself?"

Lauren removed her hand and took the glass. "I realize that but it would look bad for me to lose our new doctor on my watch."

Paxton missed the warmth of her touch. "You didn't think I would take it?"

"It's my job to see that you do." Returning to the

bathroom, she brought back a filled glass. "You need to drink it all. You lost a lot of fluid last night."

He swallowed all the water and placed the glass on the table then started to unwrap the gauze from his fingers.

"What're you doing?" A note of panic entered her voice.

Paxton didn't stop what he was doing. "I want to see what they look like. The feeling seems to have returned."

When he had difficulty with one section, she huffed and sat across from him. "Let me help." She slowly and carefully removed the bandaging.

"You have gentle hands. You must be a good nurse, Lauren."

"I like to think so." Her eyes never left her work. She turned his hands over in hers a couple of times. Using her index finger, she slowly ran it down the center of his palm and out to the end of his finger. "Can you feel that?"

"I can." It was a tingle that had nothing to do with frostbite. He removed his hand from hers and looked at it himself. "I think they'll heal well."

"Let me have the other one." She reached for his wrapped hand.

Paxton watched the top of her head as she leaned over his hand. Her hair was so dark that it shone like hot cocoa in the light. This time he couldn't resist touching it. Taking a strand between his fingers, he let it skim between them.

Her gaze met his in question.

"I'm sorry. I just couldn't resist." He pulled his hand away and finished unwrapping the gauze. What was his problem? He was going to scare her. She would think he was some needy pervert who was after her. That was the furthest thing from reality. A relationship of any type wasn't on his agenda. He'd been burnt and he had no plans to go back for more. "I wanted to see if I had all the feeling back in my hands."

Her look lingered on him, making him feel self-conscious enough that he stood and walked toward the bathroom.

"I'm hoping that fever last night was only from acute trauma and not infection. You need to take fever-reducing medication regularly for the next few days just to make sure." Lauren stood as well.

"Thanks, Doc," he quipped.

She said to his back, "It has been my experience that doctors make the worst patients."

"I might resemble that." He closed the bathroom door between them.

"I'll be right out here if you need me," she called, irritation clear in her voice.

It didn't take him long to shower. Despite his efforts not to admit his discomfort, he had to. Still having an ache in his hands was aggravating. Opening the door a crack, he called, "Hey, can you hand me my clothes?"

"Just a sec." Then he heard her say, "Hey, honey, I have to go. Yes, bye."

She'd been on the phone. Had it been with the same guy? A woman as pleasant and attractive as Lauren surely had someone. Why should that matter to him anyway?

The sound of her moving around then coming back toward him had him waiting. A hand holding his pants and shirt came through the open space.

"Here you go."

"Thanks." He took them from her.

"I called Rick. He'll be here in under two hours. That'll give us time to eat and check on Lewis and Mr. Thompson."

"I'll be ready in a minute." With his pants on and his shirt unbuttoned, he stepped out of the bathroom.

Lauren's lips were pulled in a tight line as she watched him. "You're hurting, aren't you?"

He nodded. "Yeah. I hate to admit it but my fingers don't move well enough to dress myself. And I'm hungry."

"I bet you are. You missed the pizza last night." She stepped to him and matter-of-factly started buttoning his shirt. Having no choice, he accepted it. Done with that, she fastened his pants as if it was no big deal then announced, "We need to get your hands wrapped again."

Soon she was helping him into his coat and pulling hers on, all without any emotion or physical reaction. No shaking of hands or quick breathing. Now his mortification was complete. She could dress him and feel nothing, while desire tugged at his body.

Outside the snow had ended, the air was chilly and the sky blue as they walked across the parking lot.

"I think it would be easiest to go to the hospital cafeteria for breakfast," Lauren suggested. They headed toward the hospital and a few minutes later they walked through the automatic doors, past the welcome desk and into the cafeteria.

"You shouldn't hold a tray. I'll get your food. Just have a seat. What would you like?"

She was right. Could this get more humiliating? When he got the bandages off... He gave his order without hesitation. "Scrambled eggs, bacon and toast. A large cup of coffee."

Lauren nodded and he watched her walk away. They had known each other less than twenty-four hours but he felt like he knew her better than he ever had Gabriella. Lauren was smart, efficient and capable, could take charge yet followed orders when needed. She didn't complain, which heaven knew wasn't one of Gabriella's virtues. Men were attracted to Lauren judging by the way Henry had greeted her and whoever the guy on the phone had been. Paxton certainly felt a fascination.

His own phone rang. With effort, he removed it from his coat pocket. Looking at the caller ID, he saw it was his mother.

"Hello, Mom."

"Paxton, where are you?"

"You know good and well where I am. I'm in Oklahoma."

"Did you really take that job?"

"I told you I was going to. I've already started." He wouldn't tell her it had been on the side of the road in a snowstorm.

"Pax, I can't believe you're doing this to your father. He needs you here."

"We've been through this before. There are plenty of doctors in Boston."

"But your father needs you. You know he's ill."

"Yes, but the treatment is working." His father had been diagnosed with a heart condition.

"He needs you. I need you." She paused for a second then said, "Gabriella called to say she was sorry." His mother's voice was soft.

"Mom, I'm not going to talk about that. It's done." Lauren was on her way back. "I've got to go. I've made a commitment for a month here and I need to honor it. I'll talk to you soon."

"But, Paxton—"

"Got to go, Mom." He hung up just as Lauren reached the table.

"Here you are." She placed a tray with two plates of food on it in front of him. It smelled wonderful. Her gaze fell on the phone but she didn't ask any questions.

"I didn't think to send money with you. And you bought pizza last night. What do I owe you?"

"Don't worry about it. We'll settle up later." Lauren sat across from him.

"Then maybe I can make it up by taking you to dinner one night."

She took one of the plates off the tray and set it on the table across from him. "We'll see."

Lauren had said nothing about not being able to because of a husband or boyfriend. Despite his hands and uncomfortable method of eating he dug into his meal. He took a sip of his coffee. "So, what do I need to know about Last Stop?"

She studied him a moment. "Well, there isn't much to tell. It's part of the panhandle of Oklahoma."

"Panhandle?"

Using her hand, she made a gesture of holding something. "You know when land boundaries have a strip of land that sticks out like a handle. Look at the shape of Oklahoma on a map sometime. It looks like a frying pan."

Paxton nodded. "I get it."

"There's about a thousand people living in or around Last Stop. Most are farming families or work for the oil industry. But there aren't as many of them as there once were."

"So how long have you lived in Last Stop?" He finished off his eggs.

"All my life."

He could understand that. He'd lived in Boston most of his. Except for his college years and the year in the Peace Corps. "Never left?"

"Only for a short while."

"Why'd you come back?"

A shadow of pain filled her eyes. "Because my husband died and it's home." She put her fork down on a partially eaten plate of food. "I'm going to return the scrubs to ER then check on Lewis and Mr. Thompson. Do you want to wait for me here?"

She'd been married. Her husband had died young. She'd experienced some major trauma. "I'm sorry about your husband. I didn't mean to bring up sad memories. I'm going with you to see Lewis and Mr. Thompson. They're my patients now too." If it hadn't been her husband she'd been speaking to last night, then who had it been?

The moment seemed forgotten and she nodded as if pleased with his statement about their patients. "Then we need to get going. I don't want Rick to have to wait for us. He's taking time out to come get us."

Lewis's parents were with him when they got to his room. He was now awake and seemed okay but was going to have to stay in the hospital one more night.

"I want you in my office next Monday just for a checkup, okay?" Paxton said before leaving the room.

"He'll be there," Lewis's mother promised. "We heard what you did, Dr. Samuels. We appreciate it."

"You're welcome." He'd been thanked before for care he'd given but somehow Lewis's mother's sincerity touched him more than usual.

They moved a few doors down the hall to Mr. Thompson's room. The older man was dressed and waiting for his wife to pick him up.

He stretched out his hand and quickly brought it back to his side. "Sorry, Doc. I forgot about your hands. Thanks for helping last night."

"Not a problem. They'll be better soon. Call me if you start feeling bad for any reason."

Less than an hour after their breakfast they were waiting next to a large Christmas tree in the emergency department for Rick. They didn't have to sit long. Lauren insisted Paxton take the front seat.

"Hey, Rick, I'm ready to go home." She sounded tired. Paxton spent the next hour peppering Rick with questions about Last Stop and the area. When Lauren didn't comment, he glanced back to see that she was asleep. Her night had been as exhausting as his.

His attention returned to the world outside the windshield. It was white with snow. There wasn't even a significant rise or dip in the land for as far as he could see. In his part of the world it snowed but there were buildings and roads, even mountains if he went far enough out of town. Here there was nothing but the road and fence line.

Finally, on the horizon, he could make out a cluster of buildings large enough to make up a town. He watched in anticipation as they approached. No structure was over one story high. His apartment in Boston was on the twelfth floor. Here, the stores were built of wood or cinder block. There was only one intersection, but it had no street light. A few cars were parked on the street. There were Christmas wreaths hanging from each lamppost.

"Well, I see Roger got an early start with the Christmas decorations this morning." Lauren's voice had a rough sound from sleep. It added a charming dimension to her Western drawl.

"Yeah, he was upset that the storm made him wait until today," Rick said. "You want me to drop you off at your place or with the doc here?"

She sat up in the seat. "My car's at the office. I'll just go there."

"I understand that I'm to live in an apartment attached to the office." Paxton looked back over the seat.

"It's a house. The office, a waiting room and exam room are up front. The kitchen and a bedroom and sitting room are in the back. This is it right up here." Lauren pointed ahead of them.

Rick turned right and then took a small street to the left before pulling into a drive on the left beside a clapboard house painted white. There was a sign in the yard that read "Last Stop Clinic." He stopped behind Paxton's car, which was sitting under an open shed. A large green truck with a double cab that dwarfed his car sat beside it but not under the cover.

Paxton had needed a change in his life and he'd certainly gotten it.

Lauren watched as Paxton took in his home for the next few weeks. He looked both amazed and dazed. What had he expected? She'd woken to find Rick busy telling Paxton about the area around Last Stop. She liked the sound of Paxton's voice. Deep, soothing with an occasional clip on the end of words. That was a place she didn't need to go. She'd already been swept off her feet by a man who had come to town for a short stay. Being whisked off again wasn't in her plans.

"Thanks, Rick, for the ride. Also, thanks for having my car brought in." Paxton climbed out of the car.

"No problem. See you later," Rick called.

Lauren was grateful someone had shoveled the snow off the walk. If Paxton fell, he might be forced to high-tail it back to Boston. Opening the door of the clinic, she turned on some lights.

"I'll give you a quick tour before I go home and change." She turned around in the open space. "This is the waiting room." A few chairs and a table were set against one wall, on the other a desk. She stepped to a door off the main room. "This is your office."

It was a simple room with a large oak desk in the center that she'd loved to play around as a child when she'd visited Dr. Barden. With Paxton's background, would he be as impressed with it? He was probably used to glass and chrome. She led the way down the hall. "This room—" she stopped at an open door "—is an exam room." She stepped farther down the hall. "Here is another. On down here is your living area." She moved into what was a small kitchen.

"What's all this?" Paxton's voice rose in exasperation.

Taking up every spot on his kitchen counter and small table were bags of food, casserole dishes and cakes.

Lauren giggled. "You've been visited by the welcome wagon."

"The what?" His brows rose.

"Some of the women just brought you some food to say welcome and thank you. I'm sure they all heard about what you did last night."

"But all this!" He waved his hand around in disbelief.

"Everyone in Last Stop knows you're in town."

He groaned. "I have more food than I can eat."

She grinned. "Far more. Even my mom has a casserole in here somewhere."

Paxton looked perplexed, as if it had never occurred to him that the town would be glad to see him. "Haven't you ever had someone welcome you with food?"

He was looking through the food, reading the labels. "Never."

"You'll find things might be a little different around here." Lauren stepped toward another open door.

Paxton followed her. "I'm starting to learn that in more ways than one."

"This is your bedroom and a sitting area where there is a TV."

She had to admit it wasn't much, but he would be comfortable enough for the amount of time he would be staying.

"The bathroom is through there." She walked in front of him to point out a small door inside the room. "I see someone brought in your suitcase and belongings."

There was a skeptical note in his voice when he asked, "Did Dr. Barden live here?"

"No, it's mostly been used when there has been a late night or maybe a patient needed to be watched closely until the ambulance got here. That type of thing. It's been cleaned and readied for you, though. Sorry there was no other place for you to stay."

"This'll be fine." He didn't sound disappointed. Her face brightened. She'd feared he might be upset with the accommodations.

"Is there anything you need before I go? If not, I'm

headed home for a change of clothes and will be back in an hour. Thankfully this was our morning off, but we have afternoon clinic today if you're up to it."

"I'm up to it." Paxton caught her hand as she went by him, stopping her. "I want to thank you. You were great last night at the accident and then taking care of me. Maybe I should be giving you some food."

She smiled, trying to cover her reaction to his touch. A tingle ran through her. She'd known Paxton less than twenty-four hours and she shouldn't be having this reaction. They had to work together. He wasn't staying around long. She tugged on her hand. He released it. "That's not necessary. Just be careful with those hands while I'm gone."

"I will." He raised a wrapped hand. "Promise."

She felt guilty leaving him there looking rather abandoned but she needed some space along with a new set of clothes, and most of all, she wanted to give her son a hug. "I've got to go. Someone's expecting me."

CHAPTER FOUR

WHO WAS SHE rushing off to see? Paxton would find out when she came in later.

What had possessed him to take her hand? They had been thrown together for one night. He shouldn't be reacting to Lauren on such a primitive level. For heaven's sake, he'd just come out of a horrible situation. Being attracted to another woman so soon shouldn't be happening. He couldn't even trust his own judgment. He'd certainly been wrong where Gabriella was concerned.

He'd believed his and Gabriella's affections had gone deep enough that he had asked Gabriella to marry him. Then had her cheat on him and his parents think he should forgive her and marry her anyway. All to save the family name. Was his ego so bruised he'd go after the first woman he found attractive? Lauren deserved more consideration than that. He wanted to believe *he* was better than that. Yet his physical reaction to her was undeniably strong.

He looked around the room as the sound of her footsteps disappeared down the hall. He should get his act together. First thing he had to do was put on a clean change of clothes, warmer ones. After that he would familiarize himself with the clinic.

It was a struggle, but he managed to remove his clothes and put fresh ones on. Memories of Lauren helping him dress and undress flitted through his mind. Their relationship had had a unique beginning.

Relationship?

They had no bond outside her being his nurse for the next four weeks. It would remain that way. Despite his unusual attraction to her they were just co-workers. And for all he knew, this "someone" she kept talking to and about was her boyfriend. He certainly wasn't going to encroach on someone else's woman.

Going to the kitchen, he looked at all the food. When and how was he ever going to eat it all? Still, it was nice to know he was welcome. Finding a plate of cookies, he took a few and headed to the office. It was time to have a look at the "clinic" that would be his workspace for the next few weeks.

It was nothing like what he was used to. There was no stainless steel or glass. Instead, most of the furniture was worn and as if they were leftover pieces. He made his way to the exam room. It appeared adequately stocked. There was a wooden cabinet with a small sink, and shelves above full of supplies. An exam table was located on the wall opposite. He had never seen one except in pictures. It was old but looked sturdy.

Crossing the waiting room, he entered the office. A large oak desk with a high-backed leather chair commanded most of the space. Two comfortable-looking wingback fabric-covered chairs in navy blue were stationed in front of it and behind was a bookcase filled with books and specimen jars. In the back corner was a metal filing cabinet. As he'd guessed, it was filled with patient charts. Paxton grinned. He was used to a handheld electronic tablet and paperless recordkeeping. This job meant stepping back into a simpler time. He had no real idea of what type of problems he would be confronted with but he would find out this afternoon.

The sound of the bell on the front door ringing brought him to the office door. A tall, thin man with a weather-worn face and piercing blue eyes gave Paxton a swift once-over. He held a thick-looking leather hat, wore a heavy coat, jeans and boots. He demanded in a gruff manner, "You the new doctor?"

"Yes, I'm Dr. Samuels."

He turned the hat in his hands as if nervous. "Can I talk to you?"

"Uh…would you mind waiting for a few minutes? Lauren will be here then. I don't quite know where everything is located yet." Once again he was inadequate for the job. Would he be leaning on her the entire time he was here?

An embarrassed look came over the man's face and he glanced toward the door as if considering leaving. "I'd rather this be between you and me."

Curious now, Paxton pointed toward the hall. He could at least listen. "Well, why don't we go to the exam room?"

The man walked down the hallway and Paxton followed. When they were both in the room, the man said, "I heard about the trouble last night. I appreciate you helping Lewis."

"You know Lewis?" News traveled fast around here. He suppressed a shudder. If any citizen of Last Stop learned of his humiliation in Boston, everyone would know within twenty-four hours.

"I do. People around here talk, but Lewis is also my grandson."

Paxton nodded in acknowledgment. "I see, Mr...?"

"Gerhart."

"Well, Mr. Gerhart, how can I help you?"

"I've been having trouble with, you know, my privates. Burns to pee."

Paxton nodded. Now he understood the need for secrecy. Especially since news traveled so fast in town. "Well, the first thing we should do is get a urine sample. You'll need to fill one of these." Paxton took a plastic cup with a blue top off the shelf, thankful he didn't have to go hunting for one. "There's a bathroom just next door."

The older gentleman accepted the cup with a sheepish look and left the room. He soon returned with the sealed cup in hand and wearing a pained expression. Placing it on the counter, he looked expectantly at Paxton.

He suspected Mr. Gerhart had a urinary tract infection but wouldn't know until the test results were in. "I don't know what the lab situation is yet but I'll see that it's taken care of. I'll give you a call tomorrow in case I need to see you again or call in a prescription." As soon as Lauren returned he would have her see about getting the sample to the lab.

"Thanks, Doc." The man extended his hand. "I appreciate you keeping this between us."

"I'll do the best I can." Paxton shook Mr. Gerhart's hand. "I'll be in touch."

The man nodded, placed his hat on his head and left.

Mr. Gerhart couldn't have been driving down the street long before the bell on the door rang again. This time it was a young woman.

"Can I help you? I'm Dr. Samuels. You are...?"

"I'm Margie Michaels." She raised her hand, which was wrapped in a cloth. "I'm one of the cooks over at the café. I burnt my hand."

"Come to the exam room and let me have a look."

He joined her at the exam table. "I need you to unwrap it and I'll have a look." His own bandages were going to have to go. He needed to do his job. The red angry skin on Margie's hand made him wince. "We'll need to clean it with soap and water. Then wrap it and keep it clean and dry."

"Dr. Samuels, how can I help?" Lauren stepped into the room like a warm breeze. "Hi, Margie. What happened?"

Paxton was relieved to see her. Lauren would be more efficient than he. She knew where things were, knew the patients. Could actually use her hands properly. Nothing about her appearance said typical nurse, yet he was very aware she was an exceptional one.

Her hair was pulled back from her face. She wore a coral sweater that enhanced the natural color of her cheeks and a pair of jeans that hugged her curves in a most complimentary manner. What he really gave his consideration were the Western boots on her feet with their pointed toes.

They weren't the type of footwear he was used to seeing his clinic nurses wearing, in or out of scrubs. The women in his life tended toward three-inch heels and brand names. He redirected his thoughts. "Lauren, we need saline, gauze and a pan."

A minute later she had all the supplies and was busy taking care of the burn. When Lauren finished wrapping the hand, he told Margie, "Come back in a few days and let me have a look again. Take over-the-counter pain medicine as needed."

As soon as Margie left, Paxton removed his bandages. It was time he was a doctor instead of a patient.

Lauren came back into the exam room. "You need to keep those on a little longer."

"Not going to happen. I can't do my job."

She pursed her lips but didn't say anything more. Instead, she ushered in a mother with two small children. He put on his most reassuring smile. "Hi, I'm Dr. Samuels. What seems to be wrong today?"

"They have sore throats," the haggard-looking mother answered.

He deepened his smile as he coaxed the little girl, who was half cowering behind her bigger brother. "Let me have a look and I'll see if I can make you feel better."

The rest of the afternoon went much the same. As the sun was going down he was glad to see the waiting room was finally empty. His hands were hurting, which he had no intention of admitting to Lauren. She'd reminded him a number of times throughout the afternoon that he should be conscious of his hands.

"Well, that was interesting," he said now that it was just the two of them.

"How's that?" Lauren gave him a narrow-eyed look as if she thought he was saying something negative.

"Just that I've not seen those types of problems since I was in the Peace Corps."

"Really?" Surprise lit her voice. "You were in the Peace Corps?"

"Yeah, I spent a year working in clinics all around Africa. Sobering times." And freeing. A year that had him away from his parents and their expectations. He had been his own man. Here in Last Stop he was once again.

"That must have been interesting."

"It was. I was doing good work with people who needed a lot of help."

"As you can see, we need your help here as well." Lauren went about straightening up the waiting room. "You offered good care this afternoon. Even with hurt hands."

"Thanks." It was nice to hear her praise. "Is every day like today?"

"No, sometimes we're busier. Or super-slow. Some of these people drive over an hour to get to a doctor. Dr. Barden moved to the coast four days ago so some of them have been waiting to see you for a while. You can guarantee they're sick when they make that effort."

"That reminds me. I saw a man before you got here." She turned to look at him. "Who?"

"I'd rather not say. He wanted the visit to remain between us."

"Okay." She sounded curious and maybe hurt as well.

"Anyway, I have a urine sample that needs to be run. Can you add that to the others going to the lab? By the way, how's all that handled?"

"It has to be sent to Lippscomb. They'll be picked up by a courier in a few minutes. You should have the results first thing in the morning. What name do I need to put on the sample?"

"Don't worry about it. I'll take care of it." He would process the sample and put it in the cooler before the courier came.

"By the way, is there a room or closet not used in the house that I could set up as a small lab? We need to be offering quicker results than the next day, whenever we can."

She looked back at him. "There's one off the kitchen that's used for storage but doesn't have much in it."

"May I look at it?"

"Sure. I have a few more minutes before I have to go."

He followed her down the hall. "By the way, who do I thank for seeing to it my bed was made?"

She said over her shoulder, "That would be my mom. I called ahead and she came over and put things to rights. I knew you wouldn't feel like it."

"Please tell her thank you for me."

"Will do." She led him to a small door off the kitchen and opened it.

"Why didn't Dr. Barden have a lab?"

"He didn't think it was necessary. He was happy enough with the way things were handled. You'll learn that things change slowly around here." She sounded both resigned and ambivalent. "He was a good doctor to us for forty years." This time her tone rang clearly—tread lightly.

Paxton peered into the open doorway. There were shelves on each side, creating a narrow path to a wooden workbench in the back. Stepping inside, he searched for the light switch. "Is there any light in here?"

Lauren came to stand beside him and reached beneath a shelf. Light flooded the room.

"Had that hidden, didn't you?" Paxton smiled at her.

She grinned and shrugged.

He continued on to the bench. It looked sturdy and was the right height. This space would work quite nicely.

Lauren touched one of the shelves. "Do you think

we'd need all these? There would be more room if we took one side out."

"That's a good plan. We'll need a dedicated electric line to support the centrifuge and other equipment. It won't be a fully fledged lab but it'll at least give us some basic answers faster." He moved to the back of the closet and searched for outlets.

Lauren joined him. "I know a couple of people I think would do the work for cost. I'll get in contact with them tomorrow. What about the equipment?"

"I'll handle that." He'd have what they needed shipped out from Boston as soon as possible.

Lauren turned to leave at the same time he did. Paxton bumped into her and she teetered to one side. He grabbed her forearms, keeping her on her feet. Her palms landed on his chest, feeling as if they were branding him. With wide-eyed uncertainty, she stared at him. His gaze dropped to her slightly parted full lips.

What would she do if he kissed her? Could he stop himself?

She pulled her upper lip between her teeth.

"Lauren?"

A woman's voice calling her name barely registered through the haze of anticipated pleasure racing through him.

Lauren abruptly pushed against his chest. Paxton reluctantly straightened and backed away. He took a stabilizing deep breath.

She hurried out of the closet. "Mom, I'm right here," she answered a shade too quickly, sounding breathless. And had there been a slight quaver in her voice as well?

"What're you doing in there?" Her mother stepped to the door.

"We were discussing making the area into a lab." Lauren sounded more in control.

Paxton waited a few seconds before following her out. An older version of Lauren with short hair stood in the middle of the kitchen, watching him.

Lauren's hand shook slightly as she extended it. "Mom, I'd like you to meet Dr. Paxton Samuels. My mom, Sarah Tucker."

Mrs. Tucker smiled. "Hi! It's nice to meet you. I understand you were the hero of the hour last night."

He shrugged. At this rate he might start believing the gossips. "I wouldn't quite put it that way. Your daughter was a great help. I'd take her aid in an emergency any day. It's a pleasure to meet you. And thanks for making my bed and seeing the place was ready for me."

Mrs. Tucker gave him a warm smile. "You're very welcome. I'm just sorry you had such a hard start here in Last Stop."

"Mom brought you soup for dinner. It's on the stove, warming." Lauren didn't look him in the eyes.

"Thank you." His gaze went from daughter to mother. "You've already done too much."

More food. Just what he needed.

"We're just glad you're here. I'd better go now. I know you could use a full night's rest." Lauren's mother smiled and headed back down the hall.

Lauren turned to follow her. "See you in the morning."

Paxton watched her go, regretting the interruption and yet relieved at the same time. He hated he'd missed out on that kiss but it hadn't been a good idea.

No matter how attractive he found Lauren, starting a fling with his nurse showed poor judgment.

* * *

Lauren wasn't sure a night spent in her own bed had left her any more refreshed than she had been after her stay in the hotel. Paxton affected her, stirred her passion in more ways than one.

She couldn't fault the way he interacted with the patients. He listened. Took time to hear their complaints. Had been welcoming with the kids. There was nothing of the hurry-up-you-are-a-number mentality she'd anticipated from a big East Coast doctor.

The fact he'd worked in the Peace Corps revealed a side of him she hadn't expect either. Nothing in his on-line pedigree had adequately prepared her for the flesh-and-blood Paxton who'd been right in there with her, providing emergency medical care for Lewis. Last Stop could have done worse in a replacement doctor.

His official biography had provided all the pertinent information. Paxton was more than qualified for the job. Along with that she had noticed that his last name was the same as the clinic he was associated with in Boston. She couldn't help but be impressed. On another suggested link on the search page she had read something about the wedding of the year having been called off and Paxton's name had been included.

What had happened? Had Paxton been left at the altar? Or maybe he had been the one doing the leaving. She'd been interrupted by Shawn and had never returned to read more. Now her curiosity was piqued.

To make it worse, she found him extremely attractive with his dark good looks. And that almost-kiss… She'd not been prepared for it and yet she would have welcomed it. The bump had been innocent, she was sure.

However, it wasn't like her to kiss someone she didn't

know well. A man possibly on the rebound. And there was her young son to consider. She wasn't going to bring someone into Shawn's life who would leave soon. Living in a tiny town meant her reputation was important. She'd been careful to have a good one since returning home and needed to continue doing so, for Shawn's sake.

When her husband had come to town she'd been looking for excitement, something more than had been available in Last Stop. He had offered it. There had been youthful lust and then love between them, but none of the raw sexuality she felt around Paxton. Why was she so very aware of him on that primal level? The one thing she was sure of was that her home was in Last Stop now and Paxton was merely passing through. She had no intentions of repeating the past.

That realization helped her fight the zip of anticipation rushing through her each time she contemplated seeing Paxton again. It had been so long since she'd felt that kind of male/female attraction that a sliver of fear accompanied it. Paxton was essentially her boss for the next month. Then he'd be gone. And they were from two entirely different worlds. He wasn't a man to hang her future on, and yet…he made her feel alive again. No one should know how she was feeling. Especially Paxton. What would it hurt for her to enjoy it while it lasted?

After dropping Shawn off with her mother, Lauren drove to the clinic. She entered the front door and started down the hall.

"Good morning, Lauren."

She looked into the office. Paxton sat behind the desk, studying a laptop screen.

"You're up and at it early this morning," she commented, grateful he was acting as if nothing had happened between them the evening before. For him it probably hadn't been a big deal.

"I could say the same about you. I wanted to check the lab work. My patient will need to come in and have an exam after all."

Lauren harrumphed. "Your mystery patient?"

"Yes, that's the one. But I don't know how to get in touch with him. All I have is his name."

She waited expectantly.

He regarded her with speculative eyes before conceding, "I guess I don't have any choice but to tell you. It's Mr. Gerhart."

"What? He came in. I can't believe it. I've never seen or heard of him going to a doctor."

Paxton looked back at the laptop. "It was him. Lewis's grandfather."

"That's him." She was shocked he'd come the first time and couldn't imagine him doing it a second. "Good luck getting him back in here."

"Then we'll go see him."

She was stunned by his directness. "Okay. But before we do that I'd like to have a look at your hands."

"They're a lot better." His attention returned to the computer screen.

"I'd still like to have a look." She used her firm tone that made Shawn pay attention.

His glance conveyed irritation. "You don't trust my professional opinion?"

"Not when it concerns your personal recovery. Something about you makes me think you don't give your own healthcare anywhere near the attention you give your patients."

Paxton pursed his lips but there was a slight upturn

at the corners. "You think you know me that well after less than forty-eight hours?"

"Some things you can discern about a person pretty quickly." Like the idea he might be a great kisser? Those thoughts she'd best keep to a minimum for her sanity's sake.

Paxton's eyes narrowed. "I'm not sure I like being that transparent."

She shrugged, careful to conceal her triumph. "I still want to have a look at your hands. You want me to do it here or in the exam room?"

"I'm good with here, if you are."

Lauren pulled the chair in front of the desk around to his side. "I see you reapplied bandages. Smart move."

"Okay, so they hurt a little when exposed to cold air. I needed sleep last night."

"We both did. Let me see the right one first." She held out a hand.

Paxton did as she requested. She unwrapped the gauze. His fingers were pink. "Wiggle them for me." Paxton did so. "I'd say you're right. You're on the mend. Let me check the other one."

He huffed but presented his hand. A few minutes later she sat back. "It looks like you will recover with no ill effects but you're going to need to take care of them. Keep them covered outside. This isn't the running from heated building to heated building that you're used to."

"I have to admit I should have taken the time to cover them, but I packed hurriedly and wasn't sure where to find my gloves. My decision to accept this position was rather last minute."

"Why was that?" Would he tell her about the wedding business without her asking?

"Let's just say that's a subject better left alone. So, tell me about a typical week at Last Stop's clinic. One that doesn't include a tractor accident."

She guessed that was as good as a no. So what was he hiding? Lauren wanted to pursue the mystery but instead she said, "As a general rule, the clinic is open Monday through Friday, with Wednesday afternoon off."

"So that means I'd be able to do some shopping tomorrow?"

"Yeah."

He nodded. "Good. Then I'll get some heavier pants, thick socks and adequate gloves. Is Lippscomb where I need to go?"

"That's what I'd suggest. Well, I'd better get busy. I've got some restocking to do in the exam room before our first patient shows up."

She made it as far as the door before Paxton called after her, "I've been meaning to ask you, who's this person you keep talking to and rushing off to?"

His question froze her. He'd been wondering about her personal life? Did he think she had a boyfriend?

She half turned in order to see his face before she answered. "My son, Shawn."

Only the blink of his eyes made her aware of his astonishment.

"Son," he said, more to himself than her, as if he was mulling over the idea. "That one I hadn't expected." Paxton opened his mouth as if he wanted to say more but the bell ringing signaled a patient had arrived.

Their morning went much as the afternoon before with a regular stream of patients. When they did have a break, Paxton went to his office and she did paperwork at her desk.

At noon, he asked, "How's lunch handled around here?"

She smiled. "We usually eat."

"Funny." He grinned.

"I normally bring my lunch and eat in the kitchen. Dr. Barden always went home. Since the kitchen is now your personal space, I'll just eat at my desk."

"I see no reason we can't share the kitchen table. In fact, you don't have to bring your lunch, I've enough food for a year back here." He strolled toward the kitchen. "Which reminds me, I need to do something with all this food."

"I can help with that," she offered. He did sound overwhelmed.

"I'd be grateful."

She wasn't surprised to find that all of it was still set out on the counter. He wouldn't have felt like it or cared enough last night to put it away. With her knowledge of the ladies in town, she was sure the refrigerator held the food that would spoil. Going to the refrigerator, she looked in.

"Heaven's sakes, there's more." His exasperation rang clear.

She glanced back. Paxton was peering over her shoulder. Their mouths were inches apart. For a moment their gazes met, held. Passion rose in his. There was a hint of a dare there.

It was time for her to get a grip. Lauren was old enough to push temptation away. She intended to move out from between him and the refrigerator but that didn't make the situation better when she straightened. Instead, her body brushed against his. From shoulders to hips she felt his warmth. That awareness from the day before had gone from simmering to boiling.

Paxton stepped away, as if he had suddenly realized what was happening and had thought better of it.

The cool air from the refrigerator wasn't strong enough to overcome the heat generated between them. She gestured vaguely. "I, uh, need to get that food put away. I don't know what you had planned for your lunch but there're a couple of casseroles in here you might want to try. Just put some in the microwave."

"You won't join me?"

She couldn't admit that he'd rattled her nerves and she couldn't eat. Instead, she said, "Yeah, I'll have some." Going to a cabinet, she pulled two plates out. "Why don't you sit down and I'll do this."

He looked genuinely grateful and disturbed at the same time. "Thanks. I'm going to owe you big time when I get my hands back and figure out everything around here."

"No problem. Being someplace new always means a learning curve."

She went back to the refrigerator and pulled out a dish. "This is Mrs. Clara's chicken casserole. It's one of my favorites." She put two large spoonsful of casserole on a plate, placed it in the microwave and started it. While it was heating she began putting food away in the cabinets.

At the ding of the microwave she placed the plate on the table in front of Paxton. She pulled out a nearby drawer, found forks and handed him one.

"Will you tell me about the people who live here?"

"I mentioned before that most of them are either farm-ing families that go back generations or are involved in the natural gas industry. My family happens to be a little bit of both. We farm close to a thousand acres. Some cows and growing wheat and grain for livestock. We also have gas wells." She served up her own plate and started it heating.

"I saw some wells, driving up here. First time I've seen the real thing. Before only in pictures. I was ex-pecting more of the tall iron pyramids."

"That's rigging they use when digging a well. When the well is ready to produce, all that is needed is the pump and meters to read the flow."

"Well, you learn something new every day." Paxton acted genuinely amazed and impressed. "Don't see or get much of that kind of thing in Boston."

She grinned. "I don't imagine you do."

"So I'm guessing the people around here are well-to-do."

Lauren chuckled and removed her plate from the mi-crowave. "These are gas wells, not oil. The income was good during my great-grandparents' days. The money is more supplemental now. Occasionally there's a new well drilled but not so much anymore. For the most part people here live simply."

"I like the people I've met so far."

Lauren joined him at the table. "You seem to have made a positive impression on them as well. My mother thought you were very nice."

Thought he was handsome. Asked if he was single.

All questions Lauren didn't want to respond to. It was time for a change in subject despite her own personal cu-riosity about Paxton. What had brought him here, what his life had been like in Boston…did he have a girl-friend? "Now you know about me, so what about you?"

"It's pretty simple. This opportunity came up. I wanted to do something different and here I am." Paxton had no intention of admitting he hadn't been enough for the woman he had been set to marry. His ego wouldn't let him even if he'd wanted to reveal that hard-to-swallow truth to Lauren.

"Does your wife or girlfriend mind you being away for so long?"

"I don't have either."

And I'm not looking.

"Just so you know, I sort of looked you up on the in-ternet."

"Sort of?" He watched her closely, trying to judge what she might know.

Lauren shrugged. "Well, more like read about you."

"And what did you learn?" Panic filled him. Had she seen his personal catastrophe on the internet? Hope-fully not.

"I learned you're not the only doctor in your family."

This he would talk about. "Yes, my family profes-sion is medicine, but I didn't become a doctor because of that. I wanted to help people and I was interested in medicine."

Lauren's look made him wonder if she saw through that statement, and sensed the unrelenting pressure he would have been under had he refused to become a doctor.

"So how many of you are doctors?" Lauren loaded a fork with food.

"My father and his brother, a couple of cousins and their children are involved in medicine in some way."

Her look turned thoughtful. "Apple didn't fall far from the tree."

"I guess not." Paxton wasn't sure if that was a compliment or not. He hoped he was different in some very fundamental ways. He'd tried hard enough, and was still trying. That was enough about him.

"Have you always lived in Boston?"

"I'm like you, I left for a little while but have always returned." He couldn't hide out here forever this time either. He would return to Boston. There really wasn't a choice now his father's heart disease was progressing. Paxton was needed at the clinic. There was more pressure than ever for him to take over his father's practice and place on the clinic board. Paxton could see the future mapped out for him.

"Not to pry but you said there was no wife or girlfriend but I saw something about a wedding."

He guessed he owed her some explanation. She had answered his questions. Even the personal ones. "I no longer have a fiancée. There was no wedding."

"I'm sorry."

"I'm not. In hindsight, it was something my parents wanted more than me. We'd been friends for a long time and it was more about it being time to marry than about love." At least he'd come to that conclusion on the long drive west.

His phone rang. He looked at it. He sighed. It was his father. "Excuse me a sec. I need to get this," he said to Lauren. He answered as he walked toward his bedroom. "Hi, Dad."

"How're things going out there?" For once his father sounded genuinely interested.

Paxton told him a little about a couple of cases he'd seen.

"That sounds good, but you know you have patients here as well who depend on you."

Here it goes.

"I know that but I'm in Last Stop for now."

"Son, you need to think about what you're doing. Your patients will find another doctor if you stay away too long. Can't they get someone so you can come back sooner? You're needed at the board meeting next week. The least you could do is be home for Christmas. Your mother—"

Paxton had heard all of this he wanted. "Dad, I've got to go. I have a patient to see. I'll talk to you later. Bye."

He returned to the kitchen.

Lauren gave him a questioning look. "Everything okay?"

"Yeah. Just my father checking in." Paxton glanced at his watch. "Before we get back to work, do you think you could get Mr. Gerhart's phone number for me? Discreetly?"

"I can do that." Concern filled her eyes. "Is there something seriously wrong?"

It wouldn't hurt for her to know. Lauren was a professional. She would keep the secret. "It doesn't appear to be the bladder infection I suspected. I need to do an exam for an enlarged prostate. At his age… He seemed like a really private man and I don't want to broadcast he might have a problem."

Her mouth went into a thin line. "I appreciate that. He's one of those men's men who doesn't like to show weakness."

"I think most of us are." Or at least he had been before Gabriella had cut him down to size in that area. His ego had definitely taken a hit.

They finished their meals and Lauren took their plates to the dishwasher. "I'll get that number for you."

Paxton watched the gentle sway of her hips, encased in tight jeans again, as she walked away. Her hair was tied back and his fingers itched to pull her ponytail down and see it cascade around her shoulders. Why did he find her so alluring? Maybe it was because she knew him only as himself and not the Boston socialite whose fiancée had all but left him at the altar.

His parents had made it clear his recent decision to leave town reflected negatively on the family. They believed he should have forgiven Gabriella and moved on. For him loyalty was a basic building block of a relationship. One he wasn't willing or going to compromise on, not even to make his parents happy.

Paxton headed for his office, wanting to check on the latest lab results.

A few minutes later Lauren handed him a slip of paper. "Here's Mr. Gerhart's number."

Mr. Gerhart answered on the second ring. Paxton explained the situation and asked the man to come in. He refused. Paxton told him he would come to him then and that what was going on would remain between the two of them. Mr. Gerhart agreed. Paxton finished with, "Okay, I'll see you in fifteen minutes."

Paxton went in search of Lauren. He found her in the small closet where he planned to put the lab. She was pulling a box by her fingertips off an upper shelf. "Hey, let me get that for you."

The box tilted to one side and Paxton hurried to put a hand up to stop it from falling on her. Lauren jerked away as he grabbed the box. He placed it on a lower shelf and turned to face her. Her eyes were wide as she stared at him. Electricity arced between them.

She appeared ready to run. Did the fear he might kiss her have her that skittish? Making her afraid of him had not been his intention.

In an attempt to calm her he asked, "Hey, what's so important in this box that you'd be willing to bring it down on your head?"

"Christmas decorations."

His mouth fell open. That was the last thing he'd expected her to answer. She'd caught him completely by surprise.

"You know—those things that shine and twinkle, that you put up once a year."

Her sassy tone made him grin. "Yeah, I know what they are. I just hadn't thought about them being here." He took the box, stepped out into the kitchen and set it on one of the chairs.

Lauren joined him.

"I got Mr. Gerhart on the phone. The conversation was short and to the point but he agreed to see me and I have to go to him. I'm headed out now. I'll see any patient who comes in just as soon as I return. Can you tell me where he lives?"

"Out off the Lippscomb Highway. Turn at the second road. Third farm on the left. Red barn."

"Sounds doable. After I get back I thought I'd drive to Lippscomb and get that shopping done. I know it's your afternoon off, but I'd appreciate you showing me where to go."

For a second, he was afraid she was going to turn him

down, but she shrugged. "I guess I could, but Shawn will have to go with us."

Outside seeing children occasionally in his practice, he hadn't been around them much. He liked them well enough but had never spent an afternoon with one. "That shouldn't be a problem."

She gave him a thoughtful look for a moment as if she sensed his uncertainty. "I'll go pick him up and be waiting here when you get back."

"Sounds like a plan. Wish me luck with Mr. Gerhart." Paxton started toward the back door.

She grinned. "You'll need it."

"Thanks for the encouragement," he called over his shoulder as he left. It was nice to share a conversation with a woman who made him smile when he went out the door. Whenever he'd left Gabriella, she had been complaining or telling him what social engagement she had decided they would attend next. Why hadn't he noticed that before now?

CHAPTER FIVE

PAXTON ENTERED THE kitchen through the back door. Lauren was at the kitchen table, putting an ornament on a miniature tree sitting on the table. She'd changed clothes and was now wearing a heavy-knit sweater in green with a large collar over black jeans. Her cowboy boots had been replaced by some dressier boots. She looked fashionable and sexy at the same time.

He grinned. "Success."

She stopped what she was doing and looked at him. "Really? How did you manage that?"

He put his bag on a chair and pulled his gloves off, dropping them on the table. "I can't give away my trade secrets." He couldn't help but be proud of himself.

"What did you do? Threaten to tell his wife? Make him come here? Say you would tell everyone in town?"

"Let's just say I put it in terms a man can understand." He removed his coat.

"I have to say I'm impressed. Not even Dr. Barden managed to get him to see him. House call or not. You're my hero."

Her hero? He liked the sound of that. It was like balm to his bruised ego. Paxton's grin grew into a full smile.

"Thanks." His attention turned to the table. "What have you been up to here?"

"Just putting up Christmas decorations."

He gave the tree a look. "You didn't have to do that for me."

"Well, with the exception of this tree, it's more for the patients." She hung the last ornament.

"Mommy?"

Paxton's head swung to the door of his bedroom. A little boy with dark hair and dressed in navy overalls came toddling out.

"Hey, there, honey." Lauren swooped Shawn up into her arms and pulled him to her chest for a hug. She turned to Paxton. "I hope you don't mind, I put him down for a nap on a pallet in your room. Less draft."

"No, I don't mind."

"Shawn—" Lauren looked at the boy with such love and devotion "—this is Dr. Samuels."

"That's a mouthful for a little boy. Make it Paxton." The look he received from Lauren made him think he'd said something wonderful.

"Max," Shawn said.

"Pax," he said, and Lauren shook her head and laughed. "How old is he?" Paxton asked. He'd always been ambivalent about children. With the family he'd grown up in he wasn't sure he really wanted any. He didn't want the pressure he felt to rub off on his own kids.

"Two and a half. I'll get Shawn changed and we'll head to Lippscomb." She went into his room.

Paxton stepped to the door, leaned against the door-post and watched as she changed Shawn's diaper with the same efficiency she did everything. As she worked she spoke to the boy, making him giggle.

Lauren came to Paxton and held Shawn out to him. "If you'll hold him a sec, I can get his diaper bag together."

Paxton hesitated. He didn't make a habit of holding children. When Shawn reached for him Paxton took him, holding him out from his body.

"If you hold him a little closer it would be easier." Lauren picked up a bag with tractors on the cover and stuffed some items in it.

"Max," Shawn repeated with a grin.

Lauren laughed. "You may get another name."

"Uh…yeah, I can tell that." He handed Shawn back to her with some relief.

In the kitchen, Lauren bundled the boy into a coat and hat. While she did that, Paxton put his own coat on. Lauren handed Shawn to him again. It was as if she thought everyone was comfortable holding a baby. She shrugged into her coat, which had been hanging on one of the chairs. With that done, she reached for Shawn, who happily went back to her. Paxton was glad to have her take him. Lauren pulled the bag up over her shoulder with the ease of someone who had juggled it all before.

At the back door, she said, "I'll drive. Shawn's car seat is already in the truck. Your fancy sports car wasn't made with babies in mind."

Paxton went to the passenger seat while Lauren strapped Shawn into his seat in the back before she slid behind the steering wheel. He was used to doing the driving, was usually the one in control. Here he was again at her mercy.

They were on the outskirts of town when he asked,

"So do you have a place in mind where I can get some clothes?"

"I know just the place. They should have everything you need." She picked up the speed.

"Good. I don't want to have to do this again."

"Not a shopper?"

"No. I usually order what I need. My doorman sees to my returns."

"Doorman, huh?" She glanced at him. "Why am I not surprised?"

"What's that supposed to mean?" She made it sound like he was a criminal.

"You just strike me as a man who's used to doing the everyday things in the simplest way."

At least that was a step above saying he was too lazy to do for himself. He watched her. She had her hair down but pinned back on one side so that her pert nose was clearly visible. The sunlight reflected off her soft skin, giving her a healthy glow. She was nothing like the make-up-dependent women he was familiar with.

Shawn squealed, jolting him out of his thoughts.

"We're almost there, sweetheart. I know you're ready to get out of that seat." Lauren reached back and shook Shawn's chair. He quieted for a minute then started up again. She asked Paxton, "Would you mind handing him that toy that's on the seat?"

Paxton twisted in the seat, found the truck and gave it to Shawn, who promptly threw it on the floor. This could be one of the reasons he had never shown much interest in children. Reaching around as far as he could, bringing him in contact with Lauren's shoulder, he grabbed the toy. Lauren's sharp intake of breath didn't miss his attention. Paxton handed the truck to the boy. "Here you go."

Shawn threw the truck again.

"Stop that, Shawn!" Lauren glared back at him.

Shawn continued to play the game, giggling and grinning each time he dropped the toy. Lauren finally pulled into a parking space in front of a building. Paxton was relieved—he hadn't been having as much fun with that game as Shawn had been.

They were in front of a department store on the main street in Lippscomb. "I'll need to get Shawn in the stroller then I'll be on in."

"I'll get the stroller." Paxton had seen it in the back of the truck when he'd gotten in. He went to the tailgate, released it and lifted the folded stroller out. He attempted to unfold it. It released part of the way but refused to lock into place.

"You have to pull up on the red button while pulling on the handle to get it to lock into place," Lauren called.

It took him a couple of seconds to locate the button. He tried again. Nothing. He'd seen surgeries less complicated than dealing with a stroller. Paxton was still working with it when Lauren joined him with Shawn in her arms.

He gave her a contrite look.

She grinned. "I'll admit it's not that easy."

He didn't like having his vulnerability show. He couldn't look like less of a man because of a stroller. At least she wasn't laughing at him. "Does this thing require an engineering degree to work it?"

"No, but it can be contrary."

Lauren handed him Shawn, which was the lesser of two evils at this point. Shawn patted Paxton's face as if they were new best friends. Lauren soon had the stroller open and was reaching for her son. With the efficiency of a mother who had done the job more than once, she had the boy strapped in and ready to go. She pushed the stroller toward the double glass doors.

Paxton followed, feeling defeated. He'd questioned having children and the ride to Lippscomb with Shawn had confirmed it. He should think long and hard about being a parent. He held the door open for Shawn and Lauren to enter.

Lauren said as she passed him and entered the store, "You're not the first to have a problem with that stroller. You should have seen me the first time."

That did make him feel a little better.

Inside she stopped and waved a hand in the direction of the right side of the store. "You should find what you need over there. Shawn and I are going to go over here—" she indicated the other side of the store "—to see if we can find something to wear for the community Christmas party."

"What's that?"

She gave him an odd look. "You know, where all the town comes together for dinner and a dance."

Paxton shrugged. "I've never been to something like that." He'd attended plenty of country club dances but never one where an entire community was invited.

"It's the best event of the year. Great food, kids running around and a couple of the local guys making up a band. It's so much fun. Really puts you in the Christmas spirit."

Paxton wasn't sure that or anything else would put him in the spirit. He'd never been big on Christmas or family get-togethers. And after his non-wedding he didn't care about them. He wasn't feeling warm and fuzzy about anything these days.

"Everyone is welcome. You need to plan to come. It would be a great way to meet everyone."

He shook his head. "I don't know. I'm not much on parties."

He started off toward the men's clothing. Years of required country club parties and social "must-dos" had him eager to stay away from anything that resembled one. At least if he did decide to go it would be because he wanted to, not because he was pressured into it. Not unlike what he felt when one of his parents called now.

Going to the men's department, he picked up a couple of pairs of slacks and some denim shirts but he made a point to avoid the Western-cut ones. He didn't see them as his style. Finding the socks, Paxton picked out a number of pairs of thick ones. The ties hung close by. There was a red one with reindeer heads on it. For some reason he felt daring. He didn't know where he would wear it but it was something his mother would frown on and that was enough. Conservative ties and suits had been the norm for him for so long it felt good to branch out.

He was checking out his purchases at the back of the store when Lauren walked up. She had some red fabric over her arm and a child's outfit hanging on the stroller handle. "I see you found something."

She put the clothing on the counter for the woman to ring up. "Yeah, we don't get many reasons for dressy events around here so I'm making the most of it."

Unlike the world he'd left, where his hand-tailored tuxedo hung in his closet.

"So when we do, everyone makes the most of it." She smiled. "And it's Christmastime."

She made her purchases and they returned to the car. As she put Shawn in his car seat Paxton made a show of folding and putting the stroller in the truck. It turned out it was much easier to close than to open. Puffed with pride, he got into the passenger seat.

Lauren looked at him with a grin on her lips. "Feeling pretty good about yourself, aren't you?"

His chin went high. "Yes, I am."

She giggled. A real giggle. He hadn't heard a sound like that in years. One that rang of sincerity. Women around him had made a noise like a giggle as a way of getting their way, but Lauren's was one of pure pleasure. It was a sound he wanted to experience again.

As she backed out of the parking space she asked, "Do you mind if we stop by the feed store? My father needs me to pick up a couple of bags of feed for a calf that's not eating well."

"Sure. That's fine with me."

Lauren drove out of town the way they had come. They were almost to the town limits when she pulled into a gravel lot. They faced a low building that was set well off the road and had a loading dock running across the front of it. Pickup trucks of all makes and models, including a number with stock trailers attached, were parked in the lot.

Pulling close to a ramp, she said, "This is one of the best places in town. They have everything you need from feed, to clothing, to house goods. One-stop shopping."

"So why didn't we come here first?"

She studied him up and down, wrinkled her nose and said, "Not your style. And I'd been thinking about the dress I bought."

"I get it. We were really shopping for you," he teased.

"Maybe a little bit."

Paxton enjoyed their easy banter. He'd had too little

of that in his life. Lauren had a quick wit. It was refreshing to have a woman be completely honest with him.

Climbing out of the truck, he quickly had the stroller out and ready by the time Lauren had Shawn in her arms.

"Ever been to a Feed and Seed before?" Lauren asked as she put Shawn in the stroller.

"No."

"You're in for a treat." She pushed the stroller up the ramp. "This was my favorite place to come as a child. Shawn already loves it."

Paxton joined her as they walked past a large open roller door. She continued down the dock to the double glass entrance. He held a door wide for her while she maneuvered Shawn inside.

Lauren was right. He had never been any place like it. There were work clothes, boots and hats, camping equipment, guns, feed bins for any size animal, horse tack and garden tools. He could hardly keep up with Lauren for looking around at stuff he would have no idea how to find in Boston.

She headed straight down the center aisle to the back of the store. There he saw a counter behind which stood a bearded man wearing a flannel shirt. A number of other men mingled nearby, talking to one another or just drinking from mugs. All of them wore cowboy hats, heavy coats and well-worn cowboy boots. Each man either spoke, nodded or tipped their hat to Lauren as she approached.

"Hey, Joe," she said to the man behind the counter. "Can I get a couple of twenty-five-pound bags of that special calf mix for Dad?"

The man smiled at her. "Sure. I'll be right out with it."

"Just put it on Dad's tab," she called to his back.

Paxton had wandered to a shelf filled with all types of knives. She came over to him. "Tab?" Paxton questioned. "People still do that?"

She looked surprised at the question and nodded. "Yep, people still do that. Dad pays his off on the first of the month."

Where he came from nobody would even consider running a tab for someone. That kind of trust had long gone. He liked the idea that people in the area did things based on faith. He had certainly had his shaken by Gabriella and his parents.

By the time they had arrived back at the truck a couple of strapping young men arrived with a bag apiece over their shoulders.

"Just put it in the back," Lauren told them as she strapped a wiggling Shawn into his seat. Paxton stowed the stroller. A strange sense of accomplishment came over him for having mastered it.

Lauren waved. "Thanks, guys."

They were leaving the parking lot when Paxton asked, "Before we head back, why don't we get some dinner? I owe you for the pizza and breakfast the other day."

She pulled onto the highway. "I appreciate the offer but I can't. I get too little time with Shawn as it is and Wednesday night is our family time. I really try to protect it."

Was she kidding? Family time? What he knew about family time was rushing to get in the car to head to a social event his mother said they all must attend. Actually spending real time listening and talking and finding out who he really was his parents had never done. Maybe they didn't want to know. "Maybe next time."

Their trip home consisted of mostly Lauren singing

or talking to Shawn. She was a good mother who obviously loved her child dearly. They were almost at Last Stop when the boy nodded off to sleep.

"Well, you'll at least get a mile or two of peace." Lauren laughed.

"It hasn't been that bad." To his surprise, it hadn't. "He seems like a nice kid."

"Yeah, he is. I rather like him." She looked into the rear-view mirror with a slight smile on her lips and love shining in her eyes.

What would it be like to have someone like Lauren look at him with such love and devotion? He'd never seen that in Gabriella and he'd been planning to marry her! What had he been thinking? How had he let his parents' expectations control his life so much? He was a grown man, working in a field of responsibility and he'd let others lead him around by the nose. Why?

Because he'd been brought up to honor his family heritage, because he loved his parents and wanted to make them happy. Because he'd never really thought about what he wanted. What would make him happy. He knew clearly one thing he didn't want, to be married to someone just because it was the right thing to do.

He'd already learned more about himself in less than a week while being around Lauren and living in Last Stop than he had in years of living his other life.

A few minutes later Lauren pulled into the clinic drive. "I appreciate you taking me along today." He gathered his packages.

"Not a problem. I'll see you in the morning."

Paxton watched her back out. He didn't like the feeling of being left behind.

CHAPTER SIX

THE NEXT TWO days at the clinic passed for Paxton much the same as the others, minus another tractor accident. He and Lauren were kept busy tending patients. Lewis and Mr. Thompson came in for their checkups. Both again expressed their gratitude.

Friday evening Lauren announced with a wave, "See you Monday morning."

Paxton had an unshakable sensation of being left behind again, but he needed the time to think. He'd run to Last Stop in the heat of the moment, to put distance between him and the shambles of his life in Boston, but he couldn't hide forever.

This was only a temporary reprieve from his career and responsibilities in Boston. He had a practice, positions on committees and people who expected results from him. With his father's illness, the duties had grown. While in Last Stop he had to make some positive decisions regarding his life, his future.

That evening, he had dinner in front of the TV. He couldn't remember the last time he'd not had plans for the weekend. The freedom he was discovering in Last Stop had a healthy appeal.

Though Saturday morning was overcast and gray he

went out anyway, intent on exploring. He drove along each street. It didn't take him long to see the entire town because it was only six blocks long and four wide. He had no idea where Lauren lived but he'd secretly hoped he might run into her. By the time he'd seen everything it was close enough to lunchtime that he stopped in at the café on Main Street.

"Hi, Dr. Samuels."

His waitress turned out to be Margie, who'd come in with the burned hand.

"Well, hi. How's your hand?"

She waved it at him. "I'm waiting tables until it gets better."

"Good. Are you keeping it dry and clean?"

She nodded. "Just like you told me. So, what can I get you?"

"I'd like the soup of the day and a BLT." Paxton took a seat at one of the tables.

While he ate, more than one person stopped and welcomed him to town. If he had been out for a meal in Boston no one would have looked him in the eye as they walked past, much less said hi. Here he felt appreciated. Another essential he lacked in his life.

Returning home, he checked lab results, but there was nothing that couldn't be taken care of on Monday. By mid-afternoon he was bored. Eager to start on the lab, he went searching for tools. Finding them under the kitchen sink, he proceeded to tear out the shelves on one side of the closet.

It was dusk when he started hauling them out to the backyard and heard the sounds of a band tuning up. It seemed to be coming from the direction of the high school he'd passed that morning. He looked around the house. Warmly dressed people were walking toward Main Street.

What's going on?

He wanted to find out. Washing up quickly, he grabbed his coat, gloves and beanie. He walked the block to where people were gathering along the street. Stopping beside a woman holding a child's hand, he asked, "What's happening?"

"Santa is coming," the little girl said, her face alight with excitement.

Her mother offered, "It's the annual Christmas parade. It starts in a few minutes."

Paxton nodded. "Oh." When was the last time he'd been to a Christmas parade? Or any parade, for that matter? His parents hadn't had time for that sort of thing.

Lewis, grinning and flanked by his grandfather, came up to Paxton. "Hi, Doc."

"Hey, Lewis. Nice to see you again. Mr. Gerhart." Paxton extended his hand.

The older man accepted it.

"You know my grandfather?" Lewis glanced curiously from one to the other.

"Uh, we met the other day." Paxton covered the best he could.

"Pops, I see someone I know. I'll see you later." Lewis patted his grandfather on the shoulder and without a backward glance headed straight for a teenage girl.

"So, how're you doing, Mr. Gerhart?" Paxton said, for the man's ears only.

"Better. Thanks for not saying anything in front of Lewis."

"Not a problem."

The noise of marching band instruments starting into

a Christmas carol filled the air. Paxton looked up the street toward the sound and spied Lauren, with Shawn on her hip. She wore the white coat she'd had on the first night they'd met. Her hood was over her head and pulled tight around her face. She was what he imagined a snow nymph would look like. Tiny, in white, with large expressive eyes. She lifted a mitten-covered hand in a small wave of acknowledgment.

"Mr. Gerhart, I see my nurse over there. I need to speak to her."

The older man gave him a wise, knowing look and a nod.

The band was coming down the street in formation just as Paxton jogged across the street. He squeezed in next to Lauren. "Hey."

She smiled. "Hey, yourself."

Paxton leaned in close so she could hear over the band. "Why didn't you tell me about this?"

"You didn't seem interested in the community dinner and dance so I thought you wouldn't be interested in this."

"Point taken."

"I saw you talking to your new best friend, Mr. Gerhart. Interested in getting anything off your chest?" Her look didn't waver.

"Nope." He smiled at her frustrated expression. "Patient-doctor privilege."

"You know I can keep a secret."

Paxton moved his face closer and whispered in her ear. "So can I."

"Funny."

The passing band made hearing difficult after that. It consisted of only ten people and was led by two young girls carrying a banner with "Merry Christmas" in big letters surrounded by glitter. Behind them was a pickup truck filled with cheerleaders waving their pom-poms. The crowd called out names and they responded with smiles and waves. It was followed by a convertible car with a man and woman waving from the back seat.

Paxton gave Lauren a quizzical look.

"The mayor and his wife."

They were followed by a tractor pulling a trailer loaded with a group of girls dressed in red cowboy hats, white shirts and full red skirts. They each waved to the crowd and threw candy to the kids. Again Paxton looked at Lauren.

"The Christmas Queen and her court."

"Oh." Interesting.

"I was the queen one year."

"I'm not surprised. You're pretty enough to be one." That was true but he shouldn't have said it out loud.

Lauren looked as shocked as he felt. Her eyes shone as she said, "Thank you."

Another couple of floats came by.

Lauren shifted Shawn to her other hip, putting him between them. A minute later another large tractor with a trailer attached came their way. Sitting on hay bales surrounded by presents was Santa Claus.

The crowd closed in on them. Lauren lifted Shawn to shoulder level. There was no way she would be able to hold him like that for long. Paxton took him from her and set Shawn on his shoulders.

Lauren looked at him in wonder and then appreciation. The boy fussed a little at Paxton's handling but settled when Lauren said, "Shawn, look. There's Santa Claus."

Apparently Shawn hadn't looked in the direction

she had wanted him to so Lauren wrapped her fingers around Paxton's arm and pulled close. "See, honey, there he is." She pointed to the road but she was watching Shawn, her face glowing with pure pleasure.

Paxton had never been a part of this type of parental moment yet it gave him a contented feeling deep inside, as if he were part of something special. That he somehow belonged. He looked at the people around him and across the street. This was a genuinely close-knit community. People knew each other, enjoyed the simple things in life and understood why that simplicity was important. Like having your child see Santa in a parade.

Big snowflakes started falling. Even to his jaded heart it was a magical moment.

Paxton anticipated that everyone would disperse in different directions when the parade was over. Instead, they all headed down the street in the same direction. "Where's everyone going?"

"To the church for hot chocolate. Wanna come?" Lauren's inviting grin made the decision for him.

He brought Shawn down into his arms. "Why not?"

Shawn wiggled and reached out for Lauren. Paxton handed him over. They followed the crowd.

Someone began to sing "We Wish You a Merry Christmas." The song grew in volume as everyone joined in, all headed to the white clapboard building with the tall steeple on the next block.

He and Lauren followed the line into a side door of the building. In the anteroom, they pulled off their caps and gloves. They were standing in the doorway, waiting to enter the crowded fellowship hall, when a girl of about ten years old came running up and slid to a stop.

She pointed above their heads and shouted, "They're under the mistletoe! They have to kiss!"

Virtually everyone turned to look at him and Lauren. Every expression clearly asked, *Well, are you going to kiss her?*

Paxton had been brought up to do what was expected of him. What made this situation special was his eagerness to comply.

Lauren's eyelids slowly lowered as he leaned in to find her lips. They were cool from having been outside, yet lush and smooth. Perfect. It was a chaste kiss as kisses went yet an electric jolt, warming him from the core out, shot through him.

Shawn wiggled in Lauren's arms. The kiss was almost over before it began. A few people snickered while others clapped but the moment was soon forgotten as the line formed to accept hot chocolate in plastic cups from women who were undoubtedly matriarchs of Last Stop. For Paxton the kiss lingered on his tingling lips. It hadn't been enough.

They mingled with the crowd. Lauren introduced a number of people to him and he was able to speak to some he'd seen during the week.

Soon Shawn yawned and Lauren announced it was time for her to go. They all bundled up again and headed out into the snowy night.

"May I walk you home or to your truck?" Paxton asked with confidence he didn't feel. The possibility she might say no was a bit unsettling. "I have no idea where you go after work," he quickly added, and for some reason he really wanted to know.

"Thanks, but neither are necessary. I just live a couple of blocks from here. Down that way." She pointed in the opposite direction from the one they had come. "I assure you I'll be fine."

He must have passed her house in his wanderings earlier in the day and not known it. "Just the same, I'll walk you home. I was taught to be a gentleman and to see that a lady gets home safely."

She chuckled. "I've never had anyone say that to me before."

"You should have."

Lauren gave him a speculative look then started down the sidewalk. "Well, if you insist."

"I do. And I insist you let me carry Shawn." Paxton reached for Shawn, who had fallen asleep. "He has to be heavy."

She gave her son up. Somehow having Lauren next to him as they walked through the night gave him a sense of peace he'd not known in a long time, if ever. The fact she had a child, he wasn't so sure about.

"This is me," Lauren said in front of a tiny clapboard house with a porch across the front. A single light glowed in the window of what had to be her living room.

"I'll take him now." She reached for Shawn.

"I've got him. Show me where to put him." Paxton walked toward the front door. By the time he climbed the three steps Lauren had the door open for him to enter. He stepped into her small living area. A floral sofa faced the window, an armchair filled in one corner. The TV took another and toys were everywhere.

"Down this way." Lauren flipped on a light in the hall.

Paxton trailed after her to a room decorated in cowboys and horses. A low bed was stationed in the corner.

He laid Shawn on it. Standing back, he watched Lauren remove her son's jacket and shoes.

"Tonight it won't hurt for him to sleep in his clothes," she whispered, before kissing Shawn on the forehead. She pulled the door partially closed behind her as they moved out into the hall. "Thanks for carrying him home. He's getting to be a heavy load."

"Not a problem." Paxton watched her for a moment, sort of hoping she'd ask him to stay for a while. When she didn't he said, "Well, I'd better go." It took willpower to conceal his disappointment.

She followed him to the front door. There he turned. "You know, I've been thinking about that kiss and I believe I can do a better job."

"Oh?"

He cupped her cheeks then covered her mouth with his. Her full lips pillowed his. There was a trembling hesitation before her hands slid up over his shoulders and around his neck. Her fingers tangled in his hair, nudging his head closer. His hands moved to her waist and pulled her against him. Paxton took the kiss deeper. She joined him in freefall.

Moments later he pulled back, breathless. "I think that was much better."

"Uh-huh," she said softly.

Lauren's eyes were glossy, her plump lips rosy. The temptation to kiss her again grew but if he gave in to it, he'd press for more, much more. She was too tantalizing for her own good but she didn't deserve being a rebound woman. His life was so screwed up he'd run away from it. He didn't have the right to involve her in the mess.

He stepped out the door. His voice hoarse with desire, he said, "'Night, Lauren."

An intense driving need made his heart race and held him balanced on the edge of reason. He'd never experienced this with Gabriella. Only with Lauren had he felt this new level of desire. He feared it couldn't be eased except by having her.

Doing his best to get his body under control, Paxton watched Lauren slowly close the door between them. The biting cold was welcome. It cooled his libido enough to stop him from knocking on her door.

Monday morning Lauren's body was still humming from Paxton's kiss. She had to continually remind herself that it meant nothing. It had been the mistletoe. Or him proving a point. Nothing special.

Yet her body refused to accept that. Their kiss *had* been special to her. Her toes had curled and she'd been speechless afterward. When she'd looked into Paxton's eyes there had been raw desire in their depths. It called to her even now. The second his lips had touched hers she'd lost her ability to think. What she'd had with Mark had been good but it had been easy, natural. With Paxton she felt unsure, oversensitive, an erotic excitement that was as frightening as it was new. It was as if she was walking too close to the edge of a cliff but couldn't stop herself from leaning forward to look over. It was both exhilarating and terrifying.

Was history repeating itself? Was she being swept into something where hurt would be the only outcome? It would be best if she and Paxton stayed at arm's length but she wasn't even sure she could do that. Caution should be her standard.

After dropping Shawn off at the babysitter's for the day, she drove to the clinic with some trepidation and hot anticipation. Would Paxton mention their kiss? Try to do it again? Did she want him to?

Lauren entered through the front door, consciously respecting his personal space in the back. She was surprised not to find him in the office, checking lab results. After storing her coat and purse, she still hadn't seen or heard him. Was he still asleep?

"Paxton," she called as she went down the hall.

"Hey," came faintly from the back.

He wasn't in the kitchen.

"In here."

He was in the closet. Lauren hesitated at the door. She wasn't ready to be in such close quarters with Paxton again. He wore a soft-looking flannel shirt, jeans and leather shoes. The attire made him appear relaxed, as if he belonged. Not the uptight, big-city doctor who didn't want to admit he needed her help who she'd met a week earlier. He was becoming more attractive by the day.

She made an effort to focus on the closet structure instead of him. "Hey, you've been busy."

"Yep." He looked at her from where he sat at the workbench. "I had some time on my hands this weekend so I decided to get started."

"I see that. Even painted, I see." Had he been thinking about their kiss, reliving it over and over, while he'd worked? Now she was thinking like a high-school girl in the throes of her first crush. The kiss hadn't been that big a deal for him, she was sure.

"I got that done yesterday," he was saying. "Everything's ready for the equipment. That should be here sometime today. All I need is the electric connection. I spoke to Mr. Gerhart yesterday and he volunteered an electrician guy to do it. He should be here any minute."

There was a ring at the front door.

"I'll get that. It may be a patient." She turned to go.

"Hey, Lauren."

"Yeah?"

"It's nice to see you." He watched her as if judging her reaction, as if he was unsure of what it might be.

Warmth flowed through her like the first rays of sun after snow. "It's nice to see you too."

"Anyone here?" came a deep, gravelly voice.

"Coming," Lauren called back.

The voice belonged to Mr. Adamson, the electrician. Lauren sent him back to Paxton when a patient arrived. She had barely gotten the patient to the exam room when Paxton showed up and went to work.

The rest of the day was spent caring for minor illnesses and injuries. Late that afternoon a delivery truck arrived and left several boxes in the waiting room. Paxton was visibly excited to see them. As soon as the last patient left he started opening the largest.

Disappointment doused Lauren, almost extinguishing the hope she'd been harboring, when Paxton barely acknowledged she was leaving for the day. The next day was the same. Paxton was in his new lab every second he had between patients. Her hope he'd put any emotional emphasis on their kiss was dashed. As far as she could tell, he didn't even know she was there.

She did have to give him credit for putting in the lab. Even though he wouldn't be there but for a few more weeks he was making a lasting difference in the lives of Last Stop. He had already made a couple of diagnoses that would have had to wait longer if it hadn't been for the lab on site. Paxton was a good man.

By Wednesday at noon, when they closed for the day,

she was ready to spend the afternoon with Shawn and forget about any emotions Paxton roused in her. Her plans were for her and Shawn to have some fun and decorate their Christmas tree. She went in search of Paxton to tell him she was leaving.

"No, Mom, I'll be home before New Year." Paxton's voice carried into the kitchen from the lab.

He was on the phone. She'd wait a second for him to finish his call.

Then he said, "Yes, I understand that Dad needs me. I will be home in two weeks. I've made a commitment here. I have to honor it. I can't just up and leave."

Lauren shouldn't be eavesdropping but she couldn't make herself move.

Paxton continued, "No. There's not another doctor who can handle things here. I'll be back as soon as I can. If you have something else you'd like to talk about then I'll be glad to listen but if not I have to go."

He didn't say anything for a minute and Lauren stepped into the doorway, thinking he was off the phone.

"Yes, Mother, I know where my place is. I understand my position and I know how ill Dad is. I get it. Please tell Dad to take care of himself. I'll talk to you soon." With that Paxton dropped his phone onto the bench.

"Everything okay?" Lauren asked softly.

Paxton whirled around. "Uh, yeah. You know, same old family drama."

Lauren watched him a moment. Why did she think there was more to it? What was the deal with his parents anyway? "We all have it sometime. I just wanted to let you know I was leaving."

"Where're you going?"

He really had his mind in another place. "It's our half-day today."

"Yeah, that's right, it is." He turned back to what he was doing in the lab. "See you later."

She was tempted to ask him more about the call from his mother but if the tension showing in his shoulders was any indication he wasn't going to talk to her about it.

A couple of hours later she was just getting ready to start with the tree decorations when there was a knock at her door. Opening it, she found Paxton standing on the porch with an aluminum casserole pan in his hands.

"Hey, I thought if I brought dinner you might share it with me."

"What, you're not eating in your new lab?"

He gave her a wry smile. "I do get tunnel vision when I start a new project but I'm tired of eating alone. I thought I'd take a chance and see if you'd take pity on me."

"It depends on what kind of casserole you have there," she replied in a teasing tone, keeping the thrill that went through her that he was on her doorstep to herself.

He frowned down at it. "I think it's chicken and rice."

"Okay. That sounds good. Come on in." She took the aluminum foil dish from him.

Paxton followed Lauren down the hall. Pictures of happy people filled the walls. Those must be her family members.

She led him all the way to the back where the kitchen was located. It was much like his at the clinic. The kitchen was sunshine yellow with orange accents. Despite the house being small, it had a warm, lived-in atmosphere. Her home revealed hidden aspects of Lauren's personality he'd never have suspected had he not acted on his need for company.

She turned on the oven and slid the casserole inside.

He hadn't seen or heard her son. Was there a chance he had her to himself?

"Where's Shawn?"

"He's taking a nap," she answered with smile.

He wasn't so sure that Shawn liked him but, then again, he wouldn't be around long enough for it to really matter. The only problem was that he liked Shawn's mother, but he wasn't sure about taking on a child anyway. That had never been in his plans.

"It's about time for him to get up," Lauren continued. "We're going to decorate the tree." As she headed to the front of the house she said over her slender shoulder, "I still need to get the lights on before he wakes up. There's only so much that you can do with a two-year-old and a Christmas tree, but I'm carrying on a family tradition, creating family memories."

Paxton grinned. Lauren sure was chatty. Was she nervous about him being there? He rather liked the thought his presence had her a little off center.

He joined her in the living room to see an artificial tree standing in the middle of it. Family memories weren't something Paxton had many of, positive ones anyway. Even when his family did, or had done, something together he'd always felt like he was an outsider. Didn't quite measure up to his family's expectations. There was always the burden to do as his parents wanted.

"Here, you can get started with these." Lauren reached for a strand of lights.

Paxton took them from her and studied them. He looked up to find her watching him.

"Is something wrong?"

"No. I have just never done this before." Paxton hated to admit that.

"You have never put or seen Christmas lights hung on a tree?" Her expression made him feel like he was from another planet.

He shook his head. "Afraid not. The housekeeper always took care of that." Even to him that sounded sad.

"Then you'll learn something new tonight," was her cheerful response. "Take this end and just start at the top and go around and around until you get to the bottom. I'll keep them untangled back here."

Paxton followed her directions, placing the lights in among the branches.

"My parents, my brother and I all trimmed the tree together," she volunteered with a happy face as they worked in tandem. "I want to give Shawn the same memories."

With the lights completed, Lauren turned to a box and opened it. "I love the ornaments. Each one brings back a memory."

She glanced at him. "I guess you've never hung decorations either."

He winced and shook his head. "No."

"Then you'll get to make a memory tonight in addition to learning something. So, if you didn't decorate a tree, what kind of family traditions at Christmas do you have?"

"We've always gone to the country club for Christmas Eve dinner, then opened presents at ten o'clock sharp."

"That's it?" She sounded disappointed.

"I went to my room to play with whatever toys I got. My father often had to go to the hospital and my mother would rest in her room. Holidays have always been quiet at my house."

"Mommy?" A call came from down the hall.

"Now the fun begins." Lauren had a skip in her step and a smile on her face as she left the room. She soon returned with Shawn in her arms.

"Shawn, look who's here," Lauren said.

The boy gave him a solemn look and rubbed his eyes.

"Hi, Shawn," Paxton offered.

"Are you ready to decorate the tree?" Lauren asked Shawn with enthusiasm, giving him a kiss on the cheek then setting him on his feet.

She went to the box of ornaments and pulled out a fat Santa.

"Would you like to put it on the tree?" Lauren motioned and Shawn went over to the tree. Guiding his hand, she helped the boy hang the red ball-shaped figurine. "Now we must be careful not to touch it once it's on the tree."

She picked out another ornament, a bell this time, and did the same thing. Shawn giggled when it rang. Paxton couldn't keep the smile off his face. Even with his jaded background he had to allow that Shawn was a lucky child to have such a loving mother who wanted him to grow up with happy memories.

Paxton sensed Lauren's pleased gaze on him just before she asked, "Would you do the ones up high?"

"I guess I could do that."

Lauren handed him an ornament by the hanger. "All you have to do is put this little hook over the branch."

His eyes narrowed. With sarcasm dripping from his words, he informed her, "I think I can handle it."

Her eyes were alight with mischief. "I do too."

Once he did it, Paxton found he rather enjoyed the simple task.

When they finished Lauren picked up Shawn and walked to the light switch and turned it off. She came to stand beside him in the almost dark. They stood there in silence for a few minutes, just looking at the twinkling lights on the tree.

"It's beautiful, isn't it?" she whispered, sounding almost reverent.

Though it lacked the expensive elegance of the Christmas trees various housekeepers had erected during his childhood, it was the prettiest tree he'd ever seen. Being a part of this moment with this small family filled him with a contentment and a sense of belonging he hadn't known he'd been missing.

"All it needs to be complete is some presents under it—" she looked at Shawn "—but we have to wait for Santa Claus to bring those, don't we?"

"Santa Claus," the boy repeated in awe, and looked at Paxton.

He and Lauren laughed.

"Who's hungry?" she asked.

"I would be guilty of that." Paxton raised his hand.

"Give me a few minutes and I'll have supper on the table." Lauren headed toward the kitchen with her son on her hip.

Paxton followed. "What can I do to help?"

She slipped Shawn into a highchair. "You can get the dishes and drinks together."

Over the next few minutes they worked side by side, setting their places, making a salad and putting the casserole on the table. Paxton finished by pouring the drinks.

Lauren finished a bite of food. "I thought you'd be messing around in your lab all night."

"I missed my new friend." He gave her a look meant to convey an underlying meaning.

"You did?"

"I did." His gaze held hers.

A few minutes later he looked at Lauren to find her watching him thoughtfully, tapping her fork against her bottom lip. The one he longed to kiss. "Okay, what's going on in that mind of yours?"

"I was just thinking you know a lot more about me than I do about you."

He didn't like where this was headed. "There's not much to tell that you don't already know."

"I don't believe that." She pursed her lips and watched him.

Paxton lowered his chin and gave her a narrow-eyed look in an effort to intimidate her into not pushing him for information. "I thought you looked me up on the internet."

"I did, but I'd like to hear the whole story from you. I don't want to read what others have to say."

Paxton pushed back his chair, the legs scraping the floor, but he didn't stand. It was time to face what had happened and telling Lauren would be his first step to doing so. If he had to confide in someone, she was a good choice. Even if she saw him as a pity case.

He started off slowly. "I guess I'm like most of the people in my family over the last four generations—I'm a physician. But you already know that. I love being a doctor. Have always wanted to be one. But I think that's where it ends."

"Where what ends?" She shifted so she could see him better.

"Our similarities. My grandfather and his brothers started a clinic, later a hospital that made the name Samuels mean something in Boston society. With that came the constant pressure to meet the 'obligations' attached to the family name as I grew up. I never understood that. I was an outsider from the beginning, I think. It never occurred to my parents that I might want to do something different with my life other than be a Boston Samuels. You should have seen the brawl it brought on when I informed my parents I was going to the Peace Corps. You would have thought I had asked them all to join. I feared my mother might never recover." He smiled ironically.

"But you went anyway." She sounded proud of him for doing that.

His ego had been stroked. "I did, but I had already signed all the papers and there wasn't much they could do about it then. Kind of like me coming out here…"

"They should have been happy when you returned from the Peace Corps, though, right?"

"Oh, they were, but nothing had changed. If anything, they wanted me to do more, be more. I thought I might feel different after being away, that they might have seen a difference in me and understood what I wanted."

"So when a chance to do something different came around, like coming out here, you jumped at it."

"Something like that. It was more like I needed to get out of Boston, and this was a way to escape."

"Why?"

Now they were back to the wedding business. He had no choice but to admit what had happened. "I was engaged. My family and hers had been friends forever. We'd been together since childhood. It just seemed the natural progression for us to get married. I don't know why I went along with it. I guess I was too busy trying to make my parents happy that I got caught up in the idea."

"So what happened?"

If he told it really fast, maybe it wouldn't hurt so much, or the humiliation be so great. "Two weeks before our wedding, I was shown explicit pictures of Gabriella and another man posted all over the internet. Turns out she was cheating on me."

Lauren's hiss of shock filled the air. "I'm sorry, Paxton. That is wrong on so many levels."

She was right.

"I shouldn't have pushed you to talk about it."

"It's okay. It felt good to get it out." Truthfully, it did.

Lauren put her hand over his, which was now lying on the table. "You do know that her infidelity was about her poor character and not about who you are. You're a fine man, Paxton Samuels. An excellent doctor and you have a good heart. She messed up big time in losing you."

Coming from Lauren, he found he was starting to believe it. "Along with the embarrassment that something like that had happened to me was the betrayal of my parents encouraging me to forgive her and let the wedding go on. I refused, saw this job posting and came out here to let the story die down."

"My husband ran around on me, too," she said quietly, then looked startled. "I've never told anyone that before. I guess I just didn't want you to think you were alone."

Bile rose in his throat. He was disgusted with himself. Here he was feeling sorry for himself and she'd experienced the same thing. "Do you mind telling me about it?"

She shrugged. "There's not much to tell. He came to town with the oil company. I fell hard. I'd been looking for a way to get out of town and see the world. Mark was the answer. We married then proceeded to live in five towns in a year. He was cheating on me in all of them. I told him I was pregnant the day he died in an oil-rig explosion. I came back here and rebuilt my life. I'm planning to give Shawn a good life here."

"I guess we have more in common than we thought."

She gave him a wry smile. "I guess we do. Not necessarily good stuff, but stuff."

Paxton chuckled. "You have a point there."

Shawn dropped his truck to the floor, and without thinking Paxton handed it back to him with a smile. Maybe he was getting used to this game after all.

"It's time for me to give Shawn a bath and put him to bed." Lauren stood and lifted Shawn from his chair.

Paxton stood as well. "I guess that's your nice way of saying it's time for me to go."

"That's not what I meant at all. I just wanted you to know that things will be pretty busy around here until I get Shawn to sleep."

"It's okay. I've intruded on your family time long enough. I have a couple of things I need to do in the lab anyway."

Lauren walked him to the front door. "I didn't intend to run you off."

Paxton was relieved by the convenient excuse to get going. The more he was around Lauren and Shawn the more involved he became in their lives. He didn't plan to stay in Last Stop much longer and he was confident he wasn't the man to give Lauren what she wanted or needed. She planned to stay here and he had obligations in Boston. It was his home. Just like Last Stop was Lauren's. They shared some past hurts but their futures were down different paths.

Yet there was an emotional pull between them. He couldn't help it—he leaned in for a kiss.

She pulled back, waving her hand between them. "Paxton, I don't know if that's such a good idea. You're leaving. I'm staying. You've recently been hurt. I fell for a guy who was just passing through, and look how that worked out. I think we should be careful here."

"You're probably right but I'm attracted to you. I believe you are to me. There doesn't have to be any strings attached. We could be just two people enjoying each other."

In spite of the fact he saw no future for them either, he felt a gut-wrenching desire to make love to her.

"I don't know about where you come from, but a kiss like the one we shared means something. I have Shawn to think about, and my reputation as well. You'll be gone and I'll still be here."

He met her serious gaze. "That kiss meant something to me as well. We're both adults so why can't we enjoy this while we can?"

Why did it matter so much that she agree to a brief affair? Maybe because he already knew that he wouldn't get his fill of her in a one-night stand.

She studied him a moment before her hand came around his neck and she nudged him closer. Coming up on her toes she gave him an open-mouthed kiss. Heat blazed through him. Just as quickly, she backed away and opened the door.

In a daze he walked out of the house. The cold night air was in direct contrast to the hot flow of his blood.

CHAPTER SEVEN

LAUREN COULDN'T BELIEVE she'd kissed Paxton like that. Over the next two days, she'd expected him to try to kiss her back. She'd already tossed out caution like old clothes—she wanted him to kiss her with every fiber of her being. Despite jitters of anticipation keeping her alert to Paxton's every move and word, it didn't happen. He remained professional the entire time, much to her disappointment, despite her warning that it should be that way between them. If his goal was to have her on edge, he had achieved it.

It had been years since she'd last felt that distinct feminine yearning for a man simmering below the surface. The zip that made her feel vibrantly alive. Being a mother was fulfilling but there was nothing like being desired by a man. Paxton had made it clear he wanted her and yet…

Their highly personal conversation had moved their relationship to a new level. In a sad way they had bonded over a terrible time in each of their lives. As different as their outside worlds were, their private ones had been a lot alike.

On Friday evening, she left for the day without any indication from him that he might turn up for dinner or that she would see him over the weekend. With reluctance, she gave up hope on any further intimacy between them. It was better that way. There was no chance for hurt on either side. They'd both had enough of that. Already she'd let Paxton Samuels matter far more than he should.

It was Christmastime and the community dinner and dance was tomorrow evening. She planned to concentrate on having a good time without him.

With her resolution made, she dressed for the event on Saturday, pushing Paxton out of her thoughts. Shawn looked so cute in his new outfit. She'd enjoyed putting on her red dress and knowing her appearance was at its best. The annual event was her favorite one of the year.

The community center had never looked more festive. The ladies in town had outdone themselves, decorating. A large tree stood in the corner with colorful bright lights adorning its boughs. Beneath were presents of all shapes and sizes for the smaller children. Lauren pointed them out to her wide-eyed son, who was holding on to her hand as though she might vanish.

The tables were draped with dark green cloths with red runners going down the center. Candles flickered in tall holders positioned at regular intervals. Napkins and silverware dressed each dining space.

Long tables had been pushed together and covered with matching green cloths to form the buffet table. They were so heavy with food Lauren imagined they almost groaned beneath their burden. She grinned. It was an unwritten rule that there was competition between the women over who had brought the best dish.

Everybody was dressed in their holiday finery. A small dance floor had been set up in the center of the room with an even smaller stage nearby. The overhead lights were dimmed so that miniature lights hanging from every imaginable spot on the ceiling and walls shone brilliantly.

Lauren's attention was drawn to the entrance. Her heart beat faster. *Paxton.* What had made him decide to come? Heat filled her cheeks. It didn't matter. She was glad to see him. He looked handsome in a dark suit accented by a red tie.

He strolled toward her as if they had planned this. She said with schooled politeness, "Hello. I didn't expect to see you."

With a nonchalant shrug, he offered, "I enjoyed the parade so much I thought I might like this too." He openly considered her for a moment, as if his eyes couldn't leave her. Speaking reverently, he said, "You look amazing."

She had no doubt her cheeks matched the color of her dress. The compliment shot straight to her heart. She'd taken care with her hair by pulling it back and up, leaving some tendrils loosely curling around her face. Her dress fit her to perfection, emphasizing her figure in all the right ways, but it wasn't until Paxton had voiced his appreciation that she believed she might look exceptional. His compliment she would treasure long after he'd left Last Stop.

"Thank you." Paxton brought out an uncharacteristic bashfulness in her. "You look nice also. I like that reindeer tie. Is it new?"

"It's a little something I picked up the other day when I was shopping." He grinned at her. "Festive, isn't it?"

"For a man who isn't into Christmas, that sure screams it."

He held her gaze. "Maybe I've changed my mind."

Was he talking about the tie or her? Whichever it was, she was still glad to see him.

Their attention was drawn to the stage by the mayor announcing into the microphone, "I'm not going to make a speech." A cheer went up. "But I do want to say how nice everything looks, especially the food, and say thank you to everyone who worked so hard on this evening. Also, I want to remind everyone to have their picture taken at the photo booth tonight. We want everyone's picture for the history book Mrs. Elise is putting together. Now, Reverend Bishop, will you bless our food? Oh, and Merry Christmas, everyone."

The reverend was brief, and within five minutes everyone either stood on both sides of the buffet tables, filling their plates, or were in line with plates at the ready.

"Let me have Shawn while you fill your plates. I'll come back for mine," Paxton suggested.

Lauren looked at him. She'd not really minded him not being too comfortable around her son, because the last thing she needed was for her child to become attached to a man who wouldn't be around long. But this did feel nice…

"We'll manage. You keep your place in line. Those dishes are emptying fast." Lauren didn't want him to feel like he had to take care of them.

"Don't argue. By the time I come back the line won't be that long and I seriously doubt the matrons of this town will let me go hungry."

"Thanks. I would appreciate the help." It was nice to have the assistance. Who was she kidding? Having Paxton around was wonderful. She liked the attention, the feel of walking a little straighter because she was on the arm of a handsome man.

With two plates full to the brim, Lauren looked for Paxton in the large room.

"He's over there by the tree, honey," one of the older women said. "It looks like Shawn has taken a liking to him."

Lauren just smiled. She'd found them. Paxton was showing an ornament to Shawn. Their heads were together and Paxton was listening to something Shawn was babbling. Lauren's heart caught. Did she dare hope for...?

She and Shawn had survived Mark's death to become a happy little family. Having her mother and father close, as well as her brothers, had been helpful, but something was missing. Shawn needed a father and she needed...to be needed as a woman. To give and receive what a man and woman could give each other. With Paxton, could that be possible? Would he stay and let that happen? Had he even considered it?

His face brightened when he saw her and he said something to Shawn. They came toward her. Paxton reached for one of the plates and carefully placed it on the table. Lauren put the other down.

"I'll get a highchair. I saw one over in the corner. Be right back." He was gone before she could object.

"Hey, I've been trying to get your attention," a woman said behind them.

Lauren turned. "Hi, Mom."

"I was saving you a place until I couldn't anymore, but I see you have a good one here." She looked off in Paxton's direction and smiled.

"Don't start getting any ideas, Mom."

"I didn't say anything, but it's nice to see you smile for a change."

"Hey, Mrs. Tucker. How're you?" Paxton asked after placing the highchair at the end of the table.

"Hi, Dr. Samuels," her mother responded in a welcoming manner.

"Paxton, please."

Her mother smiled. "Are you enjoying yourself?"

"I am. The parade was great so I thought I'd give this a try." He took Shawn and slipped him into the highchair like a pro. This was different. If Paxton was warming up to Shawn to get to her, it was working.

"My, you're good at that." Her mother gave her a meaningful look.

That earned her mother a warning smile. "Mom, your food's getting cold. I know ours is. We'll see you later on."

When her mother was beyond earshot, Lauren looked at Paxton. "Sorry about that. Mom means well but she can be pushy."

Paxton chuckled. "She doesn't even get in the game with my mother."

Shawn squealed his impatience and Lauren sighed. "Okay, honey. I know you're ready to eat."

They all settled in for the meal. Soon the table had filled all around them, everyone talking and laughing.

This event was nothing like the sedate and proper occasions Paxton had attended all his life. Boisterous laughter was coming from different areas in the building. Everyone here was truly enjoying each other's company, and the season. These folks weren't going through the motions of socializing in a bored haze or checking the time to see how soon they could slip away without being rude. He should have felt out of place but instead he felt at home.

Lauren wiped some food off Shawn's face and said, "Sweetpea, we need to go speak to Nannie and PaPa."

"Who?" Paxton asked.

"My parents."

Lauren started pulling Shawn out of the highchair. His legs didn't come out smoothly. Paxton quickly took over. "Let me give it a try." Seconds later he had Shawn out and in his arms.

One of the ladies sitting nearby said, "You're a natural at that."

He grinned, filling up with pride. "Thanks."

"I'll take him," Lauren offered, a tad too quickly for his liking.

Did she have a problem with him becoming friendly with Shawn? Maybe he had been a little unsure around Shawn but the boy was starting to grow on him. "I'd like to go with you and meet your father."

Lauren gave him a skeptical look. "Okay, but remember whatever happens this was your idea." They weaved through the crowd toward the other side of the building.

As they passed the photo area setup Lauren said, "I'm going to get this over with now when there's no line." She spoke to the ultra-thin man standing nearby. "Mr. John, Shawn and I are ready, if you are?"

"Sure. Come sit right here." Mr. John placed a stool in front of a backdrop scene of a tree with its branches laden with snow, a blanket of white all around and a rabbit looking out from behind a smaller tree.

Lauren took a seat, holding Shawn in her lap. He squirmed but soon stilled. The photographer stepped away. She looked at him and smiled. Shawn followed her lead.

The photographer said, "Raise your chin, just a little.

That's it." Click, click. "Wonderful." He looked back at Paxton. "Why don't you get in it? The mayor wants one of everybody."

"But we aren't…" Lauren left it hanging.

Together, Paxton finished in silence. They weren't a couple. A family. All together. But what would it really matter for a few pictures? The picture would only be seen by a few in a small-town history book that no one would ever be interested in.

Lauren shook her head in a rueful manner before motioning to him. "Aw, come on."

Paxton jogged the few steps over to join them.

"I want you to stand behind Lauren, young man. Place your hand on her shoulder. Now, all I need you to do is smile." There were a couple of clicks. "We're going to need to try that again. Shawn turned before I had it. Dr. Samuels, take Shawn," the photographer instructed.

Paxton and Lauren looked at each other a moment before she handed Shawn to him.

"Lauren, just stay put," Mr. John said. He stepped away then brought another stool close.

"Doctor, sit on the stool and spread your legs wide and scoot up close to Lauren. Now, Lauren, turn your legs this direction." Mr. John adjusted them.

Paxton relished the warmth of Lauren against him as she obeyed.

"Hang on, buddy. This shouldn't take long." Paxton grinned at Shawn and made him giggle. Lauren was close enough that his breath caused her hair to move. Had she shivered?

"Now, that looks good." The photographer started clicking the camera with zeal.

Lauren glanced back. Her gaze met his. Could she see the desire in his eyes?

She blinked and gave him a soft smile.

"That got it. Thanks," Mr. John said, breaking the moment.

Lauren didn't move, neither did he.

There were a few snickers around them.

A line had formed while they were having their picture taken. From the cozy position they were in and with him holding Shawn, they must have looked like a happy family. One that he would never really be a part of even if he wanted to, which he didn't. Stepping out of one difficult relationship into another between two people who obviously wanted different things in life would never work. His duties were hundreds of miles away from Last Stop. Paxton moved back and Lauren stood quickly, grabbed her son and walked away.

"Hey, wait," Paxton said behind her.

She didn't slow as he followed her. She hurried through and around small cheerful groups as if she were running from him. Finally she stopped at a table where the people were still eating and listening to a large man who was telling a story.

Lauren placed her hand on her mother's shoulder. Paxton stood beside Lauren. Her mother covered it with her own. She leaned toward Lauren and said in a loud whisper, "It'll be a few minutes. Your dad's stories can be long."

Paxton nodded. So the over-large man with the deep voice was Lauren's father. After seeing him, Paxton thought better of wanting to meet him. He looked intimidating. The thought that Mr. Gerhart might be a marshmallow compared to Lauren's father had been completely correct.

With most of the women Paxton dated, he'd known their fathers most of his life. He'd felt some trepidation at being around those men, but he had at least had the confidence of being a member of Boston's newest generation of socialites. In Last Stop he was an outsider, and a temporary one at that. Worse, he had a sense that fathers around this area took protecting what was theirs in a very literal, basic sense, particularly their daughters.

A few minutes later the story ended with people around them laughing. When everyone had quietened, Lauren's father turned to look at him.

"Hey, Dad," Lauren said. "I wanted to say hi and introduce you to Dr. Samuels."

"Paxton, sir." Paxton extended his hand.

Mr. Tucker accepted it and looked Paxton straight in the eyes. The man's steady stare warned him. *Don't hurt my daughter.*

Paxton let go of the elder man's strong grip. He couldn't promise that. There wasn't enough clarity about his own life to promise anything to anyone else. While they stood there Shawn reached his arms out to Paxton. He took the boy from a reluctant-looking Lauren.

"I see that you and my grandson have become friends," her father offered in an affable tone.

"Yeah, I guess we have." Paxton looked at Lauren then at Shawn. He was starting to care for them far more than he was ready to admit.

The five-person band started playing a slow Christmas carol and a few couples moved toward the dance floor.

"Why don't you give me Shawn and you and Lauren

go have a dance?" Mrs. Tucker suggested with a twinkle in her dark eyes, so like her daughter's.

"Mom!" Lauren exclaimed, embarrassment darkening her face.

Paxton gave her a pointed look. "You don't think I know how to dance?"

"I wasn't saying that. I'm sure you're a fine dancer," Lauren declared with a glare, her voice higher than usual.

"Come see Nannie." Mrs. Tucker reached for the boy.

Paxton released Shawn to his grandmother and took hold of Lauren's clenched hand before she could protest further, leading her through the crowd to the dance floor. With an experienced twirl, Paxton brought her into his arms. She came willingly and fit perfectly. He led her in the two-step around the open area. Lauren followed effortlessly, and breathlessly.

Her dress swirled around his legs as he moved her backward then pulled her to him. When that dance was over he didn't stop and instead they moved into the next one. Paxton seamlessly led her into a quickstep. He held her tight as he shifted her without a misstep. Lauren followed his lead with grace and confidence. Their partnership seemed perfect. Would it be the same elsewhere? Like in bed?

He looked into her eyes. They were watching him, smiling. That protective look he'd seen earlier had disappeared. "You're an amazing dancer."

"Thanks. Required lessons in my world. No *F*s allowed."

"That bad?"

"Only if you'd rather be outside, catching frogs in the pond."

She giggled. A lovely sound that could only be hers. "I can see your point."

"My mother didn't when the housekeeper couldn't get the stain out of my shirt."

"Well, whatever your hardship was, it's my enjoyment now. This is the most fun I've had in a long time."

"Then let me show you a couple of moves I keep hidden for special occasions." Paxton grinned then pushed her away and brought her back to him before turning her and tipping her back in a dip.

Lauren laughed deeply. The sound flowed through him like a warm drink that could thaw and dilute all the ugliness he'd brought with him to Last Stop. He pulled her to him and they started off again.

"I can't remember the last time I had so much fun," she said, her voice full of happiness. "If I could bottle this moment and keep it forever, I would."

Had another woman ever made him feel like the most special man on earth? Lauren's praise had that power.

The band went into another fast number and they separated except for Paxton's hold on one of her hands.

It was clear to Lauren that they were a well-paired couple on the dance floor, and apparently it was just as evident to everyone else because none of her male friends tried to cut in. After that the band took a break and they found their way back to her parents and Shawn.

"Paxton, you've made a mistake," Lauren's mother greeted him.

"What have I done?" He looked around him.

"You're going to have to dance with every woman in town or give the men dancing lessons!"

Everyone around them erupted in laughter.

"I wouldn't mind having one of those dances," a woman of about eighty called.

"Maybe next time. I saved my arsenal of dances for someone special tonight." The look he gave Lauren made it clear he meant her. After being in his arms, she wanted more. If he could dance so magnificently she could only imagine Paxton's skills at making love.

She gave him a shy smile. "It's time I got Shawn home to bed."

"Your dad, Shawn and I have been talking," her mother said, blocking her effort to take her son from his grandfather's arms. "And Shawn decided he wanted to spend the night with us. We could bring him home around bedtime tomorrow evening. That way you two could dance some more. You looked like you were enjoying yourselves."

Lauren felt as if she'd walked into a trap. She'd been in Paxton's arms, had been his partner. The one he'd chosen. But in a couple of weeks he'd be back in Boston, choosing some other woman to dance with. She couldn't let this go further. "But, Mom, that's too much—"

Her mother said, for her ears only, "Honey, you need to enjoy yourself while you can. You haven't in so long. Shawn deserves a happy mother."

She couldn't argue with that logic even if she wanted to. Her mother only wanted her to continue having fun, which she most definitely had been having in Paxton's strong arms.

"Okay, if that's what y'all have cooked up. 'Night, sweetpea." Lauren kissed Shawn. "See you tomorrow."

"Goodnight, Shawn." Paxton ran the back of his finger over Shawn's cheek.

Lauren's chest tightened as those what-if questions

started flowing through her mind again. She accompanied her parents to where their coats hung, helped her mother bundle Shawn up and then watched her walk away with him. Moments later she turned and discovered Paxton standing behind her.

"I take it that Shawn doesn't sleep over often." Paxton watched her with thoughtful eyes.

"No. Well, he has more in the last couple of weeks than he has his entire life."

"So that night in the hotel was the first?"

She nodded.

"That's why you kept calling him all the time."

Lauren looked at him with surprise. "I was that obvious?"

"Actually, no, but I might have been less jealous if I had known the whole situation."

"Jealous?"

Paxton grinned. "How was I supposed to know he was your son? Come on, let's dance some more before you have me embarrassing myself further."

She hesitated then took his hand. His grip was warm and strong, yet gentle. It was only dancing, she told herself. That pleasure was publicly acceptable and didn't imply they were anything more than friends. With that consolation in mind she allowed him to escort her back to the floor. They continued to dance until the number of partying people thinned.

During the last song Paxton held her close. There was comforting security in his arms. She longed for that haven. Last Stop had provided that for her and Shawn when she'd returned, but she needed human sanctuary as well. Would she be willing to leave Last Stop if Paxton asked her to? No. She couldn't take that chance again.

Whatever was happening between them now, she had to enjoy it for what it was—a passing fling. Shawn needed what Last Stop could give him. What he had around him now. The loving care of a close-knit community.

"Hey," Paxton breathed into her ear. "We'd better go. They're closing up the show."

She looked around. Men were stacking chairs. "I should help."

"I bet that you do that every time there's an event."

Lauren gave him a sheepish look. "Most of them."

"Then I'd guess they could survive one without you. Let's go look at the stars."

Her heart jumped. How long had it been since she'd look at the stars with a man? Too long. "Okay."

They pulled their cold-weather clothing on and stepped out into the chilly but clear night.

Paxton held her hand as they strolled along the road toward her house. Without saying anything, she led him around to the back of the house to where they could see over the plain for miles. There were occasional homes with lights on to mar the view but otherwise the stars were big and bright. They took a seat on the picnic table near Shawn's swing set.

Paxton placed his arm around her shoulders and pulled her close. She laid her head into the curve of his shoulder. It was perfect. "You don't get this in the city."

He kissed the top of her head. "There're a lot of things you do here that I don't get in the city. Nice things. Peaceful pleasures."

"Such as?"

"Now you're stalling for time, I think. You know you have to make a decision here, don't you, Lauren?"

"I thought I might," she whispered, unsure what to

say. She knew what she wanted, but would it be the right thing in the long run, or would it bring on hurt? But why should it? They could have a nice time together then it would all be over when he left. If they both understood that going in, then all would be fine.

"I'd like to stay the night." Paxton was watching her.

His breath formed small clouds in the cold air. Would it change things if she agreed? Or didn't? The only thing she knew for sure was that she wanted this time with Paxton, even if it was short. From it she would have enough satisfying memories to last the rest of her life.

Lauren stood and reached out her hand, "Come on, you must be getting cold."

CHAPTER EIGHT

PAXTON FOLLOWED HER up the back steps and through the door into her kitchen. A single light from the living room illuminated what little he could see. Unable to ignore his desire, he pulled Lauren into his arms. His heart throbbed against his chest as she came willingly. Even through her outer clothing he could feel her curves. Ones he sought to caress.

Her arms came up around his shoulders, her hands along the sides of his face until she'd pushed his knit cap off. His lips found her cool ones. He wanted more, so much more. She offered him entrance, which he gladly accepted, anticipating the heat to come. Her tongue met his and they danced, sending his passion soaring.

Lauren's hands tugged at his gloves, removing them. Seconds later her attention centered on the top button of his coat, releasing it. She went down to the next and down again, continuing until she could shove his coat open and step inside to wrap her arms around his waist. She wiggled against him. "It feels so good here."

Paxton felt his body hardening. He pulled her tight. "I know other ways to make you feel good."

She stepped back, forcing him to relax his hold, and studied him for a minute. Was she trying to decide whether or not to let him stay? Hadn't she already agreed or was that just him wanting the night so desperately he was reading more into her actions and words than she intended?

By the time Lauren took his hand it shook. She led him to her bedroom. He had his answer. When she didn't turn on a light, he flipped on the lamp beside the bed. "I want to see you, as well as enjoy you. I don't want anything between us, not even the darkness."

Her eyes glistened with emotion. She started removing her coat. Paxton placed his hand on hers. "I'd like that."

She nodded.

He took her hat off. There was a deep roll of humor in his throat as he fought the static electricity making her hair stand out around her head. Tenderly he ran his hands over it, smoothing it into place. "I love your hair. It's like a mass of wild silk."

Running a hand down the sleeve of her coat to her hand, he lifted it and slowly pulled off her glove one finger at a time. He did the same for the other, letting both fall to the floor.

Never breaking eye contact, she unwrapped his scarf and pulled it away from his neck, letting it slip through her fingers to pool at her feet. Using both hands, Lauren pushed his coat from his shoulders. It hit the floor with a soft thud. He met her heated gaze. Had she registered a dare in his eyes?

He hoped so. Cupping her beautiful face in his hands, he kissed her with all the fervor throbbing through him. Her responsiveness let him know she was as eager to spend time with him as he was with her. His ego and self-esteem, so thoroughly damaged by Gabriella's rejection, was rapidly healing from Lauren's ministrations.

He'd have never believed he would be able to trust again. In a few short weeks Lauren had healed his damaged ego. Helping him find the joy in life he'd been searching for with such desperation. Having lived encircled by family, he had thought well-being would come naturally, but the older he got the more aware he'd become of its absence.

During their kiss he finished removing her outer clothing. Holding himself in check was becoming more difficult. He wanted Lauren now. To feel all of her surrounding him. Holding him. Loving him.

"Please sit on the bed." When she hesitated, he kissed her neck. Her tell-tale shiver gratified his masculinity.

After she was seated, he lifted her foot and removed her red high-heeled shoe. Tossing it beside their clothes, he went after the other. It landed close to its mate. Placing her foot on his thigh, he slowly ran his hand over her calf, then beneath her knee and up under her dress. Paxton's hand abruptly stopped. His breathing jumped way up the scale.

Was that what he thought it was?

He looked at Lauren. In a teasing tone he said, "Now, what do we have here?"

A mysterious smile came to her lips. "My garter belt."

With a hard thump of his heart against his chest, he felt himself go rock hard. No woman, to his knowledge, wore a garter belt. Tight jeans and boots to black hose and garter belt, Lauren was the best of contradictions. Surprise and soft seduction. What other sweet surprises was she hiding? He wanted to find out.

His fingers paused over the belt snap. Like a knight requesting a favor from his queen, he asked, "May I?"

"No."

What? He might die if he didn't. "No?"

He raised his eyebrows. She held his world in her answer.

She grinned. "Just unsnap it, would you?"

"That I can do." Despite his inexperience, he flipped the snap and then the other. His hands shook as he slowly brushed the silky stocking down her leg; he kissed the top of her foot before placing it on the floor. "Yum, that was so nice, I think I'll do it again."

He was rewarded with that giggle he loved so much. A few minutes later her other shapely leg was bare. If he didn't have her soon his self-control would fail and he'd be humiliated. Standing, he offered his hands and she placed hers in his, allowing him to help her to her feet.

Lauren's hands flattened over his chest. She slid them up until she reached his tie. Untying it, she pulled it from around his neck in a tantalizingly slow movement. Her lips found his as she pushed his suit jacket. It fell on the growing pile of clothing with a hushed thud. When Paxton reached to take her she blocked his hands with unmistakable firmness and returned to unbuttoning his shirt down to his pants. When she went for the fastener of those he stopped her.

"Oh, no." He gently clasped her hands. "It's my turn now." His hands lightly rested on her waist and rotated her until her back faced him. Taking the pull of the metal zipper, he gently tugged downward. He placed a kiss on the exposed skin just below her neck, feeling her quiver as he opened the dress. Against her skin he breathed, "I've never seen someone look lovelier or sexier in a dress. And red. I don't know which was hotter, you or the dress."

She turned, taking his face in her small soft hands and kissing him. Instead of the sweet kiss of thanks he was expecting, this one made his blood thunder in his veins and he felt his desire rise. Her arms slipped around his neck as she opened wide to greet him with her tongue. She teased and taunted, increasing the heat from simmering to boiling.

Paxton walked her back against the bed.

"Not yet." She stopped him with a hand to his chest. "Still too many clothes."

He grinned. "I can take care of that." He reached for her.

"Not mine. Yours." She grasped his undershirt, leisurely pulling it up, then planting kisses over his heart and nibbling her way up to his chin. His discomfort shot up a couple of more notches. When she finally loosened his pants, he stepped away and kicked off his shoes, letting his clothing drop to the floor. Stepping out of the puddle of his pants, Paxton peeled off his socks with impatience and made a purposeful move toward Lauren.

In a low, teasing growl he declared, "No more playing."

It felt so good to have fun with a woman. To enjoy the moment and not think about what was next on the agenda. He'd been going through the motions of sex by "appointment" with his former fiancée for so long he'd forgotten the erotic bliss of truly desiring a woman.

Lauren turned but he caught her. She laughed when he announced, "As much as I love that red dress, it has to go."

She stood still before him as he pushed the silken fabric down her arms. The material swished as it flowed around her until it settled on the floor. Lauren was now clad in only a red skimpy bra, matching panties and a black lace garter belt.

Her beauty took his breath. "Heaven help me, Lauren, I'm glad I didn't know what you were wearing or I would've embarrassed us both."

She grew solemn and lowered her eyes, as if unsure of the compliment.

"Hey, look at me." She did. "You're the sexiest woman I've ever seen."

A shy smile covered her kiss-swollen lips.

"There's only one thing wrong." Her mouth dropped a fraction. "I'd rather see you in nothing." He lifted her and fell back onto the bed. "And I intend to," he growled close to her ear. His hand went to her narrow waist. Despite having had a child, she still had a slim figure. Her skin was as smooth as he had imagined. Perfect. Paxton followed the curve up until the pad of his thumb rested beneath one of her breasts.

The hitch in her breathing when he cupped her was gratifying. Even through the lace Paxton could feel her hard nipple erect against his palm. As he gave her a tender kiss, his hand moved around to unclip her bra. Unable to wait any longer, he pushed it up and filled both hands with the rich firmness of her breasts.

She sighed.

Paxton held one high then placed a kiss on the nipple before taking the tip between his lips. He sucked as Lauren's fingers funneled through his hair then traveled to gently knead his back, as though begging for more. Paxton shifted his devotion to her other breast, giving it equal attention.

Sometime later, as he showered her face, shoulders and neck with tender kisses, he removed the bra completely and let it slip from his fingers. Laying her back upon the bed, his hands explored all that she offered until one finger followed the tiny line of elastic low on her hips.

"You're such an amazing package of surprises." He admired her spread out on the bed just for him. "All tough looking on the outside and all sexy matching lace on the inside. Who would have thought?"

Her eyelids lowered, giving her a sensual come-hither look. "Have you been thinking about me?"

"Hell, yeah," he growled. "Why do you think I've spent so much time in the damn lab?"

"Just what've you been thinking?" she asked with a naughty note as she ran a finger down his arm.

"That I'd like to see you like this. Lying on the bed just for me. The moonlight highlighting your assets, all the ones I want to caress, plan to caress."

Lauren kissed two of her fingers and placed them on his mouth before she trailed her hand down over his chest. His manhood jumped in anticipation. He had to have Lauren soon. But she deserved better than a raging bull mounting her.

Her hand almost slipped beneath his underwear before he grabbed it. Once she touched him his self-control would fail. He leaned over and kissed her, directing her thoughts elsewhere. His hand flattened on her perfect belly. Lauren hissed under her breath. Paxton loved her reactions to his touch.

Using his forefinger, he traced the line of her panties and slipped all four fingers beneath to brush her curls. Lauren squirmed and parted her legs. That was the invitation he'd been hoping for. He gave her panties a tug, and with the lift of her hips they were gone.

Paxton's gaze met hers as he outlined her belly button. Her eyes widened, then slowly lowered to a reflective level as his forefinger slid between her thighs. Capturing her lips with his mouth before his finger entered her wet, hot passage. When it did, she jerked forward, her body tightening in welcoming acceptance. Paxton removed his finger, then slid it back in, using a rhythmic manner attuned to the thrusts of his tongue. He increased the speed. Lauren whimpered, then groaned and thrashed, her hips lifting to meet his actions. With each reaction his need grew, but her pleasure remained his focus.

With a final push that matched the ultimate invasion of his tongue, he took her over the edge. Rising up, he watched her reaction. Lauren's eyes squeezed closed then opened wide in surprise, meeting his as she flew off into bliss. Could anything be more stunning?

He'd never done that before. Sex had always been something he enjoyed but he hadn't reached the level of ecstasy he'd found with Lauren. For once in his life, perhaps for the first time, he was giving all of himself.

Lauren returned to reality to see Paxton standing and searching his pants pocket. He soon sheathed himself and joined her again.

"You're the most amazing woman I know. I can't wait…"

His passionate expression, green eyes aglow with sincerity, told her he meant every word. When had a man said something that sweet to her?

Who Paxton was, his sheer magnitude, tugged at her. Her attraction had steadily grown stronger since the night they'd first met. Each movement he made while they worked together registered in her awareness with uncommon intensity. What he might be doing on their days off had been a constant distraction to her own plans.

With Mark, lovemaking had been frenzied with lust and over almost before it began, with little time to feel. Paxton had yet to do anything significant and she was feeling too much. But that would change now. Arms wide, she welcomed him.

Without hesitation he slipped inside her. His length and bulk caught her by surprise for a second. But when he started the familiar yet unique movement that she recognized as theirs alone, she came alive. Her legs went around his waist. As Paxton moved inside her, Lauren's heels pulled him closer. He pushed her higher, applying pressure. She had been out of control before but this time as she spiraled upward toward that peak of sweet release, the journey was honeyed, oh, so sweet. Beyond anything she'd experienced or even imagined before.

Thrusting harder and faster until he caught up with her at the very edge of endurance, they joined each other in oblivion. After an almost endless perfect moment they settled, each breathing hard. Paxton pulled a blanket from the foot of the bed over them and rolled to spoon Lauren into his body. She'd never felt so secure in her life.

Sometime before daybreak, Lauren woke. For a second she was startled. There was a man in her bed. She'd been sleeping alone for nearly three years now and had almost forgotten… Yet Paxton was so unlike her memories of Mark. With Paxton her emotions were deeper, more sensual, heightened. She was more aware of every nuance of sensation. When he was gone she would miss the miraculous transformation from just existing to being vitally alive.

She wasn't kidding herself. Paxton would leave town. He had responsibilities elsewhere. He might be working on his lab as if he intended to stay yet he'd never indicated in word or deed that he was.

But that didn't matter right now. She needed this, him, their temporary union, to awaken her dormant femininity. She'd been suppressing her womanhood in an almost superhuman effort to be both mother and father to her son. This was for her.

"Hey," Paxton said in that clipped accent she knew so well.

She rolled to face him. "Hey, yourself."

"What're you thinking about over there?"

"How do you know I was thinking anything?" Was she really that predictable?

"I don't know…because maybe I've gotten to know you pretty well. I've worked with you for a couple of weeks. I've spent evenings, now the night with you. I've watched you with Shawn and the people who live in Last Stop."

He really got her. She wanted someone in her life like that. Who was she kidding? She wanted him. Would he ever consider making Last Stop his home? "You know we have a need for a good doctor here. No strings attached, I promised."

He quickly had her on her back. "Aw, but the strings would be the selling point." Paxton's lips found hers. A few moments later as his mouth moved along her neck and he cupped her breast he murmured, "Along with a few other perks."

Lauren giggled. This she could get used to. Did she dare get her hopes up that this time would be different?

The next evening when Paxton left Lauren's house he'd never felt happier, freer. It was becoming increasingly clear that he was getting attached to Lauren, even Shawn—but that couldn't continue. He would be leaving soon and it wasn't fair to any of them, yet he couldn't stay away. The more time he spent with them the more difficult it would be for him to return to Boston. If things were different with his father would he, could he stay in Last Stop?

If he could have come up with a good excuse, he would have returned to her house later, but he figured if she wanted him there she would have called him. She probably wanted to spend time with Shawn. Couldn't she do that with him there? Maybe Lauren was protecting Shawn from becoming too attached to him. Whatever her reasoning, he still missed them.

Sleep didn't come easily. All he could think about was seeing Lauren the next day. How would she react? Would there be that uncomfortable moment when neither of them knew what to say? She was the one person he had found he had no trouble discussing things with, including his fiasco with Gabriella. He still couldn't believe he told her that entire sordid story.

Monday morning when she arrived at the clinic he was busy in his office. With great effort he waited until she'd hung up her coat and come in search of him. That was one of the favorite parts of his day. Lauren seemed eager to see him, whereas Gabriella had always impatiently expected him to wait on her or be on her schedule. He'd always been an afterthought to her. Lauren made him a priority. She believed in him and therefore he believed in himself. Making him feel as if her day hadn't started until she saw him.

She hesitated in the doorway, as she always did. Paxton glanced up then back at the laptop. Confident she couldn't resist knowing what was on the screen, he waited until she circled the desk before closing the top and standing. His arm slipped around her waist, pulling her tightly to him. "I thought you'd never get here." He kissed her thoroughly. As he did, he turned her, lifted her and seated her on the desk.

She broke their kiss with a laugh.

He didn't have to worry about that uncomfortable moment any longer. Looking down at her, he asked with all the innocence he could muster, "Something wrong?"

"I was just thinking I used to play under this desk when I was a kid."

He wiggled his eyebrows up and down like a movie villain. "Now you're getting to play on it."

She giggled, placed a hand at the nape of his neck and brought his mouth back to hers. His fingers slipped under her shirt and sweater to find her warm skin. Lauren cooed her pleasure. This was a great way to start the morning.

The ring of the bell on the door jarred them apart. They both snickered into each other's necks.

"You almost got caught," he whispered in her ear as if she had been the only one to blame.

Lauren gave him a swat on the shoulder.

With a quick kiss, he helped her off the desk.

"I'll be right there," she called, straightening her clothes.

Giving her a direct look, he mouthed, "I'll be out when I can."

Lauren glanced at his crotch and grinned. She said too sweetly, like a nurse in a bad sitcom, "Yes, Doctor."

Paxton watched the sway of her hips as she left the office. That didn't help ease his pain. In Boston, he would never have dared, much less thought about sneaking a kiss from his lover at work. A Samuels didn't act that way. It was fun being naughty.

As their patient closed the door on her way out, Lauren turned to Paxton. "We're lucky Mrs. Betts's hearing has gone because she used to be the worst gossip in town."

He chuckled and pulled her in for a hug. "Would it be so bad to have people talking about us?" Paxton couldn't believe he'd just asked that. After living with concern over what people thought all his life, now he didn't care. It was a freeing idea.

Lauren gave him a long look. "It wouldn't be the first time." She shrugged. "And it would be true."

Paxton gave her a kiss. "It would be." So why had he been so uptight about the gossip in Boston when his wedding had come crashing down? He hadn't done anything wrong. Except to ask the wrong woman to marry him. He owed nobody an explanation of who he saw and what he did. His feelings for Lauren he didn't mind anyone knowing. In fact, he wanted to announce it to everyone he was going to see today. He wouldn't do that because he wasn't staying in Last Stop. She shouldn't have to answer a bunch of questions about their relationship.

The rest of the day moved along as usual, except he smiled more than normal. Lauren left at closing time, saying bye with a quick kiss. It was quiet afterward, too much so. He missed her already. What was he going to do when he returned to Boston? Could he ask her to leave everything she knew and come to Boston? That would be flipping her world and Shawn's on their sides.

Still, it would tear his heart out when he had to leave them behind. For now he had at least two more weeks before he was to leave and until then he was going to enjoy himself, and Lauren, to the fullest. The future he would worry about later.

Lauren hadn't suggested they have dinner together but neither had he. Pulling a casserole out of his freezer, he headed for her house. He walked so that his car parked outside wouldn't create any gossip. Old ideas died hard.

When he knocked he didn't have to wait long before Lauren opened the door with a smile. "What took you so long?"

He grinned. "You were expecting me?"

"Oh, about thirty minutes ago."

"Well, Miss Smarty Pants, watch out. I might surprise you and take my frozen meal elsewhere."

"Please don't do that. I was looking forward to seeing what you showed up with tonight," she pleaded playfully.

"Well, since you insist, sure! I'll have dinner with you." He stepped inside and headed down the hallway toward the kitchen.

She laughed, closed the door and followed. "Surely there's an end to these."

"I think this is the last of them." Paxton placed the casserole on the stove.

"You may have to start cooking."

He kissed her. "I was hoping maybe you would take pity on me and cook."

She pushed him away. "You only want me for my cooking skills."

Paxton grabbed her bottom with one hand and kissed her again. "Among other things."

Shawn sat in the middle of the floor, playing with a pot and wooden spoon. Paxton swung him up into his arms. The boy giggled. Something about being with the two of them seemed right. He belonged here.

"Would you mind watching Shawn while dinner warms so I can get a couple of things done?"

"I can do that." Only a few days ago Paxton would have hesitated at first. What type of spell had Lauren cast over him? This was the closest to feeling like a member of a family he'd ever experienced.

After dinner Paxton washed up while Lauren bathed Shawn. Paxton wasn't particularly confident in his ability to do dishes—he had a dishwasher and someone come over to clean his place every week—but he vowed to give it a try. Lauren had enough to do.

With them cleared to the best of his ability, he now stood in the doorway of Shawn's room, watching Lauren read "A Visit from St. Nicholas" to the sleepy boy. As he did, a peace he'd never known before settled over him. This was a precious moment and he was a part of it.

"'And to all a good night.'" Lauren closed the book, kissed her sleeping son and came to join him.

Hugging her close, he kissed her on top of the head. "Nice kid."

"Yeah, he is."

They stood there for a while then Lauren headed out of the room and Paxton left the door open a crack. Could he be a father? Did he want to be? Just days ago he would have said no but after meeting Lauren…

She started toward the kitchen. "There's not much entertainment I can offer you. TV, a movie, cards or puzzle."

Paxton had other ideas about how to spend their evening, but he enjoyed her company in and out of bed and he wanted Lauren to know that. "How about a puzzle?" He couldn't remember the last time he had put one together.

As she entered the kitchen she said, "Wow, you cleaned up."

Paxton puffed out his chest as if he'd won a sporting event. "I did. I'm not sure how good a job I did but I tried."

Wearing a small smile, Lauren narrowed her eyes. "First time?"

"Uh…" He winced. "Yeah."

She strolled to him, kissing him on the cheek. "It's perfect."

Her kiss and approval was the best reward his efforts had ever earned.

"The puzzles are in a cabinet over here." She moved across the room and opened a door, revealing three shelves packed with boxes.

"Wow."

Lauren shrugged. "The nights get long here in the winter. So, what'll you have? Hundred, five hundred or a thousand pieces?"

"How about we start with a hundred? I'm not sure I've done a puzzle since I was in grade school."

Lauren looked at him. "Really? How sad."

He couldn't disagree with her.

"So why did you say you wanted to do one?"

"Sounded fun. I'm learning to have fun." She might not know it, but she was teaching him.

"I like fun." She pulled a box out. "This is one of my favorites."

He recognized the picture of the Grand Canal in Venice. "Why's this your favorite?"

"I've just always thought I'd like to go there someday." She put the puzzle box on the table and opened it.

"I've been. It's beautiful. As pretty as this picture." His parents had given him a chance to see the world. They had traveled as a family when his father had gone to medical conferences. Maybe his parents had been better than he had given them credit for. They *had* offered him some amazing opportunities.

"I'd love to visit someday." She dumped the pieces on the table. "I've had this puzzle since I was a child."

So she'd been dreaming of going for a long time. He'd love to show her the city. But that wouldn't be. What they had was now and a few more days.

Lauren couldn't believe that Paxton was actually into completing the puzzle. They worked together, laughing when one tried to get a piece in where the other wanted to place theirs. They stopped long enough to have a hot drink.

"I hope I'm not making a mistake in asking, but I accidentally overheard part of your conversation with your mom the other day. What is going on?"

A dark shadow filled Paxton's eyes. He took a sip of his drink and put the mug on the table before he answered. "They want me to come home right now. Dad's ill and has gotten worse, Mother is worried. They are pushing me to return to Boston."

She took his hand and laced her fingers in his. "If you need to go, go. We will make do until we find another doctor."

Paxton shook his head. "I meet my obligations. I promised to be here until the end of the month and that's what I plan to do."

Unwilling to start an argument with him, Lauren let the subject drop. They returned to the puzzle. Down to the last piece, they discovered that it was missing. She panicked. Where could it be? She was always so careful not to lose any.

"Let's look around," Paxton said in a calm, clear voice. "It has to be here somewhere."

She went down on her hands and knees under the table to search the floor.

"Hey, I found it," Paxton called.

She stood in time to see him lock the last piece in place. "Where did you find it?"

"In my pocket." He gave her an innocent, mischievous look.

"Oh, you." She went after him with a smile on her face. "You did that on purpose."

He grabbed her flailing arms and pulled her to him. "How else was I going to get to enjoy you wiggling your cute butt when you climbed under the table?"

She glared at him. He looked so adorable and relaxed. "You know I'll have to get even, don't you?"

Paxton stood, letting her slide over the hard length of him. "Honey, I was counting on that." His mouth found hers for a deep, hot kiss.

Just before daylight he slipped out of her bed to go home. Lauren hated losing his warmth.

* * *

On Wednesday when it was time to close for the day, she was looking forward to spending time with Shawn. As happy as she was with Paxton, she would not neglect her son. Paxton had yet to say anything about them spending the afternoon together. Before she left, she went in search of him, finding him in his lab.

"Hey, I'm leaving," she announced as she entered the tiny lab. "Mom's expecting me to get Shawn." She put her arm across Paxton's shoulders and kissed him. Things were so easy between them.

"You're leaving?" He seemed surprised she was there.

"You know, if I had less self-esteem I might be jealous of this lab where you're always examining something."

Wrapping an arm about her waist, he pulled her into his lap and gave her a deep sizzling kiss. As he nuzzled her neck he said, "I wouldn't mind examining you."

"As nice as that sounds, I have to pick up Shawn." Could life get any better than being held by Paxton?

"What do you have planned for this afternoon?"

"I've got to run to Lippscomb. Get a couple of Christmas gifts I couldn't find online."

He made a negative sound. "More shopping." He sighed, only to brighten a moment later. "Lauren, I know you like to spend time with Shawn on Wednesdays, but why don't you let me go pick him up and have him at your place when you get back? That way he can have a nap and I'll even plan supper tonight."

Lauren leaned back and looked at him. "Are you sure? He can be a handful."

"I'm sure. You'll get your shopping done faster and I'll get more time with you."

She hesitated for a second. *Was this a good idea? Could this be the same guy who had hesitated to hold Shawn not long ago?* But he was right, she could finish her shopping a lot faster without a two-year-old along. Her mother already helped her out enough so Lauren didn't want to ask her to do more. Finally she said, "Okay, I guess. I'll call Mom and let her know you're coming."

Fifteen minutes later she was on her way to Lippscomb, unsure if she'd made the correct decision. She hoped Paxton hadn't bitten off more than he could chew by volunteering to watch Shawn. Deepening her uncertainty was the uncomfortable conviction she'd already become far too attached to Paxton. She didn't want Shawn troubled when Paxton left. It filled her heart with joy that Paxton had offered to babysit. He knew the way to a mother's heart.

Still, the fear that he might not stay niggled at her. She'd been hurt before. Last Stop was her home, her safe place. She wanted Shawn to have the feeling of security that growing up in a small town would give him. When she'd married Mark, it had been exciting to leave this tiny burg behind, but she had no interest in repeating that mistake. It hadn't taken her long to learn that Last Stop hadn't been as bad as she'd thought it was.

She and Paxton lived in two different worlds. She'd experienced some of his world and it hadn't been for her after all. Even so, she couldn't ignore the obvious. Paxton wasn't Mark. Their relationship was completely different from the one she'd had with her husband. Paxton seemed at home in Last Stop. Mark had been an outsider and that had never changed.

CHAPTER NINE

A FEW HOURS later Lauren pulled into her drive, wondering what to expect. At least the house was still standing. What would the inside look like? She entered through the back door. All was quiet. To her amazement there was a wonderful smell coming from the oven. Another casserole, she was sure. She continued down the hallway. Nothing. Shawn and Paxton were here somewhere because his car was outside.

When she came to her bedroom she glanced in. Paxton lay on the bed with Shawn curled up next to him, and both were sound asleep. Transfixed by the endearing sight, her heart swelled. Heaven help her, she was in love. With vision blurred by tears, she quietly returned to the kitchen.

The creak of the floor warned her someone was there a second before strong arms circled her waist and pulled her back against an unyielding chest.

Paxton kissed her neck. "Hey, get everything done?"

Covertly wiping the wetness from her eyes by rubbing them with thumb and forefinger, she turned without breaking his embrace and smiled. "I sure did. How'd it go here?"

"Good. Shawn and I did just fine."

"Really?"

"It might have been rocky there for a few minutes but we men came to an understanding." Paxton acted as if he'd achieved an award. "Dinner will be ready when Shawn wakes up."

"Sounds good."

"Any ideas what we can do while we wait?" Paxton's hands caressed her back.

"We could watch TV." Lauren didn't look him in the eyes in an effort to cover the emotion still filling her chest. He'd be gone soon and her heart would go with him.

"I tell you what, you watch while I nibble on you." Paxton gave her a hungry kiss that she eagerly returned.

Half an hour later Shawn was up. He was happy to see her but he gravitated back toward Paxton the moment he was done hugging her. Paxton and Shawn had become buddies. That wasn't good. Now there would be two hurting when the time came. Yet she couldn't push Paxton away.

Paxton had her sit while he served dinner. With great fanfare, he removed a large pan from the oven containing roasted beef, potatoes and vegetables. He set a plate of rolls on the table.

She grinned. "How did you know I love the café's roast beef and potatoes?"

Paxton lifted a shoulder. "What can I say, it pays to know the cook."

When he settled into the chair beside her she leaned over and kissed him. "Thank you for this. It's nice."

"You're welcome." He was a man very satisfied with himself.

They were almost through with their meal when Paxton said, "Your mother invited me to lunch Saturday."

Lauren's heart caught. She had been tempted to ask him herself but had refrained from doing so out of fear he wouldn't feel comfortable. She feared that it might be too much too soon. After hearing his stark description of his family's Christmas celebrations, she wasn't at all sure he would appreciate the simplicity of hers. "Are you coming?"

"Sure. What I wondered was why you hadn't invited me?"

She placed her hand over his. "I just wasn't sure you would want to. My family get-togethers can be loud, and that's putting it mildly. It's not something you are used to."

"Don't worry, I can handle it." He raised his head with complete confidence.

On Saturday afternoon, as they approached Lauren's parents' home, Paxton asked, "So who will be here today?"

"My brothers, their wives and children, my grandparents, a few cousins and some neighbors. The usual."

"All at your parents' house?"

"Sure. It's our family home. My grandparents used to live there but now live in a retirement community in Lippscomb. Before them were my great-grandparents. Before them great-great-grandparents who homesteaded it."

"Homesteaded? Like the Oklahoma land rush?" And his family acted as if they had cornered history.

"Something like that. A couple of my male ancestors rode out here from the east. They wrote home to say the grass was as high as a horse's belly, to come on out, that there was land to be had. They did."

"The law was that you had to sleep on your land for a certain amount of time, so they built a simple sod house. One built out of large squares of dirt. As I'm sure you have noticed, we don't have many trees. Anyway, they built at the corner of four sections."

"Sections?" Paxton was fascinated.

Lauren's pride in her heritage clearly came through in her every word. "One mile by one mile square, or six hundred and forty acres."

"I vaguely remember studying that in school." The moment in history had been a paragraph in a textbook.

"Out here we live by it. Have you paid any attention to how the roads run?"

He had, but had never thought to ask why. In Boston, there was no rhyme or reason to the streets and alleys. Here they had been mapped out.

"Anyway, a different member of the family slept in a different room in each corner of the house so that they could file for all four of the sections."

"That's a lot of land. Two thousand, five hundred and sixty acres!"

"Yeah, but to put it into perspective, in your part of the country you can feed fifty cows on an acre while here we feed one cow on fifty acres."

"That's a big difference." There were many of those between them. But that was what he liked most about her. She wasn't a carbon copy of the next woman.

"It takes more land out here, but I love these wide open spaces." She turned into her parents' drive.

When they entered the house, her mother promptly emerged from the kitchen, wiping her hands on her apron, and welcomed them.

"Thanks for having me," Paxton said in greeting.

Mrs. Tucker hugged him. "We're glad you could come. Lauren, be sure to introduce Paxton to everyone."

His own mother had never shown that much emotion when he'd entered a room.

Lauren made sure he met her brothers and their families. Both lived in surrounding counties and were farmers as well. Despite them giving him a narrow-eyed look, implying they were watching him closely, Paxton like them instantly. They had strong handshakes and were men who obviously loved and cherished their families.

The kitchen counters were loaded with food. A long wide table was set with what must have been Mrs. Tucker's best china and glassware. Nearby a smaller table sat that looked like a miniature of the larger one. He guessed it was for the children.

Lauren's father called the group to order around the enormous table. Paxton stood behind Lauren, who held Shawn. As her father continued to speak Shawn began to squirm. Paxton reached around her, taking the boy. He quieted. Looking up, he saw there was more than one set of eyes watching him. Their expressions ran the gambit between surprised to soft approving smiles on the women's faces. He had stepped through another door that was going to make his leaving even more difficult.

Mr. Tucker said the blessing. Everyone filed by the food, filling their plates. Lauren served his plate while he held Shawn. She led them to a spot at the table with a highchair. Paxton slipped Shawn into place.

"You're pretty good at that," one of her brothers stated in a flat tone.

"I've had some practice now. You should have seen me with the stroller for the first time."

Her other brother piped up, "You wait until you dress

a kid for the first time. Emily had her dress on backward when I got through." They all laughed.

"So Paxton, do you follow football?" Mr. Tucker asked.

"I do. Boston College and the New England Patriots."

From there the conversation turned to sports and became loud and animated.

With dinner finished, the family gathered around the Christmas tree. Paxton whispered to Lauren, "I didn't bring something for everyone."

"Don't worry. We all draw names for one person and bring presents only for the children. I've taken care of it."

He was sure she had. Lauren had a way of doing that. His family's Christmases were sedate and proper, while Lauren's was filled with shouts and affectionate hugs. He was fascinated, enthralled and included. He hadn't expected to receive a present, but there was one for him under the tree. It was from Lauren's parents. It was a knit blanket decorated with different places of importance in Last Stop like the oil refinery, Main Street, the church and others. He looked at Lauren's mother, almost too moved to respond, but at the last moment managed to say gratefully, "Thank you."

"I thought you could use something to remember us by," she said.

Paxton looked at Lauren. Forgetting them wouldn't be possible. It had been the best family Christmas celebration he'd ever been involved in.

Lauren slipped out of the comfortable bed, leaving the heat of Paxton to see that Christmas was all in place for Shawn. Even though he was young she wanted him to experience it all. She was just pulling the presents out of the closet when she felt Paxton's arms around her. She would have known it was him even with her eyes closed. His touch had been ingrained in her by now. She would miss it terribly when he was gone but that she would think about later. Today would be a happy one.

"Hey, I missed you." His drowsy voice was rough and sensual.

She turned in his arms. Clad only in jeans, his naked torso warmed her. "Merry Christmas."

"Best one I've ever had. I like finding such a sexy elf slipping around the room." He kissed her.

Lauren giggled. "Since you're up you can help me." She handed him the bag. "Shawn will be awake in a few minutes."

Together they arranged the presents under the tree. They had just finished when her son's sleepy call rang out. With a quick glance at the tree, Lauren hurried to get him. She soon returned with a huge smile on her face. Shawn looked at the lit tree surrounded by gifts and toys in wonderment.

"Look, baby, Santa came to see us," she cooed as her toddler rubbed sleep from his eyes.

Paxton stood to the side, as if he didn't want to interrupt the moment and was feeling out of place.

Lauren glanced at him with glistening eyes and a beaming smile. She waved him to her. His smile covered his face as he slid an arm around her waist. Moments later Shawn was on the floor, with Lauren and Paxton crouched beside him as he tried to tear open a present. He was more interested in the paper than the gift.

She picked up a package out from under the tree and offered it to Paxton. "This is for you."

Paxton looked both shocked and pleased. He opened it. Inside was a book about the history of the area.

She stood and came close. "I thought you might like it." There was a hint of hesitation in her words.

He hugged her. "I can hardly wait to read it. After being here, I'll know the places I'm reading about. I have something for you." Paxton tucked the book under his arm, went to the tree and picked up a large beribboned box.

Lauren felt more than she could put words to as she accepted the gift. Paxton had thought to get her something. When and how had he gotten it into her home and under her tree without her noticing? Sitting on the couch, she placed the present in her lap. Savoring the anticipation, she pulled the ribbon off.

"Do you always open a gift so slowly?" Exasperation was clear in Paxton's voice.

She looked at him. "I do that when it's something special." Lauren lifted the top off to find a bright orange teapot and matching cups and saucers nestled in yellow tissue paper. She lifted the pot out. Moving it one direction then the other, she examined it at eye level. It was wonderful. Paxton knew enough about her to know that it would be perfect in her kitchen. Meeting Paxton's questioning gaze, she declared, "I love them."

He grinned, looking boyishly proud of himself.

Setting the pot back in the box, Lauren patted the seat next to her. He moved to sit beside her. She gave him a kiss, hoping to convey all the love she felt.

A few hours later they were preparing to leave the house when Paxton's phone rang. He looked more resigned than pleased when he checked to see who was calling.

"It's my mom. I need to get this."

"Of course you do. I'll take Shawn to the kitchen."

"No. Stay right here."

It was as if he needed a lifeline and she was it. He sat on the bed and had her sit close as Shawn played at their feet.

Paxton answered. "Merry Christmas, Mom, Dad."

"Hi, son." A deep male voice traveled through the phone, surprisingly loud.

"Hello, Paxton," came a cool female one.

"How are you spending the day today?" his father asked.

"I'm with Lauren and her son Shawn," Paxton answered.

His mother's voice came across the line. "You haven't become involved with some woman out there, have you?"

Lauren couldn't help but tense.

"Lauren and I are friends. She's my nurse and has been kind enough to share her Christmas with me." Paxton's hand squeezed hers.

His friend.

That's right. That's all they were and would really ever be.

"When do you plan to be home?" his father asked.

"In a week."

"Can't you be here sooner than that? After all, we have the big New Year event at the club," his mother stated.

"Paxton," his father said. "I really need you here. You shouldn't have left anyway."

Lauren watched Paxton closely. How would she feel if her father was sick and she was so far away?

"I'll be home as soon as I can. Thanks for calling. Merry Christmas." Paxton hung up.

Lauren glanced at him. A dark expression covered his face. She watched him but said nothing.

"They just wanted to wish me a Merry Christmas." Paxton's nonchalance implied it was no big deal but Lauren suspected that wasn't the case. And they had not once wished him a Merry Christmas or told him that they missed him.

"If you need to go home, people will understand. I would. It sounds like your parents need you."

"Let's not talk about it today." Paxton's tone indicated that was final.

They quietly finished dressing. By the time he was loading Shawn into her car Paxton's good nature had returned. The rest of the day was spent going to church, visiting her parents and a few friends. It ended with Shawn sleeping soundly and Lauren and Paxton huddled on the sofa in the dark, looking at the Christmas-tree lights.

Lauren couldn't remember a more wonderful Christmas. Filled with family, laughter and Paxton.

CHAPTER TEN

BEFORE SUNRISE THE next morning Lauren woke to Paxton's hand brushing her mid-section. Sweet tingles ran over her and heat filled her center. His slightest touch made her feel alive. He dropped kisses along her jaw then found her mouth before he rose over her. She was waiting to welcome him.

Later Lauren watched him dress. If only she could have this every day. Her heart jolted. What was she doing? Repeating history. And not happy history. The kind that left her with a broken heart. Another handsome, intelligent man had come to town and whisked her off her feet. Heartache and devastation would be left in his wake.

Lauren climbed out of bed. She should be clothed to have this conversation with Paxton. Pulling on her robe as if arming herself, she brought the collar up around her face.

She'd allowed Paxton to become a personal part of her life. To go to her parents' house on a holiday like they were a couple and, worse, let her precious son get to know him. Moisture filled her eyes. Her heart hurt. She knew what she had to do. But could she? She wanted to eke out every single second she could have with him but this had to stop before it went any further. Heaven help her, it was already out of hand. It couldn't continue. More kisses, more touches, more of Paxton would only make it harder.

Paxton didn't look at her as he spoke. "I have to leave right after New Year's, so why don't we celebrate on Friday?"

He'd asked so nonchalantly. Didn't he know he was slowly killing her? She took so long to answer that Paxton glanced at her. "I don't think so. My brother has been begging me to bring Shawn for a visit for a few days. I thought this week would be a good time to go since you're here to cover the clinic and it's really slow between the holidays."

Paxton faced her and glared in disbelief, his shirt half-buttoned.

She loved his chest. *Focus.* The only way to survive this was to concentrate.

"You do know I'm leaving on Saturday? I have to be at work at the clinic in Boston on January the second. I'd hoped we'd spend as much of the next few days together as possible."

"To what end?"

He looked as if she had struck him. "I'm not sure how to respond to that."

"Look, things happened fast between us. We knew it wasn't going to last. Last Stop is my home. Boston is yours. We both understood that, going in. It has been wonderful. I'll always remember you. You are an amazing man." She sounded far cooler than she felt. It was becoming hard to breathe.

"Well, you seem to have given this a lot of thought.

I'm glad I could be of service this morning before you dropped the bomb on me."

Now they were both going down an ugly road. Lauren swallowed. "I'm sorry you feel that way. This morning was beautiful. I'll treasure each moment we spent together." *And relive them in my dreams, cry over them into my pillow.*

Paxton raised a pleading hand. "Lauren, can't we…?"

She shook her head. "It won't make it any better. You have obligations in Boston. Your father needs you. You're the kind of guy who doesn't let people down."

"I don't want this to end. Couldn't you come to Boston sometimes? Maybe I could get out here. Or we could meet halfway."

Lauren pursed her lips and shook her head. "I couldn't do that to Shawn. He deserves better than a mother who dumps him on his grandparents for a weekend of sex."

Paxton made a face and swung his head. "Come on, Lauren, you know it's more than that."

"How would I know that? You've never said anything about wanting more." A stricken look came over his face. He ran his hand over his hair, messing it more. At another time, during another discussion she would have reached over and moved a lock off his forehead. "I just think it's time to end this fling. I thought it would be easier on us both to say goodbye now and not have to see each other every day."

His face paled. "Are you running away, Lauren?"

This time it was her turn to feel as if she'd been hit. She *was* running, but it was the only way she knew to keep from crumbling at his feet and begging him not to go—ever. "I'm not doing anything you haven't done."

He winced. The pain in his face had her wanting to

reach out to him, but she held herself in check. Had she gone too far?

"You're right, I did run. But you did the same thing. You wanted to get out of Last Stop, and you took off running the first chance you got, with the first guy that could get you out of town. What's more, at the first sign of trouble you came running back."

She leaned toward him, her face screwed up. "I had Shawn to think about."

"An excuse. You are a smart, creative and resourceful woman. You could live anywhere. But you hide out here because it's easy, safe. You have no room to criticize me."

Anger welled in her. How dared he analyze her life when he couldn't handle his own? "And your problem is you have let your obligation to your father and family control your life. I understand you love your parents. I do too. But you are a great doctor, capable of providing excellent care anywhere, be that in Boston or somewhere else in the world. I think you deserve to be happy where you work. I'm going to take a wild guess here and say that isn't in Boston. The question is, do you know what you want? *Really* want? I don't think you'll ever be happy until you figure that out."

Paxton couldn't believe what he was hearing. Was that really his problem? How Lauren saw him? As being unable to stand up for himself, know what he wanted? Maybe he didn't know. Was that why he couldn't be completely happy in his work in Boston?

The need to take the offensive filled him. "Loyalty is important to me. I was raised to believe that came before everything." Even what he wanted. "Apparently you don't have any trouble analyzing my issues but you can't seem to see your own. What I do know is that there's a great big world out there and you're hiding in Last Stop because you're afraid of getting hurt again. You need to decide whether or not you're here because it's where you want to be or whether it's because you're too scared to try and make it without the security of what you've known all your life."

Lauren threw back her shoulders and in a snide, haughty tone said, "Well, it seems that we both have our issues. Since you're leaving in four days to deal with yours—" she waved a hand between them "—I think my plan to go to my brother's is a good one. Bye, Paxton. Have a good life. It's been nice knowing you."

Lauren stalked out of the room and turned toward the kitchen, leaving him with the sick feeling that his chance at lifelong happiness had gone with her.

A few days later Paxton drove out of Last Stop with a heavy heart. He hadn't seen Lauren since their fight. He'd been miserable but hadn't known how he could change things. He was who he was and she was who she was. Still, the feeling that he was leaving behind something central to his living and breathing dogged him. Sadly, he was confident he knew what it was. What he didn't know was what to do about it.

In Last Stop, Paxton had discovered he could describe his life as fun. *Fun.* He'd never thought about it before but now that he'd had a taste of it, he wanted it to continue. All the time. From an accident, an awkward stay in a hotel, the massive amounts of food he'd been given, his secret with Mr. Gerhart, finding out he was jealous of a two-year-old, a Christmas parade, a kiss under the mistletoe, all the dinners with Lauren and Shawn, and most of all nights with Lauren had all come together to make his life enjoyable. For the first time he'd known genuine happiness.

Christmas with Lauren in Last Stop had been more fulfilling and memorable than he'd imagined any holiday could be. Outside of his parents' call, which had put a momentary dampener on the day, it had been perfect. Now he was leaving all that behind.

Instead of sharing New Year's Eve with Lauren in his arms, Paxton had heard the fireworks from inside his little lab. He'd felt no joy. If he'd believed his life had been depressing after the fiasco with Gabriella, it didn't compare to how he felt now.

On the straight highway out of town, with dark clouds gathering in the west that could only mean more snow, he pressed the gas pedal to the floor, making the sports car fly along the road. All he wanted to do was drive so fast he could forget how much his heart was breaking.

He arrived in Boston exhausted, but with a decision made. He'd rolled over, mulled, examined and contemplated everything Lauren had said as he'd traveled. As much as he hated to admit it, she was right. He was holding on to something he didn't want and for all the wrong reasons.

She had said that he didn't know what he really wanted. Now he did. He had to make his parents understand that the path they had planned for him wasn't his destiny. His father had good medical care, extended family around him and Paxton being there wasn't going to make his disease go away. The Samuels Clinic wasn't where he needed to be. He was required elsewhere.

He'd felt more love and had had more devotion and

support than he'd ever had before from Lauren. He wanted that for the rest of his life. Life might have forced him into changes but he was going to embrace them and find that happiness again that he'd known so briefly. His first order of business was to close up his life in Boston.

Returning to work at the clinic that had his family name across the entrance the next morning, Paxton drafted a resignation letter. With that complete, he wrote a letter that would go out to all his patients, explaining he would no longer be practicing in Boston.

The next item on his list was to speak to his parents. Knowing they could be found at the club that night and that they would insist he come there to talk, he dressed in a suit, which reminded him of the first night he'd made love to Lauren. Would she listen to him when he returned to Last Stop?

Paxton entered the club with his head held high. He wasn't the person who should be ashamed. He located his parents in the dining room. His father stood as Paxton approached and shook his hand. He did look more fragile but Paxton couldn't let his father's health control his own happiness. He kissed his mother's offered cheek.

"I didn't expect to see you this evening. I'm glad you are back," his mother said as he took a seat beside her. "We have to start planning the fundraiser soon if we're going to get everything done."

"I'm going to have nothing to do with that. I'm only back in town long enough to pack up."

"What?" His father's voice carried a note of concern.

"I resigned today. I'm leaving Boston." Paxton couldn't believe how good it felt to say it.

"You can't do that," his mother said in a high voice. "Your place is here. Your father needs you."

"It's already done. I'll be leaving in under two weeks." Paxton didn't waver despite the look of distress on his mother's face.

"Why are you doing this to us?" His mother pulled the cloth napkins between her hands.

"I'm not doing anything to you, Mother. I'm finding the right place for me. Where I want to be." He hoped to set up his practice in Last Stop. If not there, then somewhere that he could be his own man. Whatever happened between him and Lauren, it was time he went out on his own.

"I've never understood you, son," his mother whined.

"I know, Mom. I wish you did. I've discovered what'll make me happy. I'm going after it."

"What is that?" His father sounded genuinely interested in his answer for the first time in years.

"I want a small practice where I know everyone by their first names. Where I can watch the children grow up. Where I'm part of the community for who I am and not because of my name. I want to feel needed."

His father nodded then asked, "You can't find that here? The position on the board will give you power to do things you can't do now."

Paxton looked around the room. "No, I can't. I'm sorry I can't be here for you, Dad. I love you but I can't take your place and I don't want to. Retire. Enjoy your life."

His mother broke in. "We've always loved and supported you. How can you do this to us? If you and Gabriella could work things out—"

"That isn't going to happen. As for support, you have

only done that if it's what you wanted me to do. It's time I do what makes me happy and not try to fit the mold you've created for me."

"Where'll you go?" his father asked.

"Back to Last Stop if I can. Somewhere like it, if not there."

"You would leave everything you have here to live in a nowhere place like that?" His mother sounded appalled at the idea.

"Yes, I would." Paxton stood. "Well, I'll be going. I have a lot to organize. I'll come by the house to say goodbye before I leave."

Paxton left with a weight he'd had no idea he'd been carrying lifted from his shoulders.

Lauren was aware she was making herself sick but had no idea how to do anything different. She was heartsick and the only remedy for that she knew of was time. Each day was about going through the motions. The only area she wasn't failing in was taking care of Shawn.

The days she was at her brother's had been bittersweet. It was nice to visit with her family but all she had wanted to do was run back to Paxton. The day he'd left she'd stayed in her room and cried. Her brother and sister-in-law had seen to Shawn and let her alone. She missed him with an ache that throbbed continuously. It was only because of Shawn she believed she might survive.

She and Paxton had said some hateful things to each other. Some she believed Paxton had needed to hear. But he'd done the same to her. At the time she hadn't thought they were true, but now she was questioning that. Was she hiding out in Last Stop or was it really where she wanted to be?

For years she'd dreamed of leaving. When she'd gotten the chance and found the outside world wasn't all that grand she had run home. But that didn't make her and Paxton's situation the same. Or did it? Was she letting her past dictate her future, too?

Paxton had been gone two days when Lauren drove out to her parents' house.

Her mother took one look at her, took Shawn and put him down to play, then gave Lauren a tight hug. "Have a seat. I'll fix us something hot to drink then you can tell me all about it."

Her mother always knew when Lauren needed to talk. Even when she'd told her parents she was marrying Mark and leaving with him they had been supportive. Maybe not happy but supportive. She knew her parents were there for her, which was something Paxton had never felt from his. That was sad and wrong.

A few minutes later her mother put a mug in front of Lauren and then took a seat with her own in her hand.

"Mom, do you thinking I'm hiding out in Last Stop? That I'm too scared to do something else? That I ran back here?"

Her mother gave her a thoughtful look. "Some."

Lauren was shocked at her answer. She really hadn't expected her mother to agree with Paxton.

Her mother continued, "I knew most of your life you wanted to get out of Last Stop. It was all you talked about. I wasn't surprised that you took the first chance you had. Your father and I weren't enamored with Mark but you seemed to love him and we could accept that. It made sense that you came home because of Shawn. You needed the help. But you never spoke of leaving again. As eager as you were to leave the first time, it seemed odd you never talked of going elsewhere, not even moving to Lippscomb. I have to admit I'm glad to have you and Shawn close so I never asked what happened."

So her mother had noticed.

"As time went by I saw you isolate yourself more. It became Shawn and you. You didn't go on dates. I know you were asked." She grinned. "After all, this is a small town. I have to say I was starting to think you'd never take a chance again. Then Paxton came to town."

"You know?"

"Honey, if it hadn't been written on your face every time you looked at him then I would have heard. You love him, don't you?"

"Yes."

"Then what's wrong? Go after him. It doesn't matter where you live as long as you're together. Step out and see the world again. This time I'd bet true love is waiting for you."

"What if he doesn't want me? I said some awful things to him."

Her mother cocked her head to one side. "What if he does and you don't tell him?"

"I can't just pick up and go to Boston." Lauren looked down at Shawn.

"Why not?"

"There's Shawn, the clinic…" Lauren's heart was beating faster at the possibility.

"Your dad and I will keep Shawn. People have managed around here before without the clinic being open," her mother said.

What if Paxton refused to talk to her? What if she didn't fit in in Boston? Could she do this? What would happen if she didn't? Her heart would never survive. That answered all her questions.

Lauren hugged her mother. "I have an airline ticket to buy."

Paxton was finishing up on the last of the boxes holding his belongings when the doorbell of his apartment rang. He made a small sound of disgust, fearing it was his mother. She'd called almost daily, asking him to reconsider leaving. Her interest unnerved him. He'd not had her razor-edged focus to this degree since he was a child. Was she now making a house call?

Dressed in a button-down shirt and jeans, which he'd taken to wearing more often than not, he went to the door. He opened it with negative words on his lips that he quickly swallowed. His heart did a tap dance in his chest.

Lauren stood there. A more beautiful sight he'd never seen. Her eyes were wide with uncertainty. Her gorgeous hair down around her shoulders. She watched him a moment as if judging her reception.

"Hi, Paxton."

Her soft Western drawl was music to his ears. She'd said the words as if she came to his door regularly.

For a moment he stood speechless with disbelief. Was she really there? He'd dreamed of her nightly. She was like water to his thirsty soul. He managed to sputter, "I wasn't expecting *you*."

"I was afraid if I called you might not see me. I want to apologize."

Paxton suddenly registered they were standing in his doorway. He reached out a hand to touch her but stopped himself. If he did he would have her in his arms whether she liked it or not. "Come in."

She did and he closed the door behind them with a shaking hand. He hadn't been this nervous since he'd seen his first patient by himself. This was his chance to get what he dreamed of in life. He couldn't mess it up. Wouldn't.

"You're moving?" Lauren looked around the room.

"I am." The question of where hung in the air. For him that depended on her.

She turned to face him. "Look, Paxton, I'm sorry for all those horrible things I said to you. You were right, I had no right to talk about your choices in life when I had my own problems. You're a grown man who can handle his relationships without my help."

But he hadn't been able to until now. She'd shown him that. "You came all this way to tell me that?"

"I did. And to get out of Last Stop for a little while. I needed to see if I could do it. Even for a few days."

"And how has that gone for you?" They stood so close yet he hadn't touched her. His hands shook at the thought. Fear held him immobile. He watched her.

"Better than I thought. I've been thinking lately I need to get out more. Move away from Last Stop. There are other places that might work better for Shawn and me."

Paxton wanted her in Last Stop but if she wanted to leave he'd ask if he could follow. "Like?"

She gave her signature shrug. "I was thinking Boston."

That was all he needed to hear. Paxton grinned and stepped into her personal space. He wasn't surprised when Lauren didn't move. He looked into her eyes. All deep, warm and welcoming. "Why's that?"

She softly said, "Because this is where *you* are."

"And that matters to you?" Paxton's hands held her elbows. He didn't miss the shiver that ran through her.

"Yes. Very much."

"Why?" He needed to hear her say the words. With his history he had to know she truly cared.

Her hands came to his chest. "Because I love you. I want to be with you. Here or anywhere else you go."

Paxton swooped her into his arms and kissed her deeply, passionately on her mouth. Her hands went around his neck and held him so tight he feared he wouldn't catch his breath. Sometime later he released her, letting her slide down him. Her eyes were like liquid chocolate as she looked up at him as if he was the most magnificent person she'd ever seen. He would work to keep that look there for the rest of his life.

"I love you with all my heart, Lauren. I promise you I'll always love you and Shawn."

She cupped his cheek. "That's all I'll ever need. Wherever you go, I'll go." Coming up on her toes, she kissed him.

After they broke apart she asked, "So what's all this packing about? Where're you moving to? Another part of town?"

He grinned. "Actually, I'm hoping to start a new practice in a small Oklahoma town. I was waiting to see if the nurse there would forgive me for being such a jerk." He looked into her eyes. "For not telling her that she is my life."

The joy was evident in her eyes before she gave him a kiss that let him know she felt the same about him.

She pulled away. "So you're moving to Last Stop?"

"Only if you agree to marry me, honeymoon with me in Venice, let me be a father to Shawn and any other children we might have."

"I can't think of anything more wonderful." She kissed him again then gave him a serious look. "I'll move to Boston, if that's what you want."

"You said I belonged here but you're wrong. I belong with you. With *Shawn*. Wherever you are is my home. Where I find happiness."

* * * * *

MIDWIFE UNDER THE MISTLETOE

KARIN BAINE

MILLS & BOON

For Catherine, Chellie, Julia and Laurie,
who helped me get this book into shape,
and a shout out to Aunt Sadie and Nigel.

A donation has been made to an ICP charity
on behalf of my sister Jemma's 'little itch'—Maisie.

CHAPTER ONE

'ANYONE WOULD THINK I had baby brain,' Iona muttered as she retrieved her perfectly good pen from the bin, where she'd tossed it along with the wet paper towel.

'Are you sure you don't?' Della, her heavily pregnant last appointment of the day, enquired with a grin.

'I'm one hundred percent positive on that score.' You needed to have had *some* sort of relations in order for that to happen and Iona had been a born-again virgin since moving to the tranquillity of the Scottish Highlands. A serious relationship was the last thing she wanted to get entangled in when she was just beginning to get her life together at last.

Although baby brain wasn't an actual recognised medical condition Iona did believe the to-do list for mothers and mothers-to-be could easily push other thoughts from mind. Her lapses in memory today were more likely to be new-house brain. She'd received the keys to her first non-share, non-rented flat this morning and couldn't wait to finish work and go home for the first time.

'That's a shame. I was hoping for a buddy to go to mother and baby club with at the church hall.'

'Sorry to disappoint. Maybe when you're planning baby number three we can co-ordinate our schedules.'

Iona took the teasing with a pinch of salt because a child of her own was never going to happen. She loved the innocence of a newborn and the pure joy they brought to families and had her personal experiences been different she would've loved to have been a mother herself.

Unfortunately, having a baby meant tying yourself to the father for the rest of your life, with no escape, and she wouldn't trust another man enough to make that sort of commitment again. She'd seen her parents caught in that trap, persevering with a long-dead marriage for the sake of their child, until they'd ended up resenting each other. In her effort to escape the toxic atmosphere she'd attached herself much too young to the dashing Andy, marrying him straight out of school. Only to find herself in an abusive relationship that she knew she would never have left if children had been involved too. It had taken her long enough just to get herself out of it.

No, Iona was happy to remain on the spectator side of pregnancy as a midwife. She was keen to help and support mothers until their babies had been safely delivered and monitor them for as long as they needed it, but her obligation didn't go beyond a medical capacity. At the end of the day the babies went home with their mothers and she wasn't beholden to anyone but herself and her job. She hadn't gone back to school and spent years retraining as a midwife to throw it all away for another man.

Della laughed, clutching her beachball belly. There was definitely a glow in the women who came to the clinic to see Iona and whilst she might experience a pang of regret she'd never get to go through the joys of pregnancy herself, she'd accepted it. Conventional motherhood dictated a lifestyle she wasn't prepared to give up her newfound freedom for.

She dipped the test paper into her patient's urine sample and checked it against the colour chart for analysis. 'Hmm, there's a slight trace of protein. Excess protein can be a sign of a urinary tract infection so we'll have to keep an eye on that in future appointments and if you experience any other symptoms, let me know straight away. Other than that, I'd say pregnancy is agreeing with you.'

Protein in the urine could also be an indicator of kidney damage or other disorders, including pre-eclampsia, but since Della's blood pressure was normal and this was the first sign of a problem, Iona didn't deem it necessary to worry her. If repeat tests showed similar readings she would send a sample to the lab for testing.

She tossed the used stick in the bin and gave her hands another wash. After Dr Irvine's retirement she'd been temporarily upgraded to using this room to treat her patients. Although she was glad of the extra space, she had been sorry to see him go. The senior GP partner—whom she suspected had been practising medicine when Highlanders had still roamed these hills—had made the decision to take her on here at the clinic permanently. It was a position for which she'd be grateful for ever when it had provided her with the financial independence she'd long dreamed about.

Jim, as he'd insisted she call him, had been a true gent with an old-school approach to treating his patients. He'd known everyone in Culcranna by name and had always had time for those who'd needed him. As a result, he'd been well loved and respected. Only time would tell about his replacement, Dr McColl, who'd taken over as senior partner now Jim was content to spend his retirement on the golf course.

Although Fraser McColl was closer to her age than his predecessor, there was a stern quality in his manner that put her on edge and had caused a few run-ins between them. The latest had been his decision to cancel the staff Christmas party usually held on the premises out of hours. He'd called it unprofessional, made noises about it not being covered by insurance and she'd fought him on the issue because she'd been so looking forward to experiencing the tradition she'd heard so much about. Her colleagues had made the annual shindig sound so much fun she'd imagined it would be the perfect way to mark her first Christmas in the village.

Fraser had refused to back down, probably because he'd never understand how much her new job and new home meant to her. By all accounts he came from a family of means, with land and a title to boot, so a tiny flat and a steady income were probably inconsequential to him when they were everything to Iona.

Despite her rallying cry to the rest of the staff to protest, Fraser had imposed so many restrictions on the celebrations they'd been forced into a staid dinner at the nearest restaurant instead. Iona thought his stance on the matter was more about him letting the power go to his head than any insurance issues and had told him so in a fit of pique.

Since then they'd had a few minor rows, more to do with their clash of personalities than to any professional discourse. Iona didn't appreciate anyone imposing unjustified restrictions on her after enduring a lifetime of that with her ex, and apparently Fraser didn't gel well with people who didn't fall into line. Which was tough luck for him because she was no longer prepared to tailor who she was to suit the needs of others.

There was no doubting Fraser's skills or popularity as one of the practice doctors but his tendency to take over certain situations wasn't a character trait she was keen on these days. With his dark, wavy hair and piercing green eyes he certainly cut a dashing figure in the sleepy village that even Iona wasn't immune to. Whilst he had some of the local ladies hot under their cardigans, he reminded her of the men in her past who'd tried to stunt her personal growth. There was too much apparent control freakery about him for her to drop her defences, or any item of clothing, and she hated herself for finding him remotely attractive.

Perhaps if he kept his mouth shut she could enjoy the view at least, without having her hackles raised along with her pulse.

'You wouldn't be saying that if you saw me in the wee hours of the morning, running to the loo every five minutes, or when my insides are on fire with heartburn.' Della shuffled her bottom to the edge of the chair before attempting to get to her feet, trying to balance the extra weight she was carrying around her middle.

Iona gave her a hand rather than watch her struggle like a turtle flipped onto its back, trying to right itself.

'Well, you haven't long to go now. I'll see you in a couple of weeks if you don't go into labour before then.' They'd discussed Della having to be induced if she went too far past her predicted due date but as this was her second pregnancy with no previous complications, Iona wasn't expecting she would require medical intervention.

'Thanks. I can't wait to have this little bundle in my arms.' That tender belly-rub every mother-to-be performed in here made Iona think about her own mum and the excitement she must've felt before her impending birth. A woman didn't carry and protect her baby for nine months expecting they'd both end up trapped in a life neither of them wanted.

She swallowed the rising sob in her chest. They were both free from those soul-destroying relationships now. It was just a tragedy it had come at the price of her mother's death.

'Your daughter will be here soon enough.' Iona handed Della's antenatal notes back to her with a smile. This was supposed to be a happy time for both of them. She had her own baby to get back to—her shiny new flat—and since they were three-quarters of the way through December she'd even treated herself to some new Christmas decorations. Some might say she'd gone overboard but she had enough to brighten up this dreary place too and really mark her first Christmas in the village.

'I need these bloods sent off to the lab, there's a pile of hospital referrals that need to be chased up, and this is Mrs Robertson's prescription. Her husband's going to call in before closing. I've informed him we usually require forty-eight hours for repeat prescriptions and we can't keep on doing this.'

'But she is eighty-three and we have to make allowances,' Sheila, Fraser's secretary, reminded him as she took the stack of paperwork from him with a nod and set it on her desk.

'It doesn't mean I have to be happy about it.' He had

enough to do without these last-minute requests to deal with too.

Taking on the role of senior partner brought with it a lot of extra form filling and bureaucracy but it was a position he revelled in. It gave him an extra say in how the practice was run and that would make him infinitely happier in his work. Structure and boundaries gave him a sense of security, an assurance he was doing things right. It was when he strayed from the rules that things fell apart. Okay, so he was no longer that over-active little boy whose parents had sent him to boarding school so he wouldn't disturb his sick mother, but he'd learned his lesson since then. If he played by the rules there was a place for him and things would work out fine. Now he simply had to get everyone else to fall in line with him.

Not all of Jim Irvine's practices adhered with that idea of running a smooth clinic. Now, there was a man who hadn't bothered too much about form filling or adhering to schedules. That kind of reckless approach had led to inevitable chaos and caused a run-on effect that could have seen the practice run into the ground if not for Fraser picking up the slack to keep the place afloat.

At least Sheila, his second-in-command, who'd been here since the year dot, appreciated how hard he was working to make these changes a success and could be relied on to keep on top of things. Sure, some of his forward-thinking ideas were going to rub a few members of staff up the wrong way. One particular community midwife with chestnut-coloured curls, who thrived on challenging his authority, sprang to mind, having made it clear she preferred his predecessor's slap dash ethos to his.

When Iona had first started working at the clinic Fraser had been pleased they'd drafted in some new blood to bring some modern thinking into the outdated practice and lower the average age of the village population at the same time. There weren't many single, young women in the vicinity but if he'd harboured any nonsensical ideas about finding someone else to settle down with again, Iona had put paid to that with her rebellion against his attempts to bring some structure to the practice.

She refused to attend his weekly meetings regarding the cleaning rota for the staffroom on the basis she ate her meals in her car and was solely responsible for its upkeep. Then there was the argument they'd had over the clutter Iona seemed to accumulate in her room. She'd told him in no uncertain terms that it was her territory and as long as it was clean and functional it was not Fraser's concern.

It seemed Iona preferred to tackle problems as they came in rather than pre-empt them. He'd been there with Caroline, his last girlfriend, and wasn't prepared to go through it again. Caroline had let him imagine they had a future together, planning that happy family with him he'd long been denied. Only she'd decided at the last minute it wasn't what she wanted at all and had blamed him for apparently not being true to her, or himself. Whatever that meant.

So he'd ploughed all of his energy back into work instead of the domestic bliss he'd been promised. He wasn't going to let another flighty woman steal his dreams from him when a new efficient way of working would better serve patients and staff alike.

Whether Iona Munro liked it or not, his new system was getting results. His last patient had been and gone and he was finishing for the day bang on time. Simply by sticking to the ten-minute time slots for each appointment, everything was running like clockwork. He'd say that was a resounding success and a score for all of the Type A personalities out there.

'I'll get on to these straight away, Dr McColl,' Sheila called after him since he'd already left the main office to check all patients had left the premises. At this time of the evening, as the working day was winding down, the hubbub outside the treatment rooms had usually died down, but there were still a few voices ringing out from the reception area. Any out-of-hours emergencies now should have been referred to the hospital or the doctor on call for the area.

The notion that his perfectly executed schedule had been thrown into disarray ploughed grooves across Fraser's forehead even before he was met with the debacle in the waiting area.

'Lift your side up a little higher. Left a bit. How does that look now? Is it straight?' Iona was balanced on a chair, trying to pin a gaudy gold-foil garland to the ceiling, with Victoria, the receptionist, as her partner in crime.

'What the—?' Fraser stopped dead in his tracks at the sight of Iona, barefoot and on tiptoe, breaking every health and safety rule in the workplace. He was in danger of hyperventilating as he did a quick risk assessment of the scene.

'Oh, hi, Fraser. I thought we could brighten the place up and make it look less sterile in here.' Unlike the rest of the staff, who quickly made themselves scarce, Iona carried on decorating as though she was perfectly entitled to do as she pleased. It was one thing managing her own caseload but she didn't have any authority outside that.

'It's supposed to be sterile!' Fraser didn't want to lose his temper when that would be a sign he wasn't in control. Although the garish garlands draped across every available space, transforming the beige room into an eyesore of gold and red, hinted he hadn't asserted his authority here as much as he'd believed.

'Lighten up, Fraser. It's Christmas. If you're worried about the cost, it's coming from my own pocket, not yours.

'Fraser.' This was exactly why she rubbed him up the wrong way. Iona gave no thought for the rules or decorum in the workplace, or anywhere else for that matter. The patients loved her easygoing persona but for Fraser that free spirit vibe was unsettling, as was anything that didn't fit into his idea of conformity. It upset that safe environment he was trying to set up here, and quite frankly he didn't know how to handle it.

Fraser had mistakenly believed Caroline had been the one person who'd understood him when they'd made their plans to get married and settle down into quiet family life, but when his father had died and he'd inherited the family estate he'd discovered the truth. Once Fraser had the means to make those dreams a reality Caroline had confessed they'd been nothing more than an idea she'd been paying lip service to, not a legitimate option. That level of deception had ultimately ended their relationship and Fraser's hope for the future.

This was different, though. Iona wasn't a love interest, so her casual attitude to life shouldn't bother him on a personal level, but she was a staff member and they had rules in place here for a reason.

'I appreciate the gesture,' Fraser said diplomatically, doing his best to remain calm. Iona didn't know him personally so wouldn't understand the issues he had with the whole palaver at this time of the year.

They'd never gone in for the whole over-the-top lead up to Christmas at boarding school and the death of his mother on Christmas Eve had cemented Fraser's dislike of the season. It was a reminder of the childhood he'd lost and the family that had never recovered from the devastation of cancer. Now he dreaded that last week in December more than ever since it was also the anniversary of his break-up with Caroline.

He'd made the mistake of trying to embrace Christmas last year in an effort to make it special for her with an over-the-top marriage proposal, including a horse-drawn sleigh and carol singers serenading them along the ride. Only she'd turned him down on the basis that he was 'being fake'. Fraser couldn't win and was now even less likely to get caught up in the fuss, reverting back to his true Grinchy self, unwilling to be one of those people who lost their minds for the sake of one anti-climactic day.

On the rare occasions his parents had retrieved Fraser for the holidays it had been a non-event anyway. They'd gone through the motions without ever getting bogged down in the sentiment. Whilst he'd yearned for this infantile nonsense as a child far from home, he'd learned to live without it.

Iona carried on making her mark on the recently painted ceiling, humming Christmas carols and reminding Fraser what a very long month December could be when you weren't in the festive spirit.

'As I said, I appreciate the gesture but we can't have all of this cluttering up the surgery.' He would've told her that if she'd sought his permission in the first place.

'I think the patients will love it. It gives them something to focus on other than their aches and pains.'

Sure. They'd all end up with tinsel blindness on top of everything else.

'I'm sorry, it'll all have to go. It's a health and safety hazard.' Fraser began to detach the string of fairy lights from the reception desk.

'Okay, I'll give you the lights. They haven't been assessed by a registered electrician but they are bonny. Perhaps I could bung more tinsel there instead. I have some neon pink somewhere...' Iona clearly wasn't going to give this up without a fight and, as had become the custom, Fraser would have to get tough to have his opinion heard.

He ripped down the cardboard Father Christmas she'd stuck to the counter and hoped it wouldn't leave any sticky marks behind. 'It's all going to have to come down.'

Iona stopped this time. 'You're kidding me, right?'

'I don't kid.' He reached his hand up and tugged the large blue and silver foil star dangling from the ceiling until the tack holding it in place dislodged and pinged to the floor. This was exactly what he was talking about. One drawing pin in the wrong person's foot and they could be facing a lawsuit. Luckily for them both he spotted the gold pin glinting on the dark carpet and retrieved it before it damaged more than his peace of mind.

'What harm can a few decorations do?' Iona faced him, her displeasure flaring in her big brown eyes and her full lips pursed into a tight line. It didn't thrill him to note he was the one with the power to steal away the twinkling smile she wore for everyone else.

'They're a breeding ground for germs with so many

sick people coming and going. Then there's the dust. Think of how many asthma patients we have. Our appointment list is full enough without putting it under more stress.' Deep down Fraser knew he was grasping for excuses but coming into the clinic every morning and being reminded of the worst days of his life was too much for him to bear.

'Okay. Okay. I get it. I was only trying to do something nice. Talk about dampening the mood,' she muttered as though he wasn't there, and began dismantling her ceiling display.

'I know, but perhaps next time you could check with me first instead of going rogue?' Fraser understood her intentions had been good and would've preferred not to fuel this animosity between them, but Iona's spur-of-the-moment actions were infuriating when they impeached on his carefully laid plans and tugged on emotions that needed to remain dormant for the remainder of this dreaded month.

'Yes, sir.' With her anger clearly still bubbling away, Iona yanked down the bunting she'd only finished hanging.

Fraser watched in horror as she tottered on the chair, clearly off balance, her arms freewheeling in the air as she fell.

With lightning-fast reflexes he rushed over and caught her in his arms before she hit the floor. Iona's yelp softened to a gasp as he hooked a hand under her knees and one under her arms. Instinctively she latched her arms around his neck but that contact and the strong grip she had on him almost startled him into dropping her again.

The adrenaline rush was making them both breathe heavily and in that moment, holding her in his arms, their faces almost touching, it was easy to forget what they'd been fighting over, or even where they were.

She weighed very little, reminding him how delicate she appeared to be beyond the bravado. Despite her petite frame, she projected herself as a larger-than-life character but, with their clashing personalities stripped away for the time being, he was reacting solely as a man with an attractive woman pressed against him and was too stunned to do anything other than enjoy the sensation.

Iona blinked first. 'You can put me down now. I think I'm safe.'

'Sure.' Fraser abruptly set her back on her feet and tried to compose himself. 'Like I said, a health and safety nightmare.'

He ignored her tutting as she tore down the rest of the decorations, thankful that this moment of madness had passed, letting normal, tense service resume between them. It was easier to view her as a threat to his plans for a new, improved workplace than through any inappropriate romantic haze.

CHAPTER TWO

As she did every morning, Iona arrived at the clinic with plenty of time to spare before she was officially on the clock. Due to the unpredictable nature of midwifery, scheduled meal breaks were impossible and she often had to eat on the road, if she managed to eat at all. So having a quick cup of tea and a bowl of porridge in the morning as she checked her schedule for the day ensured Iona had at least one proper meal in peace.

Today she was especially keen to get on the road as she'd booked the afternoon off. It was moving day and she was bursting with the excitement of transferring her belongings from her rental to her very own home. It wouldn't take more than a few runs in the car with the meagre possessions she had, and some of her male colleagues had volunteered to give her a hand with the heavy lifting. The sooner Iona got around her patients, the sooner she'd get settled into her own place.

Except as she lifted her first spoonful of thick, oaty goodness to her mouth, a note in the blood results of one of her patients immediately threw her plans into chaos. Iona shovelled in her breakfast as quickly as she could while digesting the news that had come in.

At around five days old, babies were offered newborn

blood spot screening, or a heel-prick test, where a small amount of blood is taken to screen for certain genetic disorders. In this case, the baby had tested positive for one of the listed conditions—phenylketonuria, or PKU for short. Although Iona had done some research into the illness during the course of her training, it was a rare metabolic condition she'd never personally come across before, with approximately only one baby in ten thousand in the UK a sufferer.

The genetic mutation for phenylketonuria was passed on by both parents who might not even have been aware they were carriers. PKU patients, unable to break down the amino acid phenylalanine, a building block of protein, could have a build-up of protein leading to brain damage without adherence to a strict low-protein diet. It was imperative the child be referred to the metabolic unit at the hospital as soon as possible to begin treatment and prevent any long-term damage.

Although modern advances thankfully kept the condition under control with the restricted diet and amino acid supplement to ensure normal development, Iona was aware the news would have a great impact on the family. Every new mum wanted to believe her baby was perfect and to be told otherwise could be difficult to accept and overwhelming.

She took a gulp of tea before pouring the rest down the sink and gave the dishes a quick rinse. There wasn't liable to be a spare minute today but she had one more thing to do before she could hit the road and she wasn't looking forward to it.

Every time she had thought about Dr McColl since last night her blood had boiled, sure his intense dislike of the season was to spite her. She'd made no secret of her desire to make this Christmas one to remember but Fraser seemed determined to thwart those efforts at every turn.

Iona told herself it was this battle of wills that made her react so passionately when she thought of him and nothing to do with whatever frisson she'd imagined when he'd caught her in his arms yesterday. She was no longer the kind of woman who let common sense be overridden by such a romantic cliché. It would take more than being swept off her feet and a handsome face for her to fall for another dominant male. Her sense of self was now defined by her home and her job, not by some fool idea of romance, love and that non-existent fairy-tale ending.

With a deep breath and a sharp knock on the door, she entered Fraser's room out of courtesy rather than a desire to see him for the first time today. In too much of a hurry to waste time on pleasantries, she didn't wait for him to acknowledge her.

'I thought I should give you the heads-up on one of your patients, Marie Gillen. Her baby has tested positive for phenylketonuria.'

There was a slight rise of Fraser's eyebrows before surprise was overtaken by furious typing on the computer keyboard.

'Is this something you've encountered before?' he asked over the sound of the printer whizzing into life.

'Not first hand.' The discovery of rare conditions always brought a range of emotion to the fore, with sympathy for the family at the top of the list. As a medical professional, though, Iona became curious to learn as much as she could to pass on to the parents so they were equipped to deal with whatever challenges were thrown at them. It had to be the same for the GPs who would go on to treat these patients, probably for the rest of their lives.

'Nor me.' Fraser ripped out a handful of printed pages, stapled half together and passed them to Iona, keeping the remainder for himself.

'I'm going to speak to the metabolic unit before I see Mrs Gillen. She'll need a referral straight away.' Since Marie and her newborn were Iona's patients, she would be the one to oversee the initial handover to the hospital.

'This is some basic info on PKU you can give to her. I'm sure you have it all in hand but it will do us all good to reacquaint ourselves with the challenges ahead.' The way Fraser said it made it sound as though he expected her to make a home visit straight away when she'd intended to wait until she'd spoken to a consultant.

'You know I'm on a half-day? I'm only here until lunchtime because I'm moving house today.' Iona didn't know if he was aware of her time off so she gave him the benefit of the doubt that he wasn't deliberately trying to antagonise her again.

'You can see her first and put the rest of your appointments back. The family need to know and this kind of bombshell is best delivered in person.' When Iona didn't respond immediately, stunned that he was pulling rank on her, Fraser added, 'You know this is a time-sensitive condition and we need to begin treatment as soon as possible.'

She knew he was right and if she hadn't been so caught up in her moving plans she would have suggested the same. As the only midwife at the practice, she didn't have anyone else to delegate to so the responsibility was solely hers to deliver the news to the family. That didn't mean she couldn't be irritated at losing her time off.

The slightest brush of his fingers against hers as he handed her the information started that prickling sensation beneath her skin she'd experienced for the first time last night when he'd held her in his arms just a fraction longer than necessary.

That spark of awareness in Fraser's eyes said he'd felt it too but it only served to annoy Iona more. The GP who'd stolen Christmas was now dousing cold water on the plans for her afternoon off so she shouldn't find anything remotely attractive about him.

'I'm sorry for yesterday but, you know, we have to have a code of conduct in the workplace or all hell would break loose.'

She stared at him, unblinking, wondering if he was trying to justify nixing her time off by blaming her for making a move on *him*. Her cheeks burned all the more when she realised he was talking about her dalliance into interior decorating and she was the only one whose thoughts had strayed elsewhere.

'It's all sorted now. Don't worry about it.' Although Fraser deserved more flak over his over-the-top reaction to a few baubles, it would keep until she'd got over this bout of madness.

'If you need an appointment for me to see Mrs Gillen, let me know and I'll fit her into my schedule.'

There were a lot of things about Fraser that frustrated Iona no end but she couldn't fault his devotion to his patients. Their mutual patients were a shared interest. Somehow that didn't give her any more comfort. Iona greedily snatched at more reasons to dislike him to erase the memory of the tenderness she'd felt in his touch and the desire she'd seen in his eyes when he'd held her close.

In that brief moment she'd understood those defences she'd built up against this man were because she was afraid of liking him too much. She had enough physical and mental scars to be wary of any man, especially the bossy kind, but she worried even that mightn't be enough to save her.

'I'll let you know. I guess moving day will just have to wait.'

Fraser nodded and with her last obligation here taken care of, Iona was able to make her escape from the claustrophobia of these four walls.

There was nothing akin to driving out on the open road, radio blasting and singing along at the top of your voice where no one could hear. Iona loved her job. Sure, it was challenging, the hours long with no discernible time for breaks, but it was rewarding. Not only did she get to accompany these women throughout their pregnancies and sometimes get to welcome their babies into the world herself, she was able to enjoy her independence on a daily basis.

She was free to drive out here in the beautiful Scottish countryside, often travelling for miles between each of her appointments. It gave her that sense of empowerment over her destiny, even though she was still technically an employee.

Her freedom was everything to her after her marriage, during which Andy had practically held her prisoner. She'd been blinded by love in those early days, unable to see how he was slowly isolating her from friends and family, insisting he was the only one she needed in her life. Cut off from anyone who could've helped her, she'd been at the mercy of his temper when it had shown itself. He'd used any excuse to lash out at her—if the dinner had been overcooked or she'd been wearing too much make-up—but towards the end he hadn't even bothered making excuses to beat her it had become so commonplace.

Iona flinched, almost able to feel those blows raining down on her after all this time. It was then she had understood why her mother had endured her own loveless relationship for so long. She'd been worn down, cut off from the outside world with no means to support herself financially when she'd sacrificed everything for her family. It had been Andy's talk of babies and her mother's death that had finally galvanised Iona into action. She could never have brought a child into that toxic atmosphere when she'd grown up in similar herself and had followed the pattern into adulthood.

It had taken death to enable her mother to leave her own marriage and Iona hadn't been prepared to wait for the same fate. The strength she'd found to walk out on Andy and file for divorce had carried her on to university and to carve out a whole new life for herself.

Placements during her training had seen Iona working in hospitals and birth clinics but that environment had been a conveyor belt of women passing through her hands with no room to get to know them on a personal level. Life as a community midwife gave her much more of an intimate connection, visiting the patients at home and being on hand as they settled into family life.

She took a bite of the pre-packed sandwich she'd bought at the garage on the way back from Mrs Gillen's. Car picnics were Iona's speciality, if not the hearty dinner she'd been hoping to have in her own place tonight. Now all she wanted was to get back and collapse into bed.

It had been a tough day all round with having to deliver baby Gillen's diagnosis. The family had been rocked by the news and it would take some time to come to terms with what it meant for them but they had family close to provide a good support system.

With some liaising with the hospital team she'd managed to arrange a meeting for them tomorrow morning so hopefully that would ease their minds that their son would still live a full and active life with proper guidance.

She'd talked them through the basics of PKU, as outlined in Fraser's printouts, leaving the experts to discuss the day-to-day realities. There had been no need to panic them by overloading them with information when they couldn't do anything until they'd seen the metabolic consultant and dietician who'd be overseeing the treatment.

The circumstances, however, dictated Iona had stayed with the family much longer than she'd anticipated and she'd been forced to push the rest of her appointments back. It wasn't something she was happy doing to people waiting in for her but given the cold weather her patients had assured her they'd no intention of venturing outside today. She didn't blame them. Given half a chance, she'd have stayed indoors with a mug of hot chocolate and a cheesy Christmas film on the TV.

Of course, the extra time had meant not only had she missed out on her afternoon off but the surgery would likely be closed by now and she'd wanted to stop by to grab a few things for tomorrow.

After eight months in the village Iona knew the area

pretty well but in the dark, with the first flurry of snow visible in the car headlights, these remote roads were daunting, to say the least. When she saw the lights on at the clinic ahead she breathed a sigh of relief that she'd made it back in one piece and she could stock up on supplies for tomorrow's excursions.

It would be an early start tomorrow again in order to keep up to date with all of her patients and paperwork. Being a midwife required stamina and not for the first time she was glad she didn't have to go home and go straight into wife and mother mode to keep others happy. As soon as she was done here she could go home and slip into the guise of knackered singleton guilt-free.

'Hello. It's Iona. Can you let me in?' She rapped on the clinic window, hoping whoever was here, cleaning or catching up on last-minute paperwork, would open up.

'I hope you're not expecting overtime.' Fraser's dour tone almost tipped her over the edge into a rant about putting her patients above financial gain and her own plans, until she saw the tease playing on his lips. In her exhausted state Iona wasn't sure she was prepared to deal with the sight.

'I just want to restock with supplies for tomorrow morning.' Iona didn't rise to the bait, not willing to prolong her working day any longer than necessary. With his large frame filling the doorway, she chose to duck under his arm as he held the door open, rather than take the chance of touching him again by pushing past.

'How is Mrs Gillen?' Unable to take the hint that she didn't want him near her, Fraser followed her into the stockroom. Iona should've known he'd want a full account to analyse if she'd handled the situation correctly, no doubt concerned he'd be the one to pick up the pieces if Marie fell apart.

'Shocked, obviously, but reasonably calm. I passed on the printouts you provided.' He could give himself a pat on the back that he'd participated in some way if that's what he was interested in.

'Good. Good. Would you like me to make an emergency appointment to discuss any concerns with her?' With his arms folded and resting casually against the shelves, Fraser left scant breathing space in the small room. There really was no reason for them both to be crammed in here so Iona forced her way past into the corridor so she wasn't suffocated by his spicy aftershave.

'No, I've made arrangements for her at the metabolic unit. The consultant and dietician will take over from here.'

She doubted he'd be one hundred percent happy about being out of the loop but there were areas even out of his expertise.

'They know best,' he conceded politely.

'How come you're here so late?' Usually you could set your watch by Fraser, who tried to keep office hours when he wasn't on call. He'd never have made it as a midwife.

The idea of him in blue scrubs, tootling around the countryside in her small car, made her grin and she had to turn away so he wouldn't see her amusement.

'I thought I'd swot up on PKU while I was waiting for you.'

The admission made her do an about-turn. 'Me? What on earth for?'

Their contretemps over the decorations immediately sprang to mind, along with that back-of-the-neck tingling sensation. Her pulse apparently thought she was in a sprint and other parts of her were reminding her it had been a long time since she'd been with a man and she should simply acknowledge this growing attraction for her colleague. If the opportunity arose to get close again, she couldn't be certain common sense would get any say in the matter when her hormones were currently doing all the talking.

'I thought you might need help moving in.' The expression on Fraser's face displayed concern rather than an intention to seduce her. He was the innocent party in the lurid fantasies her overtired mind insisted on conjuring up.

'I'll just have to reschedule for the next time I'm free. Whenever that might be.' Her need for sleep now was more vital than assuaging Fraser's apparent guilt that she'd been held up and she wished she'd never broached the subject with him. It put her in a no-win situation. Saying no to him wasn't going to help their already strained relationship but letting him trespass into her private life wasn't going to be comfortable for either of them.

'Call it my apology for yesterday. I could've handled things better.' Hands in pockets, he gave a shrug and appeared even less of a tyrant than ever. None of that was helping Iona maintain that wall of steel she tried to surround herself with at the merest hint of a too-alpha male. Sincere apologies and taking responsibility for anything weren't traits often associated with such domineering personalities. She should know.

On this occasion Iona had to consider the possibility she might have been mistaken in her assessment of Fraser McColl. Then she could stop being so hard on herself for being drawn to him. Unfortunately this humble side of him decreed a compromise on her part lest she become the sort of obstinate-to-a-fault twit she despised.

'Me too. I should've asked before I did my sugar-plum fairy act. I got a bit carried away.'

'Really? I hadn't noticed.' There was that grin again and Iona wondered if it was reserved for the privileged few or it only made appearances out of working hours. It was unnerving that she even wanted to know what her relevance was to the rare sighting.

'It's my first Christmas in my own home, free from demanding family members, messy flatmates and fussy co-workers. Excuse me for being a tad over-excited.' It spoke volumes that the first purchases for her new place had been an abundance of Christmas paraphernalia instead of essential household appliances.

'I can't say I understand the need for the fuss but each to their own as long as it doesn't leak onto the premises again.' Fraser verbally slapped the back of her hand but she'd had much worse from other men she'd inadvertently ticked off in the past.

'What do you have against Christmas anyway?' Since they appeared to have embarked on a truce, Iona thought it best to find out as much as she could about the elusive doctor before the clock chimed and he transformed back into his monstrous alter-ego.

She could see the inner struggle he was having as to whether or not to share the reasons behind his anti-Christmas stance in his hesitation to reply. He was watching her as though judging if she was trustworthy enough to keep his secrets.

Eventually Fraser sighed and said, 'My mother died on Christmas Eve. I was six when they first discovered she had breast cancer. I haven't really celebrated since, packed off out of the way to boarding school when she first became ill. Come to think of it, I don't remember ever celebrating even before I associated her death with Christmas. It's just not a point in my life I'm keen to relive every year.'

The heartfelt explanation shook Iona to her core— she had never expected such an honest and bleak insight into his background. As someone whose job was all about families and protecting young children, it was only natural Fraser's story should get her choked up. She knew how traumatic it was to lose a mother but at such a young age he must've suffered dreadfully.

It explained a lot about his negative outlook on the season and she winced at how tactless her actions now seemed with hindsight. The shock of seeing those decorations would've brought those painful memories flooding back to him and it was no wonder he'd been angry at her. She was sorry that he'd been denied the joy in sharing Christmas with family but she didn't want to pry too far into his personal life and jeopardise their ceasefire. It wasn't as though she was keen to discuss Christmases gone by either.

'I understand that and I'm really sorry for your loss but if you ever need someone to sprinkle a little Christmas magic, you know where to find me.' It wasn't a serious offer when it was probably too late to change his opinion on the subject but she did manage to get him to smile.

'I certainly do but don't let my hang-ups encroach on your obvious enthusiasm. You're perfectly entitled to celebrate however you choose, in your personal life.'

'It is a big deal for me this year,' Iona said apologetically, understanding his point of view but also determined to go all out for herself.

'In that case, we should start with getting you moved in properly.' Fraser turned off the lights and ushered her towards the door so he could set the alarm.

Ready or not, her new best friend was coming home with her for the night.

CHAPTER THREE

'LET ME GET that for you.' Fraser made a grab for the door while balancing a heavy cardboard box in his other hand.

'It's fine. I can manage.' Iona, who could barely be seen over the top of the stacked boxes in her arms, insisted on doing it herself.

'No problem.' He took a step back so she wouldn't think he was trying to crowd her. Iona was so independent Fraser always felt he was in her way somehow, even though she would never have managed to move all of this on her own.

None of this had been in his plans tonight. He had, instead, been anticipating another quiet night in with nothing but the clock chimes echoing through the house to disturb him. It had been his guilty conscience preventing him from walking away from the whole situation when he'd heard from other staff members how excited she'd been about moving in tonight.

Iona nudged the door open with her bottom but he wasn't sure how they were going to manoeuvre her belongings up the narrow staircase leading to the flat above the shop.

'Sorry. I didn't mean to snap. It's just…this is a milestone for me.' The apology was as much of a surprise as the tears he could see making her eyes shine like glossy chocolate. It was clearly an emotional moment for her and probably for more than the reasons she'd given him. He'd experienced something similar when he'd taken over the family home after his father had passed away, believing it was going to be the start of his new life with a wife and children, surrounded by love for the first time. Before then, being on his own had been something he'd simply taken for granted because he didn't remember life before it.

Even if he hadn't had his hands full, Iona didn't give him a chance to pry any further as she made her way upstairs. Clearly the sharing of personal information was only coming from one direction tonight. Fraser had surprised himself by telling her about his mother's death. It wasn't something he usually told people and certainly not those he had trouble getting along with. However, he did want to explain his behaviour surrounding the Christmas issue so she wouldn't hate him too much. Since she hadn't slammed the door on him, Fraser had assumed he'd made the right move.

He'd kept finding excuses to stay behind at the surgery tonight—paperwork, the weather, waiting for news on the Gillens—but as soon as Iona had arrived he'd realised he'd been waiting to see her again so he could make it up to her for spoiling her plans. He had been sure she would come back to make preparations for the next working day and he suspected his overtime had been driven partially by curiosity over that frisson between them last night. It had definitely been attraction on his part, unexpected and somewhat inconvenient since they were co-workers and not harmonious ones at that.

Wandering the empty corridors of his family home,

Fraser had little else to focus on other than his work and now that it had become entangled in his personal life it was impossible not to spend the night thinking about Iona.

He didn't know what he'd expected to come of seeing her after hours but he certainly hadn't imagined going home with her. With their history he'd never thought she'd actually agree to let him help.

It wasn't immediately obvious if her concession was for purely practical reasons or if she, too, was keen to explore that new chemistry between them. He wasn't about to ask when any possible answer was sure to unsettle him more. A dalliance with a colleague was totally out of the question, too disruptive, too close to home, and it had disaster written all over it. He couldn't afford to have his love life screwing things up at work when he was just beginning to get things the way he wanted.

'I know what you're thinking.'

Fraser nearly dropped Iona's belongings at being caught having inappropriate thoughts about her.

'What's that?' He aimed for a neutral 'I have no idea what you're talking about' tone as he stacked his box on top of the ones she'd positioned on the floor. There was still a car full of bric-a-brac outside but he reckoned he could unload it into the hall in double-quick time if he incurred her wrath.

'Why would I leave a pretty chocolate-box cottage for this only a few days before Christmas?'

Once it became clear his thoughts remained private, Fraser deemed it safe to engage in conversation again. 'It's none of my business.'

Since she'd pointed it out, the contrast between the

homely bungalow he'd helped her empty to come to this shell of an apartment did raise questions.

'I mean, Mrs Dunlop said I was welcome to stay as my rent is paid up until the New Year.'

'But you're excited about having your own place? I think you mentioned that.' Fraser could tell how happy Iona was. Her smile was warm enough to heat the whole building—which was just as well because he doubted the central heating had been on since the last tenant had vacated the property.

Personally, Fraser couldn't see the attraction but, given how Iona had no qualms about making her mark at the surgery, he was certain she'd quickly make it a home. As soon as she bought some furniture. Unless this was one of those futuristic, space-saving apartments where the fixtures and fittings popped up from the floor at the touch of a button, she really didn't have any furniture of note.

Iona's quirks were in danger of bringing Fraser out in hives, her inability to plan ahead making him itch. When he'd transferred his stuff from his bachelor pad to the family home he'd allocated a specific timescale for completion, with all his things boxed and labelled accordingly for the removal company. Iona had randomly chucked things into cardboard boxes and bin liners with no forethought given to how she expected to find anything again. Even if she hadn't got caught up at work, there was no way she'd have managed to get things in order in the space of one afternoon.

'I do have a bed, well, a mattress, and there's a kettle here somewhere.' She began rifling through everything, unwrapping the contents until the floorboards were littered with bits of newspaper and kitchen paraphernalia.

'I'll go and bring the rest in.' Fraser couldn't stand back and watch this level of chaos without wanting to fix it. Something he knew Iona wouldn't appreciate. This wasn't his mess or responsibility and he had to get used to the fact Iona had chosen to live this way.

By the time he'd lugged the rest of her trash chic luggage into the flat Iona had moved into the kitchen. It would be generous to call the space open-plan, it was more in keeping with a student bedsit or, in its current state, a squat.

He shuddered as he set the bags down in the one space he could find amongst the mess she'd already created.

'If that's everything, I'll head home.' Back to his pristine house, which didn't look as though it had just been burgled.

'Look what I found!' Ignoring his plea to be released back into civilised society, Iona held up the elusive kettle and two mismatched mugs.

'Great,' Fraser muttered through clenched teeth, accepting his fate. It wouldn't help relations between them if he declined her hospitality when she was trying to be friendly.

'For a job well done.' Iona clinked her mug to his once she'd completed her task, oblivious to his discomfort in the corduroy beanbag serving as his seat during their tea break. The chipped cartoon cat mug he was drinking from was a world away from his mother's fine china he'd become accustomed to.

'So, er, what are your plans for the place?' The old outhouse, long forgotten somewhere on the family estate, was more inviting than these four bare walls, yet Iona was so pleased with it Fraser wondered what kind of place she was used to.

Iona shrugged and slurped her tea. 'I'll get some paint to freshen it up a bit for Christmas and I'll pick up whatever bits and pieces I need along the way.'

Fraser snorted in disbelief at her *laissez-faire* attitude to being a homeowner. For someone so fastidious about her work and keeping track of her patients, Iona was very blasé about her own personal life.

'We're very different creatures, you and I.' Fraser supposed she would be as ill at ease with his set-up—with the family heirlooms giving it that look-but-don't-touch vibe that made people hover nervously—as he was here.

'I thought we'd figured that out a long time ago.' She was teasing, even though there'd been nothing funny about their previous arguments.

'We've had our moments.' This insight into Iona's chaotic world, such a contrast to the one Fraser had created around himself, made sense of their feisty exchanges. They were completely different people and living up to that adage about opposites. Last night they'd finally recognised the attraction even if they hadn't acted on it.

Somewhere across the room Iona cleared her throat and he knew her mind had ventured into the same dangerous territory as his.

Fraser drained the last of his tea. He'd become too comfortable in Iona's company, if not her new dwelling. 'Time to go.'

'Thanks again for all your help.'

He struggled to clamber out of the shape-shifting cushion trying to swallow him whole, which didn't help the growing sense of panic clawing at his chest. He had to get away from here, be somewhere safe and orderly where he wouldn't be ambushed by the furnishings or unexpected emotions.

'Perhaps I'll start my purchases with a chair or two.' Iona came to his aid, holding out her hand to hoist him out of the man trap.

'Not on my account,' Fraser insisted. He had no intention of coming back here and certainly not to relive those distracting feelings he kept experiencing around her. If only he'd stuck to his schedule, all of this could have been avoided. This kind of havoc was exactly what happened when he didn't abide by his own rules.

'You never know who's going to drop in and, as I've just witnessed, not everyone's used to slumming it on beanbags.' Unlike his, Iona's place was the sort people would be dropping into whenever the notion took them. She wasn't the type to be governed by social etiquette outside work, which made her home so much more appealing than the formal invitation one would require to gain admittance to his. Fraser couldn't remember the last time he'd even had a house guest but that isolation was part of the charm as far as he was concerned.

Fraser negotiated his way through the detritus on the floor, waved goodbye at the door, but for the entire journey home he couldn't help worrying on Iona's behalf about her lack of preparation for the move. Neither could he put out the thought of the contents of his own apartment sitting in storage now he had no use for them. Iona was so pleased with so little but she really deserved better, and with a small effort on his part he could provide it for her *and* have her think of him a tad more fondly. He didn't know why her acceptance had suddenly become important to him but it might have had something to do with her smiling at him instead of the usual scowl he elicited.

It warmed him on the inside, reaching parts of him he'd thought frozen in time along with the contents of his family home.

Even though he was worn out after his impulsive house removal, he knew he'd be returning to that compact residence before the night was over. Whatever spell had been cast on him the minute he'd taken Iona in his arms Fraser couldn't seem to stay away from her and that definitely didn't fit in with his plans for a carefully organised life.

Iona sank back into her bubble bath and closed her eyes. This was just what she needed after such a fraught day. Okay, so she'd had to wait for a while for the hot water to come through but like everything else wrong in the flat she was happy to put up with it when she was now the proud owner of all she surveyed.

A secret smile played across her lips as she thought of Fraser's reaction on seeing the place. The outright horror on his face had been comical and she'd admit to intentionally pushing his buttons by leaving everything lying around to see if he'd try to tidy her up outside work. Iona knew he preferred everything spick and span as he was forever rearranging things in the waiting room, but since he'd insisted on stepping into her personal life, this was her way of marking her territory, creating a boundary. There was a chance she'd also been trying to rile him so he would overstep the mark and criticise her so she could stop thinking of him as anything other than her tyrannical boss.

To his credit, he hadn't risen to the bait, proving

there was some restraint and positive qualities behind his fussy, bossy exterior. He'd been generous with his time and support for her tonight and, coupled with yesterday's revelation that her urges towards him weren't only of a violent nature, she was losing track of the reasons to give him a wide berth. At least he'd made it clear he wasn't in a hurry to come back any time soon so she wouldn't have to worry too much over the consequences of inviting another man into her life.

It was easy to recall the feel of Fraser's hands, strong and capable as he'd cradled her after the fall, and imagine how they might feel on different parts of her body. Iona soaped a flannel up her arms and across her chest, startled that her thoughts of Fraser had turned so…carnal.

She let out a groan and covered her face with the cloth. It wasn't as though she'd become a nun on leaving her abusive ex but she'd put her career ahead of any notions of settling down again after being bitten, and a relationship of any kind had been the furthest thing from her mind. As far as she'd discovered, they only brought pain and heartache to everyone involved and she'd had enough of that to know she was better off unattached.

Now she'd settled into her position here and got her foot on the property ladder, it seemed her neglected libido was making a bid for freedom too. Its untimely reappearance around a man with the uncanny knack of riling her temper was entirely inconvenient—a weakness in the armour she'd built around herself since her reinvention. This warrior queen no longer needed anyone to give her life meaning.

Iona ducked her head under the suds, letting the hot water envelop her whole body in a warm hug. It had obviously been way too long since she'd enjoyed the physical benefits of a relationship of any description when her mind was dragging her towards that riptide with the potential to pull her back under.

In her watery cocoon Iona thought she could feel a dull vibration coming from somewhere beneath the flat. She sat upright, listening to the rhythmic drip, drip, drip of the tap, which almost lulled her back down into the depths of soapy luxury until the shrill ring of the doorbell and more thumping noises downstairs prompted her to action. Someone was desperate for her attention.

'I'm coming!' she yelled, pulling on her dressing gown with no heed to the water sluicing onto the bathroom floor. There was no time to dry or dress if she was to get to the door before they left so she simply belted the robe around her naked body to protect her modesty.

Fraser was the last person she expected to find on her doorstep.

'What's wrong? Did you forget something?' She couldn't think of any other reason that would have brought him back again so soon.

'No. I…er…thought you could use these.' He glanced over his shoulder towards the stack of chairs Iona hadn't noticed currently blocking the path.

'And they couldn't wait until tomorrow?' Although it was a nice gesture, it hadn't warranted an immediate return visit tonight. The impulsive act was so out of character she was thrown by his possible motive. Was this intended to impress her or an attempt to impose his authority in all areas of her life?

Iona folded her arms and did her best to make Fraser realise she wasn't impressed that he'd interrupted her 'me' time for the sake of a couple of chairs so he wouldn't get used to the idea of dropping in at will. It did the trick as he grimaced and gave her his best game-show-host impression in trying to sell her the quality of his wares with a flick of his hands.

'I couldn't bear to think of you here in this empty flat when I have a load of furniture sitting in storage.' He gestured to the vehicle behind him, having apparently exchanged the practical car he drove to work for a gas-guzzling four-by-four packed with other household goods.

'Really? This has absolutely nothing to do with you trying to *fix* me? I know you, Fraser, and how much my empty apartment was probably keeping you from sleeping.' Her cynical eyebrow took on a mind of its own as she searched for a dark ulterior motive behind the selfless offer. He'd made it obvious he had issues with her laid-back approach to her interior décor but she hadn't realised it was to the extent he'd empty the contents of his home to spruce hers up.

'Sorry. I was trying to do you a favour. I probably should've asked first.' Fraser took a step back, shoulders slumped with such dejection Iona may as well have told him never to darken her doorstep again. It was a trick she'd seen her ex use time and again to garner her sympathy and she'd always fallen for it, believing she'd been judging him too harshly and accepting an apology for whatever misdeed he'd committed against her. Only for him to exploit that weakness, lull her back into a false sense of security and strike even harder next time around.

She was less trusting these days but she had absolutely no obligation to Fraser so if he did overstep the mark in any way, she wouldn't hesitate in bouncing him back down the path.

'I'm not dressed for company, or furniture delivery.' Standing here in the cold, face to face with the subject of her recent fantasies, made her aware that she was clad only in a layer of terry towelling.

'No problem. If you want to put some clothes on, I can bring the stuff inside for you then I'll get out of your hair.' There certainly didn't appear to be any sign of anything untoward going on behind his earnest expression and she could use the items he was offering. This would be no run-of-the-mill second-hand furniture either, having probably been vacuum packed in plastic wrap to prevent it being spoiled.

'If you insist.' She left the door open and scarpered back upstairs to put some clothes on. Things were awkward enough without hanging around him semi-naked and partially aroused.

Iona did take her time getting ready, going as far as drying her hair before venturing out of her bedroom again. Fraser deserved a hard time for trying to organise her life for her so she let him sweat for a while. Literally.

When she walked back into the living room he was breathing heavily, the sleeves of his once pristine shirt now rolled up and her flat looking as though someone actually lived in it.

Not only had he carted all the heavy furniture up a flight of stairs single-handed, he'd arranged it all and tidied up the mess she'd left on the floor earlier.

'You really didn't have to do this,' Iona protested, tightening her grip on that theory Fraser was only doing it to exert some control over her. Yet, amongst the seats and the table he'd set up, there was also a small electric fire and a television solely provided for her comfort and not any obvious ulterior motive. Perhaps he deserved some credit for his thoughtfulness but that meant accepting she'd been on his mind tonight too and she certainly didn't want to contemplate the implications of that.

'I wanted to,' Fraser said simply, and continued unpacking a bag onto her kitchen worktop.

'What are you doing?' As far as she was aware, she was the only one named on the mortgage and she hadn't advertised for a lodger but here he was, making himself at home.

'I didn't think you'd had time to do a shop so I picked up a few essentials for you on the way over.'

Bread, bacon, butter, eggs, milk and a huge chocolate bar lined the counter as though he knew her shopping list off by heart. Although he was providing the means to christen her new home with all her favourites, Iona didn't want him to think she was a pushover, someone who could be trained with titbits of chocolate. She was in charge of her life now and didn't need anyone making decisions on her behalf. It would be easy to take all his efforts at face value, and as much as she wanted to believe he only had the purest of intentions at heart she had to protect herself by assuming the worst. Andy had made it impossible for her to trust anyone, especially handsome men who seemed too good to be true.

'You really didn't have to. I'm quite capable of going to the shop myself, thank you.'

'I know. I just thought—I wanted you to feel more at home. Sorry.' He started to pack the groceries back into the bag and the waver in his confidence about being there had guilt gnawing at Iona's insides that she'd got him wrong. Perhaps Fraser *was* simply trying to do something nice for her after all. Learning to trust new people was a long and difficult journey every time, no matter how hard she wanted to speed up the process.

'No, it's okay. Leave them.' Iona reached out and touched his hand to get him to stop and show him the gifts were appreciated. His sharp intake of breath and her reluctance to move back out of his personal space drew them back into that fizzing awareness of attraction to one another.

This thing between them was nothing either of them could control but she knew Fraser didn't want to act on it any more than she did. They were complete opposites; they'd drive each other crazy.

Every nerve ending in her body was drawing Iona closer, telling her to submit once and for all. Yet, with Fraser refusing to succumb too, she held her ground. A rejection now would be humiliating every day for the rest of her working life here. If he declined her advances now, it would give him the perfect excuse to undermine her the next time they clashed at the clinic, blaming her hurt feelings for her next bout of stubbornness. A risk she wasn't willing to take if it could jeopardise any future decisions regarding her patients' welfare.

Eventually Iona forced herself to return to the less dangerous task of putting the groceries away in the cupboards.

'How did you come to have so much spare furniture?' She kept her tone casual, even though her heart was pounding with as much adrenaline and arousal as if they had kissed because she'd imagined it so vividly.

There were a few beats before she heard Fraser move away. As though it had taken him that time to shake himself out of the daze too. 'My dad died a couple of years ago and I inherited the family home. I sold my apartment and moved back but I haven't decided if it's what I want on a permanent basis.'

Keeping hold of the contents of his place if he'd sold it didn't make much sense to Iona, but she understood the death of a parent was such an emotional upheaval it brought about huge life changes. It had been her mother's death that had prompted her to strike out on her own regardless of not having anywhere to go or anyone to help her.

'Sorry for your loss.' It was a sentiment she'd heard so often herself yet seemed so inadequate when it passed from her own lips. Those four words could never hope to comfort someone who'd suffered such a devastating event. She'd never known how to respond to it either. It wasn't the done thing to burst into tears or go off on a rant about how unfair it was so she'd learned to graciously nod and thank people for their condolences.

'We weren't really close. Not since Mum died. Or ever, really.' Fraser was disarmingly frank about his relationship with his father and Iona was shocked to discover they had more in common than either of them had realised.

'I know the feeling. It's hard to bond with a parent in those circumstances. Almost as though you're being forced into a relationship you never had because the one you were closest to has gone for ever.' In those early days after her mother's death Iona had done and said all the right things expected of a dutiful daughter trying to make sure her dad wouldn't feel the loss as acutely as she did, filling that role of caregiver left empty by the woman who'd sacrificed everything for her family. None of it had come naturally and she had soon come to realise it had been fear and grief fuelling her actions, not love. She'd rather be alone than submit to another man's whim again.

Fraser was such a strong, confident individual she didn't imagine he'd been in quite the same position with his family but it would explain that frostiness he exuded at times. She knew she'd erected a lot of barriers to keep herself safe when she'd moved away. It had taken a lot of time to make herself accessible to people again, and only because she'd wanted to work in such a people-friendly environment. She was still working on the walls she'd barricaded around her heart, which weren't dismantled so easily. She wasn't sure she'd ever be ready for them to come down again.

Fraser's loss and the anger and sorrow that surely had been part of that were relatively recent and raw. Something he would have to work hard to get past. It wasn't so unbelievable that it formed part of the reason he hadn't moved in for that kiss when the opportunity had arisen. That lessened the sting slightly but also flashed more warning lights that this complex man was the last one she should set her cap at.

'I can't say I was really any closer to my mother but it's all in the past. We're supposed to be celebrating your future.' Fraser smiled but there was a sadness behind it that touched her heart so deeply she couldn't tell if she wanted to reach out and hug him or rip off his clothes.

His decision to move back to the family home rather than stay in his own place seemed all the more bizarre if it held such dark memories for him. Given the same opportunity, she'd prefer to slum it in her Borrowers-sized flat than move back to a house echoing with tears of the past. A clean break was the only way to leave those ghosts behind.

'You didn't think about selling up?' A senior partner in a thriving GP practice with no discernible dependants that Iona knew of should've had the means to live wherever he wanted. Unless he had some debilitating addiction syphoning off his pay packet but she couldn't picture Fraser with any vices that would have seen him spiralling into that kind of desperation.

'It—it's complicated. Walking away isn't really an option, being the last of the McColls.'

She'd heard the rumours that he came from a wealthy background so there was a chance his father had written a clause into his will that Fraser would only inherit if he remained in situ. The kind of emotional manipulation that made it difficult to leave an abusive relationship. Including one from beyond the grave, it would seem.

Iona was lucky that she'd had her mother in her corner, trying to provide some sort of stability, when her father had made no attempt to hide the fact he'd rather have been anywhere than at home with his family. If both of her parents had been demanding and continually messing with her head, she would never have survived this far.

'What about you? No other family or friends nearby who could help you out?' Fraser turned his back on her to go and play with the heater he'd provided, an orange glow flickering in the fake fire screen at the touch of a switch providing a cosier atmosphere already.

'I see a lot of my ex-patients but they've got young families to take care of. Then there's Katherine, but she's not in any condition to do anything but waddle these days.' Katherine was her recently widowed, pregnant colleague currently on maternity leave and probably Iona's only real friend here. She didn't mind her social calendar being pretty much empty when this was supposed to be her new start away from the demands everyone else put on her time.

'I meant outside work.' Given Fraser's usual gruff demeanour, it was difficult to picture a queue of people lined up at his door, waiting to take him out for a night on the town either, so this interest in her out-of-hours activities seemed unnecessarily intrusive.

'I'm a long way from home and, as you know, our line of work can be very demanding. It's not a typical nine-to-five job. Colleagues, and patients to some extent, are my friends.' Iona became so involved with the families it was impossible to sever ties completely and she often received calls in the middle of the night, asking for advice. There wasn't space for her to be lonely and she happened to enjoy her own company. Having anyone in her home, especially of the male variety, was a novelty and not something she wanted to get used to.

'Now you're in the centre of the village I'm sure you'll get to know everyone very well.'

Iona got the impression he was encouraging her to socialise to get himself off the hook from having to bail her out again. Which wasn't a bad idea if it limited those sparky moments between them, although he'd been a great help tonight. She couldn't pinpoint the exact moment when they'd moved from foes to making cow eyes at each other, or which one was more damaging to her well-being. Particularly when she didn't want him to leave.

This was one of those occasions when Fraser was grateful for his bolthole in the hills. There had been many times when he was on call or the roads were treacherous with snow and ice that his location was a nuisance.

Tonight, however, it would be good to put some distance between him and Iona.

They'd become too close, too soon, in the space of twenty-four hours for him to be comfortable. Not that the effort of the drive had put him off coming over for a second time tonight. The sight of Iona fresh out of the shower, hair wet and wearing nothing but a robe, had made the trip worth it. He'd fallen over himself to install his long-neglected furniture, which he'd retrieved from the converted barn at the back of the main house.

If he got her set up tonight, spread the word that she'd moved into the centre of the village and needed a few friendly faces to come and welcome her, he'd have no more excuses to make himself available.

He crouched down by the heater to demonstrate and relay instructions so there was no confusion on how to operate it and no need for him to worry about her shivering here.

'It's very straightforward. This is the on switch—'

'And, let me guess, this turns it on?' Iona knelt beside him, their thighs almost touching as she made fun of him.

They were back to where all this trouble had started, locked in that lustful gaze, battling between their libidos and common sense, desire pulling them closer than the world's strongest magnets, their mouths and restraint venturing into the danger zone.

That red-blooded male trapped inside the body of a man described by his ex as 'too buttoned-up to love' was screaming out to kiss her. Well, for once Fraser wasn't going to hold back and would be true to himself and his feelings instead. If that's what it took to be with Iona,

he was willing to change from the stuffed shirt he had
a tendency to be.

He kissed her. Hard.

Her hands cupped his face and she returned the kiss
with equal abandon.

Fraser couldn't remember the last time he'd felt so
alive, so aware of his every breath, every beat of his
heart, quickening with each flick of her tongue against
his. If this was what he'd been missing out on by playing by the rules all this time, he'd be throwing the etiquette book right out the window.

Iona fell back onto the floor, bringing him with her
until he was splayed across her body, every soft curve of
her lush body hardening his. He wanted her to the point
where nothing else mattered except exploring this walk
on the wild side with her.

Somewhere in the depths of his hormonally dazed
brain Fraser registered her hands pushing against his
chest and he wasn't so far gone he'd ignore any hesitation
on her part. He immediately rolled away and apologised.

'I'm so sorry. I thought you wanted this too.' He'd
never forgive himself if he'd made an unwanted advance.

Iona sat up looking every bit as dazed and confused
as he was about what had just happened. Or had almost
happened. 'I do, I did, but let's be honest, this isn't me
and I'm fairly certain this isn't you. Thanks for your help
with everything but I think we should call it a night. We
have work in the morning.'

She got to her feet and headed towards the door without looking back at him, leaving Fraser in no doubt that
she wanted him to leave now so they could revert back
to solely work colleagues tomorrow. He didn't blame
her when he was at a loss to explain what had come

over him other than pure lust. That didn't make the re-buff any easier to take when he'd put himself out there in a way he hadn't done in a long time. If only he could rewind the clock back to earlier in the night when he'd first left the premises and avoided taking another blow to his confidence and their working relationship! Then he wouldn't be returning home with an even worse opin-ion of himself than if he hadn't tried to help her.

The irony of this was, of course, that Fraser was try-ing to be himself, acting completely on impulse without moderating himself as he usually did, or trying to be the person he imagined people wanted him to be.

Yet Iona had rejected him just the way Caroline had when she too had accused him of not being true to him-self. Perhaps he simply had to face facts. There was no one willing to love him for who he was, or who he tried to be for them.

CHAPTER FOUR

IONA WAS LOATH to leave her new flat the next morning, wishing she had some time off to fully immerse herself in unpacking. The task itself wouldn't take her more than a couple of hours but she could spread that out to last a full day with a chance to binge-watch some of the DVD box sets she had waiting for her.

Since she'd decided to keep her days off for the Christmas period Iona had to carry on her working day as usual and save her solo housewarming party for then.

Her unusual reluctance to get to work might also have had something to do with Fraser's unexpected late-night visit and their nocturnal shenanigans.

She'd finally conceded that his attempt to furnish her flat had been thoughtful, generous and more than appreciated, but it was the re-ignition of that heat between them that had made the night especially unforgettable. Every time she thought of Fraser now, her blood boiled for more than their clash over the Christmas decorations in the clinic. It wasn't a secret they had a clash of personalities but who knew it had been the build-up of such immense sexual tension between them? That kiss, and her reaction to it, had been as much as a surprise as the wild passion Fraser had apparently been hiding under his buttoned-up shirt.

A fluttery sensation started in the pit of her stomach and quickly spread throughout the rest of her body as she recalled the intensity with which they'd dived on each other. As though they'd tired of pretending the chemistry didn't exist and had abandoned themselves to it instead. Desire for Fraser had hit Iona so hard it had literally knocked her off her feet and she could have given herself completely to him at that moment.

Their time together last night proved that first encounter hadn't been a one-off and it scared her half to death. Iona wasn't so damaged by her ex that she believed every man who crossed her path was going to physically abuse her but she remembered how it was to have to constantly think about the other person in a relationship—their moods, their feelings, their needs—and how exhausted it made her. There was little joy in it for her and on balance there was more benefit for her to remain single.

Although she couldn't shake off the knowledge that chemistry between them would be equally as explosive in the bedroom as it was in the workplace. Fraser's kiss alone had had more heat and passion than she'd experienced in her marriage or any college dalliances since but she wasn't going to get burned again. This was the same man who liked to 'take an interest' in her patients, as he put it, whereas she thought of it more as checking up on her. Enough reason for her to give him a wide berth.

If she ever got involved with another man it would have to be with someone who was content to let her be herself, without a desire to bend her to his will. Fraser McColl would never settle until she'd come to heel. The food and furniture delivery was proof enough he was incapable of letting her run her own life without his interference.

Going into the surgery this morning, Iona's stomach was tied in knots wondering how he'd respond to her after her epic rejection and if his bruised ego would make life more difficult for her at the clinic.

'Morning, Victoria,' she called to the receptionist, not stopping for her usual chat in the hope she would manage to dodge Fraser on her way through the clinic.

She knew he was there on the discovery of his labelled, neatly stacked plastic containers in the communal staff fridge. The sight always gave her the urge to mess up his arrangement out of sheer badness. This morning, however, she resisted targeting the regimented meals and fruit snacks since he had gone out of his way to help her before things had spiralled spectacularly out of control.

This morning she had her antenatal clinic so it wasn't unheard of for her to run into Fraser at some point, or indeed consult on the treatment of mutual patients. On walking past his room, she noticed the door was firmly closed, a sign he didn't want to be disturbed by anyone. Fraser didn't normally shut himself off from the outside world until his first patient of the day had taken a seat. It was going to be awkward facing each other after that wanton display they'd put on in her living room but they'd have to get over it when they still had to work together. Regardless of how difficult it was going to be to put the thought of that spine-tingling kiss to the back of her mind.

Her day was taken up with the usual pre-pregnancy checks keeping her too busy to dwell on what was going on behind Dr McColl's closed door. It wasn't her business to know what was going on in his head but it was her job to be professional and supportive to every mum-to-be and make sure her ladies and their babies were progressing as they should.

'Roughly how often do you feel the baby move?'

'Have you given any thought to breast-feeding?'

'How are you feeling generally?'

There'd been no complications or referrals so far today so that meant she'd get out for her home visits on schedule. There was no better way to leave Fraser and that lapse in judgement behind than to get onto the open road and put the vast rural Scottish countryside between them. At least her next patient was bound to close her clinic on a high.

'Katherine!' Iona rushed to give the heavily pregnant woman a hug, or as close to it as her protruding round belly would allow.

'Having a rough day or are you just happy to see me?' Katherine backed herself into the nearest chair and sat down with all the grace of a reversing truck, leaving her other two charges hovering nervously at either side of her.

Hamish and Poppy were too old to be pacified with the box of toddler toys here to entertain the children who often accompanied their mothers, yet were too young to be left unattended in the waiting room for the duration of this appointment.

'Both.' Iona helped Katherine with the shoes she was struggling to take off and pulled a couple of extra chairs over for the little ones.

Iona handed out the lollipops she kept for restless children and improvised some art supplies with printer paper and whatever pens and pencils she had lying around in order to keep their minds and hands occupied so she could have a proper discussion with their mum. Once they were ensconced at her desk she helped Katherine up onto the bed and pulled the curtain partially around her for at least the illusion of privacy.

'Sorry. They've been playing up this morning and I didn't want to send them to school only to get a phone call to drive back and collect them again. They're complaining about tummyache, but as you can see…' Katherine indicated the empty lolly wrappers and the hands dipping into the jar for seconds '…it comes and goes. I think they're just missing their dad.'

'It's only natural.'

Katherine was one of their own, a practice nurse at the clinic who'd taken Iona under her wing when she'd started. The excitement over her new pregnancy had been matched with that of sharing it with her new friend.

Neither of them had expected she'd lose her husband so early to brain cancer only weeks after his diagnosis. The loss and grief had caused Iona to keep a close eye on Katherine, providing a shoulder to cry on and her mobile number for whenever she needed to talk. They'd become firm friends over the course of these past months, especially because neither of them had any other family close by to rely on. The bond they'd developed had gone beyond a work or a patient/midwife relationship.

'Noel did all the decorations at this time of year. He went all out until you could probably see our house from space with the number of lights he put up outside the house. It's not the same now. It's never going to be the same again.' Iona could see Katherine was trying hard not to get upset for the sake of the children, including the one who was due in the not-too-distant future.

'No, it's not, but that doesn't mean it can't still be good. You're a strong woman with two beautiful children and you'll get through this, I promise.' Iona's heart went out to the family. They had moved here from the city with the intention of providing a better environment in which to raise their kids, unaware their future would be cut short and leave Katherine to cope on her own with them.

Iona couldn't in good conscience turf Katherine back out to her husbandless home after a ten-minute checkup when she was this low. Her mental health was as important as the baby's welfare at this point; any distress could impact on the pregnancy.

'Listen, I have some time before my home visits. Why don't I go and make us a cuppa before we take all your measurements? I think we might even have a few chocolate biscuits stashed somewhere too.' An image of Fraser's rectangular plastic tub with his biscuits counted to the last crumb came to mind. This was an emergency. He'd understand, and if he didn't, well, he'd just have to come and tell her so.

'Fraser's?'

'He's a medical professional. He knows chocolate cures all ills.'

Iona returned with a tray of sweet tea and biscuits for the two adults and glasses of milk for the children.

'Now, tell me how you're really feeling.' Iona made sure the kids were distracted enough not to eavesdrop on their conversation before she dug deeper.

That head start on her visits wasn't going to happen after all but it was more important for Katherine to be in a good frame of mind before she left here. Iona worked mostly on instinct and her gut was telling her she needed to be here.

'Stressed. Knackered.' Now she'd let the façade drop, the bags under Katherine's eyes were more noticeable and she was slumped against the pillows, crumpled under the weight of her woes.

'Let's start with the source of your stresses at the minute and we'll see if we can't tackle them one by one.' Tiredness wasn't unusual at this stage of pregnancy when the baby bump was so large it was impossible to get into a comfortable position for a good night's sleep. However, depression could also be a factor and given recent events in Katherine's life it would be surprising if her mood hadn't been affected. The important thing was to recognise and acknowledge it so she could get help. Being a counsellor was one of the many unofficial roles a midwife was prepared to undertake to ensure a happy, healthy mother and baby.

'Apart from the obvious, there's all of the practical things I'm left to deal with now Noel's gone. I mean, I was expecting him to pick up the slack with the shopping once I was at the whale stage. I can barely carry my own body weight, never mind lug bags of shopping around, even if I did have time, what with the school runs and the housework I've to do too. I can't keep on top of any of it and I've still to get the place ready for the baby coming.' Katherine let out a long, ragged sigh then helped herself to a biscuit and ate through the rest of her feelings.

'First things first, is there anyone who can give you a hand until the baby comes?' A good support system played a huge part in any pregnancy but here, with a grieving family heading into their first Christmas without their husband and father, they were going to need people around them more than ever.

'My parents are on a cruise over the holidays. They'll be back nearer my due date to help with the children but we're on our own until then. They weren't going to go but they've been so looking forward to it and I persuaded them we'd be fine. Unfortunately, Noel didn't have any family.' Katherine crammed another biscuit into her mouth.

'At least you'll have someone around when you're in hospital. Until then you know I'll help out wherever I can, and I'm sure everyone else in the village will want to offer a helping hand.' Everyone was fond of Katherine here and though she would never want to impose on people, Iona knew they'd fall over themselves to do what they could for her.

'Thanks, I appreciate that but I know we're not exactly local and everyone has their own family to focus on.' There was that note of resignation in Katherine's voice that everyone would be too caught up in their own lives and Christmas preparations to even think about driving out into the wilds to do a bit of vacuuming. She probably had a point. Everyone except Iona had a life outside work and mightn't be as readily available as she was.

'You could put an ad in for a cleaner for a couple of weeks. I know it might seem like an extravagance but you don't want to be wearing yourself out. You should be taking it easy. It doesn't matter if your house isn't pristine in the grand scheme of things. You've done an amazing job of keeping your family going these past months so don't give yourself a hard time over a bit of dust. Order takeaways, let the kids decorate with cut-out snowflakes and finger paintings. Whatever it takes to get through the holidays. Remember Christmas is only one day and you've got a much more significant one coming up. Trust me, you'll all be more excited about welcoming a new baby into the house. Until then, stick a DVD on for these two and get a nap when and where you can.'

'That feels like such a copout.'

'No, it's called self-care. Your little ones are much more likely to remember you spending time with them than what decorations they did, or didn't, have this year. Speaking of which, did you hear Scrooge McColl enforced a ban on any festivities here so I have an overflow of garlands and sparkle? I'll come over and blitz your place with some magic fairy dust next time I'm passing if you want.'

'Ah, yes, I'd heard Fraser had put his foot down this year about the staff party too. I suppose he has a point. The drinking has had a tendency to get out of hand. It's better to keep these things separate so they don't muddy the waters at work.'

Iona couldn't help but being piqued at her friend for taking Fraser's side, no matter how on point her insight was, but she'd rather stay mad at him than think about that amazing lip-lock and the effect it had had on her last night. With his mouth on hers, his body pressed close, she'd been close to throwing away everything she'd worked towards, and walked away from, in a rush of hormones.

'Mu-um. I'm bored.' The first rumblings of discontent sounded from beyond the blue curtain as the children tired of their improvised art session.

'We'll be done in a wee minute or two. Get my phone out of my bag and you can play that game you like on it until I'm ready to go.' Katherine shouted instructions to her offspring and handed Iona her now-empty mug. 'See? I wouldn't get a minute to relax.'

It was probably true but at least those few minutes of normalcy over a cuppa with her friend had evened out the frown lines on her forehead. A chat seemed such a small thing but it could do wonders for mums, or anyone else feeling low or isolated. Once the baby came Katherine could socialise at the mother and baby club in the community centre but Iona would provide her company in the days leading up to the big event so she wasn't completely on her own.

If nothing else, this brief respite should have given Katherine some time to de-stress before she had her blood pressure checked, along with everything else. 'In that case, we'll get on with what you came in here for.'

'Sorry. I didn't mean to turn this appointment into a counselling session.' The small laugh was an improvement on the near-tears mood when Katherine had come in and proved Iona's theory that a listening ear could make all the difference.

'That's what I'm here for, to make sure you and bump are all right. You can call me anytime you need a friend. Now, do you have a sample for me?'

'Yes.' Katherine handed over the bottle with her urine sample for her to test.

'If you just pop on the scales, we'll make a wee note of your weight.' Increased weight was expected, indicating that baby was thriving, but as Iona plotted the digits on her chart they became cause for concern. Compared to the reading from the week before, Katherine had put on five pounds.

'I don't think I want to know.'

'You are growing another human being in there.' The dipstick she used to test the sample indicated the presence of protein and, combined with the excess weight, called for action.

Unbidden, Katherine lay back down on the bed and uncovered her belly so Iona could check the baby's size and position.

'Have you noticed any unusual swelling lately in your hands or around your ankles?' As Iona felt around the bump she could tell the baby remained in the head-down position and, compared to the last measurement, the growth seemed normal. If the baby appeared too big or too small she would need to order an ultrasound for a more accurate evaluation of its growth and check the levels of amniotic fluid.

'My ankles are puffier than they have been but that's not surprising with all the extra weight they're carrying.' With some help from her midwife Katherine took off her socks so Iona could see for herself.

The alarm bells were deafening now Iona could see the oedema causing the ankles to balloon and Iona was sure the skin around her patient's eyes were puffier than usual too.

'Any headaches, nausea or problems with your vision?' All the symptoms so far were pointing towards a diagnosis of pre-eclampsia that, if severe enough, could potentially cause serious, sometimes life-threatening problems and often warranted early delivery.

It was constriction of the blood vessels that caused the high blood pressure and this reduced blood flow could affect the liver, kidneys and brain. Such changes caused small blood vessels to leak fluid into the tissues, resulting in the swelling, and these leaks in the kidneys caused the protein from the bloodstream to spill into the urine. Although it was normal to have a small amount of protein in the urine, more than that signalled a problem. Less blood flowing to the uterus could lead to growth problems for the baby or placental abruption, where the placenta separated from the uterine wall before delivery. Early delivery was often needed to protect the mother's health and prevent a stillbirth.

'I suffer from migraines anyway and nausea comes with the territory. I just assumed it was the stress of the holidays. Why? Should I be worried?' If Katherine had had her nurse head on and not her busy mum one she would've recognised the signs for herself. Then again, all symptoms individually were common enough during pregnancy and it was only when they were added together they suddenly became something sinister.

'I'm going to check your blood pressure.' Choosing to avoid the question until they knew for sure there was a need to worry, Iona wrapped the cuff around Katherine's upper arm to take the reading.

With the tea and chat she'd had time to settle so elevated blood pressure now would solely be down to medical reasons and not outside influences.

A blood-pressure reading was considered high when the systolic upper number was greater than one-forty or the diastolic lower number was higher than ninety. Katherine's readings far exceeded acceptable figures. One high reading in isolation might not give an accurate picture, and results could fluctuate throughout the day but, combined with the other symptoms, Iona wasn't content to wait longer than necessary. The same reason she was willing to go with her gut instinct on the initial urine screening instead of waiting for the requisite twenty-four-hour sample collection.

'It's high, isn't it?' There was such resignation and understanding of the consequences in Katherine's question Iona didn't even have to answer it.

'Do you have any errands to run in town, or anywhere you could leave the kids for a while? I'd like you to come back this afternoon so we can do more readings. I think another urine test might be in order.' In place of twenty-four-hour monitoring there was another one-time test that could be carried out on a random sample. The protein-creatinine ratio could show signs of pre-eclampsia if it showed at least point three of a milligram per decilitre in results, creatinine being a waste product the kidneys should have filtered out.

'I was going to get a few groceries while I was here.'

Iona unfastened the cuff and noted the readings, which had cemented her suspicions. 'You go ahead and do that and I'll nip in and have a chat with Fraser about the next step.'

'If it's pre-eclampsia, we could both be in trouble, right?' Katherine lowered her voice as she stroked a hand over her bump, illustrating exactly where her fears lay.

'At the minute I'm simply being cautious. We need to do a few more checks but since you're not yet at thirty-seven weeks and your baby's developing well, it could be we just need to monitor your blood pressure closely for the rest of your pregnancy.'

If Katherine had been at the end of her term they would have had to think about inducing her but Iona didn't want the complications of an early delivery for any of them unless absolutely necessary. In certain situations a Caesarean section would be performed if there were signs mother or baby wouldn't be able to tolerate labour, but that would create more difficulties for Katherine when she had to cope back home alone with two other small children after the birth and the impossible task of resting.

'I'll see if I can find a babysitter for a few hours.' Katherine set her mind to practicalities and Iona was grateful for her calm acceptance as anything else could have exacerbated the condition.

'Good idea but don't over-exert yourself and I'll see you again in a couple of hours.' With the most reassuring smile she could give her, Iona helped Katherine down off the bed.

An official diagnosis was going to plunge the family into even more chaos over the festive period but this baby had to be delivered safely wherever, or however, that might happen.

'Right, kiddos. What do you say we go and get some comics and sweeties?' As most mothers were prone to do, Katherine hid her own worries so as not to upset her children and did her best to carry on as normal, so strong on the outside whilst inevitably crumbling on the inside. A widowed single mum with another baby on the way, facing a potentially life-threatening illness, couldn't help but draw compassion.

Before the family trooped from the room Iona threw her arms around her friend and hugged her close. 'We've got this, okay?'

She meant every word of the promise, even if that entailed having to consult Fraser on the case.

Fraser closed the door after his patient, even though there was no real need for continued privacy after he'd completed his paperwork and made his triage calls. On any other day he'd have been content to have an unimpeded view of clinic life but he wasn't ready to face Iona, or whatever new feelings he'd developed for her over the course of the past forty-eight hours.

Even when he'd been loading his old furniture into the vehicle last night he'd known it was a mistake to return. That hadn't stopped him. Going against his own judgement was never a good idea and not an oft-practised one for this very reason—acting without considering all potential outcomes that could affect those around him was what drove everyone away from him in the end. Somehow he had to find a way to exercise some damage control with Iona for the sake of their working relationship. For his own peace of mind in future, one of their hot-tempered arguments would be preferable to the attraction that seemed to be drawing him closer and closer to her.

The knock on the door was a reminder he had more pressing matters to attend to than a romance that could never happen.

'Come in.' Fraser brought up the notes for his next patient on the computer screen to maintain a modicum of professionalism.

That pretence lasted merely seconds as Iona strode into the room full of purpose and Fraser's heart lurched at the first sighting of her this morning. With her uniform on and her hair tamed into relative submission, she was a different woman from the one who'd greeted him on the doorstep fresh out of the shower, but she had no less of an effect on him, his pulse leaping with the recollection of how she'd tasted on his lips.

'I…er…' Fraser had spent half the night and most

of the morning in between consultations trying to construct a speech to excuse any behaviour that could have been misconstrued as inappropriate or an opening into a budding relationship. Only now, seeing Iona again, those words eluded him. He was fighting a losing battle when his better judgement was overruled at every turn by that primal need she'd unleashed within him.

'Katherine was here for her check-up and she's showing signs of pre-eclampsia. I know this is my jurisdiction but I wanted to consult with you on the matter since there could be certain complications for her family if she's admitted to the hospital.' If thoughts of their time together was on her mind, Iona didn't show concern for anything other than her patient. It was a serious enough condition that she was prepared to let him in on the case, not for his opinion but so they could work together on the best outcome for the family.

Fraser sat back in his chair and gestured for her to take the seat across from him to discuss their colleague's situation. 'How so?'

If she wasn't going to acknowledge what had transpired last night, he was more than happy to follow suit. He didn't need to give himself to another woman who had no qualms about rejecting him. It was a mercy in a way that it had happened before any notion of a romance had got off the ground, instead of waiting to deliver the blow when he'd invested everything he had emotionally in a relationship.

Iona cleared her throat, showing an uncertainty that he'd never seen her demonstrate before. She fidgeted with the hem of her skirt, unable to sit still, making her discomfort obvious.

A silver dagger engraved with guilt stabbed at his

insides with the thought that stepping out of his regimented way of life and into hers had somehow caused her apparent distress. Although Iona would be the first to say not everything had to be about him.

'You know she lost her husband not that long ago and they have two other children?'

'Yes, we were all devastated for her.'

Fraser wasn't heartless and as the doctor who had treated Katherine's husband he was acutely aware of the loss she'd suffered. The death of a patient always stayed with him, in this case not only because the family was known to Fraser but because of the sense of powerlessness a terminal illness brought to everyone involved. Even doctors weren't immune to that frustration when all they could do was make the patient comfortable and pain-free where possible before the inevitable end. Any death felt like a failure on his part when his job was to treat illness and save lives, regardless that in such tragic circumstances no one had the power to stop fate in its tracks.

The conversation stalled with Iona waiting expectantly for him to say more on the subject than merely expressing sympathy. She didn't give him long to figure it out before she rolled her eyes and tutted at him.

'There's no one to mind the kids if she goes into hospital.' Iona spelled it out to him with a heavy dose of exasperation.

'Right. Of course. That's the last thing Katherine needs. She already has so much to deal with.' The family had had more than their fair share of bad luck and tragedy recently and it seemed it was going to continue for now.

'I've asked her to come back in a couple of hours for

further blood-pressure and urine checks before I make the hospital referral. I thought that would give us some time to make a few phone calls to see what options are available so we can present her with the facts when she returns.'

'There are definitely no friends or family members she can call on since this is an emergency? I'd hate to think of the children being sent away to strangers when they are still grieving for their father.' Fraser wouldn't wish that on another young soul, having been through it at much the same age. Bereavement was such a confusing concept for children to deal with and they needed guidance and security—something that had been sadly lacking from his own father when he'd needed it most— to help them get through it. More upheaval and stress would have long-term consequences for the family unless someone was able to step in and find a way to smooth their path.

Unfortunately, Iona was shaking her head. 'Her parents are in the middle of the Caribbean somewhere on a cruise and not expected back before the New Year. Katherine might be able to hire a babysitter for an hour or two but there's no one close enough for her to ask to care for them long term. Two small children is a lot for anyone to take on in a village where nearly all the residents are over retirement age and those that aren't have young families of their own. With the exception of present company, of course.'

'So, that only leaves…'

'Temporary foster care.'

A solution they both knew would only upset Katherine more and terrify the children at the prospect of being sent away from the only person they loved to be at the mercy of strangers. That frightening journey into the unknown was something Fraser had been through himself when he'd been sent to boarding school away from everything he'd ever known. He'd much rather the children were able to stay with a familiar face, and together, if possible, to make the experience less traumatic.

It was difficult for a child to see the necessity of such actions, often blaming themselves for events as though they'd done something wrong and the decision to banish them from home was a form of punishment.

Although Katherine had no other options here, unlike his parents who'd simply decided they preferred not to have him around, Fraser doubted her little ones would understand it any better than he ever had.

'I hope it won't come to that and we might be able to sort things out for her. That's not something a member of our staff, a friend, should have to consider for her children. Have you broached the subject with her yet?' It wouldn't be the first time he'd had to contact social services regarding the welfare of children he suspected were being neglected, but it was a different story dealing with someone he knew personally was a fantastic mum going through a rough time.

'Not yet. I wanted to be clear in my own head about what would happen first before I overwhelmed her with information. Katherine isn't some addict or neglectful parent who doesn't deserve her children and I don't want her ever to be made to feel that way.'

'I'll do whatever I can to prevent that.' Not that either of them would sleep easily if her children were taken into care at all. 'Her parents really can't get home any sooner?'

Fraser didn't know what type of people they were but

most parents, with the exception of his, would rather cut short a holiday to care for their daughter and prevent their grandchildren going into care.

'I'll try and convince her to contact them today. Perhaps I'll have more chance if she knows the alternative but even then, it's doubtful they'd make it back before she's admitted to hospital.'

Fraser could see why she'd brought the matter to his attention. Katherine was one of their own and they had to explore every available avenue before succumbing to the inevitable conclusion. He intended to do whatever he could to help.

'Have you spoken to the consultant at the hospital?' Fraser was already going through his list of contacts to see who he knew that could assist them in the matter.

'I'm going to phone now and get her booked in.' Yet Iona wasn't making any move to leave and start the ball moving.

Fraser lifted the phone on his desk and began punching in numbers. 'You do that. I have a friend who's a social worker. I'll ask her advice off the record about what can be done before we make anything official.'

It was a long shot but he was willing to try anything if it would ease Iona, Katherine and the children's suffering in some small way during this difficult time.

Her soft, 'Thank you for understanding,' and slight upturn of the mouth was sufficient payment.

How he wished someone like Iona had fought his corner for him to remain at home when his mother had become sick, and after her death, when his father had seemed to find his presence even more unbearable. If the McColls had had a family friend close enough to persuade them their son would be better off at home, his life might not have been ripped apart, never to be the same again.

CHAPTER FIVE

By the time Katherine arrived back at the clinic alone, Iona had already made arrangements for her to be admitted to hospital. The specialist Iona had spoken to was keen to monitor Katherine closely and try to get her blood pressure lowered.

'One pregnant lady reporting back with a full bladder as requested.' The humour wasn't quite covering up Katherine's fear and she was even paler than she'd been this morning.

'If you want to pop into the bathroom, we'll get another sample for testing.' In the meantime, Iona would call on Fraser for his input and find out if he'd heard anything from his social worker friend.

It was strange lapsing straight back into professional coolness towards each other after the heat they'd generated in her flat last night but it probably was best they didn't acknowledge anything had gone on and set aside their personal entanglement to focus on Katherine. Fraser had been very sympathetic to her predicament, most likely because of what he'd told her about his own childhood and losing a parent himself. Still, he didn't have to get personally involved and it said a lot about his character that he wanted to help get them out of this situation. His empathy with Katherine and the children was all the more remarkable given the cold relationship his parents had apparently fostered with him.

There'd been a couple of other things that had surprised Iona about their earlier meeting in his office. First, that he'd suggested making the call off the record, which was unusual as he wasn't known for going against procedure. In all likelihood it was his familiarity with the patient and the situation the family were in but there was a part of her wishing he'd done it for her sake too.

She'd also been rattled by the mention of his friend, a *she* by all accounts. A casual phone call to chat about the situation suggested he was acquainted with this woman on more than a professional level and that thought burrowed so far under Iona's skin to possess her soul that not even a priest with his Bible and crucifix could have driven it out. Obviously the upheaval of these past few days must've messed with her head if she was seriously thinking of herself as the spurned lover when she'd been the one doing the spurning. She had no right to have her claws out for his other potential suitors.

Iona's green-eyed imagination might have had something to do with the way she burst into his office. 'Katherine's back. Did you manage to speak to your *friend*?'

Fraser did a double take but didn't comment on her intrusion or her surly tone. 'I did get hold of Sandra, as a matter of fact.'

So he was on first-name terms with her.

'Iona?' An unusually timid Katherine appeared behind her and she cursed herself for not closing the door behind her.

Fraser rose from his chair and ushered them both in. 'Come in, Katherine, this concerns you too.'

He pulled another seat over so Iona could sit next to him and they could discuss this together.

She leaned forward so she was closer to her patient. 'As you know, there are some concerns about your current symptoms. The high blood pressure, protein in your urine and the nausea are all adding up to a possible diagnosis of pre-eclampsia.'

Katherine broke eye contact with him to focus on the hands clasped in her lap as she fought to hold it together. 'You still have the other test to do, though?'

'I've already spoken to the consultant at the hospital and they want you to come in. This afternoon.' There'd be more blood tests and if her uric acids were high, they might have to induce her.

The tears dripping down Katherine's face were a silent acceptance.

'They need to keep an eye on that blood pressure and treat it with whatever medication they deem necessary to bring it down to acceptable levels.'

'How long for?'

'As long as it takes. If things settle down they might permit us to monitor you at home but if they think you or the baby could be at risk there's a possibility they could keep you in until you're full term.'

This was out of Iona's hands now and solely down to the severity of the condition. She didn't want to scare Katherine any more than she wanted to give her false hope she could be home by dinnertime, but Katherine was in the profession so she knew the score and that they didn't have all the answers immediately to hand.

'What about the children?' As the implications of her impending hospital stay finally hit, Katherine fidgeted more and more in her chair, panic setting in. Iona should've taken her blood pressure before scaring her half to death.

'Where are they now?' It wasn't as though they were going to spirit her away without letting her say goodbye, as though she was going into witness protection.

'I managed to get Mrs McAdams to watch them for an hour at the coffee shop but I couldn't possibly ask her to do that indefinitely. I can phone my parents but they'll have to arrange flights. What am I going to do, Iona?'

Iona had to swallow several times to prevent her airways closing as her friend implored her to help. 'There's a possibility they'll have to go into temporary care. Just until you're discharged or your parents get here.'

'No. No!' Katherine rose along with the pitch of her voice.

Tears were pinching the backs of Iona's eyes too as she attempted to calm her down. 'Social services will have to get involved once you're admitted. They have to make sure there's someone to take care of them.'

'I can do that. You said it yourself you can monitor my blood pressure at home. I can come here every day if I have to but nobody is taking my babies away from me.'

'We don't want to do that but you need to go the hospital for the sake of the baby. You'd never forgive yourself if something happened.' It wasn't a threat, it was a truth Katherine had to face. They weren't about to handcuff her and frogmarch her to the hospital but it was in her best interests to let them do comprehensive checks and begin the necessary treatment.

'I will never forgive myself if I have to put my children into care.' With her head now in her hands, she was sobbing so hard Iona was afraid she'd go into labour.

'It'll be okay, Katherine. Come on, sit down.' Fraser

guided her back into her chair. 'I put in a call myself to a social worker friend of mine for some advice. Now, there's a chance we won't have to get them involved if you can come to an agreement with a family member to take care of the children.'

'It's not an option. I told you, there's no one until my parents get here. I need someone in the interim.'

'To be honest, Sandy confided in me that it's going to be difficult to place them in emergency care so close to Christmas. If there's anyone you trust to mind them, I'm sure you could come to some arrangement with the local authority.' Reading between the lines, Iona could sense that it wasn't going to be easy keeping them together. Two young children who were still grieving for their father were a lot to take on when most people had already made their Christmas plans. Even those without family had an idea in their minds of how the festive period should pan out.

Katherine's children had done nothing wrong to find themselves in this situation and they deserved a better end to such an awful year. They needed to be spoiled and having so much fun they didn't have time to think about who was missing from their dinner table. Once their mother went into hospital they were going to be even more afraid and confused than they already were, and being split up and shipped off to strangers was going to make it harder to recover from for them.

All those horrible childhood experiences stayed with you long into adulthood, as Iona knew very well, and it was about time they had some positive memories of this year to cling to.

'I'll take them.' She didn't know who was more shocked by her outburst, Katherine, Fraser or herself.

There'd been no thought to the practicalities of the suggestion, merely an emotional reaction to a situation she couldn't bear to witness without trying to do something about it.

'Are you serious?' The minute Katherine's face lit up with hope, her fate was sealed. There was no way she could back out now, even if the practicalities would have to be ironed out. She had no experience of raising small children but she could remember what it was like to lose a parent and it was that empathy that was making this decision for her.

'You need time to think this through.' Fraser was staring at her as though she'd gone mad, but why recommend a close friend should help if he didn't expect one to put themselves forward?

'Sometimes we just have to go with our gut feelings, and mine's telling me to do the right thing here.' Such was the common theme of their clashes, Fraser wanting to do everything by the book when she was happier to trust her instincts. Iona was usually justified in her actions and she hoped this time would not be the exception. Katherine literally had no one else and she certainly wasn't going to start analysing the pros and cons of her decision in front of her. This was one argument she wasn't prepared to give him.

'Can we really do this? I mean, the kids know Iona and it will only be for a few days…'

Damn Iona for giving Katherine this hope without proper consultation. Fraser didn't want the two mites to enter the care system any more than she did but he didn't want her to rush into something else without thinking, only to regret it. These were small children with real feelings who couldn't be picked up and set down on a whim. He was an adult and even he was having trouble keeping up with Iona's changeable moods.

Yet he couldn't deny he'd be happier to see the children go to Iona than imagine them spending Christmas without fun and love, the way he had too often.

He sighed and assumed the position of chief negotiator in the deal. 'There is the possibility of short-term foster care but you will have to notify children's services and request they assess you as a foster carer as soon as possible.'

'That shouldn't be a problem, surely? Iona is acquainted with the children and she's a medical professional. What more could they want?' In Katherine's mind at least, it would be the perfect solution to her current crisis.

Fraser wouldn't deny her peace of mind but it was going to involve more than signing a few pieces of paper. Thanks to Sandy, he was aware of some of the scrutiny Iona would be subjected to in order to assess her suitability as a carer. 'They don't know Iona as well as we do and they'll want background information for the social worker to submit a report for approval.'

'What sort of background information?' For the first time since riding to the rescue, Iona was frowning and perhaps thinking seriously about what was being asked of her. It sparked the embers of suspicion that there might be something she wasn't keen to share in her past. Maybe she wasn't as much of an open book as he'd assumed.

'Stage one will go into detail about your health, marital status, employment and accommodation.' They exchanged glances, fully aware her flat was barely adequate for a busy midwife without the addition of two small children.

'That could be a problem.' Despite her previous pride in her new home, even Iona could see the unsuitability of the premises for the purposes of raising children.

'They won't turn you down on the grounds that your flat's too small or you don't have a garden. I think it's more about ensuring the children have their own space.' It was going to be tight for sure, but Fraser could see Iona whipping the furniture back out if it would secure a place for Katherine's little ones to stay.

'Couldn't you just stay at our place?' It was natural Katherine would want to keep things as normal as possible but that didn't take into consideration the day-to-day practicalities of Iona's job.

'It's too far out for me to commute from every day. They're forecasting one of the worst storms of the year next week and neither I nor my expectant mothers can afford for me to get stranded up there. I don't think it would make practical sense unless you have a snow plough I can drive to work?' Not even the usually optimistic midwife could salve the crushing blow of disappointment falling on the plans of everyone in the room.

Crazy as this plan was, it was the only one available to save the children from going into care. It didn't matter to either of them where the children stayed as much as who they were with. They needed someone familiar enough that they felt safe and that could only be Iona, regardless of how unprofessional that was for a member of staff.

Fraser was acquainted with Katherine in much the same capacity as Iona. She'd been at the clinic longer than both of them, yet after these past couple of days he felt closer to Iona. Perhaps it was down to the time they'd spent together outside work, or because he'd already done her a favour he wouldn't have dreamed of doing for anyone else, but he was compelled to get involved. If only to make sure she wasn't taking on too much.

The kids deserved the best Christmas ever but her empty flat wasn't the right background to frame that happy scene.

As a child Fraser had seen both sides of the coin during the holidays. Either left at boarding school with those whose parents had lived abroad, going through the motions without any of the sentiment supposedly attached to the holidays, or at home, where his parents hadn't bothered about making a show for his benefit any more.

He'd always told himself that if he'd had a family of his own, they'd know they were loved, have all the joys most other children took for granted. After his disastrous attempt at a relationship this could be the closest he got to make that dream come true for some other frightened youngsters who didn't have a clue what was going on beyond missing the stability of a family home.

That big house, full of furniture and possible adventure, had always been missing the laughter of children and this could be one way to exorcise the loneliness there. It was vast enough to provide a solution and a home for the holidays. He could give Iona and Katherine a gift money couldn't buy.

He took a deep breath, contemplated getting a fellow doctor to prescribe him anxiety pills before he said what was on his mind. 'They could come to my place.'

The two women swivelled around to stare at him, mouths agape.

'Pardon?' It was Katherine who found the words to

speak first. 'I could've sworn you just offered to take my kids in.'

'My house is closer to the clinic than Katherine's and bigger than yours, Iona, with a garden and rooms for each of the children. It makes more sense. On the understanding that Iona moves in too as their primary carer.' That covered all bases and though Fraser didn't have much experience of children outside the clinic, he was sure he'd do a better job than his parents had. Iona had made it clear in no uncertain terms that she didn't want to get involved with him on a personal level so that was the end of that issue. The focus would solely be on doing the right thing by this family and he wouldn't let any personal conflict impact on that.

'Iona?' Katherine turned to Iona for approval of this new radical plan.

The decision now rested with her and if she fought him on this it would be for more personal reasons than any excuse she could come up with.

'You'd have to go through an assessment too.' If she thought that would unnerve him, she didn't know him at all.

'Not a problem. I've got nothing to hide.' Even if they brought in a crack investigative team, all they would dig up on him was a list of disappointed exes who hadn't been fans of his regimented approach to relationships.

'You're really prepared to do this? To have me and two children move into your house indefinitely?' Iona was challenging him in front of Katherine to deliberately put him on the spot but he'd made up his mind.

'I don't say things I don't mean, Iona. Katherine needs someone for the children, you need a place for all of you to stay, and this way I can make sure you get to your shifts on time. It sounds logical to me.'

It wouldn't be beyond the realms of possibility for her to believe he was only doing this to ensure the running of the clinic wasn't affected by this madcap scheme. That was safer than letting her know he wanted to help her when he was doing that way too often to go unnoticed by anyone, including himself. He didn't understand what made Iona different from any other colleague that he put himself out to this extent, and he couldn't say he was happy about the disruption, but he'd become a slave to his conscience. Along with other parts of him he didn't wish to acknowledge.

'I'm sold. I'll be much happier having them in such capable hands. I can't thank you enough.' He'd managed to convince Katherine that his intentions were honourable, even if Iona continued to eye him with a certain scepticism.

'If we're all in agreement, perhaps I should put a call in to Sandy and see if we have to make this official?' He directed that at Iona, prompting her to give him a response confirming she was on board.

'I guess so. Katherine, you'll need to pack a bag for the hospital and get some of the kids' belongings together.' Hopefully as a sign of things to come, Iona was on her feet and setting the plan into motion. Since this was work-related-*ish* she would put more thought into this than she had over her last house move.

'Do I have time to take Hamish and Poppy somewhere first so I can break the news to them? I don't want to scare them by just disappearing in case they think the same thing's going to happen to me as their daddy.'

'We'll make time. The longer we take explaining to

them what's happening, the better they'll understand it and make it easier for all concerned.'

As Katherine disappeared out of Fraser's office to get things organised, Iona hung back.

He supposed they weren't going to get far if he didn't deign to give away the keys to his kingdom again. He pulled out his desk drawer and retrieved his spare key, scribbled down his address on a scrap of paper and slid it across the desk towards her. 'If you put the postcode into your satnav, you should be able to find it.'

Iona closed the door and sat down again, clearly wanting a private conversation with him. Fraser braced himself to hear her regret over what had happened between them the previous evening and prepared to give her assurances it wouldn't happen again.

'Is there something else I can help you with?'

'It's about this background check for social services…'

There was a restlessness about her as she alternated between wringing her hands and rubbing her palms on her knees. He'd thought she'd seemed uneasy when he'd mentioned it but now he was worried that whatever she was about to tell him would jeopardise the whole plan, maybe even her position here if it was as serious as it appeared.

'Is there something bothering you, Iona?' Fraser couldn't begin to imagine what it was she was about to tell him but he knew it wouldn't leave the confines of these four walls if she trusted him enough to confide her secrets.

She stared at her hands, avoiding eye contact, her shoulders rising and falling with each shuddery breath, her usual confidence deserting her. 'I…er, I was in a difficult relationship a few years back. Married, in fact. The police were involved.' She took a deep breath. 'There are hospital records too.'

Fraser knew what she was trying to tell him, yet he didn't want to accept it.

'Iona,' he said softly, 'did he—did he hurt you?'

She lifted her head, the haunted look in her eyes breaking his heart. The idea that anyone could lift a hand to harm a curl on her head was as devastating as the thought of her cowering under the threat of violence. It took a special kind of coward to hit a woman and a worse one still who'd feel the need to crush her spirit. Someone obviously threatened by strong women who needed to exert some sort of power over her. Someone who'd never deserved to have her in their life.

'Andy exerted his control in physical form but he also inflicted mental torture on me too until I was a prisoner in my own home. It took a lot for me to leave him and retrain as a midwife so I could get my life back.'

In his position as a GP Fraser had witnessed a lot of domestic abuse cases, knew how quickly they could es-calate into physical violence and how emotional abuse could cause as much damage. He'd referred countless patients to counselling as a result and treated many oth-ers for depression. For some the scars never healed but Iona was one of those rare survivors who'd used that trauma to become stronger and more powerful than the man who'd tried to dominate her through fear. It ex-plained the mystery that had surrounded her move to the village as well as her habitual defiance against any form of control.

He was completely in awe of her strength. 'You're an amazing woman anyone would be proud to have in their life.'

With a swipe of her hand Iona erased any trace of the tears he'd seen forming. 'Anyway, I'm only telling you this because I'm worried it could affect my suitability as a guardian for Hamish and Poppy.'

There was no evidence of self-pity in her words when goodness knew she'd be entitled to it. It must've have been a serious domestic situation for police involvement and injuries to warrant hospital treatment. His urge to track down the person responsible for hurting her and give him a taste of his own medicine was almost as strong as his wish to hug her and comfort her when she was having to relive the nightmare. Neither of them would endear him to her. Instead, he did his best to allay her fears.

'I'm sure that will have no bearing on your current situation. You're not in contact with this individual any more, are you?'

Iona gave an emphatic 'No. We're divorced', letting him know she'd cut all ties with her abuser and giving him some peace of mind that there was no chance she'd let herself be dragged back into that nightmare again.

It was a very personal and painful matter she probably wouldn't even have shared with him but for her concerns over Katherine and her family. Fraser was thankful she'd been brave enough to walk away and start her life over again here in Culcranna.

'You've done nothing wrong and you have absolutely nothing to be ashamed about.' He wouldn't call her a victim when he knew she'd hate to be thought of in that way but that's exactly what she'd been. Now she was a survivor, a warrior who'd fought the battle for her life.

'Perhaps you could ask your friend if she thinks it could cause any problems down the line.'

'I can certainly do that if you want or we could ask Katherine about keeping this as a personal favour, without getting social services involved?' He knew fostering wouldn't be a problem, after all Iona wasn't at fault for an error in judgement. If that was the case every person who'd ever fallen in love with the wrong person would be barred from the process, himself included. Although this would go against proper procedure, he knew they'd all be happier with a more informal arrangement.

'Thanks, Fraser. I'll have a talk with her.' She didn't have to say any more than that as she left for him to understand how momentous this was for her, and him.

'No problem.' Fraser felt honoured Iona still trusted him enough to share the deeply personal information even after last night. Perhaps it was meant in some way to explain her reaction. She'd been hurt in the worst possible way and her fierce fight for independence had been her survival strategy up until now. It helped him understand her a little more and, just like that, he knew he'd been thrown back into the path of oncoming chaos.

CHAPTER SIX

'IT'S NOT TOO late to change your mind, Iona. I don't want you to feel obligated to do this because I have no one else.'

Iona and Katherine were sitting in the hospital car park, the children chattering away in the back seat at the prospect of their adventure in Fraser's grand house, with Katherine expressing her last-minute doubts about the arrangements.

'Definitely not. You heard Fraser. Between us we've got it all sorted.' Iona was still trying to get her head around his involvement in all this. Not only had he assured them they could manage this without outside interference, he'd managed not to treat her as a victim when she'd confided in him about her abusive past. He had been sympathetic without suffocating her, understanding that she didn't need a white knight to ride in and rescue her, offering help only when she'd asked for it. That alone was a big step for Iona after all this time of going it alone.

Fraser was full of surprises today. When he'd first suggested they stay at his house she'd nearly fainted. That wasn't in his senior partner's handbook and made him more human beneath that starched shirt.

'I thought I sensed some tension between you two and I wouldn't force you into a situation you're not comfortable with.'

Katherine was twisting the handle of her bag, which reminded Iona that the prospect of spending the next however many days in residence *chez* McColl was creating the same mass of knots in her stomach, but she couldn't let Katherine fret. Whatever was going on with Fraser, it certainly wasn't going to happen in front of the children. She'd shut down any notion of something happening between them and she'd never drag innocent minors into a potential messy relationship when she was proof of the damage that could do.

'Hey, neither of us would do this if we didn't want to. It's not in our DNA. Fraser's not that bad once he's off the clock. He helped me move into the flat and brought me some furniture to fit it out.' That was when the trouble had started and now she tended to forget he was a danger to her sworn singleton status.

'Maybe I really did read the signs wrong. Is there something else going on I don't know about?'

'No!' The denial came too fast and felt so wrong it was obviously a lie, but so much relied on this plan neither of them questioned it. 'Honestly, there's nothing to worry about.'

Although Iona veered between wanting to kiss or strangle Fraser at times. It was a blessing now that they hadn't fully given in to temptation when they were going to be shacked up together as stand-in parents for the foreseeable future.

She couldn't actually believe she was moving out of her home only a day after she'd moved in to live with another man. So much for the quiet Christmas she'd planned for herself but she could always do that next year, or the one after that. Katherine and the children certainly weren't having the jolly time they'd anticipated this time last year and they took precedence over Iona's self-indulgence.

'You will bring these two up to see me, won't you?' Katherine reached around the back of her seat and fumbled to find the hands of her precious babes.

'Every day if I can.' It would be the only way to convince them that, unlike their father, their mum would recover and come home again.

Iona got out of the car to retrieve Katherine's things from the boot, allowing her some privacy to say her goodbyes. Understandably she was teary when she did eventually step out to join Iona.

'Take care of them,' she sobbed before swamping her friend in a hug.

'We will. Now, are you sure you don't want me to come in with you?'

Katherine shook her head and wiped her tears on the back of her hand. 'No. I'll be fine. Take them back to Fraser's and get them settled in. I'll call as soon as I can.'

'I promise I'll do everything I can to make sure they're happy.'

Things would work out fine if Fraser could straddle the line between senior partner and the guy she could rely on. If he swayed too far into the realm of either persona, their new arrangement could be in serious trouble.

'It won't be long now, guys,' Iona shouted into her rear-view mirror to the bobbing heads of the children, who couldn't sit still. Thank goodness they were comfortable enough around her to see this as a holiday of sorts rather than something to fear.

It was Iona's nerves that were stretched tight enough to snap at any second in the unfamiliar surroundings. The night was creeping in and as they drove further and further into the wilderness there was a sense of being swallowed up by the darkness.

The lack of lighting out here wasn't helping. All it needed now was for the car to break down and this would have all the markings of a horror movie.

Eventually they came to a set of gothic black wrought-iron gates, which opened on their approach. The security cameras mounted either side of the gates turned and followed her progression up the long, winding driveway. The security measures were good for the children's safety but not exactly a warm welcome to visitors.

Iona's jaw almost dropped into the footwell of the car as Fraser's fortress loomed into view.

'Is it haunted?' Hamish leaned forward between the two front seats to peer through the windscreen.

'Don't be daft. It's just a lovely big house with plenty of room for you and your sister to run around in.' The huge mansion sitting in the moonlight was the sort of place she imagined a gang of pesky kids and their Great Dane might come to solve mysteries but this was no cartoon, this was their real home until further notice.

The trio made their way to the front door and as it creaked open Iona half expected a tall, deathly pale butler, who'd probably been spying on them since their arrival at the gates, waiting to greet them. She was more surprised to find a hunky doctor in casual wear on the other side, imagining Fraser would have employed someone else to answer the door rather than have his usual routine disrupted by meeting his guests personally.

'You're here?'

She hadn't expected Fraser to be home, having thought he'd wait until they were in bed and less likely to disrupt his usual routine before he came back.

'I finished up earlier than expected and it occurred to me I didn't give you the security code for the gates.' There wasn't a hint that he'd come back for anything other than practical reasons. Yet the faded denim jeans and soft sage-green wool jumper he was sporting projected a friendlier image than his formal shirt and tie ensemble. He'd taken the time to change and since he wasn't expecting any other visitors she had to assume it was for their benefit.

'Can we come in?' The wind was beginning to howl around them on the doorstep and she pulled up the collar of her coat to act as a barrier against it.

'Yes. Sorry. The heat's on and dinner's in the oven. It's only chicken and chips, I'm afraid. I'm not much of a cook.'

'That makes two of us.' Iona followed the children, who'd run ahead, into the house, the idea of someone making dinner for her heavenly. He'd picked a child-pleaser too and although Fraser could deny it all he wanted, what mightn't be a complicated meal was something he'd gone out of his way to do for his house guests when undoubtedly he was more of a gourmet diner.

Hamish stopped dashing in and out of the rooms long enough to address Fraser. 'My mum says I'm the man of the house now and I have to take care of my wee sister.' He puffed out his chest in an attempt to appear bigger and braver than his young age portrayed.

'That's right but Iona and I are here to help out if that's all right with you?'

'Sure.'

Fraser played the big brother role perfectly, instead of barging in and taking over as he was prone to doing at work, so Hamish was suitably reassured Fraser wouldn't usurp his position.

'This is some place you have. I didn't know you ran a hotel business on the side.' They followed Fraser through the halls of his home, Iona as mesmerised by the elaborate décor as the two little ones.

'Very funny. I told you, it's my parents' place. I inherited it and I'm not entirely sure what I'm going to do with it yet.' When anyone else would've been jumping for joy over the riches bestowed upon them, Fraser didn't seem particularly happy about it. Up until yesterday she might have believed his resistance had something to do with being beholden to someone else's plans but he'd indicated there'd been some bad blood between him and his parents. On his part anyway. She couldn't imagine him inheriting the family fortune if they'd held a grudge.

'Complicated, you said. I can sort of see why. It's not everyone who has a couple of million spare to buy you out.'

'Not self-funded, I'm afraid. It's the family business.' He gestured towards the stern portraits lining the walls whose faces bore some resemblance to their casually dressed descendant leading the way to the kitchen.

Places were already set around the farmhouse-style table in the middle of the floor, which wasn't in keeping with the opulence on display elsewhere. The children were directed to their seats so Fraser could dish up dinner.

'This is cosy. I would've expected one of those mile-long dining tables in the Great Hall where you need a megaphone to be heard from one end to the other.' Iona poured drinks for everyone from the water jug on the table and watched Fraser's cheeks stain red at the joke.

'I prefer to sit in here.'

This old house had every cliché in the book and if she went exploring she'd be sure to find servants' quarters and maybe a housemaid or two hidden away. If he'd owned up about his status, he could have saved them a lot of trouble and provided a live-in nanny.

Whether from habit or a conscious decision to fit in, Iona noticed he didn't sit at the head of the table and pulled up the chair next to her. 'Tuck in, everyone.'

In an effort to set a good example to the other guests, Iona lifted her knife and fork and helped herself to the first hot meal of the day or, in her case, the week. She couldn't remember the last time she'd had a home-cooked meal and this didn't taste as though Fraser had tipped a couple of bags of frozen chips and chicken strips onto an oven tray. The giveaway was that it tasted of the food it was purported to be. He'd made them from scratch and added corn on the cob to their plates in an attempt to get the children to eat some sort of vegetables.

'This is lovely, thank you, Fraser.'

'Have you got loads of money?' Hamish, obviously taking a keen interest in the new surroundings, blurted out what anyone would've assumed on setting foot in the house.

'Hamish, it's not polite to ask that.' Iona scolded him, although it was human nature for that to cross a person's mind. There was no reason for Fraser to work at all as far as she could tell from the house and land he'd inherited. He was clearly dedicated to his profession since he could've retired at any point since his parents' passing. She was sure he could spend many happy hours alphabetising and arranging every expensive knick-knack here, instead of tending to the sick.

'It's all right,' Fraser said placatingly as the young lad leaned back on his chair, arms folded, potentially gearing up for his first showdown with authority.

'Hamish, please sit on your chair properly so you don't damage it.' If Iona had been aware this place was full of priceless antiques she wouldn't have taken responsibility for two small children and the damage they could do running amok here. It was surprising that Fraser had agreed to it at all. Along with being a babysitter, she was going to have to be a disciplinarian too. Neither she nor Fraser were parents to these children and there were going to be times the kids would no doubt push the boundaries so they had to set them early on.

'For the record, I'm not rich, but I do own the title of Laird and the land. As for the house, I'm trying to decide whether to break centuries of family ties and tradition and sell up. Anyway, if you're all finished, I'll show you up to your rooms.'

They traipsed up the grand staircase and along a carpeted hallway until Fraser stopped at a door on the landing. 'I thought Hamish would be comfortable in this room.'

The plush bedroom could've come straight out of a five-star hotel brochure but it wasn't very homely. Hamish set his superhero backpack on the bed. It was lost in the furnishings of a very adult room.

'It's very grown up, isn't it, Hamish?' Iona acknowledged Fraser's effort in preparing a space for Hamish and at the same time tried to convince the boy this was all one big adventure.

'There's plenty of space for you to put your things away and your bathroom is through there.' Their host gave a whirlwind tour, pulling out drawers and opening doors. An en suite bathroom was a luxury for Iona, who was used to house-sharing.

'You could put your pyjamas on, Hamish, and we'll come back when we get our own rooms sorted out.' They left the door slightly ajar so he wasn't completely abandoned.

'Poppy, you're next door to your brother.' The second room was less intimidating, smaller and decorated in neutral tones. Once they'd dotted Poppy's toys around and covered the bed with the favourite fluffy pink bunny blanket she'd insisted on bringing, it would be more child-friendly.

The door creaked behind them and a worried little face peered out at them.

'Come in, Hamish. Don't be shy. You're free to come and go as you please.' Fraser was usually so meticulous about everything being in its proper place it was strange to hear him being so welcoming to the boy. It was clear he wanted the children to be comfortable here, a magnanimous gesture on his part when Iona had the impression he never had been before.

'It's just a thought, Fraser, but could we bring another bed into this room? Perhaps Hamish and Poppy would prefer to stay together as he's promised to look after her for his mum.' She didn't want to embarrass the boy by suggesting he might be scared in that big room alone but wanted Hamish to think she was doing this to keep his sister safe.

'Sure. I'll show you to your room before I start shifting the furniture around,' Fraser said, striding out of the room at breakneck speed.

Iona took some pleasure in seeing Fraser disconcerted at the suggestion because it reminded her this congenial host act could be a façade and she shouldn't let her guard down just in case.

'This was my mother's room.' Fraser didn't give her the same warm introduction as the others into her new living quarters and she didn't dare enquire why his mother had had a separate room from his father.

'It's beautiful.' The scene before her was straight out of every little girl's fairy-tale. A four-poster bed and closet space big enough to fit her flat in, not to mention the rolltop bath in an alcove, was a fantasy come true. The floral wallpaper and thick pink carpet underfoot weren't to her taste but fitted perfectly in here.

'And where's your room?' She'd have to know in case of emergency, not because she was curious where he spent his nights.

'I'm down the hall.' In the other direction, she noted as he spun away from her.

'Thanks for this, Fraser. You didn't have to do this.'

'Neither did you.'

'No. We're a regular couple of heroes.' Iona laughed, not seriously fooling herself she was doing anything more than any other decent human would do.

'Or two people with nothing better to do over the holidays,' Fraser muttered, and left her to her own devices.

Iona heaved her bag onto the bed and unpacked the few things she had. There had been no way to predict how long they'd be here so they'd only brought the essentials for now. If anyone needed anything else, they could call home and get them. She eyed up the tub, wondering when she'd get an opportunity to use it. It wouldn't be tonight. She was exhausted and in danger of falling asleep and drowning in it and she had to get the children tucked up in bed at some point too. Although, judging by the thumping and banging coming from down the hall, they'd no intention of sleeping tonight. She had visions of them using the antique bed as a trampoline and Fraser presenting her with an extortionate bill for damages at the end of their stay.

'Hey, guys, can you keep the noise down in there?' Putting them into a room together might have been a bad move after all.

There was another loud thump against the wall, followed by the sound of muffled voices.

Iona sighed. She'd have to put her foot down tonight or they'd never get any sleep. She whipped the door open, fully prepared to read them the Riot Act if they carried on wrecking the place, except it was the Laird himself making all the racket and being reckless with the furniture. He had a bed base tipped on its side and was sliding it through the door, so focused he didn't appear to see Iona peeping at him. That's exactly what she was doing here, watching him as he stripped off his jumper—being a peeping Tom.

Fraser tossed his knitwear aside, revealing a tight white T-shirt layer. Iona scrunched up her face at being denied a sneaky glimpse of what lay beneath. Her stealth, however, was rewarded seconds later when he lifted the hem to mop the sweat from his brow.

Darts of lust targeted Iona's erogenous zones, the sight of his taut stomach and that sexy V where his jeans rode low on his hips hitting bulls-eye after bulls-eye.

When she realised the heavy lifting had ceased and she dragged her eyes back up his body to find she'd been caught ogling, she forced her buckling knees to carry her forward.

'You didn't have to do this on your own. I would've helped.' The belated offer of assistance should've been enough to deflect the fact she'd been gawping where she oughtn't, but the smirk on his face suggested otherwise.

'It's no problem. I can see you're busy.' He flipped the bed upright and manoeuvred it adjacent to Poppy's, mesmerising Iona with every flex of biceps she hadn't known he possessed under those buttoned-up shirts. Then he was on his hands and knees, tightening all the nuts and bolts and giving her a good view of his taut backside.

'I'll bring the mattress in.' She excused herself from the sight and the too-hot room to drag the mattress in from the hall.

Unfortunately her muscles weren't as well developed as Fraser's and she had to employ a combination of shoulder charges and kicking to move it.

'Let me try.' A large hand rested on her shoulder and almost collapsed her into a puddle. She hoped this hormonal mess incapable of functioning would return to her normal competent self soon once she got used to seeing a man around the house.

'Right, you two, into the bathroom to brush your teeth.' Leaving Fraser to the manly bed-building, she shut herself away to compose herself and remember who she was and who he was.

'Why's your face all red, Auntie 'Ona?' Poppy's scrutiny made her blush harder so she was forced to splash herself with cold water at the sink.

'It's hard work, moving furniture.' That was plain to see from the trickle of sweat making Fraser's hair curl at the back of his neck.

Another splash of water and Iona kicked the door shut. She was too young to start getting hot flushes and needed her brain to compartmentalise this man back into his 'unsuitable dating material' box. The best way to stop daydreaming about his body was trying to wrangle two small kids into bed in a strange house but she knew once she did that the adults would be left alone and there were no guarantees her mind wouldn't start to wander again.

Fraser made up the spare bed and exited sharply back to his own room, collecting the jumper he'd cast aside along the way. Iona could put the kids to bed while he took some time to cool down.

He tugged his shirt over his head and tossed it into the laundry hamper in the bedroom with the rest of his clothes. At the last minute, before he stepped into the shower, he locked the bathroom door. He was going to have to remember he was no longer living alone.

His mind flitted back to Iona standing in the doorway, watching him so intently he may as well have been naked. The first blast of ice-cold water took away his breath along with the mixture of manual labour, anger and lust making him sweat.

While he lathered his body with soap, it was easier for him to fixate on never being able to please her than the memory of her predatory gaze sweeping over his body or he wouldn't leave this cubicle until he'd found some satisfaction.

He didn't want to be assigned a significant role in this scenario that he wasn't ready to accept. He was, however, considerate of the children's plight, and how they'd left the warmth and familiarity of home to be here. This wasn't a school full of stern masters and other frightened children but it could be equally as imposing. As an adult, and the owner, there were times it scared the hell out of him too.

Fraser had done everything he could to make them comfortable by cooking dinner and preparing their rooms, all the time wishing he'd retained some of the household staff after his father's death.

His best hadn't been good enough for Iona and though he'd shifted things around to suit he didn't think she'd find favour with anything he did. Ordinarily it didn't bother him if people took to him or not but he was sharing more of himself than ever with Iona and he wanted her to see the best in him. If he'd had any sense he would've volunteered for on-call duty this weekend and avoided crossing paths as much as possible then he wouldn't have to be constantly under her scrutiny.

Fraser slammed off the shower and towelled down before throwing on a clean shirt and jogging bottoms and padding barefoot downstairs to the kitchen. It was odd expecting to hear the chatter of other people when at any other time he imagined every creak and murmur might be the ghosts of his past come back to haunt him.

The house was quiet except for the sound of the kettle as he waited for it to boil and he assumed the others had all gone to bed after their fraught day. For the umpteenth time he wondered how he'd got himself into this mess. Iona. His life had been thrown into turmoil from the moment he'd held her in his arms and fried the logical side of his brain. How was he supposed to sleep now when the same woman was only down the hall from his bedroom?

'Oh. Sorry. I didn't realise you were down here. I fancied a cup of tea before bed.' Iona's unexpected arrival made him spill the hot water over the kitchen worktop and he had to move quickly before it scalded his feet too.

'Great minds…and all that.' Fraser grabbed some kitchen towels and crouched down to mop up the mess he'd made on the floor.

Iona reached for another mug from the cupboard he'd left open.

'Sugar?' she asked, and it took him a few seconds not to respond with an equally sweet nickname to the one he'd imagined she'd bestowed on him.

'Not for me, thanks. It's in the container there beside the kettle if you want some.'

'I didn't mean to disturb you but you should know I'm a night owl.' Iona justified her appearance so late, even though this was to be her home too for a while.

'I'm more of a morning person myself but I suppose we should take the quiet times when we can get them, huh? Are they both down for the night?' Actually, Fraser didn't usually sleep long enough to have a preference, only catching a few hours in between when exhaustion finally overwhelmed whatever problems or memories had been keeping his brain awake. New people in the house were bound to bring him additional thinking time in the small hours.

'Out for the count.'

'We can take this into the lounge if you want. If we leave the door open, we can hear any little feet wandering around upstairs.' If they took their tea in there they'd have extra room to spread out and create much-needed distance between them.

'Are you sure you trust me not to spill anything on your antique rugs?' Iona was teasing but she didn't realise how close to the mark she was—Fraser was still afraid of causing damage to the family heirlooms. It had taken a long time to get used to being in charge around here and this was an act of defiance against the house rules for the sake of those he'd invited to treat his home as their own. It was just difficult for him to understand what that truly meant. Not long ago he'd thought that was having a wife and children and now he didn't know if he'd ever have the right to the deeds without either.

'It's okay, I'll have the staff come in and clean up after you leave.' Fraser's deadpan delivery made her almost snort her tea back out.

'Do you actually have people who do that?'

'My parents did but I didn't see the need. Most of the time I only use the lounge and the kitchen, which I'm quite capable of cleaning myself, as you know.'

Iona's giggle, which came at his expense, nonetheless lifted his spirits. If they could find the funny side in his compulsions they were making progress.

Iona sat in the chair opposite him, her legs curled up under her. 'I know you have very valid reasons for not celebrating Christmas but you don't even have a tree.'

Which, apparently, was the crime of the century. It suggested his life was in some way lacking because he hadn't bothered chopping a tree down to stick in a bucket in his front room.

'Last year wasn't a great Christmas for me either. My…er…girlfriend left me. Just after I proposed to her. I wasn't in a hurry to be reminded of it.' It hadn't crossed

Fraser's mind to decorate because he was supposed to be the only soul in residence. When he'd had a partner, a vision of a future together and there'd been something to celebrate, he'd done the whole festive frivolity along with everyone else, but, as in his childhood, it had turned out to be fake and a waste of time pretending Christmas was something special.

Talking about it now wasn't as painful as it once had been. It was a positive sign that he was beginning to move forward and not letting either event define who he was. That should probably include no longer allowing bad memories to taint future holidays.

'I'm so sorry. I don't want to make you uncomfortable in your own home but the children could be here for Christmas. It's only a few days away and I'd like to try and make it special for them. Would you mind if I decorate? I could limit it to their room if you'd prefer and you wouldn't have to do anything except say yes. They're still little enough to believe in the magic and I don't want to spoil it for them. Your house is beautiful but it's not very child-friendly.'

Didn't he know it. When he hadn't been at school, abiding by the rules there, he'd been restricted by the list of dos and don'ts at home. Don't make too much noise. Don't leave toys where people could trip on them, dress smartly, don't talk back… He'd never been free to explore childhood without a scolding. There hadn't been much reason to change anything in the house once he'd found out a family was off the table for him.

'This has never been a fun environment for raising children.' He'd been more of an intruder when he'd been home, having to be careful not to disturb his mother, who had invariably been in bed, exhausted at the very thought of having him here. These walls echoed with the loneliness of his childhood and he'd have changed everything in a second if Caroline had accepted his proposal and set up home with him. After she'd left there hadn't seemed any point in changing anything.

'My mum used to put on the whole show with the tree, the presents and the big family dinner. It was wonderful. Except for the ever-present threat of my dad's temper, which would explode when he found fault with the smallest thing. Then that lovely tree, the thoughtful gifts and the dishes of food would end up smashed on the floor.' Iona clutched her tea close to her chest and looked smaller than ever.

Their constant battle over power seemed to be about asserting their right to be heard when they'd both been nothing but casualties of their past.

'I guess a domineering father is as damaging as a disinterested one,' Fraser mused aloud, although Iona's experiences of ruined celebrations had taken her in the opposite direction from his attitude.

'So you can see how important it is we get this right?' Iona didn't have to guilt-trip him. Fraser had accepted that responsibility when he'd agreed to host them here. That's why he was so afraid of getting it wrong. He trusted Iona had enough experience of at least one loving parent that she had more clue than he did about how to do this.

'You have free rein. Go tinsel crazy around the house with my blessing.' He was sure he could stomach it for a few days.

'Are you serious?' As soon as he said it her eyes lit up like fairy lights and she dropped the defensive body language.

Fraser winced as she set her cup on the floor, flattening a circular patch of the deep-pile carpet, but let it pass since she looked so happy. He didn't want to be another man to make Iona miserable. Her enthusiasm was contagious, his smile growing to match hers. What harm could there be in letting her loose with a few ornaments? The house wasn't governed by the health and safety rules of the workplace or even those set by his parents. As he had to keep reminding himself, he was free to do as he pleased and now so was Iona.

'I'm serious. Honestly, I'm not the monster you think I am.'

She bounced out of her seat and launched herself at him. 'Thank you. Thank you. Thank you.'

She landed a smacker of a kiss on his cheek before she whispered, 'I've never thought of you as a monster.'

In that second all his icy edges melted and he would've let her redecorate the whole house if she'd asked. There was something about her and her quest to fix everyone that made him think she might be able to fix him too.

'Let's try and keep it that way,' he eventually managed to get out after the shock of her touch and his need to please her ebbed away.

He ignore the urge to nuzzle into the cloud of soft curls falling around his face and waited until she backed off before he could breathe again.

'I'll make a list of everything we have to do. I've never planned a family Christmas before.'

'Neither have I.' Fraser had never even considered he'd truly been part of one and now there was a possibility he'd always be of the opinion it should include Iona and a kid or two.

CHAPTER SEVEN

'I HAVE TO make a few patient calls then I'll pick the kids up from their after-school club.' Iona checked in with Fraser after ensuring he didn't have any patients in with him.

'Should I expect a lorry load of fake snow and a herd of reindeer to meet me on the drive when I get home?' He spun around in his chair, arms folded across his chest and giving her that bright smile that was fast becoming a familiar fixture. They'd come such a long way since the day they'd fought over the decorations here at the clinic and she was glad of it. Now she was comfortable enough to walk into his room and plant her backside on his desk.

'Unfortunately, it was too short notice to get the reindeer. They're fully booked until the New Year. You might get the snow, though—I hear they're predicting a white Christmas this year.'

'I'm sure the kids will love that. Not so good for the rest of us who still have to work. Speaking of which, I've managed to get cover in for Christmas week in case we're still playing happy families.'

That's exactly how it had seemed this morning as she and Fraser had teamed up to get the children ready for school. She'd made sure they were washed and dressed before they all sat down to a Fraser breakfast special of freshly made French toast and bacon. He'd also packed lunches for everyone as they headed out on the school run. There was definitely something to be said for being organised when they were all benefitting from it and starting the day calmly instead of the chaotic mess it could've been, left to her.

'Oh, good. I'm not planning on going anywhere but babies have a habit of not sticking to the schedule. With you at home that means we've got things covered.' She high-fived Fraser.

Home. How quickly she'd come to think of that huge house and the inhabitants as somewhere she'd every right to be and wanted to be. Not every housemate was someone to dread, just as living alone didn't have to be everything. Last night, chatting with Fraser, had reminded her there wasn't always something to fear from sharing her personal space. It could actually provide a sense of well-being to have someone to unwind with and talk to. Until now Iona hadn't realised the extent to which she'd isolated herself. Outside work and patients she didn't have anyone to call on for a chat or a shoulder to cry on if she needed one, and there was something reassuring, therapeutic even, in having company other than her own.

For too long she'd associated any form of relationship as a hassle, something to be endured or avoided at all costs. Simply having someone who understood her, who was willing to compromise his needs to accommodate hers, showed her there was something different out there if she wanted it.

'Should I bring something home for dinner?' He'd swivelled around again and tossed that word casually over his shoulder, which made her shiver every time she thought of him waiting there for her.

'That would be great. I've promised Hamish and Poppy we'd make it to the hospital for visiting later then we can start decorating. I'll get some Christmas supplies with them after school.' They'd have more than enough to keep them busy until bedtime and hopefully seeing their mum would help settle them. According to the staff member she'd spoken to this morning, Katherine's blood pressure remained high and they weren't prepared to send her home yet.

Fraser stopped typing momentarily to glance at her. 'Is there anything else I can do for you?'

Iona was aware her continued presence, sitting here, was disturbing his otherwise perfectly arranged desk but she was enjoying this new easy atmosphere between them too much to leave.

'Um, no, I don't think so.'

'You're sitting on my notepad.'

She shifted her position slightly so he could retrieve his precious notepad but hadn't anticipated the effect his hand brushing against the curve of her backside would have on her. The joke had well and truly backfired and her attempt to provoke him had succeeded in raising her own temperature.

She leapt off the desk as though someone had started a fire beneath her, things suddenly feeling too hot for her to handle.

'I'll see you at home,' Fraser called after her, and now she really couldn't wait to finish her shift.

Iona phoned around her patients to give test results and check in with her ladies before she clocked off for the day. Once she'd finished her shift, any emergencies would be down to the duty midwife. The midwives from neighbouring clinics took turns at covering nights and although it was a large catchment area they weren't overly stretched with callouts.

She was already putting her coat on as she dialled Angie, one of her first-time mums, so she could get started on her evening plans as soon as possible.

'Hi, Angie, it's Iona here. I'm just calling to tell you your last test results were all clear. The antibiotics seemed to have cleared up your UTI so there's nothing to worry about.' She turned off the light and grabbed her car keys from the desk.

'Thanks, Iona, that's a weight off my mind. It's been one urine infection after another lately.' The heavy sigh was a standard response from most of her patients in the later stages of their pregnancies as they struggled to even tie their own shoelaces. Although she'd never been pregnant, Iona could understand the frustration of not having a say in what happened to you. Andy had taken that right away from her with the physical and emotional torture he'd put her through until she had been too frightened to make any decisions for herself in case he disagreed. Thankfully, those days were long behind her and she was a different person now from who she had been then.

'How are you feeling otherwise?' It had only been a couple of days since Iona had seen Angie at the clinic but it was a question it was always necessary to ask in case anything untoward crept in between appointments.

'Some heartburn at night and I don't know if this is anything but my hands and feet have been really itchy. It could be an allergic reaction, I suppose, but I haven't changed my washing powder or anything recently. It's probably nothing.' While Angie was talking herself out of the significance of any symptoms, the comment managed to stall Iona's exit.

'What about the baby? Is he still moving about plenty?' Adrenaline was rushing through her system at the prospect of what this could mean for her patient but she didn't want to scare her.

'Not as much today but I was up late last night because I couldn't get comfortable at all.' There was a yawn to illustrate the lack of sleep.

'The itching was more noticeable at night?' Iona retraced her steps back into the office, turned the light on and retrieved Angie's file.

Mild itching itself wasn't uncommon during pregnancy as the skin stretched to accommodate a growing belly but it could be symptomatic of a more serious condition.

ICP, intrahepatic cholestasis of pregnancy, was a potentially serious liver disorder, often characterised by itching when bile acids, which should have flowed from the liver to the gut to aid digestion, built up elsewhere instead.

To get a conclusive diagnosis they would need a variety of blood tests to check liver function and measure bile acid levels but time would be of the essence, especially if the baby's movements had reportedly slowed. There was a high risk of stillbirth for those with an elevated BAL. There was no cure and with Angie in her thirty-seventh week of pregnancy it was possible the hospital would want to induce labour to prevent the worst from happening.

'Angie, is Chris there with you?' This would go much easier if she had her husband there to support her.

'No, he's at work. Why?' That element of fear Iona hated hearing in her patients' voices when she had to deliver distressing news was there, turning her own blood to ice.

'I don't want you to panic but I would prefer it if you went to the hospital to get checked out and make sure everything's all right.'

'Why? What's wrong? Chris won't be home for hours—he's working in Aberdeen. Is my baby in trouble?' The panic gradually picked up pace and there was only one thing Iona could do.

'Everything's going to be fine. I'm being cautious but I'd prefer to get you to hospital for a scan to make sure the baby's not in any distress. I'll drive you myself.'

'Should I have my overnight bag ready?' Angie sniffed back the tears but she already sounded calmer that she wouldn't go through this alone.

'That mightn't be a bad idea.' Not only would it give her something to distract her until Iona got there, the obstetrician might decide to keep her in.

'I'll phone Chris and let him know.'

'I'll be with you as soon as I can and, Angie, please don't worry.' Words were never enough to soothe a scared mother-to-be but the presence of an experienced midwife often put her mind at rest that someone knew what they were doing in the circumstances.

Iona was in the car and on her way before she'd hung up. Technically the call should have gone to the duty midwife, who probably would've told her to phone for a taxi or rung straight through for an ambulance, but Iona thought there was more chance of keeping her calm by doing it herself. She would do the handover, of course, leaving Angie in the care of the consultant lead team at the maternity unit, but having a familiar face for most of the journey could make all the difference to a woman's first experience of pregnancy in such difficult circumstances. On speakerphone, she managed to call ahead and let the hospital know she was bringing Angie in.

This kind of crisis was the reason Iona could never be a normal wife and mother with responsibilities. It would only take her back to those dark days of having to account for her every move outside the house until it was easier to simply stay put.

Wait. This week that's exactly what she was supposed to be and she'd failed at the first hurdle. Not only was she going to be late for the school run but she was going to have to renege on the promises she'd made to her surrogate children.

The steering wheel took the brunt of her temper as she lashed out and swore. It was going to be harder to juggle motherhood and work than she'd imagined, as she'd become so accustomed to doing what she wanted when she wanted. Iona wasn't used to thinking about other people outside work or relying on anyone but herself.

Now she was going to have to depend on Fraser, her pseudo-husband, to jump in and save the day. It was going to take hours to get to the hospital and back, by which time she'd have missed visiting time, dinner and Christmas decorating. She wasn't looking forward to disappointing the children or putting in an SOS call to Fraser. Already she could see there was a fine line between controlling and being in control when it came to family obligations, and she was a long way from both. Fraser might have the better temperament for taking care of children after all. Gut instinct was all well and good but she had others to think about now and a flaky parent was as damaging to the bonding process as an overbearing influence. She prayed he'd step up to cover her inadequacies until she could make it up to everyone later. If she made it back at all before bedtime.

'You're rubbish at this.' Hamish provided the harsh critique as Fraser lifted the tray of charcoal that purported to be the walls of their gingerbread house.

'I'm doing my best.' He dumped the charred remnants on the draining board along with the other gingerbread rubble from their last attempt. They'd managed to stick three walls, and Fraser's fingers, together with the icing before it had collapsed on itself.

'It's yummy.' Poppy helped herself to a broken piece of the front door and wandered off again. It was nice to know it hadn't been a complete waste of time.

'My mum makes good gingerbread. I wish she was here.' Hamish kicked the leg of the kitchen table with the toe of his scuffed shoe, which ordinarily Fraser wouldn't have stood for but he understood that feeling of being let down by Iona tonight.

How many times had he stood waiting at the school entrance, bag packed and ready to go home, only to be told at the last minute no one was coming for him after all? Enough to stop him trusting a word his parents had said. Young children didn't understand the reasons you flaked out on them, they didn't care about anything except the fact you didn't stick to your word. Once that trust was lost it was difficult to get back. These two had every right to be annoyed. It wasn't as if Iona couldn't have arranged for someone else to provide a taxi service, no, she'd chosen who'd deserved her attention and it certainly hadn't been the master gingerbread builders here. Still, it wasn't going to help lift the mood if he let rip at Iona when she did come home. Parenthood was new to both of them and they were learning on the job.

Fraser pulled over a chair and sat down so he was at eye level with the disgruntled seven-year-old. 'Listen, this isn't easy for us and I wish it was your mum here baking for you, and she will be, soon. I know you're disappointed you didn't get to see her but I'll do my very best to get you there tomorrow.'

'Sure…' Hamish didn't look up from his feet, already cynical about trusting the word of an adult.

It took Fraser to physically tilt his chin up to make him look at him. 'Hey, I mean it.'

Hamish didn't seem convinced but he did stop taking out his anger on the furniture and ran off to find his sister.

Tonight had been tough, thanks to the last-minute change of arrangements. By the time Fraser had finished at work and picked up their new dependants it had been too late to make it in time for visiting at hospital. Hamish had been in a foul temper since and Poppy much too quiet for a five-year-old.

Fast food hadn't managed to lift their spirits and neither had the impromptu art class he'd set up. The lack of decorations they'd been assured would be up today hadn't gone unnoticed by the children so he'd persuaded them to make their own. Although their paintings were colourful, they weren't enough to brighten up the huge room.

He'd let them stay up well after their bedtime in the vain hope Iona would show up before they retired for the night. The kitchen massacre could be dealt with after that.

'I think it's time you put on your pyjamas and brushed your teeth.'

'Iona said—' It was Poppy's turn to protest.

'I know, Iona promised we'd decorate but she got caught up at work.' In her brief call she'd told Fraser she was driving her patient to the hospital but, knowing her, she'd stayed on for moral support too. A quality he'd admire in her if it wasn't for the two disappointed faces staring at him.

It was better for him to imagine she was hand-holding a frightened pregnant woman than that she'd been in an accident on that dark, potholed road back to civilisation. Like it or not, they were a makeshift family as a result of their recent decisions and apparently that entailed worrying about all members, every minute of the day. It wasn't a responsibility anyone should take lightly and, in hindsight, it had probably been fortunate Caroline had changed her mind about the prospect of family life before they'd married or he could've been left as a single father.

As Fraser began seriously contemplating reporting Iona as a missing person, car headlights slowly made their way up the drive. Although relieved she was safe, he was going to have to confront her about the childcare situation.

Hamish and Poppy ignored his request, watching Iona through the window with him. When she turned the key in the front door there was a posse waiting for her.

'Hello. Sorry I'm late, everyone. I had to take a very poorly patient to hospital and I didn't want to leave her on her own.'

'Hi. How is she?' Fraser rammed his hands in his

pockets after he noticed they were covered in icing and glitter.

'They're keeping her in to do a trace but her husband is with her now.' Iona flung herself into a chair and kicked off her shoes.

'I hope everything works out all right.'

'Me too.'

'There's some dinner left in the oven if you're hungry.' He'd saved some leftovers as he'd never seen her take a proper meal break in all the time she'd been at the clinic.

'Starving. Thanks. How did you get on today?'

'We did some painting and tried our hand at building gingerbread houses. It didn't go very well.' An understatement she'd see for herself next time she stepped into the kitchen but it was important she knew he'd done his best to keep the children entertained in her absence. Despite the fact that they were still upset, he'd genuinely wanted to get involved with them and had shaken off any notion he'd be as bad a parent as his own. Far from putting the idea of fatherhood far from mind, he was afraid it was strengthening the case for having children of his own. Unless he found a partner who was completely committed to the idea with him, it was a nonstarter anyway.

'Sounds fun. Sorry I missed it.'

'Did you get Christmas stuff?' Poppy piped up with the question that had prevented her from going to bed, afraid of missing something.

'I didn't get to the shops in time, sweetheart. I stopped off at the petrol station but this was all I could get for now. We'll get more tomorrow.' She handed a bag to

Poppy, who proceeded to sit cross-legged in the middle of the floor and empty out the contents.

One by one she held up the items—strands of silver and gold tinsel, a packet of foil-covered chocolate tree decorations, plastic mistletoe and a tree-shaped car air freshener.

'You said we'd have a proper tree.'

Iona attempted to hug the little girl but was brutally shrugged off. 'We'll get one tomorrow after school.'

'Unless you have something better to do.' Hamish gathered up the unwanted gifts, stuffed them back in the bag and dumped it at Iona's feet. Fraser was beginning to feel sorry for her. She hadn't intentionally hurt them, had simply tried to do the right thing by everyone. The last thing she would've wanted after a long day, and evening, was to face more stress at home.

'You heard Iona, we'll do everything tomorrow. It's late and we're all tired.' He gave his child-minding partner a hand up so they were both imposing their authority together from a higher vantage point.

'We couldn't see Mum tonight because of you,' Hamish spat, and caused Iona to flinch.

'Enough, Hamish. Tomorrow, you were told. Now, go up to your rooms and get ready for bed.' It went against all his instincts to scold the children but he couldn't let them attack Iona. It would undermine their position as the adults in charge if they didn't set boundaries from the start.

Unfortunately, it also put him into the doghouse alongside Iona as far as the sullen child was concerned.

'You're not my dad and you're not my mum. I hate you both.' Hamish stomped out of the living room and up the stairs. Fraser's heart ached for him as he was clearly missing his two parents.

Iona stared open-mouthed as Poppy trotted after him and the sound of the bedroom door slamming echoed through the house. 'Now what?'

'Let him cool off for a while then I'll go and have a talk with him.' Fraser had never wanted to get emotionally involved but since he had some understanding of what the boy was going through he might be in a better position to talk him round.

A dazed Iona sagged back down into the chair.'

'I really didn't mean for them to feel like an afterthought but Angie had suspected ICP and this is her first baby. I'm an idiot for thinking I could get away with postponing their evening and making up for it with a bag of tat from the garage.'

'Don't be so hard on yourself. We're dealing with two vulnerable young children. They're scared and have had such upheaval they need to lash out at someone and, unfortunately, that's you tonight.' Fraser put an arm around her shoulder and gave her a squeeze to let her know he was on her side.

'You heard Hamish, he hates me, and I'm pretty sure Poppy's right there with him. Even if he hadn't said it I could feel the animosity in the atmosphere as soon as I stepped into the room.' Years of walking on eggshells had finely tuned that skill, anticipating shouldering the blame for whatever perceived misdemeanour she'd committed to justify Andy's foul mood. Although, in these circumstances, the anger directed at her was understandable.

'Now, now, don't go getting all sorry for yourself. I do believe he said he hated us both. Something I'm choosing not to take seriously or personally when he's clearly upset.'

Iona appreciated Fraser's attempt to make her feel better but so far it wasn't working. 'Nice try, but we both know this is my fault. I just hope you won't hold it against me. I'm trying, I really am, but it's difficult for me too. I'm not used to factoring anyone else into these last-minute decisions, or trusting anyone other than myself. That's why I felt the need to take Angie to hospital myself and why I'm struggling to work as part of a team here with you. It's going to take time, Fraser, for all of us. I've relied only on myself for so long none of this is coming naturally to me.'

She was bone weary, leaning into him and making him wish they could put the whole saga behind them and relax until tomorrow, when they had to do it all over again.

'For me neither. They'll forget all about it once they get to see their mum and they have a lovely sparkly Christmas tree to stare at.'

'I hope you're right.'

'Always,' Fraser said with a grin. 'Look, I can identify with the kids but that doesn't mean you should be punished for doing what you thought was the right thing. My parents sent me to boarding school at an early age and let me down time and time again, telling me they were coming to pick me up, getting me excited, only to change their minds at the last minute. At that age you're left feeling as though no one cares, that your feelings don't matter, even when there's a perfectly reasonable excuse.'

'Gee, thanks for making me feel better.' Now she

had the added guilt of making Fraser relive his abandonment issues too.

'I'm simply trying to explain the fear hidden behind the surface anger. As long as you follow up on your word tomorrow, I'm sure they'll forgive you.' Fraser's wounds obviously still ran deep from his experiences but that was probably why he'd bonded with the children so quickly.

Iona was afraid her actions would somehow exclude her from the circle of trust they'd been working on together.

'What about you, Fraser? Will you forgive me?' She'd hurt him on several occasions and eventually she'd run out of lives with someone who'd obviously been so let down in the past.

'I did, the moment you came home safe.' Fraser tilted her chin up so she was looking into his eyes, and seeing the truth of his words reflected there made her heart melt. The knowledge that he cared enough about her to worry made her want to wrap herself up in his arms and the warmth of that beautiful sentiment.

He dropped his hand away so quickly she thought she'd imagined the whole exchange. 'Now, come on and we'll get you some dinner.'

It was obvious he wanted to keep things light between them so she simply had to file away the moment along with all the other ones they couldn't talk about. 'I wouldn't say no. I didn't dare stop for any on the way home. The wind is picking up out there and I had visions of my wee car being blown into a ditch or a tree falling on my roof.'

'In that case, we should get your dinner on in case there's a power cut. You start reheating and I'll hunt

for candles and torches.' They made their way to the
kitchen, where Iona picked at the gingerbread ruins lying
around as she waited for the microwave to ping.

From now on they had to work as a team. It was the
only way they'd survive.

The reheated pizza and fries were no substitute for Fraser's home cooking the previous night but Iona's rumbling belly was past point of caring.

She'd expected disappointment and guilt about not
following through on her plans with the children but the
full blast of Hamish's rage had almost finished her off.
Judging by the bomb-hit worktops she wasn't the only
one who'd had a tough day.

'Thanks for covering for me,' Iona said after swal-
lowing a mouthful of the wine Fraser had poured for
her. He hadn't had much say in the matter but he hadn't
tag-teamed the others to point out the extent of her failure so she was grateful.

'What did you think I'd do? Leave them somewhere
with a sign around their necks saying, "Please take care
of me"?' Fraser was trying to make her laugh and he
succeeded.

She'd been expected an 'I told you so' once she realised what a great undertaking this whole thing had
been. If they'd been in this position a month ago she'd
have been horrified at the thought of leaving Fraser in
charge of the children. It wouldn't have been a stretch to
imagine him marching them around the house in regimented fashion, issuing commands. Since getting to
know him properly, she'd almost become too compla-
cent that he was up to the job.

The paint-splattered surfaces and baking attempts

showed how hard he'd tried to cover for her without expecting, or receiving, a gold star for his efforts. Thank goodness he was in this with her because it was clear now she'd never have managed them, and work, on her own.

'Maybe you should do that to me.'

'Something tells me you wouldn't be willing to let anyone take care of you.' Fraser's insight was spot on but she was willing to let him clear away her dirty dishes for her.

'Take care of me, yes. Take charge of me, definitely not.' It was a warning shot that he shouldn't dare to try but as she locked eyes with him he didn't look away. As if he was telling her he was up to whatever challenge she set him.

CHAPTER EIGHT

AN ALMIGHTY CRASH interrupted Iona's late supper, so loud it made her jump out of her seat. 'What the hell was that?'

She'd seen plenty of horror films to know big houses were playgrounds for ghosts, ghouls and everything else that went bump in the night.

'That was the front door being slammed.' Fraser bolted in the direction the noise had come from but his explanation didn't put her any more at ease. The solid wooden door didn't open and close by itself. Either someone had come in, or gone out, and both scenarios sent chills through her cold enough to freeze her bones.

'I'll go and check on Hamish and Poppy.' She left Fraser walking out into the night and took the stairs two at a time in her haste to make sure they were safe.

On opening the door, she was relieved to see Poppy was fast asleep. Hamish's bed, however, was empty and his backpack missing along with the few personal possessions he'd brought with him.

All the blood seemed to drain away from her body until she was sure her empty Iona shell might collapse at any second. It was only the fear of Hamish being outside alone in the dark keeping her upright and propelling her downstairs.

She ran out onto the porch to locate Fraser, not taking time to find her shoes when it was her fault the child was out there somewhere exposed to the elements. 'Hamish is gone and he's taken all his things with him.'

'There's no sign of him out here. I'll grab a torch and head down to the gate. He can't have gone very far.'

'Let me come with you,' she begged, cursing herself for not keeping tabs on him when he'd been so upset. Katherine had told her she'd need eyes in the back of her head to watch the children but she'd seized the quiet to wallow, not realising it had been the calm before the storm.

'Not unless you put on some warm clothes first.'

Iona complied without fuss, fetching her coat and shoes before meeting him again at the door.

'We'll lock the door behind us and if we don't find Hamish soon, you come back here and I'll carry on the search myself.' Fraser handed her a torch and pre-empted her fears about leaving a second child alone.

Hamish would never have entertained the idea of leaving the comfort of the house to venture out into the wilderness if he'd been happy, and she was accountable for his current state of mind regardless of anything Fraser said to the contrary.

'Hamish!'

Every now and then they caught a glimpse of beady eyes watching from the edge of the trees, which turned out to be woodland creatures curious about who else was out here with them. With each crunch of the undergrowth in the distance, every creepy sound of forest wildlife, she drew closer and closer to Fraser's side, sure he'd protect her from any assailant who might come from the shadows. Goodness knew how a small boy was coping out here when a grown woman was letting her imagination scare her half to death.

'What was that?'

'It's an owl.'

'Did you hear that? Anything could be lurking out here.'

'It's the countryside, Iona. You have to expect some noise from the neighbours. We are sharing their habitat after all.' Fraser was right, she'd been brought up in the city with a soundtrack of speeding cars and emergency sirens, not living, breathing creatures. Unless you counted the drunks who had sometimes serenaded her outside her bedroom window. This relative peace took some getting used to.

'What are we going to do when we find him, Fraser?' *If* wasn't an option. They had to find him but they also had to get him to come back with them and to want to stay with them. Otherwise social services would have to get involved and it was disheartening to think Hamish would rather do that than spend another night under the same roof as them.

'Get him into the heat as soon as possible before he ends up with hypothermia, tell him off for scaring us, then have a talk about the position we've all been put in.'

'How come you're so sensible about all this?' Fraser was managing this all so much better than she was and more than she'd given him credit for. Anyone would think he'd had experience in caring for children it came so naturally to him. The total opposite of the father figure and domineering partner she'd assumed he'd make.

'It might be difficult for you to accept but I was a boy

once too. One who found himself in a similar situation. Except my parents chose to send me away to live with strangers.' The explanation didn't make it sound any less heartless. Unlike Katherine, his parents had had a choice. It was gut-wrenching to picture any child in that predicament but more so of Fraser as that lost little soul when he was such a source of strength to her now.

Iona had been afraid and unhappy too but she'd had her mother to remind her she was wanted and loved, even if her parents hadn't demonstrated it to each other. It was no wonder he gave off that defensive vibe that made it difficult to get close to him. She counted herself lucky he'd let her see the real Fraser, who was warm and caring and everything his parents apparently hadn't been for him. Instead of launching herself at him and forcing a hug on him, she cleared the ache in her throat and simply said, 'Childhood sucks.'

'But it makes us who we are today. You want to know why I'm such a stickler for the rules and doing everything by the book? It's because I thought, by being the perfect son, my parents might love me more and want me around. I thought I'd been too wild, too unruly for them to have at home. Clinging to the rules, projecting that perfect image in the hope people will like me has become my way of life. I don't know why when it's never worked.' He gave a bitter laugh but there was nothing remotely funny about what he'd shared with her.

Iona knew that kind of loneliness and uncertainly intimately, along with that constant worry about trying to please people who neither deserved nor appreciated it. Yet, since coming here with the children, she'd never had any sense he'd been pretending to be anyone else other than himself. It might be because he'd abandoned his rule book for their sakes.

It was proof of his strength that he'd become such a success yet had retained that compassion that endeared him to his patients, and now her too. A lesser mortal might have rebelled against the idea of school and authority but Fraser had turned it to his advantage and applied it to his career to get him to the position of senior practice partner. Every day revealed new layers to Dr McColl, making it impossible for her to deny her growing affection for him. The longer they were under the same roof, the closer they became physically and emotionally. It was lucky they had two small children to act as a buffer between them. As long as they remained safe, she was sure her heart would too.

'Listen. Do you hear that?' Fraser stopped beside her.

'Don't you start. I thought I was the paranoid one here.'

'Shh. Listen.'

She was about to tear strips off him for shushing her when she heard the faint cry for herself. They stood motionless, holding their breath, hoping to locate the source.

'Help.'

The plaintive cry was so full of pain and exhaustion she cursed the McColl family for not having the foresight to install floodlights out here for such emergencies.

'Hamish? Where are you?' Fraser's voice carried easily through the night, ensuring the boy would hear it no matter which direction he was in.

'At the gate.'

They sprinted the last few yards to reach him, their torch beams picking out a crumpled figure lying on the other side of the metalwork. Iona clamped her hand over her mouth to smother her gasp. 'What on earth happened? How did you end up down there?'

'He's tried to climb over the gate.' Fraser jabbed the security code into the control panel and they waited for an eternity for the gates to open and allow them access to the child.

'Where did you think you were going out here?' Iona knelt down beside him and brushed the dirt from his face, glad to see him again.

'I want to see my mum.' Hamish's face was streaked with tears and mud and Iona had to catch her own sob before it escaped with his.

'Can you stand?' Fraser was focused on the injuries Hamish had sustained during his not-so-great escape. Shock was probably the least he'd be suffering from the height he'd fallen.

Hamish sat up and Fraser attempted to disentangle the backpack from around his shoulders only to prompt an ear-piercing scream.

'My arm hurts so bad.' The unearthly squeals subsided into equally disturbing whimpers. Each agonising sound was like a fist in the gut. Hamish would never have been hurt if Iona had come home as planned.

'He might have broken it.' Fraser tossed her the backpack and scooped the boy up into his arms, careful not to jar the arm he was cradling.

It wasn't a life or death emergency but they took him back to the house with no less urgency, guided by one torch now that Fraser had his hands full.

'The key is in my pocket.' He turned to her in the porch lights and she stuck her hand in to fumble for it, trying not to acknowledge the solid muscled thighs beneath her fingertips.

Once back in the house Fraser laid Hamish gently on the sofa and Iona switched on every light and lamp she could find so they could examine him.

'We're going to have to get your coat off so I can check that arm, Hamish.' Fraser didn't want to hurt him any more than he already had been, but he had to assess the damage to prevent further injury. Hamish was responsive and breathing and Fraser didn't want to think about what could've happened if they hadn't found him out there.

Hamish wasn't his son but after a couple of days of taking care of him Fraser worried just the same. It was impossible not to draw comparisons with his own parents and their apparent lack of compassion for their only child when the severity of Hamish's injuries was taking priority right now.

Iona put her hand to the boy's back to help him upright and between them they managed to remove his outer layer with the minimum of discomfort. Hamish peeled his sleeve back to expose the skin, every whimper reminding him this was more than a scratch. Although Hamish's complexion was grey from the shock, there was no blood and the bone hadn't broken the skin, minimising the risk of infection.

Fraser confirmed that Hamish could move his fingers with no sign of numbness or blue tinge to suggest otherwise. The swelling, bruising and tenderness around the deformed area he was protecting so vehemently did, however, suggest a fracture of some description.

'I think you've broken your arm, Hamish. We need

to stabilise it here, support it so there won't be any further damage done until we get you to the emergency department.'

'It hurts.' The fear and pain wasn't just from Hamish's arm—it was clearly also about not having either of his parents here to comfort him when he needed them.

'They'll put a cast on it at the hospital, you know.' Iona leaned over the back of the couch, trying to find a silver lining in this for him.

'They will?' Hamish stopped crying to mull that over.

It occurred to Fraser that those unfortunates who had come to school with broken bones encased in plaster had suddenly become the most popular pupils there. 'Yeah, and everyone will want to sign it.'

Fraser winked at Iona for her quick thinking as it could keep Hamish distracted from his injury for a while and get him to co-operate.

'Will it hurt?' he asked, narrowing his eyes, suspicious they were conspiring against him.

'Not at all. They'll just want to protect your arm. As I do.'

'I think your mum packed some liquid paracetamol for you so that should help with the pain. Fraser, do you have ice in your freezer to bring that swelling down?' Iona, satisfied that Hamish was going to let them help, took the first step to stabilising the injured limb.

'Yes. Top drawer. You'll find towels and tape in the bathroom.' Fraser was going to have to improvise a splint for the journey. There were a lot of household items they could utilise, such as rolled-up newspapers, but towels would provide some padding and relieve some of the discomfort.

'Hang in there, pal, we'll hit the road as soon as we get that arm supported.

'Then I can visit my mum?' Whether this injury had been a deliberate attempt to get Hamish to his mother, or an unfortunate coincidence as he'd tried to run to her, there was no question of his desperation to see her.

'I'll see what I can do.' Fraser couldn't bring himself to be angry about it. If he'd had an inkling his parents would've welcomed the sight of him at any given moment he'd have broken out of boarding school in a heartbeat.

Before Fraser was forced into making any promises that might be beyond his ability to carry out, Iona returned with supplies.

'Would you believe Poppy's still fast asleep?' She shook her head as she deposited the ice, towels, bandages and tape on the coffee table and administered a spoonful of medicine to Hamish for the pain.

'Thank goodness for small mercies.' With the smallest one of them safe and sound, they could concentrate on the one they'd failed. Parenting was hard and they weren't perfect by any means but the important thing was they were doing their best.

With some manoeuvring and cajoling they managed to get Hamish to lay his arm down on the folded towel, covering the distance from his fingertips to slightly past his elbow. Fraser tied the towel around the arm, making sure it was completely wrapped and snug, tied at either end and avoiding any pressure on the injury site.

'Can you wiggle your fingertips for me?' He rechecked circulation, sensation and motion to make sure he hadn't tied it too tight but the arm remained immobilised.

When Fraser was satisfied Hamish was as comfortable as could be expected, Iona fashioned a sling from the bandage to cradle his arm, fastening it around his neck to make it secure.

'That's not too tight, is it?' she queried before backing off.

'Thanks.' Fraser could've handled this on his own but it was reassuring to have her here, backing him up. They were a team, and for the first time in forever he no longer felt alone. This was how he imagined a family would be, all pulling together to make life more than bearable for one another. He wasn't looking forward to the time when Iona and the kids moved out and he was back to rattling around the house on his own with no one to think about but himself. It did much more for the soul to be around people, helping when and where he could.

Iona draped Hamish's coat around his shoulders, presumably to stave off some of the cold facing them on the other side of the front door.

'If you're happy to stay here with Poppy, I'll drive Hamish myself.' It wasn't that he wanted to leave her but it was more practical than waking the little girl to make the long journey Iona had already done once today.

'Sure. Let me know that you've got there safely.' That made him smile. He wasn't used to having someone worry about him and to know he'd impacted on her in some small way meant the world to him.

'I will.'

It wasn't easy getting Hamish into the back of the car but eventually they got the seat belt around him so it wasn't jarring his forearm. He had more colour in his cheeks now and he'd stopped whimpering. In fact, he was having trouble staying awake, so the car ride could put him over into sleep soon.

'I'm sure you're exhausted after the day you've had. Get yourself to bed and we'll let ourselves back in. Whatever time that might be.'

With the car door closed on Hamish to keep the wind off him, they were left facing each other in the driveway.

'I'm sure yours has been equally as eventful. Thanks for taking him. Just make sure you take care.'

'I will,' he assured her. He had a lot to come back for.

Iona threw her arms around him for a hug and kissed him on the lips as though she was afraid she'd never see him again.

Fraser embraced the contact, catching her around the waist and finally admitting to himself that he was fast falling for her. He lost himself in the kiss, fuelled with the desire which had been rising in him for days.

Her warm mouth on his, her tongue seeking his, turned the goodbye peck into passionate foreplay. There was nothing he wanted more than to sweep her up in his arms and carry her off to his bedroom and close the door on the rest of the world but it would have to wait. They had responsibilities and he wasn't the sort of man who'd put his wants before the needs of a child.

With great reluctance Fraser pulled back while he could still think straight, rested his forehead against hers and waited for the white noise in his head to subside.

'I'll see you when I get back.' His voice was thick with emotions he'd long thought dormant.

They extricated their limbs from each other until they were only holding on by their fingertips and they finally had to let go or he'd never get in the car.

Kissing Iona went against all the restrictions he'd imposed in order to protect his heart. Yet it was one of the best moves he'd ever made.

He set off for the distant city lights with a spark of hope in his soul that he might not be alone for the rest of his days after all. Unlike the little boy so often shunned by his parents and the adult orphan forced to return to the ancestral home alone, Fraser was finally excited about coming back. That was down to Iona being there and for once he didn't want to have his future all laid out for him. It excited him more to wait and see what could happen.

Iona stumbled back to the house in a daze and gave one last wave at Fraser driving away before going back inside. She touched her fingers to her softly swollen lips, which were throbbing from Fraser's tender kiss. For days they'd been fighting that recurring desire for each other but there was no denying it was there and she had no will to fight it any more either.

On a day when everything had gone wrong, Fraser had ended it on a high for her. Who knew where that kiss would lead to? But she wanted more. Now she was convinced he wasn't the prison jailer she'd assumed him to be there was no reason to keep her feelings for him on ice.

Deep down she'd known he was nothing like Andy even before he'd shared the painful truth behind his need for order in his life. It was his security blanket, as her solitude was hers. These past days, however, had shown her it was no longer enough to simply exist in her safe bubble and to really embrace her new life she had to let someone step inside it with her. She could honestly say so far that living with Fraser had only been positive and those long-held fears about allowing a man to get close to her again were beginning to ebb.

Fraser knew she wasn't a woman who could be pushed around and he seemed to respect that, making her fears about repeating past mistakes redundant. The timing was awkward but a relationship shouldn't affect the children if they kept it quiet. They were going to have enough on their plates anyway with the aftermath of Hamish's exploits.

Not only were there physical restrictions on him now but they were going to have to explain the accident to his mother.

She groaned. It would be a miracle if Katherine agreed to let her continue as his interim guardian after this.

Once she'd peeked in on their younger, less troublesome charge again, Iona stripped the pillows and cover off her bed and brought them downstairs.

With the lounge curtains slightly parted she'd be able to see the others coming back from her makeshift bed on the sofa. Fraser's ancestors wouldn't have approved but the man himself would only want her to be happy and that seemed to overrule his sense of decorum these days. A quality she simply couldn't find fault with, regardless of how hard she'd tried to.

CHAPTER NINE

IT WAS THE early hours of the morning before the travellers returned. Outside it was dark and gloomy, the kind of winter morning when you didn't want to get out of bed, even if it was only a blanket on a sofa. Iona wouldn't have been surprised if Fraser had decided not to drive back until the sun came up but now that she could stop fretting about him falling asleep at the wheel, her tension headache was easing off.

Iona had managed a couple of hours' sleep but she couldn't say they'd been particularly restful, on alert for Poppy upstairs and the sound of the car coming back outside. Not to mention the adrenaline pumping around her body in anticipation of embarking on a new phase of her life with Fraser. Bit by bit he was helping her see relationships didn't have to be toxic. She could have someone by her side, enriching her life with support instead of trying to snuff out her spirit. Perhaps in time she'd get to do the same for him and show him he deserved to be loved for exactly who he was.

Fraser stepped out of the car looking as spritely and alert as if he'd had a full eight hours' sleep and opened the rear car door to emerge with a sleeping Hamish in his arms. Iona smoothed down the crumpled clothes she'd slept in and tried to tame the nest of snakes she called her hair before she ran to the door.

'Is he okay?' she whispered, spying the cast covering most of his forearm.

'He'll be fine.' Despite the possibility he must be running on empty, Fraser summoned the energy to flash her a reassuring smile. Iona couldn't believe she'd ever believed this man to be selfish when he'd shown her a hundred different ways how wrong she'd been, setting his own comfort aside to give them all whatever they needed at any given time. Other than her mother, she'd never known anyone else to do that for her and it comforted her knowing she wouldn't be on her own with whatever the next crisis was.

Out of the blue it occurred to her he'd make a great father one day and made her wonder why he wasn't one already. He had a successful career, a title and an estate, he was drop-dead gorgeous and a natural with children. Unless he had some horrible, dark secret locked away in the cellar, she couldn't understand why his ex hadn't snatched him up, having fallen madly in love with him. A few days in his company and Iona knew she was well on the way there herself.

Perhaps it was his childhood experiences preventing him from settling down. She could empathise when her knowledge of parenting had come from two people who should never have stayed together. Both she and Fraser had to figure out who they were in their own right, away from the influences of the past.

She watched him carry Hamish to bed, her blood pumping so fast in her veins as she acknowledged those strong feelings there was every chance she might pass out. The man was carrying a sleeping child to bed after driving for hours so she could get some rest. Andy had never shown her such consideration from the day they'd married. The problem was she and Fraser had gone past the point where a quick fling would satisfy, too involved in each other's lives now for anything casual. If they acted on that kiss, picked up from where they'd left off, she had no doubt it would be the start of something so serious and meaningful it made the hairs stand up on the back of her neck. Yet she was intrigued by the possibility of something new and exciting to spice up her life.

To take her mind off the shock at the new direction things had suddenly taken, and wanting to thank Fraser, Iona set about making some breakfast in the kitchen. She lifted out some eggs and bacon and proceeded to cook them while waiting for the toast to pop and the kettle to boil. This house had been designed and built to be an intimidating status symbol, yet Fraser had made her feel part of it and she was no longer afraid of breaking something or forgetting proper protocol. There'd been a marked change in Fraser's behaviour since they'd moved in and it showed how hard he was working to overcome his hang-ups rather than force them all to conform. Something she appreciated to a level he couldn't possibly understand.

'Something smells good.'

Iona's stomach flipped along with the bacon and eggs at the sound of Fraser's voice and she wondered how they were going to be able to work together again when she went gooey inside every time he spoke.

Viewing the scene through the eyes of a third party, it could be construed as the very picture of domesticity, sharing a quiet breakfast together after a rough night with the kids, and she couldn't find a thing wrong with it.

'I'm starving. All I had was a curled-up sandwich from the vending machine and the dregs left in the coffee machine. It's so nice to come home to a cooked meal and good company.'

The compliment was likely born primarily from his hunger but Iona knew herself it was much preferable to returning to an empty flat and a microwaveable meal for one.

'So, no complications with Hamish's arm?' Normally she'd refrain from bringing up medical matters at the table but he was a doctor and wouldn't be as squeamish as the average person.

'A small fracture. It should heal in no time.'

'That's good news, I suppose. We'll still have to tell Katherine about it, though.' It wouldn't say much for their ability to take care of her children if Hamish had broken his arm already and Iona wouldn't blame her if she decided to discharge herself to do the job properly herself.

'It's all sorted,' Fraser said once he'd swallowed his huge bite of toast. 'I managed to sneak Hamish in to see her while we were there.'

'How on earth did you manage that? On second thoughts, maybe I don't want to know.' It wouldn't take much for a handsome doctor to sweet talk his way in anywhere and she didn't want to hear the details of him charming some other woman who wasn't her.

'Katherine was awake, she's still not sleeping, so I explained what had happened. She understood, had a chat with Hamish and he's promised to behave. He's much happier now he's seen his mum.'

'I'm glad. I trust you told her how sorry we are?' The

development lessened the burden of guilt lying heavily upon her.

'I did and it only succeeded in making her cry and thanking us again for taking them on.' Fraser shrugged then proceeded to clear his plate and drain his cup.

'I suppose you'll want to get some sleep?' After last night they were all entitled to a lie-in. Everything else could wait until they had clear heads again to think about where they were headed next.

'I managed a nap when Hamish was getting X-rayed but I'm probably better staying up now or I'll end up with night-lag. Actually, I was thinking about Christmas here.'

'Oh?' In all of yesterday's drama Iona had forgotten about the very event she'd been building up to and which she'd done a very poor job of preparing for so far. Unforgiveable for someone who'd promised not only herself but two young children she'd make the Yuletide special.

'I think we need a make-over. Especially with Hamish. Perhaps if we give them Christmas we could all learn to forgive and forget the mistakes of the past twenty-four hours.'

'What do you suggest?' He'd obviously been concocting some sort of plan to bring it up now.

'Well…' He shifted in his seat, appearing restless to get on with it as soon as possible. 'Christmas here was never the jolly family fun time most people associate with the season. Even when my parents did deign to bring me home for it, we merely went through the motions. I always knew their heart wasn't in it but that doesn't mean we didn't decorate accordingly. The house made a picture-perfect Christmas-card scene if it didn't go beyond the superficial exterior.' His description of his strained family time tugged at her heartstrings for the young Fraser who'd been denied a childhood.

The way he'd looked after her and the children made it clear he was someone who had so much love to give and deserved buckets of it in return. To feel unwanted, unloved and confused by what was going on in the adult world around him must have been frightening for him. Each time he did something to make them feel safe here, Iona knew it was because he wished someone had been around to do the same for him at that age. For all the money and land he'd been surrounded by, his life sounded as lonely and messed up as hers had been and the emotional damage done in those formative years wasn't easy to shake off even as an adult. They had more in common than anyone would've guessed from their vastly different backgrounds.

'In that case, what are we waiting for?' Iona was wide awake again and ready to get started now he'd put the thought in her head that they might actually be having their first proper Christmas. Together.

After all he'd been through, Fraser was offering so much by opening his home to them and Iona wanted to show him the best of the season along with the children. It would have been easier for him to lock himself away here on his own for the holidays, the way she'd planned to. Or, worse, taken out his pain and dislike of Christmas on those around him. He was better than that, stronger, and if he was prepared to stand up and reclaim his life back from fear, it gave her the impetus to do the same.

Opening the door to the attic made Fraser's heart pound just as much now as it had when he'd been a bairn. That creak giving away his location to anyone who happened to be searching for him, that blast of cold air bringing goosebumps to his skin and the dust filling his nostrils as he disturbed the family mausoleum of memories.

The only time he'd been up here as an adult had been shortly after his father had passed away to store boxes of his personal papers and belongings until he decided what to do with them. He'd been alone then, Caroline playing no part in his actions then, when Iona was the very reason he was up here now.

'Watch your step. There isn't much light up here, I'm afraid. We didn't spend much time in this part of the house.' Fraser took Iona's hand in his and guided her steps with the aid of the single light bulb hanging in the middle of the vast space. A scary place for a child with a vivid imagination. Scarier still for a grown man who hadn't fully dealt with his father's death and the unanswered questions he'd left behind.

Once she was on a firm footing he had to let go of her hand even though he liked the feel of it there, soft and warm and comforting that he wasn't here alone.

'Where should we start?' With her sleeves rolled up, Iona was gung-ho about tracking down these vintage decorations he'd told her were here. Hands on hips, ready to excavate, she could've been standing at the entrance of a pharaoh's tomb, ready to create history, she exuded such excitement. It was refreshing to see her embrace that inner child when he'd gagged and bound his long ago.

The contrast of her exuberance in the midst of this stuffy environment helped Fraser see it was possible for the two to exist together here. If anything, her sense of freedom brightened the whole house and Fraser wondered if by stifling his childish enthusiasm back then he hadn't done his family a disservice. Perhaps if he'd been allowed, by his parents and himself, to explore the boundaries more he could have brought light into the place to combat the sombre spectre of his mother's illness.

He kicked out at one of the boxes but there was nothing could be done now to salvage his relationship with his parents. All he could do was focus on those people who were important in his life now.

'What about here?' He headed to the far side of the room where neatly stacked boxes were labelled for convenience. An act he doubted either of his parents had undertaken. His father would've deemed such manual work demeaning to a man of his standing, and his mother had never ventured far from her bed for much of his childhood. Yet he recognised her handwriting on the containers, tracing his fingers over her elegant letters and wondering when she'd handed over responsibility to the staff instead of sharing it with her only child.

'Let's see what we've got,' Fraser said, dismantling the tower to place the boxes side by side on the patchwork carpet underfoot, comprised of offcuts and old rugs his father had refused to throw out.

'May I?' Iona sat cross-legged in the midst of the display, itching to unwrap whatever treasures she imagined they'd find.

'Go for it.' Fraser didn't have any sentimentality for any of this stuff and if he needed the space he wouldn't think twice about getting rid of everything. If they could fulfil one promise to the children, though, and create the sort of wonderland Iona had envisaged all along, he was willing to finally sort through it. With the children fast asleep in their beds they had plenty of time to do it.

It had been on his mind the whole way to the hospital and back to do something that would lift everyone's spirits. After all, they'd all been orphaned in one way or another for the holidays. As the adults, it was down to him and Iona to make the place feel like less of a foster home when none of them had planned to be here.

Of course, that hadn't been the only thing on his mind. Kissing Iona had ensured he stayed awake and alert for the entire journey. He didn't know why he'd done it any more than why he'd brought her up here with him.

Only that it felt right. There'd been no faking the concern she'd shown for Hamish when he'd gone missing, or her willingness to co-operate with him when it had been desperately needed. No more reason to keep hiding from his growing feelings for her.

'These are beautiful.' Iona reverently unwrapped a box of vintage baubles, each decorated with snowy scenes on their fragile glass shells.

'We should have a tree somewhere to hang them on.' Behind another stack of boxes he eventually found the artificial Christmas tree that, at some point, had replaced the real pine they'd once picked out together.

Flashing images of those times flickered at the back of his mind when they'd been happy, together as a family, which he'd long forgotten. He couldn't figure out if it was better or worse to discover the atmosphere around the season hadn't always been as strained as he remembered in those early days before it had turned into such a chore for all of them.

'Your handiwork, I presume?' Iona dangled a pipe-cleaner reindeer complete with googly eyes and a tiny red pom-pom nose from her finger, delighted with her find.

Fraser took the handmade decoration and stretched out beside her, fighting back the emotion suddenly trying to burn a hole in his chest. 'I remember making this with Mum.'

He pulled up his legs and laid the reindeer on his knees to see it better.

'You did have some good times with her, then?'

'When I was very small—I hardly remember—I think we used to have craft days. We made silly animals and space rockets out of whatever she had in this big wooden art chest. It was full of cards and stickers and glitter, and all sorts.' The memories came flooding back, almost drowning him with images of them playing together, actually going out as a family, his mother and father either side of him, swinging him by both arms and laughter ringing out all around.

'That's lovely, Fraser. She sounds as though she really loved you.'

'At one time. Then she got sick and no one seemed to want me around any more. After she died, well, Dad was old-fashioned and he didn't know how to raise a child on his own, he'd left all of that to Mum. I suppose it was easier to let the masters at boarding school do his job for him but we were never close again. He paid my school fees and put me through medical school but we were more acquaintances than father and son.' Tears were burning the backs of his eyeballs for that boy once surrounded by love who had somehow ended up abandoned miles from home and for the relationships he'd lost with his parents.

He spotted a rare family photograph lying at the bottom of the box and lifted it out. It had been taken at Christmas, these same decorations hanging downstairs in the background. He couldn't have been any older than Poppy—it was before he'd been sent away from home. They were all smiling, opening presents under the tree like any other normal family. Fraser's insides flipped over at the sight. There were probably no other happy snaps of them together after that and with both parents now gone there wouldn't be another.

Fraser could feel the warmth of the tears falling down his face but he didn't wipe them away, finally letting the emotions of the past run free. It was Iona who softly brushed away the evidence of his pain, stroking his face and giving him the comfort he desperately needed.

'Is it possible they might have sent you away because they thought they were protecting you in some way from your mother's illness? Neither of us can know for sure what their reasons were but when I look at that photograph and hear how much your mother loved spending time with you it does make me wonder if they thought it was best for you. We both know the toll cancer takes on a family and they might not have wanted you to watch her decline.' Iona clasped both of his hands in hers, trying to make him look back on the time from an adult standpoint instead of as that confused little boy.

He'd blocked out those happier times because he'd had tunnel vision about being to blame for being sent away. Deep down he must have known they'd loved him at one time but he'd spent more of his life with stern strangers so those memories had gradually faded. The only vivid recollections he'd had were the traumatic ones because they'd had such an emotional impact on him. Perhaps he'd perceived the separation from his parents as neglect because he'd been angry at them for leaving him. It wasn't surprising he'd become an afterthought to his parents with the surgeries and treatments that had gone hand in hand with the breast cancer and the later, secondary cancers that had spread throughout his mother's body.

This new theory that they'd tried to protect him, not cause him pain, didn't lighten his heart, only made him sad for the time with his parents stolen from him. These days they would have had counselling, talked through their feelings and had other help to pull them through the sickness and bereavement. Instead, illness had devastated the whole family piece by piece, the same way cancer had taken his mother. It was such a waste.

'I suppose it's possible but it can't change what happened or how I felt.'

'Can't you find it in your heart to forgive them?' Iona rested her forehead against his, their hands still clutched together between their chests.

'I can try.' Fraser didn't want to hold on to a grudge or remain trapped in this guilt any longer. It would be time and energy better spent focused on the future.

'It might help you find some closure. I know it sounds hypocritical when I've come out here to escape the people who were supposed to love me most in the world. I lost my mother too but my father's still alive. I can't say he ever showed me any such affection. If he had I might think more kindly towards him and might not have let myself get swept up into an abusive relationship myself.'

Fraser knew how much her experiences must have impacted on her given that he was still in recovery from his last break-up. But Iona had been married, physically hurt by the man she'd intended to spend her whole life with, and that wasn't something easily forgotten.

'You're the strongest woman I've ever met.' While

he'd remained locked in the house with his resentment and anger, Iona had moved on and somehow managed to leave the issues of her early life behind to focus on her future. Not only that, she'd devoted herself to helping others and proving she was better than the man who'd claimed to be her father.

'I've had to be. I don't have anyone else.' She turned away from him and busied herself with putting the decorations back in the box, including his prized reindeer, but she didn't fool him. That tough façade was protecting a fragile heart identical to his.

'Hey.' He caught her chin between his thumb and finger and turned her head so he could drop a soft kiss on her lips to let her know he wasn't going anywhere. 'You've got me.'

'Have I, Fraser? I don't want to get into something I'm going to regret. Do you promise you're going to be here for me?' The question was so full of residual pain he knew she couldn't bear to have it inflicted on her again.

Right here, talking about and raking through the remnants of his past with her, the wind rattling the old bones of this house, it was the only place he wanted to be. She'd messed up yesterday but she'd owned it, wanted to make amends, and that was more than anyone who'd wronged him in the past had ever done. Being with Iona, he didn't have to think about the next step, free to do whatever came naturally without fear of being judged.

He was beginning to see what Caroline had meant when she'd accused him of not being true to her, or himself, when he'd been unwittingly projecting an image of the man he imagined he *should* be, instead of the one he was around Iona. He needed to embrace every part of who he was to fully enjoy life, including that inner child who'd been stifled for too long. He had nothing to lose and everything to gain.

'Always,' he promised, and kissed her again. It was the sweet reward he'd been waiting for since last night, the thought of which had got him to the hospital and back without incident, knowing she'd be at home, waiting for him.

He felt her soften at his touch then she kissed him back with such urgency and desire he didn't want to think about anyone other than the woman back in his arms where she belonged.

He shifted her onto his lap, never breaking the seal between their mouths because he couldn't get enough of her. She unbuttoned her blouse and Fraser helped tug it over her head to reveal her full breasts cupped in wisps of black lace. Every part of his body tightened to attention, begging to be freed with her.

He pulled off his sweater and Iona stood up to remove the rest of her clothes, leaving her breathtakingly naked before him. He barely had a chance to drink in the beautiful sight or unzip his trousers before she straddled him again and lowered herself onto his straining erection.

The immediacy of the act jolted him, body and soul, every nerve ending ready to explode with satisfaction. The intimacy wasn't purely physical as they stared into each other's eyes, rocking together in search of that place of utter peace. They needed each other, needed to find a release for all of those pent-up emotions and replace the pain with something much more enjoyable.

Iona bore down on his shoulders, riding him with relentless urgency, her breasts bouncing as Fraser thrust ever upwards to meet her. He caught her tight, pink nipple in his mouth, sucking hard enough to make her gasp and contract her inner muscles around his shaft. The sensation urged him on to tease the other pinched bud but she arched her back, increased the pace of her hip grinding and drove him to the brink of insanity much too quickly.

With one swift movement he flipped over so she was on her back and he was deep inside her, his movements no longer restricted between her thighs. Unencumbered, he drove deeper and harder inside her, Iona lifting her hips to accommodate every inch of him. Bodies slamming together, Iona's nails clawing his back, each of them making those animalistic noises that only came with raw passion, Fraser knew they were out of control. Neither of them held back about what it was they wanted, or demanded, from each other.

He prided himself on being a considerate lover, aiming to please his partner as much as himself. Yet, with Iona, he was acting on pure, carnal instinct. As she was. At the end of this no one would be left wanting.

Iona knew exactly what she wanted, him, and he was more than happy to oblige. Their chemistry hadn't been a figment of his imagination when they were living out the hot, frenzied truth of it together.

As the wind picked up outside, so too did the ferocity of their coupling. Iona's moans grew more frequent and higher pitched, her muscles tightening to let him know she was almost at breaking point. With every bit of strength he had in him, Fraser drove into her again and again and pushed her over the edge, tumbling with her into that all-enveloping ecstasy of release.

He'd never lost himself so utterly with a woman before and he knew this was more than great sex or physical attraction. It was love for who she was, how she made him feel, and who he was when he was with her. The sort of connection a man was lucky to find once in a lifetime and would be a fool to ever let go.

Iona curled her naked body around Fraser's, certain that was all the activity she was capable of for the foreseeable future. He'd reached parts of her she hadn't known still existed, the most significant of which had been her heart. Sure, this was, and would probably remain for a long time, the most erotic and passionate encounter of her life but she wanted this to be the start of something between them, not simply the culmination of all the drama and emotion they'd been dealing with.

Fraser had shared a lot with her, including those poignant memories of his parents. Then there was all the passion she'd somehow unlocked from within him. She shivered, the feel of him so new, so recent and so very pleasurable.

'Are you cold?' He mistook her goosebumps for something entirely different and wrapped his arms and legs around her to share his body heat. She wasn't about to complain. This was the most content she'd been in an age and if it wasn't for their sleeping babes downstairs she'd happily stay locked in here for the rest of the day.

Every now and then Fraser kissed the top of her head, reassuring her he was there, all the while she was wondering if he'd become distant, lost in his thoughts. She was confident that he wasn't regretting the tryst but if there was something else bothering him she wanted to put his mind at rest.

'I…er… I'm on the Pill. Thought you should know.' In her line of work she'd seen plenty of women caught out by the same rush of lust causing them to lose common sense and gain a surprise bundle nine months later not to take precautions herself. Although she'd never been so carried away before that the idea of contraception had never entered her head. Fraser wasn't the sort to overlook something as important as protection either but apparently the buttoned-up Dr McColl was just as hot-blooded as the next male. More so, judging by her limited experience.

'Oh. Right. Good. Sorry. I should've taken care of that.' His embarrassment at being ill prepared was as obvious as the fact that wasn't the subject monopolising his thoughts.

'Is there something wrong? You seem so far away.' She rolled onto his chest so she could look into his face and see for herself if he was having second thoughts about getting involved. It wasn't in her nature, or her plans, to be the needy, clingy girlfriend. She simply preferred to know where she stood. There was nothing to be gained for either of them by embarking on another sham of a relationship.

'I'm right here.' He deliberately misinterpreted her comment and tried to distract her with another one of his swoonworthy kisses, which, although gratifying all the way down to her toes, didn't answer her question.

She let him distract her a while longer, until she was in danger of not caring about what had snagged his attention as much as the new yearning he was awakening inside her.

In between smooches and desperately pretending she hadn't noticed the hand tangled in her hair and the one caressing her breast, she asked the question again.

'Where did you go, Fraser?' *Without me*, she wanted to add.

She lifted her head off his chest as he drew in a ragged breath.

'I was just thinking...the kids will be up soon.' He wasn't telling her the whole truth but he was back in the present with her and thinking about the future. Even if it was only the immediate one.

'I know but I don't want to move.' She drew her fingernail around his nipple, teasing the sensitive skin and watching it pucker with arousal.

'Neither do I but we, uh, came up here for a reason.' He grabbed her hand and gave her a half-hearted scolding, his ever-darkening eyes and swiftly recovering libido telling her what he'd much rather be doing. Unfortunately, he was all about doing the right thing, not always necessarily the most fun thing, but on this occasion she had to concede he was right. They'd had their quality time together, which, if all went well, they'd get to repeat somewhere more comfortable and at a more convenient time. That didn't give her any more motivation to move.

'Spoilsport. Don't you have house elves who come in and do all the work while you're asleep?'

'We call them staff, sweetheart, and, as you know, I don't employ any here. It doesn't sit well with my conscience.'

'Damn you and your principles. With one ring of a bell we could've summoned someone to bring us a bed up here and sent a nanny downstairs to see to the children.' She burrowed further into Fraser's side.

His chuckling eventually ended with an abrupt 'Up!', and her clothes landing item by item on top of her naked body. There was something sexy about when he was being bossy, especially when he was naked and she'd had experience of what it was like letting him be on top.

For once she did as he asked.

CHAPTER TEN

IONA HAD A renewed burst of energy once they'd transported their festive finds down to the living room. Running on pure adrenaline since she'd had next to no sleep, she set to work creating a sophisticated winter wonderland as much for Fraser as the children.

He might not have been invested in the aesthetic design but she set him to work where his height was an advantage.

'Hang that garland from the ceiling...

'Drape that bunting around the lintel...

'Find somewhere to put the mistletoe...'

That last instruction drew a lascivious grin from her co-worker as he held the plastic spray somewhere that would make a Christmas angel blush. 'I think custom dictates you're supposed to kiss me under this.'

He'd grown bolder now they'd shared intimate knowledge of one another but she knew he was joking. For now. The next time they had the place to themselves she'd call his bluff and kiss him everywhere south of his impressive sprig.

'You wish.' She tossed some tinsel at him and set his mind back to the task rather than the contents of his trousers. Although that was easier said than done for her too.

'Wow! Did you do all this while we were sleeping?' An animated Hamish walking in on them soon extinguished all explicit thoughts circulating in the atmosphere.

'Iona did most of it. What do you think?' Fraser credited her with the display when it had been his idea to work through the morning in an attempt to get her back into their good books.

'It's cool. Thanks.' Hamish was back to being the good-natured boy they'd first met, thanks to Fraser's uncharacteristic bending of the rules at the hospital. She trusted he was beginning to see the benefits of acting on instinct and not always following the rules. Making love on his attic floor wouldn't have been scheduled into his daily planner and it was all the more memorable for it.

'It's so pretty.' Poppy came to stand beside her at the tree, marvelling at the delicate baubles and tartan bows.

'Do you want to put the fairy on the top of the tree?' Iona handed over her favourite task to the bleary-eyed child in her pink pyjamas, imagining her mother doing the same thing with her every year.

The McColl fairy was altogether different from the Munro one, which was a chubby-cheeked, soft-bodied angel. She wore scarlet felt trimmed with gold and berries instead of white netting and Poppy was enchanted with her as she placed her carefully on the tree.

'Look! It's snowing.' They all followed Poppy's gaze out of the window to see snowflakes falling like confetti outside. It was the perfect backdrop to their Christmas scene but the snow was always more welcomed by children than the adults. Especially out here where there were no road gritters to clear a path for people who had to get to work in a hurry. Thank goodness they had no plans today beyond keeping the children entertained.

'Can we go out and play?' Hamish had his nose pressed up against the glass with longing.

'After breakfast. What would you like?' Fraser took a turn at being the grown-up and temporarily put the fun and games on hold.

Poppy tugged on his jumper. 'Can we have pancakes?' she asked, as tentatively as though she'd asked for diamond-encrusted cereal. Her plea caught Hamish's attention back from the snow to stand beside his sister.

'They won't be the same, Pops.' The scowl on his face aged him beyond his young years and the scolding soon made Poppy's head drop too.

'I can make pancakes. It's no problem.' Fraser was quick to put any fears to rest and Poppy beckoned him down so she could whisper in his ear. He nodded, took her hand and led her to the kitchen.

'Dad made them shaped like Christmas trees for us.' Hamish's chin wobbled as he explained the significance to Iona.

She put an arm around him and followed the other two. 'Then I'm guessing you'll have to show Fraser exactly how to make them.'

Breakfast was a raucous and messy affair as they all got involved in trying to re-create the perfect tree pancake. This apparently included decorating with a combination of maple syrup and chocolate chips. It wasn't the healthiest start to the day but the sound of their laughter was glorious to hear after last night's unpleasantness.

The sugar rush soon had them bouncing in anticipation of a day playing in the snow and by the time they were bundled up in appropriate layers, Fraser and Iona included, the snow had formed a thick white blanket as far as the eye could see.

They were heading outside when Poppy spotted the mistletoe Fraser had stuck above the door at the last minute.

'You have to kiss Iona!' She clapped her mittened hands together while a disinterested Hamish—with his cast wrapped in a plastic bag so it didn't get wet—went on to make the first footprints in the snow.

To the squealing delight of their little matchmaker, Fraser planted a kiss on Iona's lips and, satisfied he'd fulfilled his obligation, Poppy ran out to join her brother.

Iona tried to follow her out the door, only to be pulled back under the mistletoe.

'Where do you think you're going?'

'Out-outside,' she stuttered, seeing that glint in Fraser's eye that took her right back to what they'd been doing, rolling about on the attic floor.

'Not until I get a proper kiss.'

With the two mischief-makers busy piling snow into the beginnings of a snowman Iona saw no reason to deny herself. Fraser kissed her long and hard and passionately enough that her knees wobbled when she did finally make it outside.

The four of them worked together, rolling and patting mounds of snow into a head and body shape.

'He needs eyes.' Hamish pulled off his glove and used his finger to dig two eyeholes into the blank face.

'Put that back on before you get frostbite and lose the use of that hand too.' Iona wasn't willing to take any more chances when there'd be no clear roads back to the hospital now.

'Can we use these for his mouth and nose?' Poppy opened her hand to display a selection of small shells and stones.

'Where on earth did you find these?' The nearest beach was miles away and they certainly hadn't had the weather recently for a leisurely stroll around the coast.

'They're her lucky finds. She used to collect them when we went beachcombing with Dad and she carries them everywhere.' It was clear Hamish didn't want Poppy to part with them and Iona wouldn't want to deprive her of her link to such precious memories either.

'We could use those, or you could put them back in your pocket and we'll find something else from around here.' She left the decision to Poppy, who stared at the handful of mementoes before stuffing them back into the pocket of her duffel coat, much to Iona's relief.

'Poppy and I are going on a nature hunt, we'll be back soon,' she called to the boys as they headed off to excavate body parts for their new creation. They weren't paying attention, too engrossed in dressing Mr Frosty, as Hamish had named him. Fraser took off his woollen hat and perched it on Frosty's head.

'He needs a scarf too.' Scotland's latest fashion expert stared pointedly at Fraser's neck covering, which he untangled with a sigh. If Iona and Poppy weren't quick he'd be stripped bare and in danger of hypothermia. Only half of that thought was appealing so she grabbed the first things she found and, along with Poppy's new finds, they trudged back.

'There. Excellent job, everyone.' With his twig arms and pine-cone features, Frosty was finally complete, providing a much-needed bonding session for her and the children.

'High five!' It was Fraser who led the call for self-congratulations with the others. When he got to Iona, it wasn't a high-five she got but a face full of snow.

'I. Am. Going. To. Kill. You!' she spluttered through the icy face mask.

Fraser was bent double, laughing with his co-conspirators. Not to be outdone, Iona scooped up a handful of loose snow and stuffed it down the back of his trousers. The snow-in-the-pants dance was the best form of revenge she could have wished for as she watched Fraser trying to get it out without mooning at his impressionable young audience.

Taking their cue from the adults, Hamish and Poppy took off screaming and throwing snowballs at each other.

'I suppose you think you're funny?' Fraser advanced on her, eyes narrowed and lips pressed tightly together.

'Hilarious.' Iona folded her arms, determined to stand her ground, but the second she clocked him scooping up more ammunition she took off, shrieking.

He reached her in seconds to launch another icy attack, this time down the back of her neck. She screamed with shock and the weight of Fraser bundling her down onto the ground. They landed together, panting and laughing and so carefree she didn't care about the cold soaking through her clothes.

Her heart fluttered with the possibilities that lay ahead with this man who understood her need for space and provided a little order in the midst of her chaos.

The sound of a vehicle crunching through the snow interrupted this new discovery and had them scrambling back onto their feet.

'I'll go and see who it is.' The weight and the heat lifted from her chest as Fraser jogged off to open the gates. Their future was on hold so they could deal with whatever new guests had arrived. With the bad weather closing in, there was no way this was a casual visit but Iona had the uncharitable thought she wanted them gone already so they could continue with their Christmas fantasy.

'Hamish! Poppy!' she called to get them back inside the house to get warmed up again while Fraser established what was going on out here.

They were wrapped up in front of the fire in the lounge when he returned with the visitors.

'Mum!' The children flung themselves at Katherine as she walked in, accompanied by an older man and woman.

'Easy.' Fraser stepped in before they knocked her off her feet.

'They didn't tell us you were getting out this morning or we would've had the children ready for you.' Iona was as gobsmacked as the children to see her since they hadn't said anything other than she was improving on her last check. Whilst she was happy for their sakes that they were reunited, she did feel as though she'd been caught out rolling around in the snow with Fraser when they'd arrived.

'My blood pressure's down and Mum and Dad managed to get a flight in this morning. They agreed to let me out as long as I rest, but I wanted to surprise these two.' The colour was back in the young mum's cheeks at having her children back again and Iona wouldn't have denied her a second with them.

'I think you did that all right but you should be taking it easy. Have a seat. Can we get you something to eat or drink?' At least Fraser remembered his manners, playing the host and introducing himself to her parents. Iona was glad the children were going to have their Christmas after all but she had a horrible premonition hers had come to an end.

'I really just want to get home. I'm sure you understand, Iona.'

She did but it didn't make it any easier for her to say goodbye. 'Of course. I'll go and get their things.'

It was silly to get upset when this was the best present the family could have received but it didn't stop the tears falling as she folded their clothes and packed their bags to leave. It marked the end of their pretend family and she didn't know what that meant for her and Fraser.

Iona composed herself when the time came to see them off. It wouldn't have been fair to spoil their moment when they were so happy to be going home together.

'Thank you for everything.' Katherine insisted on hugging her and Fraser as tightly as her huge pregnant belly would allow and Hamish and Poppy followed suit. Iona managed to keep her quivering smile in place until they finally drove away.

'You'll see them again.' Fraser slipped an arm around her waist and held her close.

'I know. It's just…' If she was honest she didn't know why their departure was hitting her so hard other than the absurd notion that he mightn't want her now they weren't part of the package. As if having a ready-made family to fill his house was the only reason he'd fallen for her.

'You got used to having them around? Me too.' Given the noise and disruption two small children managed to make, his admission would've been surprising once upon a time but not any more. Not since she'd seen the tolerant, nurturing side of him that she'd fallen for.

He closed the door on the outside world so there was only the two of them left to fill the home.

'This is our time now and as the lady of the house I wonder if you might care to join me in the master bedroom?'

Her heart wasn't the only part of her flourishing back to life with the promise he was making her. Time alone with him wasn't a luxury she had yet explored to its fullest potential.

'I'm not really looking my best after rolling around in the snow. Perhaps the Laird would prefer to wait for me to freshen up before he ravishes me?' A girl wanted to look her best for such auspicious occasions. Even those where her clothes wouldn't be required for too long.

'The Laird would not. He does, however, think it would be more fun to freshen up together.' He wiggled his eyebrows in a comically suggestive manner, totally unsuitable for a laird or a doctor, which made her laugh and practically run into the master bedroom along with him.

The Laird's Chamber was as grand and masculine as Iona had imagined, with swathes of tartan and the family crest everywhere to tell the tale of Fraser's heritage. Yet if it had been cast entirely of gold and diamonds she would still have been more impressed with the sight of Fraser undressing in the room.

Without saying a word, he stripped naked, the sound of a bath running the only prompt Iona needed to mirror his moves. There could've been some awkwardness standing here staring at each other's naked bodies but

Fraser watched her with so much admiration and desire that any inhibitions were quashed before they had time to manifest themselves. With such a fine body himself, Fraser had nothing to be ashamed of and clearly wasn't, striding confidently to the bathroom.

Iona felt more of a queen than a lady stepping into the cloud of bubbles in the tub, the warm water inviting her to sink deeper. Fraser's long legs enveloped hers and she relaxed back against his chest, letting the water and her lover wash over her.

She couldn't remember the last time anyone outside a salon had washed her hair but he did so, unbidden. He lathered the shampoo in her hair, his fingers massaging her scalp with a tenderness that made her want to weep. By all accounts, no one had ever taken care of him, yet here he was expressing his love for her by touch alone.

She closed her eyes as he rinsed out the suds and though she was content to remain where she was, she was obliged to give him the chance to experience this bliss too. 'Do you want me to wash your hair for you?'

'In a minute. I'm enjoying taking care of you without you trying to bite my head off for it.'

Now she knew there was no call to rebel against him through fear he was trying to get the upper hand over her, Iona had to admit it was nice having someone look after her. She'd been on her own for so long, untrusting and suspicious, she'd forgotten simple pleasures like this.

Fraser took a flannel and began to wash her body with long, sensual strokes across her neck, over her breasts, slipping further down between her legs. She closed her eyes and gave herself over to his ministrations. After giving so much of herself these past few days, she figured she was entitled to some pampering.

Under the water he continued to move the cloth along her thighs, teasing across the part of her so desperately aching for his touch. She let out a whimper as he abandoned the flannel and carried on, using only his fingers to stroke her.

He kissed his way across her shoulder to that sensitive spot at her neck that automatically increased her arousal tenfold. It was then he pushed inside her, drawing a gasp and a groan as he soothed her ache.

She writhed against him as he stretched and filled her with his fingers, the swell of his erection pressed into the small of her back turning her on beyond measure. He wanted her but he wasn't going to have her until he'd driven her to climax first. A selfless lover was the best aphrodisiac known to womankind.

With one hand pushing her towards the brink of oblivion, the other was at her breast, pinching her nipple to provide that oh-so-pleasurable pain. Her orgasm slammed into her, the blinding flash behind her eyelids and shudder of gratification taking her breath away with the sheer force of it.

She was so lost in that spiralling bliss she didn't realise those erotic cries echoing around the walls were coming from her.

'Are you okay?' Fraser whispered in her ear, his hot breath sending another aftershock of rapture rippling through her body.

'Uh-huh.' Apart from having lost the power of speech, her mouth dry and her brain having exploded with the sensations he'd drawn from her.

'In that case, let's get you dried off.' Water sluiced over her and the floor as he stood up and that weightlessness in her body disappeared at once.

'What about your hair?' Fraser wasn't going to cheat her out of doing something for him in return. She wanted him to experience the same moment of pure happiness he'd just given her.

'It's not my hair that's needs tending right now.' He grinned and held up a towel, waiting for her to get out of the bath.

There was no place for her gaze to linger other than at his manhood standing tall and demanding her attention.

Fraser swamped her in the fleecy warmth of the bath sheet, carried her into the bedroom and laid her down on the covers as though she was the most precious thing in the world. At that moment that's exactly how he made her feel.

He unwrapped her painfully slowly, taking his time to appreciate every inch of her he uncovered. There was no mistaking his desire for her, it was there for her to see in all its physical glory, but so was the love in his eyes for her, and that was her undoing. Fraser wasn't the same as the others, he wouldn't hurt her or try to change her, and he loved her for who she was, regardless of how difficult it was for him at times. In the few days they'd lived together they'd learned the art of compromise. Learned to love and live in harmony.

It was an unconventional match but it kept things so exciting and passionate between them that Iona never wanted to leave his bed.

Anticipation was throbbing through her body with that one look promising all the things he was going to do to, and with, her.

She pressed herself tightly into him, teasing them both as her nipples rubbed against his chest and Fraser groaned, his erection grazing where she craved him most. He swallowed her breathy pleas with a tongue-tangling display of desire that did nothing to quench the fiery lust coursing through her veins.

'I need you, Fraser.' She begged him to fill that part of her that was incomplete without him now.

'I need you too.'

They belonged together and now they'd found each other it was unthinkable that they should ever be parted again.

Last night had been the culmination of their pent-up yearning for one another, a frantic endeavour to release that pressure and find ultimate satisfaction as quickly as possible. Being together here, Iona knew, was an expression of the depth of their feelings for one another, tender and loving as they took their time climbing towards that peak of absolute contentment together. It carried them both in quick succession over the finish line, leaving her breathless and euphoric.

She watched the rise and fall of his chest as he lay down beside her and the smile spreading across his face adding his own glowing review of their endeavours.

'Has it—is it—always this way for you?' It was the sort of question one might attribute to a naïve virgin but she'd never experienced this level of impact on her heart and her body.

She'd had lovers and the occasional relationship but none of her previous partners had reached her or taken her to such heights the way Fraser had. It made her question if she'd truly been in love before or if he was simply an exceptional lover. Perhaps he had this effect on every woman who'd ever shared his bed but she wanted what they had to be special for him too.

Fraser rolled over onto his side, propping his head on

his hand, and reached out to brush a tendril of her still-wet hair from her face. She turned her cheek into his palm and closed her eyes, afraid to know the answer in case it ruined this for ever.

'Never.' His soft voice reached in behind her closed lids and travelled all the way to her soul. He was hers and hers alone and if every time was like this she never wanted to wake up alone again.

CHAPTER ELEVEN

IT WAS DARK when they finally decided to leave bed in search of sustenance. Iona walked over to the window to close the curtains and found the world outside glowing with a fresh fall of snow.

'Winter has well and truly arrived.' The night was so peaceful and still, they could've been perched atop their own private glacier, miles from civilisation, and content to be so.

'In that case, we should stock up on food supplies to see us through our hibernation.' Fraser jumped out of bed and began to pull on his clothes.

'What are you doing?' She was dismayed that he was hiding his beautiful body back under layers of fabric when it was so unnecessary.

'Er…getting dressed so we can go down and get something to eat.' The absurdity of what he was doing was completely lost on him so Iona took it upon herself to make the point. She walked over to his side of the bed, making no attempt to hide her own nakedness, and began to unbutton his trousers.

'This is your house, Fraser. We're alone and there's no one around for miles. We don't need clothes.' He put up no objections to her pulling his trousers off—indeed, he appeared very happy to let her do so. There was hope yet he'd learn to abandon some of his stuffy ways with her to lead him astray.

Fraser approved of Iona's naturist tendencies and with her every effort she was making this into a place he was comfortable to be in. It was early days to bring up the idea of her moving in when she'd barely unpacked in her own flat but she was the sole reason he'd decided he was going to stay in this house.

Iona would certainly blow away the cobwebs here and shake things up as she had done for him. A lot of his old habits and compulsions for order no longer seemed important and no longer dictated his daily schedule. They were no competition when pitted against spending time with Iona instead. With her by his side it was as if his brain had been reset, no longer conditioned to worry about the consequences of every tiny action. It could take a while for him to be a live-in-the-moment kind of guy but with Iona's infectious zest for life he would get there.

They stole downstairs, laughing in the faces of his staid ancestors and making him feel like the naughty child he'd never been here. He'd never done anything intentionally to upset his parents or Caroline. His inability to change had inevitably pushed her away but he'd changed for Iona after only a short time together. Deep down he must have known Caroline wasn't the one for him.

'Houston, we have a problem.' Iona flicked the light switch on and off in the kitchen but they remained in darkness. It was the same in the living room, their beautiful Christmas tree shrouded in shadow instead of twinkling fairy lights. The only light was coming from the fireplace, which would also be their only heat supply too until the power came back on.

'The storm must have brought the lines down. Not to worry, we have plenty of candles.' All those elaborate candelabra around the house would come in useful after all.

'I take it the oven's out of use too?' The desperate call for food from Iona's rumbling belly was the only downside to the situation but Fraser was used to stocking up for those late nights when he came home and couldn't face cooking.

'Ah, but we do have a selection of cheeses and cold meats. Speaking of which, as much as I appreciate the view, without central heating there's a danger of us contracting pneumonia.' Fraser stacked plate upon plate and loaded a tray up with goodies to take into the lounge and spread out their makeshift picnic in front of the fireplace. Iona snagged the throw from the back of the couch and draped it around their shoulders as she sat down beside him.

It was moments such as this, wrapped up with his lover, feeding each other sustenance after a day spent in bed, that were worth more than money could ever buy.

'Is it wrong of me to want the snowstorm to last for ever so we can stay holed up here?' Iona took a sip from the bottle of water he'd taken from the fridge and a trickle of condensation splashed onto her chest and over her now erect nipple.

'I'd say that sounds perfect.' He leaned down and lapped the droplet with his tongue, thirst quickly overtaking his hunger.

Since having Iona here, he'd decided to make this his permanent residence but it only felt like a home with her in it. If she'd taught him anything over these past days it was to stop over-analysing everything and do what made him happy. He knew they'd only been together a short time, most of that accompanied by two minors, but it was sufficient to know this was right. It wasn't fair to keep ignoring his feelings any more when it had already cost him so much wasted time. 'Why don't you move in?'

Iona's brow knitted together in an expression that showed anything but enthusiasm for the idea. 'I know it's a big house but in case you haven't noticed, I've been living here for a few days now.'

'Well, I didn't think it was the Christmas elves who'd taken over... Seriously, though, think about it, but not for too long. I don't want to waste any more time. I want to be with you, Iona, share this house, and my life, with you.' He'd been here before with Caroline but this was different. He was being truer to himself than he'd ever been, putting everything he was on the line for Iona when he'd never done it for Caroline.

Sweat broke out over his skin the longer he waited for an answer when he'd thought the idea was a no-brainer. They were good for each other, anyone could see that, and their time together in the bedroom, and on the attic floor, had been every bit as exciting as the emotional connection they'd made.

'Fraser...that's—that's...' She was clearly as overwhelmed as he was, struggling to find words.

He knew he was risking a lot on what was primarily a gut instinct they would make this work. The opposite strategy from how he usually lived his life. Iona wasn't the kind of person to be blinded by the expensive trappings that came with him and he trusted her enough to base her decision on the strength of her feelings for him alone.

She stood up, wrapping the blanket around her to cover her nakedness, and Fraser rose with her for the warm hug he anticipated along with her acceptance.

'That's a ridiculous idea.'

He'd stepped towards her before the words slammed into his chest, causing serious internal damage. Optimism and a pitiful hold on the last vestige of hope he could rescue the situation and his heart prevailed. 'I know it's a bit out there but it seems like a natural progression to me when we already know we make a great team. You can ditch that dingy flat, move in here—'

'Quit my job, pop out a couple of kids...' Her tone definitely wasn't in keeping with his earnest endeavour to show her how he felt about her.

'I would never ask you to leave work but I won't lie, I'd like to be a father someday.' He hadn't been thinking quite that far ahead but since she'd brought the subject up he wanted to be honest about his dreams for a family. It had been the deal breaker for Caroline but the way Iona looked after all the children who came into her care hadn't gone unnoticed. He could see a future with her or else he would never have asked her and risked another rejection.

'Fraser, I've only just moved into my own place. You know what it means to me to have my independence. If you're expecting me to sacrifice everything I am for your benefit then you don't know me at all.' Despite everything they'd shared, it appeared Iona was still unwilling to compromise anything for him. Clearly he'd completely misjudged the situation and the baggage she had yet to unpack from her previous relationship if she didn't warrant him worthy of a permanent place in her life. A common theme unfortunately being played out again by someone he loved.

'I was merely asking if you wanted to move in. I've got my answer. That's fine. It was just a thought. Forget I said anything.' Fraser didn't want to cause a row or make her think he was anything akin to her ex when all he'd done was act on impulse. An area in which he apparently still had some work to do.

'No, Fraser. I can't forget it. This is exactly what I was afraid would happen. One small opening into my life and you try to bulldoze through everything. I think we've probably got caught up in this fantasy life we've built around the kids. Let's be honest, before them we didn't really have a lot in common or much to say to one another that wasn't an insult.

'Now they've gone I think we're clutching at straws in an attempt to keep the fairy-tale going by jumping into bed. But it's not real. I think we've both been too damaged to ever make this work. You need someone here to give you that security you've missed and I can't give up my freedom when it's all I have. I'm going to pack my stuff and go and we'll keep this time together as a fond memory.'

She turned away from him and he knew this was more than a lovers' tiff, she was serious about leaving him and was trying to reduce what they had to a casual fling.

Fraser willed his feet to move, to run after her and beg her to stay but his body was uncooperative, shut down in a complete state of shock. The whole scene was a re-enactment of last year with Caroline, except this was so much more traumatic. Although he hadn't been with

Iona long, he knew beyond doubt he was in love with her in a way he'd never loved anyone before. The rejection was not only of him in his truest form but the idea of a future together. Now he'd seen a glimpse of the family and home they could've had together here, he'd never want it with anyone other than Iona.

Nausea undulated through his body as his whole world collapsed around him once more. He reminded himself he was a grown man now, not that little boy who'd been parted from everything he loved without a say. Although Iona's decision to walk out felt very much like being abandoned all over again.

Iona was breathing heavily, her chest tightening with every step she took upstairs to escape the life Fraser was trying to create around her.

Yes, she fancied him like crazy and was maybe even falling in love with him, but the second her defences were down he'd swooped in and tried to exploit that weakness. Living together? Babies? That was a one-way ticket back to that prison she'd broken out of once already.

Iona needed to get back to her own place, her own space, where she could think clearly without abject terror clouding her judgement. Cooped up here, fostering that idea of family with Fraser and the children had messed with both of their heads. Once she was out of the picture again he'd realise that himself. Hopefully by the time they were back at work after the Christmas break they'd remember who they were.

Iona dressed quickly, gathering her belongings as she whipped around the bedroom. If she didn't leave now there was every chance she'd end up back in bed with him at some point and completely forget why her 'dingy flat', complete with borrowed furniture, should be more appealing than Fraser's bed.

It was far too tempting to ignore the distant sound of her phone ringing but she was never really off duty and a call this late could be an emergency.

'Hello.' Her response to whoever was on the line may as well have been an expletive she said it with such aggression but she wasn't in the best of moods, having just ended a relationship with a man she'd come to care for deeply.

'Iona, this is June Lowe, the community midwife on call. I'm sorry to phone out of hours but I understand you're staying with Dr McColl at present and we have an emergency out there. Claire McKenzie is desperately in need of assistance but the main roads there are blocked with fallen trees and downed power lines. We're trying to get an air ambulance out but with the storm... Anyway, we were wondering if you could get through from your end to check on her?'

Iona didn't want to spend long analysing what scenario the rumour mill had dreamed up for Fraser and her being shacked up here together when they would be correct in all of their assumptions. They were consenting adults and it shouldn't matter to anyone else what they did in their private lives as long as it didn't impact on their professional duties. Which it would have done had she not just called a halt to everything.

'Give me the details.' She grabbed a pen and paper from the bedside table and jotted down everything June told her.

Fraser appeared at the door but she didn't have time to feel bad about the forlorn look she'd put on his face.

She put her hand over the phone to let him know what was going on. 'There's a patient in trouble. Claire McKenzie's in advanced labour and her last child was stillborn. I have to get to her. She's not far from here anyway.'

Once she hung up, she forced on her boots and prepared to brave the outdoors.

'Geographically, yes, but we're under several feet of snow in the middle of nowhere. It's not easy terrain to negotiate.'

'I do this for a living, don't forget.' She grabbed her coat and bag, fully aware of the dangers she faced as she walked to her car but nothing was going to stop her from getting to her patient.

'You can't go in that. You'll never make it down the lane.' Fraser insisted on following her outside, criticising her every move.

The compact car was ideal for village life, although probably not conducive to extreme weather conditions, but she didn't have a choice right now.

'Please don't tell me what to do when it comes to my job.' It was easier to leave him when he was trying to undermine her and she started the car regardless of his concerns.

She could see him give chase in her rear-view mirror as the gates opened and she drove away with tears in her eyes and lead in her stomach.

Even at a snail's pace the car tyres slipped and skidded down the lane, gaining no traction at all on the ice, and she was helpless as the vehicle veered off the road and into a ditch.

Before she'd had time to assess any damage to the car, or her pride, she heard the sound of Fraser's four-by-four making its way down the road towards her. Given the circumstances, Iona was going to have to set aside her personal differences with him in order to do her duty to her patient. She'd make sure he didn't take that as a sign she was willing to give him another chance when that was a weakness that had seen her burned too many times.

Once they'd transferred her equipment from the boot of her car into Fraser's I-told-you-so-mobile, Iona got in the passenger side and slammed the door. 'Don't say a word.'

She was in a bad enough mood without another lecture. In the space of fifteen minutes she'd been reminded none of this fairy-tale romance was real, that this relationship couldn't survive reality.

CHAPTER TWELVE

THEY HAD SOME hairy moments during the journey to the patient's house, despite Fraser's careful and methodical driving. There were times when even he couldn't control what happened as the car hit a patch of black ice but the lack of other vehicles in the area at least prevented any serious accident.

If pushed, Iona would have admitted his jeep was better equipped for the road conditions than her runabout, but she didn't think the choice of driver made a difference regardless of Fraser's opinion on the subject. He could have easily handed his keys over to her and gone home but that apparently wasn't something he had been ready to do.

'That's the McKenzie place up there.'

They were forced to stop at the bottom of a particularly hilly stretch of road, their journey brought to an end by the huge tree and assorted debris strewn across their route. The McKenzies' car had been abandoned halfway between the obstacles and their house.

'Could you help me carry my equipment up to the house, please?' Iona could have been churlish and insist she manage on her own, leaving Fraser freezing down here, but that wouldn't achieve anything. By giving him a task, it was also asserting her position in this situation. She was in charge.

'No problem.' He fell into line and Iona loaded him up with any kit she might need. Only time would tell how long this compliance would last once they were confronted with whatever was going on behind that front door.

Mr McKenzie met them at the door, wearing the panicked face of a father-to-be. 'Thank goodness you're here. The baby's on its way. We can't get out and after last time…' He didn't have to say any more as he ran a shaking hand through his hair. Claire had recounted to her the trauma the family had gone through in her last pregnancy, which had ended in the stillbirth of their precious baby. Despite reassurances there was no medical reason the same would happen again, the couple had been understandably anxious for the duration of this pregnancy and this setback wasn't going to allay any of those fears. That was her job.

'Where's Claire? I'll have to examine her and see what stage we're at.' Nothing else could be helped now and the importance of mother and baby's welfare had to come before anything. If they were trapped up here for the entirety of her labour, Iona had to be prepared for any eventuality.

'She's up in the bedroom. Said she was in too much pain to try and get out again.' The understandably anxious birthing partner led them up to what was about to become the delivery suite, but he was so tense Iona wasn't convinced he'd do anything to put his wife at ease.

Regardless of the urgency in the situation, Iona took

the time to knock on the door and introduce herself. 'It's Iona. The midwife.'

It was important patients maintain some dignity and privacy where they could so they weren't made to feel little more than a baby-making machine in the process.

'Come in. I'm so glad you're here.' Claire's fears were evident as she welcomed her into the room. Iona didn't know any more than the rest how this was going to play out but she had to act as confidently as she could manage to keep Claire calm. Stress could cause more complications if her blood pressure spiked now and there was only so much Iona could do without the conveniences of a hospital labour ward.

'You've got a midwife and a GP on hand so there's no cause for alarm. Now, how far apart are the contractions?' She left the two men hovering in the doorway to come and examine her patient.

'It feels as though they're constant.' Claire groaned as her belly tightened with another.

'Every two minutes. I was timing them before you came,' Craig chimed in.

'In that case, baby shouldn't be too long.' Iona wasn't worried about delivering the baby at home, she'd done it plenty of times, but she usually had more time to prepare. Especially if there'd been complications in previous pregnancies.

'What if the same thing happens again? Instead of bringing our baby home last time, all we had was a memory box. If something goes wrong here…'

Iona understood Craig's concerns and she'd had the same thought herself but there was nothing they could do but deliver the baby into the world. This constant reminder of their loss was going to prevent Claire taking any good memories from this labour and she had to get him out. He could be a part of the birth experience when the time came but for now it was better for all concerned if he took a back seat.

'We'll have it covered. Fraser, why don't you go and stick the kettle on for all of us? There's a gas cooker downstairs if you don't mind making it the old-fashioned way. Craig can fill you in and I'll get Claire comfortable here.' The message to Fraser was twofold, get Craig out of here and if I need your help I'll ask for it.

As one might have predicted, he wasn't prepared to relinquish the medical lead as easily as that.

'Craig, if you could do the honours, I'd like to have a word with Iona first.' His lips were drawn into a tight line, such a contrast to the soft mouth that had covered her body with tender kisses only hours earlier.

Iona trusted he wasn't so blinded by ego he couldn't see the serene atmosphere she was trying to create here, but she did step out onto the landing to have the conversation in private.

'What's up? I'm kind of busy here.' She kept one hand on the doorknob, making it clear she wasn't going to be detained long.

'I know you're ticked off at me but please let me help.' He could have called her out on the fact she'd relegated him to tea boy, put on some display of anger towards her based on the way she'd treated him since he'd asked her to move in with him. Instead, she could see he simply wanted them both to work together for the best outcome.

'I know what I'm doing but if I need you I promise I'll call.' Thinking of Claire lying behind the door, already afraid of what was going to happen, she knew she couldn't let her personal problems jeopardise the labour should anything go wrong out here.

'Thank you.'

She couldn't resist one last needle before she went back into the bedroom and closed the door. 'Mine's milk with one sugar, thanks.'

At least now she couldn't see or hear him she could get on with her job and bring this baby safely into the world.

'Okay, Claire, I'm just going to do a wee check and see how dilated you are.'

Dismissed from the scene, Fraser was forced to join the anxious Craig downstairs, cursing Iona for her pig-headedness. All he wanted to do was protect her, not that he could tell her that when she'd made it clear she thought he was trying to take over her life.

'Tea or coffee?' Craig greeted him at the bottom of the stairs, clutching a jar of coffee and a teabag.

'Neither. Have you got a snow shovel or heavy chains or something?' Fraser wanted to be more pro-active than simply sitting here, sipping tea.

Rather than rushing off to source essential tools to dig them out of here, Craig was still staring at him blankly, choice of beverages in hand.

It was tempting to try and shake some urgency into him but there was no need to see another display of his headless-chicken routine. He needed clear direction and something constructive to keep him occupied.

'Teatime can wait. We could be doing something useful, such as trying to move that tree. Your wife and child are going to need a clear path out of here at some point.'

That evocative reminder of why they were all here

galvanised Craig into action. He turned back into the kitchen and tossed the tea things on the worktop. Iona probably wouldn't have liked the way he made it anyway.

'I'll take a look in the shed and see what I've got.'

'Great. At least then we'll feel as though we're doing something to help.' Iona mightn't want him here in a personal capacity but he could still be useful. With any luck they would all come out of this unscathed then he could set his mind to trying to win her back.

The sounds of scraping and revving car engines outside weren't going to distract Iona. Whatever Fraser was up to, at least it was keeping him out of her business. She had enough to deal with here, without dealing with Fraser's ego too.

It had become clear Claire's contractions had been going on for some time with little progress. On examination she'd detected a problem that could explain the delay.

'Claire, I think the baby is in what we call the asynclitic position, where baby should come into the pelvis and rotate into position but in this case the head hasn't engaged properly. That's putting pressure on your pubic bone too.' There were certain positions with the foetal head that couldn't be delivered vaginally, which would be grave cause for concern here without proper intervention They were going to have to go back to basics to try and get the baby moving to where it needed to be.

'What do we do?' Claire's sobs were a mixture of fear and exhaustion, her hair stuck to her face with sweat, labour taking its toll. There were still a few tricks Iona could try to get junior to move before there was any reason to start stressing.

'I can tell you what we're not going to do, we're not going to panic. I'm going to go and see what's keeping your husband with the tea and get him to give us a hand to direct baby to the way out.' The attempt at humour took some of the focus off potential danger. Whatever happened, Claire was going to need the support of her husband to get through it, and despite Iona's resistance to engage Fraser in proceedings she would require his assistance if the baby was in distress.

She didn't waste any time locating the men, following the racket outside.

'Both of you come upstairs, now.' She had to yell to get their attention they were so engrossed in clearing the snow from the road.

'Is something wrong?' Craig came running first, with Fraser close behind, his cheeks so pink with cold it made her yearn for that time they'd spent wrapped up in front of the fire. It was too bad she'd learned the hard way there was no point in looking back.

'Baby needs some encouragement to move into place so Claire's going to need some assistance to get into a better position. She's a bit emotional right now so it would be good if you could just reassure her and support her through the contractions in the meantime.'

Fraser hung back to discuss the matter out of Craig's earshot. 'We've cleared a path down to my car. We could try to get her down.'

Iona shook her head. 'We're way past that stage. You're going to have to take my word for it, she's not going anywhere. Unfortunately, neither is the baby. Now, if you really want to help you can come up and run her a nice warm bath.'

She wasn't going to hang around to argue the point.

The baby was dictating what happened here, not her and certainly not Fraser.

'We're going to move you so you're on all fours, Claire. It might help tilt the baby's head forward. Craig, can you give me a hand here to move the pillows and get her more comfortable?'

Between them they manoeuvred Claire onto her hands and knees, with the pillows to cushion the front of her body. She was too exhausted to put all the weight on her arms, panting through each contraction with Craig rubbing her back and making encouraging murmurs. It must be nice to have a supportive partner willing you on through such a momentous event but Iona doubted she'd ever experience it through any stage of her life.

'How's she doing?' Fraser wandered in, drying his hands on a towel, having actually followed instructions and drawn a bath for Claire.

'Working hard. Claire, could we get you into the bath for a while? It's not the traditional birthing pool but it might relax you and encourage our long-awaited arrival to drop down.'

Once the next contraction passed they had a small window to make the move before the next one hit. They encouraged her to lean over the edge of the bath in much the same position as she'd been on the bed. It was a tight squeeze with the four of them in the bathroom but they were all working towards the same outcome.

'You're doing great, Claire.' Iona reached down with the Doppler device so she could listen to the baby's heartbeat, which was still fast and strong.

Craig was holding her hand and helping her to pant

through the contractions and Fraser was scooping warm water over her back so she didn't get cold.

As the contractions became more powerful it became increasingly clear the baby was finally ready to make an appearance. They had to wait for that brief respite again before transporting her back and in the end the birth was quick, Iona catching him before he slid onto the bed.

'Daddy, would you like to cut the cord?'

'We did it, Claire. We have a son.' Happy tears were streaming down the proud father's face as he did the honours.

Iona placed the baby on the mother's chest so they had that precious first skin-to-skin contact, welling up herself now that the danger had passed and he was finally here. It was always a privilege to be part of people's lives and follow their journey, more so to see it through to a happy end.

'Congratulations. All of you.' Fraser's praise was welcome but it was also tinged with a little sadness for Iona because when this was over she was faced with the prospect of going home. Alone.

Once she was sure the baby's Apgar score determined it was in good health they could leave the couple to enjoy the new member of their family until the next check-up. A low score now would suggest baby needed extra medical care but indications so far were good.

'Iona?' Fraser no longer sounded full of the joys of a new baby but concerned as he drew her attention to the scarlet stain spreading rapidly across the bed covers, enough to suggest a post-partum haemorrhage.

She nodded an acknowledgement, trying not to scare the McKenzies, but the amount of blood being lost constituted an emergency. Even when births seemed to go to plan they were notoriously unpredictable. These days a woman was very unlikely to bleed to death giving birth, but this hadn't been a planned home delivery and currently they had no way to get her to hospital where they would be best equipped to deal with all eventualities.

'Okay, Claire, you're losing quite a lot of blood and we need to find the source so we can deal with it as quickly as possible. Craig, could you go and phone for an ambulance again and see what's happening out there?' She remained calm and in control of the situation for the benefit of the new parents, who were currently wide-eyed with fear, even though her own pulse was hammering away with the implications of the situation.

'Do you need me to take the baby?' Craig dithered by the bedside, ignoring her request. Thankfully Fraser had his mobile in his pocket so he went ahead and phoned in the emergency. In hindsight it was probably best to have him chasing up some medical support when he understood the severity of the situation.

'It would actually help contract the uterus if we could get the baby to breast feed. Do you think you could try that, Claire?'

She nodded, and with her husband's assistance they tried to get the baby to latch on, leaving Iona the important job of finding out why this had happened using the *T*s—tissue, tone, trauma and thrombin. She hadn't needed stitches so that ruled out trauma, and thrombin, an issue with blood clotting, was rare and would've been known prior to birth. Although the placenta had been delivered there was a chance a bit had been left behind or that the uterus didn't have enough tone to contract and stop the bleeding.

They might not be in a conventional hospital setting

but she would follow the same steps regardless. She encouraged Claire to pass urine so she didn't have a full bladder and massaged the top of her uterus to stimulate it to contract, but blood was still gushing at an alarming rate.

'They're on their way. What can I do?' Thank goodness Fraser was here, offering another pair of hands where she desperately needed them.

'I'm going to administer an oxytocic drug but if that doesn't stop the bleeding we should put up an IV. Everything we need is in my bag.' Ordinarily the drugs were enough but if they had to transfer her to the hospital they needed a vein open and ready for easy access if necessary. Any issues with clotting would need to be treated and blood products administered.

With Fraser available to set up the IV, Iona was able to continue to massage the uterus in the hope it might help expel any retained tissue preventing good uterine clamp-down.

'You're doing great.' Fraser was doing a good job of reassuring Claire everything was going to be all right, then Iona felt the warmth of his hand on her back and she realised he was talking to her.

That unexpected support when she was so accustomed of weathering the storm alone almost made her cry at his kindness after the way she'd treated him today. She knew in that moment that no matter what happened between them romantically, he'd always be there, supporting her. It put her earlier rant into perspective and her hysteria that he was somehow trying to railroad her into another painful relationship. Fraser would never hurt her. She'd simply been projecting her own fears onto him because she was so afraid of making another mistake.

She couldn't bring herself to respond to him, afraid she'd burst into tears and never regain her composure at a time it was needed more than ever. Instead, she continued bi-manual compression, continually pushing on the uterus externally and internally until they heard the sound of the ambulance siren in the distance and she nearly collapsed with relief.

'I couldn't stop the bleeding, Fraser.' Iona was beside him, watching the ambulance make its way cautiously back down the path he and Craig had shovelled, with the McKenzies loaded up inside.

'You did everything possible. You were amazing. I'm sure she's going to be fine, thanks to your actions.' If Claire required a blood transfusion or surgery to remove any remaining placenta, it was down to the hospital staff now to continue her treatment. Iona had done her best given the circumstances and he was proud of how she'd handled everything in such a potentially life-threatening situation.

It was easy to take midwives for granted when he wasn't actively involved with their practices every day, but having now seen first-hand how fraught a home birth could be, Fraser respected her even more. Especially since she didn't seem to have the confidence in her actions that she'd portrayed to the worried couple. He was sure her calm exterior had prevented them all from losing it and making matters worse, even if her own stress levels had been through the roof.

'I'm glad you were there with me. I couldn't have done it without your help.' After their earlier parting,

Iona's words meant more to him than ever. He hoped in some small way he'd shown her he'd never do anything to interfere in her life and only wished to be part of it in some way.

'I'm pretty sure you could. You've managed all this time without me. Now, let's get back to my place out of this cold.' He understood where she was coming from. They were both perfectly capable of doing their jobs on their own but there was something reassuring about having that extra body nearby in case they were needed. It took the pressure off when you were able to share the experience with someone who understood the situation on the front line of medicine.

Neither of them had to go through life alone, if only they'd open up and accept they deserved the kind of love and support they could offer each other. It was something they really should discuss back at his place if Iona was willing to hear him out.

'Well, my car is still in a ditch there so I suppose I'll have to go with you.' That hesitation remained but she did lift her bag, indicating she would follow him.

He saw her legs begin to buckle as the enormity of the day seemed to hit her all at once. She wasn't as immune to the stress of the ordeal as she pretended. Not that anyone else would have known as she'd waited until her patient was safe before she'd given in to her own feelings. On this occasion at least she didn't have to go through it alone. He swooped down and scooped her up into his arms, just like that first time they'd found themselves thrown together.

'What are you doing?' Iona put up a half-hearted protest but he could tell she no longer had the strength to fight and that in itself was cause for concern.

'I don't care if you hate me for it but someone has to look after you. You're exhausted and in need of a strong cup of tea.' Everything else could wait until he was certain she had recovered from the trauma of the birth herself.

The drive back was as quiet as the outward journey had been but the atmosphere seemed more of a comfortable silence than the frosty drive out to the McKenzies' place.

'I'll get your car fixed up for you later,' he promised as they passed her abandoned vehicle.

'I can do it myself. I was just in a hurry to get to Claire earlier.' Even in her current state she was asserting that independence at any cost.

Fraser sighed. He couldn't understand why she didn't see he only ever wanted to help but he wasn't going to get into another argument with her now.

They pulled up outside the house and he went around to Iona's side of the car to help her out.

'I can walk, thanks.'

'Sure.' Glad she was coming inside at least, Fraser gave her some space and went on ahead.

The scene greeting them in the living room was like something out of a tragedy. The power was back on, the Christmas tree twinkling in the corner of the room and illuminating the remnants of their post-coital picnic on the floor. It was a reminder of the happy times they'd had together and those they could still have together.

Everywhere he went in the house Fraser would be faced with more painful memories. Except now they'd be full of Iona's smile, her kiss and the sense of having her close to him.

The room smelled of Iona's sweet perfume and

Christmas and he knew packing away those decorations she'd so lovingly hung for the children would kill him. All the fairy-lights and mistletoe would now become symbols of loss and regret.

Fraser thought of the pain caused by his parents never truly opening up about their feelings to him. If only they'd been able to talk things over, at any stage of his life, it could have saved them all a lot of heartache. He understood now they had been trying to protect him in their own way, but by shutting him out he'd only imagined the worst. They'd missed out on so much, all for the want of better communication. Such a waste of precious time that could have been spent together in his mother's last days. Perhaps he would've even been reconciled with his father at the end of his life too.

He didn't want to make the same mistakes with Iona when she meant so much to him, and he wasn't prepared to give up on love without a fight. This house was a shell without her in it and he could never be happy here alone.

'Please don't go, Iona. Can't we just start again?'

'We're so different…' Instead of the definitive no she'd given him earlier, she seemed to be mulling over the idea of a second chance. Perhaps the visual reminder of their time here had had a similar impact on her too.

'We've known that from the start. That's what makes the sparks fly, remember?' Life would never be boring between them and he wanted to remind her that their personality clashes could be a whole lot of fun at times.

Iona managed a wistful smile. 'Passion might disguise the real problems for a while but they show themselves in the end. I can't be with someone who thinks they can run my life for me. I'm never getting into that kind of toxic relationship again.'

'I would never try to control you. In my clumsy way I was trying to show you how much I cared for you.' Fraser's stomach rolled as he realised his misplaced faith in rules and order had fed directly into Iona's fears about everything she thought he represented from her past, and he didn't know how to fix it. Nothing meant as much to him as Iona and he'd give up anything for one more chance to prove it.

Previous experience had shown Iona that controlling men didn't change their behaviour for anyone. They might pretend for a while to be charming and contrite but that was all part of their manipulation. Their way of maintaining a hold on their victims by showing they were capable of redemption but always under an atmosphere of fear. Her mother had been afraid of her father and Iona would've left her ex sooner if not for the underlying threat of violence. She'd never once been afraid of Fraser. Annoyed, frustrated and downright angry at times with him but never had she seriously considered that by voicing her opinion on anything he would do her harm.

'It took a lot for me to walk away from the last man who tried to control me and it's taken me years to get where I am now. I have no intention of going back there.' Despite how desperately she longed to rewind time back to when they had been wrapped up here together with the world at their feet.

'I'm sorry. Did your ex ever say that to you and mean it? I'm truly sorry.'

Iona had heard the words before but never with the genuine remorse she saw shining in Fraser's eyes.

'I'm afraid to put myself in that position again when my life is very much my own now.'

'And you're not willing to share it with me at least? That's all I'm asking, Iona. I love you. If nothing else I want you to know that and believe it.' The catch in his voice gave away the truth of what he was saying and though hearing it made her heart soar and gave validation to her feelings for him, it couldn't completely heal her scars.

She wasn't used to having someone looking out for her unless they were trying to use it against her for their own means.

'In case you missed it, I'll say it again. I love you, Iona. I want us to be together.'

She was afraid that if she told him how much her heart was swelling with love for him too she might start ugly crying again and he might change his mind about loving her.

'Asking you to move in here, I suppose, was symbolic. I was offering my heart along with the key to my home. I mean, we can forget the whole living-together thing. I know you just moved into your own place. Just tell me you feel the same about me and it'll give me hope I haven't totally messed this up.'

His rambling was endearing and she knew he'd never try to force her into doing anything when he was doing his best to give her her own space. Today had shown how much he loved her even before he'd said it out loud. Not only had he been there to assist her during Claire's labour in a professional capacity, but he'd been an invaluable source of emotional support to her. Something she hadn't realised she'd been missing until he'd rubbed her back and reassured her she was doing everything right.

His kindness in the face of her hostility towards him said everything about his character that she needed to know. It made her see her reaction towards his offer had been because she'd feared the strength of her own feelings for him, brainwashed by past experiences into thinking it meant she was opening herself up to get hurt again. She was still letting Andy isolate her from people who really loved her.

Iona would never love anyone the way she loved Fraser for everything he'd done for her, and how he loved her. He'd gone against all his own fears to open his house up to her and the children, had decorated for Christmas regardless of his own personal issues and had abandoned his rule book so they had all been comfortable here. He'd sacrificed a lot to try and make her happy.

So she had two options. She could throw herself whole-heartedly into a relationship with him and take the risk along with him that love would win out and make everything worthwhile. Or she could walk away now and protect what was left of her heart, back to the safe life she'd left behind in her one-bedroom flat. If she wanted to live life to the fullest she could no longer hide away from everything it had to offer.

She leaned in to whisper in his ear, 'I love you too.'

As the truth left her lips that veil of suspicion finally lifted. She loved him with every fibre of her being. Fraser McColl was the part of her she hadn't realised was missing until she'd tried to walk away from him.

He gathered her up in his arms and peppered her with kisses. 'You don't know how happy that makes me.'

She had a fair idea with the grip he had on her and the size of the grin on his face. 'Is that offer to move in still on the table?'

He stopped hugging and kissing her long enough to stare. 'Does this mean—?'

'Yes. I want to live with you. I want to spend Christmas here with you and every day after that if you still want me.' There was that slight wobble in confidence that he might have grown tired of her drama.

'Always,' he said, and planted one of those delicious long kisses on her lips.

Fraser McColl was the best Christmas present she could ever have wished for.

EPILOGUE

'Okay, the tree's up, the dinner's in the oven and we have cover for the holidays. Is there anything we've forgotten?'

Fraser had his hands on his head, searching his mind for things they might still have to do, but Iona was certain they'd made provision for every possible eventuality.

'Relax. They're going to be here soon and we don't want you stressing them out. This isn't our first rodeo, remember?' Iona handed him some fresh towels to set out in preparation for their new arrivals so he had something to keep him busy other than driving her mad with his constant worrying.

'No, but it is our first *official* Christmas as foster parents. I want everything to be right for them.' Fraser's compassion for the unfortunate children who'd found themselves in the care system through no fault of their own hadn't lessened over the years and she loved him for it.

'It will be.' She kissed him gently on the lips, hoping it would go some way to settling his nervous excitement. He always gave one hundred percent to the children who came to stay with them, no matter how short their time here, but Christmas was particularly special to him as he wanted to give them the special memories he hadn't had as a youngster. After their experiences with Hamish and Poppy they'd both been keen to offer the same safe environment to others and it had given him a reason to keep on the family home other than through obligation alone.

Iona had moved in shortly after their first Christmas together, shipping her barely opened boxes from her beloved apartment, but Fraser had never put her under pressure to do anything she didn't want to. When it came to those big decisions they always had a lengthy conversation so there was no room for misunderstanding and it had worked out pretty well for them so far. They'd taken their time with their relationship, only committing to marriage when they had both been ready, and doing it on the quiet because it was for no one else's benefit but their own.

Since then it had been a whirlwind of activity in the big house, redecorating and turning the place into a home where everyone was welcome. A family remained on the agenda for both of them but for now they were content to parent on a temporary basis for those who needed it.

'Here they come.' Fraser set the towels on the hall table to open the door for the terrified little faces peeking out from the back of the car pulling up in the drive. He wrapped a hand around Iona's waist and pulled her close, their united front to put the eight-year-old twin girls at ease as they ventured towards the strange new house. His heart was so full of love to give to these children for whom it had been so lacking, Iona knew it wouldn't be long before they started their own family. Fraser had proved time and time again he'd make as good a father as he did a husband. For now, though, these children were theirs to look after and nurture until their circumstances improved, and they'd devote all of their time and energy into doing that.

'Have I told you how much I love you?' she whispered to her husband, doting on him more every time she witnessed his devotion to helping others.

'Not in the last five minutes.' He grinned and left one last, lingering kiss on her lips before their visitors came to meet them.

'Welcome.'

'Merry Christmas.'

They greeted their new family with warm smiles and a desire to make some new, cosy Christmas memories with them to last a lifetime. It was only right they should share their happiness with those less fortunate when they had so much of it to give.

* * * * *

COMING SOON!

We really hope you enjoyed reading this book. If you're looking for more romance, be sure to head to the shops when new books are available on

Thursday 29th November

To see which titles are coming soon, please visit **millsandboon.co.uk**

MILLS & BOON

Coming next month

THE BILLIONAIRE'S CHRISTMAS WISH
Tina Beckett

'Theo?'

'Actually, I'm struggling with something.' Maybe it was the revelations about her mom that cast Madison in a different light—the reasons for the slight standoffishness he'd noticed from time to time suddenly making sense. Or maybe it was the stress of dealing with Ivy's illness that had his senses out of whack. But he found himself wanting to do something crazy and impulsive, something he hadn't analyzed from every angle before acting on it.

'With what?'

'The way your thoughts dart from one thing to the other so fast that I can barely keep up.'

'I—I'm sorry.'

'Don't be. I like it. But it also drives me…insane. In ways I should be able to control.' Letting go of her hand, he curled his fingers around the nape of her neck, his thumb sliding just beneath her jaw to where he knew her pulse beat. He let his fingers trail down the side of her throat, along skin that was incredibly soft. 'But right now I don't want to control it. And that's the struggle. So…I need you to tell me to back off.'

She moistened her lips and started to say something, then stopped. Her eyes met his. 'I don't think I can.'

Something inside him leaped to attention and he lowered his voice, aware that they were still completely alone. 'You can't tell me to back off, or you don't want to?' He leaned forward, employing light pressure to bring her nearer until their lips were a mere centimeter away.

'I don't want to tell you…want you to…' Her hand went to his shoulder, fingers pressing through the thin fabric of his button-down shirt. Warmth bloomed and traveled. And then, with a feeling of déjà vu, her mouth touched his.

Senses that had been dormant for years erupted in a huge array of lights that rendered him blind for several seconds.

When he could see again, he was kissing her back and Theo knew at that moment he was in big trouble. He should stop this before it went any further, but his limbs wouldn't co-operate. Neither would his mouth.

So there was nothing else to do but sit back and enjoy the ride. Because any time now Madison was sure to realize what a mistake this was and call a screeching halt to it.

All of it.

And when that happened, Theo had no idea what he was going to do.

Continue reading
THE BILLIONAIRE'S CHRISTMAS WISH
Tina Beckett

Available next month
www.millsandboon.co.uk

LET'S TALK
Romance

For exclusive extracts, competitions
and special offers, find us online:

- **f** facebook.com/millsandboon
- 🐦 @MillsandBoon
- 📷 @MillsandBoonUK

Get in touch on 01413 063232

For all the latest titles coming soon, visit
millsandboon.co.uk/nextmonth